**W9-BYZ-290**

DATE DUE

# THUNDER
# AND
# RAIN

## Charles Martin

**CENTER
STREET**

New York  Boston  Nashville

Copyright © 2012 by Charles Martin

Center Street
Hachette Book Group
237 Park Avenue
New York, NY 10017
www.centerstreet.com

Printed in the United States of America

First Edition: April 2012
10 9 8 7 6 5 4 3 2 1

Center Street is a division of Hachette Book Group, Inc.
The Center Street name and logo are trademarks of Hachette Book Group, Inc.

The Hachette Speakers Bureau provides a wide range of authors for speaking events. To find out more, go to www.hachettespeakersbureau.com or call (866) 376-6591.

The publisher is not responsible for websites (or their content) that are not owned by the publisher.

Library of Congress Cataloging-in-Publication Data
Martin, Charles, 1969–
    Thunder and rain / Charles Martin.—1st ed.
        p. cm.
    ISBN 978-1-4555-0398-8
    I. Title.
    PS3613.A7778T48 2012
    813'.6—dc23
                            2011029527

*For Charlie, John T., and Rives*

# ACKNOWLEDGMENTS

I'm indebted to some rather talented people:

My editor, Christina Boys. You are tireless, uniquely gifted, and you made the book better—by a good bit. My sincere thanks.

The team at Center Street—most of whom I've not met and who work unselfishly in the shadows. Thank you for what you've done, and are doing.

Chris. My friend on the journey. I think this book would make a good movie. I'm just saying.

Dave. Thanks, pal.

Bill and Jason. Thanks for making the effort. Smitty's is only a day's drive. Probably quicker if we let Pat do the driving.

Clint and Heidi Smith. Portions of this book began to surface while standing on the range deck in a sideways snowstorm—a good day. I'm lucky to have been trained and befriended by you both. We all are. If there's truth in this story with regards to weaponry, and its proper use, the credit is yours. Where there is error, the fault is mine. Many, many thanks.

Art Scharlach. Thank you for educating a stranger about cows, for your patience in answering umpteen questions, and then for taking me on my first cattle drive—albeit a short one. A dream come true.

Brantley Foster, Texas Ranger. A modern-day John Wayne, one tough hombre, and my friend. Texas is lucky to have you. Thank you for opening your home to a stranger and sharing with me your love of the Rangers and all things Texas.

Christy. I love you. *You'll do to ride the river with.*

Charlie, John T., and Rives. I love you. Psalm 91. *Come heavy.*

# THUNDER
# AND
# RAIN

# PART ONE

In a sort of ghastly simplicity we remove the organ and demand the function. We make men without chests and expect of them virtue and enterprise. We laugh at honour and are shocked to find traitors in our midst. We castrate and bid the geldings be fruitful.

—C. S. Lewis

# PROLOGUE

*Five years ago.*

Andie grabbed the pommel, slid her foot in the stirrup and hopped up on May—a fifteen-hand black cutting horse with white socks. I handed her the reins while she glanced at me below the brim of her hat. A slight smirk. She walked to the door of the barn where the last of the sunlight danced on her shoulders. She ducked below the beam and the saddle creaked. An M. L. Leddy's we'd found at a flea market. I checked the knot holding her saddlebags and the picnic inside. She clicked her mouth, heeled May in the flank, pressed her hat down tight and May launched her out of the barn. Half laughing, she hollered over her right shoulder, "Last one down brushes them both." I laid the left stirrup across the saddle, adjusted the breast collar, and watched her. Full gallop. Swirling dust in her wake. I'd seen jets on aircraft carriers do much the same thing. If ever woman was at home on a horse, it was Andie. Heels deep, back straight, ponytail bouncing, arms straight. When we first married, she'd done some barrel racing. The insides of her thighs grew so strong from holding on that she could hang upside down on a fifty-five gallon barrel like a kid on monkey bars. I tried it once and ended up with three stitches in the top of my head.

She rode across the pasture then disappeared through the mesquite and scrub oaks. I led Cinch to the door and climbed up. I stroked his mane. "Let's don't keep her waiting." He turned toward the river and blew through his nose, ears forward. I laughed. "Well, she can wait a little."

We ambled to the river, waded in, crossed over and climbed up on the island that had become our oasis. A scrub oak canopy rising up out of a sandbar known to few. Time spent here was once plentiful. Now rare. The echoes of laughter had long since faded downriver. I climbed down and tipped my hat back. She had spread dinner out across the blanket. I'd be up all night and the spread was her attempt to make sure I didn't go hungry.

I washed my hands in the river and sat across from her. She handed me a plate. Her cheeks were thinner. More hollow. Black circles under her eyes. Jeans loose. The nights had worn on her. Being alone did that. She said, "You'll be careful?"

I nodded. The trick was to give her enough detail to satisfy her while not causing more concern. Or showing my own. "Everyone'll be asleep. Most will be drunk or high. There's more of us than them."

"And if they're not asleep?"

"Then"—I laughed—"it'll get exciting."

She turned away. I should learn to keep my mouth shut. I tried to remind her. "This is four years in the making."

"But you always told me you can't control every variable, every angle."

"And, we feel like we've got most of them."

"But, what about—?"

"Honey."

"But..." She pushed the food around her plate.

"Andie." I set down my fork. "This is what I do."

She nodded, which meant she heard me but didn't like it.

Maybe all this was unavoidable. Maybe it couldn't be helped. Occupational hazard. Or, casualty. Happened to lots of guys. I had tried to be a good husband. Father. Least, that's what I told myself. She turned and swallowed the pill she had told me was a women's multivitamin prescribed by her doctor.

I knew better. It was not.

We ate, stepping silently around the elephant on the island. I scooped the cobbler and passed it to her. The silence loud.

My pager sounded. A thunderclap. I muted it.

She shook her head. "You can't do that."

Five minutes later, it thundered again. I read the callback numbers: "60." I had an hour. I gathered the plates, began packing.

She stopped me. Set the dishes aside. Reached across. The vine-thick vein on her neck pulsed rhythmically. On a blanket beneath a deep Texas sky, she slid off my hat and pulled me to her. Once tender and warm, her love had been an offering shared, a discovery, a pursuit.

This was not that.

I'd already lost her.

# CHAPTER ONE

Dad?"

"Yeah, big guy." The sun had fallen and hung bright orange rimmed by dark mango, filling the sky from Amarillo to Odessa, drawing long shadows across rusty oil derricks.

"I don't understand something."

"What's that?"

He was whittling. A yellow-handled two-bladed Case trapper. Three miles beyond the end of his knife sat Jack McCarter's pasture where the last few years he'd grown melons. "I don't understand why some people put salt on their watermelon."

It was not yet March. Watermelons were still a good ways off. "A watermelon'd be good about now."

"Why would people do that?"

His legs dangled off the end of the tailgate, hanging to below the bumper. He was eleven now and his boots looked to be getting small. The river slipped silently by. Wood shavings sprinkled his lap. A few rode the river. The Brazos River falls into Texas off the

Cap Rock, or the end of the Great Plains, in northwest Texas then meanders some eight hundred miles to the Gulf of Mexico. Below our feet it still had some six hundred to go. He waved the blade of his pocketknife in a circle in front of him, an extension of his hand. "Why would you want to put salt on something sweet?"

I shook my head, ran my fingers through his hair. "I'll be gone when you get up in the morning. Dumps'll fix your breakfast. Get you to school." He nodded and didn't look up. The fishing pole next to him leaned against the side of the truck bed, its line connected to a red-and-white bobber floating midstream and a piece of hotdog resting on the bottom. The fish had yet to find it. "I should be home tomorrow night."

He shrugged, digging his knife into the wood, marring it. "Can I go?"

I shook my head.

He looked up. "But I'm old enough."

The weight of the world lay hidden in his question. "Yes, you are, but I need some time with her."

"You always say that."

"You're right, I do. But it's true."

"When can I see her?"

"I don't know, son."

"She don't call much."

"I know that."

His eyes narrowed. "You taking her some flowers?"

Beyond the river, the pasture was dotted with the first of the bluebonnets. *Lupinus texensis.* The Texas state flower. Another month and God would paint the earth blue and the sky red. "Think I should?"

He nodded.

"Okay. I'll pick some. Take them down."

"You get her some for me?"

"Yep."

I reeled in his line, held it while he fed a worm onto the hook. He cast farther upstream and set it back against the truck bed.

He returned to his stick.

"Dad?"

"Yes."

"How much longer does she have?"

I put my hand on his shoulder. He looked away. I tried to speak quietly. "You should know."

He'd hung a calendar on the refrigerator. Every morning he'd mark another "X" then announce the number of days remaining. "Thirty-five." He looked up at me. "When she's done, is she coming home?"

I pulled him to me, tucking his shoulder under mine. "I don't know, son." The sun slid. Orange bled to crimson.

"Do you want her to?" The world hung in his question.

I squeezed him. I'd never lied to him. "I don't know." He cut deep into his stick. "I don't know."

# CHAPTER TWO

I-10 westbound. Louisiana in my rearview. Texas beyond my hood. The rain had returned. Grape-sized drops pelted the windshield. I couldn't see past the end of my wipers. The manila folder sat on the dash. Yellowed. A coffee stain on top. The weight of the papers inside drew my eye. Such finality. Two signatures...I could almost hear the "sign here" tags talking. I shuffled it off to the side. Wedged down where the windshield met the plastic. But it did little to dull the conversation. Nothing silenced that.

I slowed, watched my mirrors for lights and mopped off the fog on the inside of the glass with a dirty T-shirt. I slowed to a crawl, nearly stopping. I couldn't see anything. The flowers lay on the seat next to me. Wilted.

I hadn't left them.

My mind was distant. The Polaroid stared up at me. I'd taped it next to the gas gauge. When full, the needle pointed to Brodie's ice cream–covered face. He was sitting on my shoulders, wearing my hat, arms raised. He was so proud. My mind was distant—half of me was driving, and half of me was walking up the front porch trying to find an answer to Brodie's question. That distance only partly explained why I bumped the car in front of me. The rest of the explanation had something to do with it being parked in the middle of the highway.

I hit my flashers, pulled off to the side, pulled on my slicker and hat and walked toward the driver's window. The car was once a 1970s wood-paneled station wagon. Most of the wood was gone. A woman—young, maybe early- to midthirties—climbed out of the driver's side as I approached. She was soaked to the skin. A muffled and tight cough rose out of the backseat.

The driver was tired. Haggard looking. Medium height. Five-eight or so. Skinny. Light brown, even blond, hair. Faded T-shirt. Glasses. She wrapped a dirty towel around her shoulders. She pushed wet hair out of her eyes. Rain dripped off her face. One lens of her glasses was fogged up and the rain was causing them to slide forward on her nose. One of the nosepieces had broken off so they sat at an awkward angle. She shoved them up with her finger. She was not happy. "Why don't you watch where the hell you're going!" The word "hell" was two syllables and sounded like "hale."

I looked behind us. Two lights approached in the distance. Closing faster than I liked. Sometimes the best way to disarm somebody is to come in around them. "Will it crank?"

More coughing from the backseat. Her eyes narrowed. "If it would, do you seriously think I'd be sitting here?" Her accent wasn't Texas. More Alabama. Maybe south Georgia.

"You steer. I'll push."

She bit her lip. This confrontation wasn't going as she had planned. I glanced at the lights behind us. She hopped in, I leaned against the rear bumper and pushed her onto the shoulder of the road as a moving truck passed in the left lane. I walked to the window. "Hit the engine one time and let me listen." Rain puddled alongside the road.

She turned the key and the engine turned over but wouldn't

start. She palmed her face, locked the door, and began rolling up the window. She spoke through the glass. "Thanks for your help." She tried to smile. "We got help coming."

I'd "read" a lot of people. It's helped me stay alive. 'Course, I've missed a few, too. I knocked on the window. "You sure it's got gas?"

She cracked open the window and tapped the gauge. "It's broken. Doesn't register right."

"When was the last time you filled up?"

She paused, staring through the windshield. Black circles around her eyes. She sat back, crossed her arms. "A while back."

I lifted a five-gallon can out of the back of my truck, and began pouring it into her tank. Doing so allowed me to see the person in the backseat. She was small, hidden in a blanket, eyes wide and knees pressed to her chest. Her face was pale and her breathing shallow. While the empty tank drank, I listened. The coughing came in violent, spastic spurts. Sometimes hard and deep. Other times, short and shallow. Sounded like it was coming from down in the lungs and it sounded like everything else was swollen and tight. I'm no cough-reader but it needed a doctor. I screwed the cap back on, patted the roof. "Okay, hit her one time." She turned the engine over and over. "Pump the pedal." She did and the engine sputtered, backfired, then the big block roared to life, sending white exhaust out the left bank. It idled rough and the timing needed adjusting. I knocked on the hood and spoke over the rain, which was thundering. "Pull the latch."

She did and I lifted the hood. I shined a light. The engine was leaking oil like a sieve and one of the engine mounts was broken and banged every time the engine revved and torqued. I hollered around the hood, "Your timing's off."

I heard a mumble from inside, "You're telling me."

The door opened, she came around the side, wrapped in the soaked towel, arms crossed. The rain was bucketing. It was cold and getting colder. "Is that expensive to fix?"

Water was dripping down my back. More hacking erupted from the backseat.

I leaned in, and turned the distributor counterclockwise.

The engine settled but little improved. White clouds blew from the right rear pipe. I shut the hood and held the door while the lady climbed back in the car. An empty quart of oil lay on the passenger floorboard. The gas gauge was bouncing off "E."

She cracked the window again. I spoke above the rain. "You're burning a lot of oil. Your right head gasket is leaking like Swiss cheese. You push this thing very hard and you're liable to blow the engine."

"Can it be fixed?"

"Yes, but..." I glanced at the car. "I'm not sure the car would be worth whatever you'd have to pay to fix the engine."

The woman seemed distracted, nervous. Like she was looking over her shoulder. She was rubbing her hands together. The person in the backseat had pulled the blanket over her head, crossed her legs Indian style, and was writing in a journal. The pages were covered in words. Lots of words. She looked up once, eyed me, but never quit writing.

The woman pushed the hair out of her face. Unzipped a small black backpack that looked like it served as a purse, and pulled out her wallet. Crow's-feet formed in the corner of her eyes. She said, "What do I owe you?" Given the concert of her life—the torn upholstery, bouncing gas gauge, empty oil can, kid coughing, bald tires, smoke billowing out the exhaust pipe, smell of burning oil— I had my doubts.

"Not a thing."

She let out a breath. "I'm sorry about your truck. Is it very bad?"

My truck is a Dodge Ram one-ton, 3500 series four-wheel drive, powered by a Cummins turbo diesel. Its color was in the gold family but with a little over two hundred thousand miles, it's more a dull satiny remnant of that. If there is such a color. It's what I like to call a highway tank. It has a crew cab—four doors—a topper that keeps everything dry in the bed, including me when I sleep back there, and aftermarket BFGoodrich all-terrain tires. It is designed to pull cattle trailers, which it has done much of, and if forced, could probably slide a house off its foundation.

"Where I come from that's called a cattle guard and it takes something akin to a nuclear blast to ding the thing. A few exits down, you'll find a truck stop. Greasy place, but it's dry, they serve a good egg sandwich and they got a mechanic who will be in tomorrow morning. He's almost honest. If you can't wait, then you might ought to stop and pour some oil in this thing. Maybe buy a few quarts for the road. It's burning as much oil as gas."

Another push on her glasses. They were stretched out and didn't fit her face well. She tried to laugh. "Don't I know it."

Another painful swallow. She proffered her wallet. "Sure I can't pay you something?" Another muffled hack sounded behind her. The shape moved slowly, obscured by the fogged-up windows. The woman glanced over her shoulder, then returned to me and slid her hand back into her purse. "I can."

Rain was flooding the side of the road. "I'll follow you to the truck stop. Just stay in the right lane and click your flashers on."

She nodded, smeared the rain off her face and rolled the window up. She tried to take a deep breath but it didn't get very far. She opened and slammed the door, which did little to lock it shut. She shut it again, but the hinge was bent and, judging by the sound of metal on metal, had been for a while.

She dropped the stick to drive, rolled up her window, and eased off the side of the road, slinging mud out of the right tire. The left spun on the asphalt. The car fishtailed. Two eyes stared at me out of the backseat.

# CHAPTER THREE

Dear God,

I figure you already know everything I need to tell you. If you don't then you ain't much of a God. Certainly not The God. Momma says God would know. And if God was really God then He would be pissed. I'm writing you 'cause we don't never stay nowhere long enough for me to find a real pen pal. Plus, Momma told me to. Remember the train station? We were sitting on that bench in that town with the name I can't remember, just Momma and me, and she was rubbing her hands together, and we didn't have no ticket to nowhere and no money and no nothing and I kept bugging her and asking her to tell me who to write 'cause somebody needed to know about us. Somebody other than us needed to care about our life, which was real bad but it was ours so anyway she's rubbing her face and sweating and pacing back and forth and trains are coming and going and nighttime was coming and I

*15*

didn't want to sleep in that station another night and I jabbed my pencil into this book and I said Momma, who can I write? And she looks at me and tells me not to raise my voice at her. Can't I see she's got enough going on. And when I started crying and threw this book at her she went and picked it up and straightened all the pages and then she sat down and put her arm around me and she cried too, which she don't do much 'cause she's trying to be strong but she cried then and she cried hard, I know 'cause she was shaking and she couldn't catch her breath and then she was quiet a while and finally she picked me up and carried me through this door that said "chapel" and it wasn't nothing more than a broom closet without the broom but with a stained-glass and bleeding Jesus hanging crooked on the wall that reminded me of one of those velvet Elvises you see hanging at closed gas stations and we spent the night in there and a couple hours later when the trains had quit coming and going and she was combing my hair with her fingers she looked at me and said, God, baby. He'll listen. He'll be your pen pal. You can write God. So, you're stuck with me. I know you're busy with hungry people and folks dying and disease and all kinds of bad stuff but when I asked Momma about you and having the time for me she just smiled and told me that you can walk and chew gum at the same time, which I think means you can do more than one thing at a time so if I'm bugging you then just tell me and I'll try to write shorter letters.

I haven't written much lately 'cause, well—I guess you know. Anyway, I can't talk to Momma about it 'cause it hurts her too much to hear it and come to think about it it hurts me too much to say it and, well, I don't really know where to start so I'll just start right here—Momma found out about the... you know, and she blew a fuse. Like I ain't never seen. She grabbed me and we took off. Said we were "getting the hell out of there." Sorry to cuss at you but that's what she said as we ran to the car. I'm just repeating it and repeating it ain't a sin 'cause it didn't start with me.

She stole this car. It was the neighbor's and she wasn't driving it. Just letting her cats sleep in it. She won't miss it none. Anyway, we stole it and Momma's been breaking every speed limit we see. By a lot, too. She says we're headed to her sister's. Told me not to worry. Says when we get there, she can get a job and we'll be fine. Just fine. She said it twice, which means she don't believe it none neither. Says there's lots of jobs in New Orleans. She can go back to Wally World and they'll transfer her job to wherever she's living at the time. She says they're good about that. They like her 'cause she's always on time and never stole nothing like the other cashiers. And at her sisters, she says we'll have our own room. Upstairs. Overlooking the water and the lights of the city. And we can have clean sheets every night 'cause her sister's got a washing machine. Says there's always something going on in New Orleans. Always a party. I'm not so sure. I know I'm just ten, but sometimes I think she tells me things to make me feel better even though they ain't true and they ain't never gonna be.

My blanket is dirty. I asked Momma if we could get a new one and she rubbed her hands and put her hand on her forehead, which told me it cost money and we didn't have none of that so I took it in the bathroom at the rest area and tried to wash it out with the pink hand soap and then held it under that hair dryer mounted on the wall but it didn't do no good. I tried to find a word to describe it. I think I found one. "Bedraggled." I think it fits. Anyway, it's real dirty and looks like I been dragging it in the mud.

It's raining. I better go. Momma just cussed, twice, 'cause the engine quit and now we're sitting in the middle of the highway with headlights getting closer.

*   *   *

It's been a few minutes. This man stopped to help us. Actually, he bumped into us, Momma cussed him out and he just tipped his hat and helped us, which I thought was strange. He looks like a cowboy. Wears one of those long raincoats you see in the movies. Gave us some gas. Looked through the window at me. Momma pulled the hood latch and he fiddled with something. The engine don't sound as bad. He told us about a truck stop up ahead. Said he'd follow us.

He is. I just looked.

Momma once told me she's got a tumbleweed heart. I didn't know what it was so I looked it up. It's a bush that dries up 'cause its water source goes away, then, once it's sucked dry and dead, it rolls around in the wind. Or, tumbles. That's how it got its name. You've seen them in old Western movies.

Momma just asked me how I'm feeling. I said fine. But between you and me I feel like a dirty tumbleweed. Just rolling 'round in the wind. No roots. No place to set down. Nothing to call home. And you know when you see a tumbleweed rolling around those old movies, the movie always ends before you get to see what happened to it.

But, looking back on it, I don't think it's real good.

# CHAPTER FOUR

The rain had driven most of the trucks on I-10 off the interstate and into the flooded truck stop parking lot. Must have been two hundred trucks sitting in six to eight inches of water. She parked underneath the canopy overhang and sat long enough for the windows to fog up. I tapped on the window. A crack appeared. "There's oil inside." The landscape was a tightly packed sea of parallel trailers. "If you have anything valuable, I wouldn't leave it lying around."

She nodded and rolled up the window. Her eyes were darting all over the place.

I grabbed my bag, and headed for the showers. Twenty minutes later, shaved, clean, and feeling more human, I dropped my bag in my truck and saw that her car was gone. Nothing but a big black oil spot remained. She wouldn't make it far.

I took a seat at a booth in the corner and a waitress named Alice appeared with a pot of hot coffee, a dirty apron, and an empty mug. I looked up. At one time, Alice had been good looking. The "A" in her name tag had worn off. She smiled. Several teeth were missing. "Baby..." Her voice was sweet, and cigarette raspy. "What you need?"

"Just an egg sandwich with cheese. Please, ma'am."

She set down the cup, filled it, and patted me on the shoulder. "You got it, baby." Her white uniform shoes were run down. Greasy. Yellowed. The years had not been kind to her.

I bought a paper and made it halfway down the first column before the picture of that wood-paneled station wagon reappeared in my mind. Then my mind played a trick on me and I heard that cough. I made it to page two before I heard it again. I looked up over the paper and caught movement out of the corner of my eye.

She was wrapped in a worn fleece blanket that, at one time, had been cream-colored and printed with Disney characters. Now it was a dirty brown and most of the characters had blended in or worn off. One frayed corner dragged the ground. Something red had dried and smeared in one corner. She coughed slightly, one hand covering her mouth. Tight, labored, and mucus-filled. She crept around the far end of the diner, away from Alice, slowly eyeing each tabletop. When Alice disappeared toward the kitchen, the girl approached a table where a tip had been left. A few dollar bills and some coins. Glancing over her right shoulder, she slipped her hand out of the blanket, across the table and took one quarter. Six minutes later, when the two guys down from me stood and left a similar tip, she reappeared, quickly scanned, and stole a second quarter.

Alice appeared at my table with my egg sandwich just about the time the girl's fingers clasp around the coin only to disappear back under her blanket. Alice put her hand on her hip and muttered, "Well, I'll be a—"

I put my hand on her arm and shook my head. Alice watched the little girl leave, and muttered, "What's the world coming to?"

I reached in my wallet, and gave her a ten-dollar bill. "Will this cover it?"

Alice smiled at me and slid the money into the top of her bra. She leaned on the table and the front of her dress hung open exposing two sagging bosoms. "Are you married?"

"No, ma'am."

Alice raised one eyebrow and shook her shoulders. "You want to be?"

"It's tempting, but . . . I'm still trying to get . . . unraveled from the first one."

She patted me on the shoulder. "Baby, I know what you mean." She stood, ran her fingers through my hair and walked back toward the kitchen keeping her eyes on the girl.

The girl walked the aisles of the convenience store next to the restaurant. She paused in the medicine aisle, then walked down to the trinket aisle where they sell all the crap that kids look at and bug their parents about but is absolutely worthless. She stopped a long time at one thing but I couldn't tell what it was. She pulled it off the rack, flipped it over, looked up at the counter and then she eyed the Lottery sign. She hung whatever was in her hand back on the rack, wrapped the blanket around her shoulders, coughed three times hard enough to bend her double at the waist, and then took a long look into the restaurant. When she walked around the aisle and disappeared from sight, I emptied a handful of change and six dollar bills on the table two down from me.

The girl reappeared at the end of the row of booths, shuffling close along the edges of the tables with her head low. Wrapped in the blanket, I still couldn't see what she looked like. About this time, I started wondering what happened to her mother who I hadn't seen since the side of the highway. Least, I assumed it was her mother.

The girl reached the table two down from me and paused, looking at me out of the corner of her eye. I hunkered over the sports page. She reached out, grabbed one quarter, then returned her hand to inside the blanket. She took one step, then stopped and looked down into both her hands. Her lips moved, then she turned her head to look at all the money remaining on the table. She coughed again, covering her mouth, then slipped her hand out, grabbed a second quarter and walked out of the restaurant.

I finished my sandwich, paid Alice, and meandered into the convenience store, stopping in the children's crap aisle. Didn't take me long to find it.

Tinker Bell stickers.

I pulled two packs off the rack and approached the counter where the girl stood swaying back and forth—her head just extending over the counter. She laid four quarters on the laminate surface. Her voice was constricted, "I'd like to buy a lottery ticket, please."

The woman at the register laughed and tapped the sign above her head with a pencil she slipped from her beehive. "Child...you got to be eighteen. How old are you?"

Her eyes never left the lady at the register. "Eighteen...minus the eight part."

The lady leaned on the counter. "Child, if I sell you a ticket, I could lose my job."

I laid the stickers on the counter next to the four quarters and paid no attention to the kid. "Howdy. I need sixty on pump seven, these stickers, and one lottery ticket."

The kid stepped back and eyed her quarters. She shook her head, mumbled something I couldn't hear, slid the quarters off the counter, and shuffled back toward the restaurant. I walked out the side door and began pumping the gas. I leaned against my truck, and stared back through the window at the kid crouched in a corner watching Alice. When Alice disappeared into the kitchen, the kid crept into the restaurant, laid four coins on the table nearest the door and walked out.

I scratched my head and stared down the highway. I have a thing in the back of my brain that starts dinging when something doesn't set right. At the moment, it was banging pretty good.

I refilled the five-gallon tank in the back, screwed on both caps, and walked back toward the trashcan where the kid was leaning against the window. The glass had fogged up in front of her mouth. I walked inside and laid the lottery ticket on the frame next to her cheek. She stepped back, looked at the ticket, wrapped her blanket tighter around her and didn't look at me. I spoke softly. "I was a kid once, too."

Dirty fingers came out of the blanket and hovered over the ticket. "My mom told me not to take stuff from strangers."

"Did she also tell you not to talk to them?" The kid nodded. "Good. Don't talk to us, don't take anything from us, and don't ever, not ever, get in a car with one. You understand?"

A slow nod.

"Where's your mom?"

She shrugged and her eyes darted left and right, skimming the floor. "Don't know."

I stared out over her shoulder, over the fogged-up section on the glass, across the parking lot and toward the intersection that led into the truck stop. At the corner, where the four lanes intersect, a woman stood in the rain holding a cardboard sign. I swore beneath my breath.

The girl looked up at me. "You shouldn't cuss." A weak cough. More of a tickle. "God don't like it."

"Seems like I remember hearing something about him not liking thieves neither."

She flushed and shot a glance toward the restaurant. She pulled her hand back inside the blanket, leaving the ticket on the window-sill. "It's not for me."

"Yeah? Who?"

Her eyes darted to the intersection.

I reached in my pocket and set a penny on the sill next to the ticket. "Well...some lucky stranger might win..." I stared up at the marquee. "This is one of those quick pick deals where you can win a couple million bucks when three of the numbers match."

Two hands came out. One grabbed the penny. The other, the ticket. She scratched furiously then turned it sideways, studying the numbers. None matched. She flicked it like a playing card and walked off. The ticket fluttered, spun, and returned like a boomerang, landing on my toe.

The girl was making her way toward the far corner of the parking lot where the station wagon sat in the shadows. She skirted a puddle, pulled away the sheet serving as the right rear window, climbed in and pulled the soaking sheet back across the window frame.

I swore again. This time louder.

# CHAPTER FIVE

I cranked my truck, dropped it in drive and sat watching the intersection through my binoculars. The sign she held read, PLEASE HELP. GOD BLESS. The rain had slowed but was still falling, as was the temperature. Upper thirties. I could see her breath from the warmth of my seat. Maybe the last cold front of the year. The kid in the car had to be cold, too. I rubbed my forehead.

One of the passing trucks threw a hamburger wrapper at the woman on the corner. I pushed my hat back, and backed into a corner of the lot where I could see.

Thirty minutes later, the parking lot filled with trucks and the intersection quiet, the woman sailed her sign like a Frisbee into the ditch and then started making her way down the long row of semis—knocking on doors. Her clothes were drenched.

I rolled a cigarette and watched her talking with the drivers. The first seven shook their heads. The eighth deliberated, then shook his head. The ninth—a big man with an even bigger gut, looked around the parking lot, rubbed his hand through his beard, scratched his behemoth belly, then smiled and welcomed her up into the cab.

That was my cue.

I pulled on my slicker and my hat and set the unlit cigarette on the base of a lamp pole on the only dry spot I could find. I wove my way around the trucks, through clouds of spent diesel fumes, stopping just shy of his cab. His trailer was sitting low on the rear wheels. I waited, listening. About sixty seconds later, I heard the raised voices followed by the smacks and screams.

I didn't used to be a flashlight nut but you spend enough time walking around in the dark and you come to appreciate a good light. SureFire makes one of the best. Something the size of your palm can light up the world. Mine did. I put my foot on the step, took a deep breath, put the flashlight in my left hand, and pulled on the door.

I swung into the cab, lit up the sleeping quarters and found him trying to do to her what he was paying her to let him do. Problem was, the thing he needed to do it with wasn't cooperating. Or, if it was, it had a funny way of showing it. She lay on her back in front of him—available.

He shielded his eyes. "What the...?" He was not happy but his pants were crumpled at his ankles so I knew he wouldn't be making any drastic movements. At least any that were successful.

I clicked the switch above my head and turned on the cabin lights. He liked that even less. She reached for her clothes and covered up. Her nose was bleeding and her lip was already puffy. Her glasses hung bent on her face. She turned and spat blood on his sheets. She needed to shave her legs a week ago. He made a move to pull up his pants, but I did something I'd done a hundred times before and his response was much the same. I drew from the holster and pointed the muzzle at him.

Deer in the headlights.

A large frame handgun like the 1911—the GI's .45—has several impressive features, the most eye-catching is the inside diameter of the barrel—it's bigger around than many folks' pinky finger. And you get a pretty good view of it when the fire-breathing end is aimed at you.

His eyes crossed and he started stammering. I cut him short.

I waved the muzzle slightly left to right. "Not a word out of you."

He nodded.

I turned to the woman. "You okay to move?"

She turned on her side and spat again, dark red. "Yes."

"You ready?"

She pulled on her panties and wet clothes and then climbed out the door. I was about to hop down and then remembered. I looked down at her. "Did he offer to pay you?" She crossed her arms, looked away and nodded. "How much?"

He piped in, "I ain't paying noth—"

I steadied the muzzle six inches from his face. "I'll let you know when it's your turn. This ain't it."

She didn't bother to wipe the rain draining off her face. "Fifty."

He screamed again. "That lying whore...she said 'twenty.'"

His wallet was chained to his pants. I ripped it off the chain and opened it to find it empty. Not a dollar in sight.

He laughed. I shook my head. Figures. She turned, said something beneath her breath, and began walking off. I turned to him. "Out."

"What?"

"Now."

"But I ain't—"

"That's your problem."

When he climbed over the seat, his pants fell on the floor. I pushed him out of the cab where he tumbled into a puddle on the asphalt. He stood up, cussing.

I grabbed the keys off the console, locked the door, and slammed it shut. He stood wearing a T-shirt, two wet socks, and his birthday suit. The two trucks facing us had heard the commotion and clicked on their headlights. Fenway Park wasn't as well lit during game time. Laughter rose all around us. One of them blew a horn.

I holstered only to watch her turn, walk back to him, and stand in front of him. He laughed. "Just what do you think—" He got the word "think" out of his mouth about the time her boot landed squarely in his groin. His heels lifted four inches off the ground and his voice rose about that many octaves. He crumpled and fell to writhe in a puddle. She turned and began walking to the restaurant. I turned to follow her and he screamed, "What about my keys?"

I threw them into the retention pond just opposite the truck. He lay in the puddle, moaning, hands holding his tenders.

The woman began walking toward the lights of the truck stop— cold, wet, and no closer to the money she needed. I stared at my truck, and followed her at a slow walk.

Behind me, I heard the sound of a man vomiting.

She walked the length of ten trailers in the direction of her car. I was about to take a deep breath, I even raised my finger to get her attention and ask her if I could talk with her a second—seems like she and I ought to have some closing conversation—when a man dressed in all black with the hood of his sweatshirt pulled up over his head, walked out from behind a truck, grabbed her by the hair and threw her up against the side of a tractor trailer. Her head hit the trailer, her glasses clattered on the asphalt. Rag-doll limp, she slid into the mud. He picked her up, threw her over his shoulder and, with fast, strong strides, disappeared between two parked trailers.

The whole thing took less than two seconds and went a long way to explaining why she was constantly looking over her shoulder.

# CHAPTER SIX

I don't know how he found them. It's not too tough to put out some sort of alert on a stolen vehicle, especially one that keeps breaking down, but even that was hit and miss. No guarantee. Despite some unknowns, I was absolutely certain about a few things: He had been waiting, which meant he had a plan, he was physically strong, he was experienced, he had in fact found them, which reminded me of the proverbial needle in a haystack and, once he did, he wasted no time. Lastly, I had a pretty good feeling she didn't want to go with him and he knew that, which would explain why he didn't waste time talking about it.

I skirted around one trailer, sprinted the distance of six more and paralleled his shadow along two more. He walked to the fence and slipped behind eight other trailers en route to the corner of the fence and a parked van. Flat-black paint, dark window tint, even dark wheels and tires. The thing disappeared in the shadows. He pulled open the back door and dropped the woman into the back.

When he did, the screaming voice of a frantic, gagged, and coughing girl rose up beneath her.

A brachial stun is taught by most martial arts and self-defense schools. It's performed by striking someone on the side of the neck, just below the ear. Doing so blocks—in theory—the electrical impulses traveling from the brain to the rest of the body. One being the ability to stand up. If performed correctly, it can completely immobilize a very large or strong threat for a few seconds. Maybe several if you're lucky. If performed incorrectly, you run the risk of making them mad.

He shut the door and I stunned him. He collapsed like the Scarecrow. I rolled him to his stomach, quickly untied his boot laces, folded his legs behind him so his heels touched his butt, pulled his rather muscular arms across the lower part of his back, fed the laces beneath his belt and tied the ends around his hands. Given the size of his arms, that only gave me a few seconds. I opened the door and found the woman unconscious and the girl wide-eyed and hysterical. Fortunately for me and unfortunately for him, the door of the van was lined with industrial-strength zip ties. The kinds tactical units use on crowds when they don't have enough handcuffs to go around. Held in a can mounted to the door just above a sign that read, HIGH SPEED—LOW DRAG. Some law enforcement folks have been known to carry them inside the crown of their hat for such a purpose. Not even the Hulk can break them.

I zip-tied his hands, his feet and then zip-tied those together. In Texas, we call that hog-tied.

Because wolves hunt in packs, and more than half of all assailants have a partner, I wasn't sure if this guy was flying solo or traveling with help so I dragged him off to the side next to the fence, knelt down and got quiet. Listening. Muffled cries rose from the rear of the van. When I didn't hear footsteps, or shots fired, I appeared at the rear of the van, held my finger to my lips, cut the girl's ties and pulled the gag off her mouth. I scooped up the unconscious woman and whispered to the little girl, "Can you walk?"

She nodded.

"Follow me."

I carried the woman back through the spent diesel fumes to my truck and laid her across the backseat. She was regaining consciousness when I sat her up. The girl climbed in next to her. I touched the cut above the woman's left eye.

She recoiled.

I reached down along my ankle and pulled out a Smith & Wesson model 327 from an ankle holster. It's an eight-shot revolver chambered in .357. I load it with Barnes triple shock. While not a .45, you don't want to get hit with it. When you do, it feels like you're being lit on fire. Keeping the muzzle pointed away from us, I handed it to her. I placed the grip flat inside her palm and stretched her trigger finger straight along the frame and away from the trigger. I didn't want to get shot giving someone my own gun. "If anyone other than me opens that door, point that at them and pull this trigger until it stops going 'boom.' Can you do that?" She wrapped her left hand around her right and nodded. I pushed the door closed and said, "Be right back."

I don't know if she trusted me but I was pretty sure she didn't trust the other guy. I returned and found him trying to wiggle his way around the van. I put a boot in his rib cage and drove the air out of his lungs. He coughed and cussed. I knelt and pressed the muzzle of my 1911 against his temple. Unlike a lot of folks in that same predicament, he didn't go crazy. Didn't scream. Didn't writhe uselessly. He was cool. Collected. Measured. That told me a lot.

I studied the shadows. If he had help, it was slow in coming. He was studying what he could out of the corner of his eye. He hadn't seen, and couldn't see, my face but he was taking a mental picture of everything else. He was good. He also liked being in control—which he wasn't.

And that he didn't like.

I straddled him and drove my elbow down onto his neck, pressing his face into the mud. He shook his head and spoke around the mud. "Don't know you. Don't really care. I do know that I'll hunt you. Find you. Rid you of whatever and whoever you love." He laughed again. His anger was growing and he was losing his self-control. I reached in his back pocket and slid out his wallet. A bifold. On one side I found his driver's license. On the other, his badge. Told you he had experience. I slipped it in my shirt pocket.

He had yet to see my face and I didn't really want him to see me drive away so I sunk my arm under his chin and dragged him into the corner of the fence where the grass was tall. He knew what was coming. I locked my right hand on my left bicep and applied pressure to the back of his head with my left hand. He grew frantic. He knew he didn't have long. In martial arts circles, this hold is called a "rear naked choke." It's painless, quite effective, and the problem with it is not that law enforcement folks use it but rather that they don't use it enough. He, evidently, had used it. Through gritted teeth, he managed a smile. He was thick, all muscle. I'd not want to face him on even terms. He spoke through gritted teeth. "You are now…my life's mission."

I clamped down on both sides of his neck with my bicep and forearm and continued to push forward with my left hand. It only takes a few seconds. Just before he went to sleep, I whispered, "Be careful what you wish for."

He slumped forward and I laid him in the grass. He'd recover. I walked a different route to the truck and approached slowly—from the front so she could see me through the windshield. I made eye contact with the woman holding my gun, opened the door slowly, and gently took the pistol from her hand. I grabbed a dirty T-shirt and an old towel off the passenger's side floorboard, and draped them over my front and rear license tags. I didn't know if this truck stop had video monitors or not but I wasn't taking any chances.

The girl was shaking uncontrollably and the woman wasn't altogether conscious. I put it in drive, turned off all lights, and began pulling out of the truck stop.

The girl pressed her nose and palms to the glass and screamed, "Wait!" She was trained on the station wagon. "Turbo!"

The woman held out a hand. Stop sign. "Wait, please."

I stopped and stared in the rearview.

She opened the door and the kid ran back through the puddles to the car. She reached in the back and returned with a cage filled with what smelled like old cedar shavings. She set it on the backseat behind her mother, then ran back for her blanket, her notebook, a small black backpack, which her mother held on to and set in her lap, and a thick paperback. As she opened the back door I could see the pages were dirty, the corners were curled, and both the front and back cover were missing.

She hopped in and we drove out, through the lights and onto the highway.

A quick glance in the rearview. The woman was looking at me out of the corner of her eye. The look on her face told me she didn't trust me any more than the guy behind us. Her face above her left eye was cut and needed stitches, her glasses were gone, her nose was dripping blood, her left eye was black, her bottom lip swollen, and she was still spitting blood.

We drove in silence. After fifteen minutes with no headlights coming up fast behind us, I turned off onto a smaller state highway, then again onto a country road. When the pavement ended, and the road turned to dirt, I pulled over, cut the lights and sat with the truck running. I turned around and scratched my head. "Are you okay to talk?"

Her wall had returned. "What do you want me to say?"

Her accent was rich. Thick. Syrupy. Mixed with a little attitude and sprinkled with spunk. Reminded me of Jo Dee Messina singing "Heads Carolina, Tails California." I shrugged. "How about a name?"

"I'm Virginia. This is my daughter, Emma." I doubted it, but if I were her I wouldn't trust me, either.

The girl looked up at her.

"And, what are you two doing out here tonight?"

A quick look in the rearview. "Running from him."

"And he is?"

"Was…a guy we lived with."

"Until what?"

"Until I decided I didn't like him anymore."

"Where are you from?"

"Cordele, Georgia."

Thought so. "Why's he chasing you?"

She looked away. " 'Cause he…didn't want us to leave."

There's always more to a story than what surfaces on the first go 'round. Even the second and third. The best scenario for me would be to get them some place safe, get back on my way, and never ask her for her real name.

I tapped my chin, considering my options. "You got any family?"

"Sister in New Orleans."

"Will she take you in?"

She paused, nodded.

"When was the last time you talked to her?"

"Couple months ago."

"Why so long?"

She pursed her lips. "Phone's disconnected."

That should have been my first clue. "You know where she lives?"

She nodded.

I pushed her. "As in…you can point me to the exact address?"

Another nod. The rain was coming down again. I spoke to myself as much as to her. "I hate New Orleans."

She pressed gingerly on one side of her mouth, talking as much to herself as to me. "I hate a lot of things."

I did the math. Almost four hundred miles. About a six-and-a-half-hour drive. "Would it help if I drove you to your sister's?"

Her head tilted to one side. One eyebrow raised. "You'd do that."

It was a question embedded in a statement. "Yes."

"Why?"

"How else are you going to get there?"

She stiffened. "I got no money. Can't afford to pay you."

"I figured."

"Well, you don't have to sound so smug about it."

"I didn't mean it like that. I just meant that after everything tonight, that you... probably didn't have much of anything. That's all."

"My sister can't pay you, either."

"I'm not looking for money."

Her eyes darted away. "Are you wanting the same deal I gave that truck driver?" It was an offer embedded in a question.

I shook my head. "No."

Her eyes narrowed, forcing a wrinkle between. "You gay?"

I laughed. "No."

"What's wrong with you?" I picked up on the fact that when she got wound up, her accent got wound, too. It took a second after she quit speaking for the words to settle in their rightful place of meaning.

I laughed. "We're going to need a longer highway for that conversation." Her shoulders relaxed and a crack in her wall developed. I looked at her—the whole of her. She was dead tired. "How long have you been awake?"

She spoke without looking. "Couple of days."

"How many is a couple?"

She thought. "What day is it?"

"Tuesday."

"I slept some last... Friday."

I thought about her car at the truck stop. "Do you have Triple A?"

She frowned. Her head tilted. "Do I look like I have Triple A?"

"What about your car?"

"Not mine."

"Whose is it?"

She shrugged. "No idea. I stole it."

"From?"

She rolled her eyes. More of the story she didn't want to tell. "An old woman lived behind...where we were staying. She's in a home. They were letting her cats sleep in it."

"Well..." I glanced at my watch, thought about home, and dropped the stick into drive. "Come on...let's get you two to New Orleans."

I pulled back onto the highway. Her head turned on a swivel as she checked all the signs. A few minutes passed. She grew more jumpy. Her eyes squinted as she tried to read the passing road signs. "Are you really driving us to New Orleans?"

I figured we didn't need any more sarcasm. "Yes."

She sat up a little. "You're not dropping us"—she tried to read another sign that disappeared into the blackness on the side of the road—"the first place you come to?"

"No." She sat back, confused and deflated. "Why don't you get some sleep. When you wake up, we'll stop and get something to eat."

She closed her eyes. "I already told you...I don't have any money."

"I can afford McDonald's for three."

For the first time, she noticed the bluebonnets I'd picked. Lying on the front seat wrapped in plastic. "You going somewhere?"

I shook my head once. "Been there."

"What happened?"

"Nothing."

"Want to talk about it?"

"Not really."

She fell quiet. Maybe even dozed. After a few minutes, she jerked slightly and lifted her head. I spoke softly. Tilted my hat back. "It's okay. You're safe. Still headed to New Orleans." She put her head back down and took a deep breath. Drunk with sleep, she turned to check on her sleeping daughter, then stared out through the windshield at the wreckage that had become her life. "I don't have real good judgment when it comes to men." I didn't say anything. She spoke without looking. "Are you a good man?"

"My son thinks so."

She stared at the Polaroid taped next to the gas gauge. "That him?"

I nodded.

Minutes passed. She spoke, "That driver tonight…the truck… that was the first time I'd—"

"Lady, I'm not judging you."

"That'd make you different than most men I've met."

No response.

She fought to keep her eyes open. "You're pretty good with people in duress. I mean, you didn't lose your cool when a lot of others would." She was asking how, not stating a fact.

"I've had some practice."

"What, being cool or handling stressful situations?"

"Well, both."

Her tone changed. "Is that why you carry a gun on your ankle and one on your hip?"

I shrugged. "I'm from Texas."

"You a cop?"

"Do I look like a cop?"

She eyed me. "Not really."

Unimpressed, she studied my truck. "What do you do?"

"I'm retired."

"You don't look retired."

"What's it look like?"

"Knee-high socks, Sansabelt slacks, pudgy belly."

"I'm not that kind of retired."

"What'd you used to do?"

"I worked for the DPS."

"DPS?"

"Department of Public Safety."

"What, you drive a bus or something?"

I laughed. "Something like that."

Her words were slow, even slurred. "You have a name?"

"Yes."

"Well?"

"Tyler. Most folks either call me Ty or Cowboy."

She chuckled. "Are you?"

I nodded. "I've done some cowboying."

"That gun you gave me... would it stop him?"

I nodded.

"How do you know?"

I rubbed my thigh. "Well..." I smiled. "It stopped me."

"What happened?"

I shook my head and shrugged. "Wrong person got a hold of it."

I watched her in the rearview. The whites of her eyes shone in the glow of the dash. A pause. She squinted, looked away. "My name's not... whatever I told you."

I smiled. "Virginia."

She nodded. "Right."

"Didn't really think so."

"It's Samantha, or"—a shrug—"Sam." She scratched her head. "This is Hope."

My father once told me that the truth will eventually find its way to the surface if you don't muddy the water. "Nice to meet you."

A longer pause. I'm not sure the whisper was meant for me. "I doubt it."

She drifted off. I heard some strange scurrying behind me so I flashed my light into the cage where I saw a fat rat-looking thing covered in brown and white hair. Enter, Turbo.

I glanced in the rearview. Under the passing streetlights, I saw the journal tucked beneath the girl's arm. The paperback lay next to her leg. I looked closer. It was a dictionary. I reached back and picked it up, held it beneath the light. The "A"s were missing. A word was circled. It read, "bedraggled."

Fitting.

After an hour or so, it struck me that the girl hadn't coughed since she'd climbed into this truck. But that wasn't the thought that was bugging me. The thought I couldn't shake was wondering if Mr. Tattoo-SWAT-Hulk-man knew about the sister's house. Then I thought the thought that stayed with me all the way to New Orleans, which was: What was I going to do if she wasn't there?

# CHAPTER SEVEN

They slept to the city limits. I was humming a Don Williams tune when she stirred. She muttered, "Yeah, I hope this day is good, too," then dozed again. It wasn't until the truck came to a stop at a gas station that Sam jerked. She sat up, sleep heavy on her face, and stared at me. I was standing at the pump, topping it off. I could tell she was waiting for her brain to assemble the pieces. I tipped my hat back so she could see my face. I registered somewhere in her brain and she let out a shallow breath.

There was a McDonald's tied to the station. I opened the door and spoke first, moving slowly so she wouldn't recoil. "You hungry?"

Hope was staring at me from under the covers. I said, "Hi." A hand appeared and she waved but said nothing. I pulled the Tinker Bell stickers out of my shirt pocket and laid them on the seat. "Thought you might like these." She waited for me to step back, then slid her hand out, grabbed the packet, and returned to the safety of the blanket.

They stepped out looking rather haggard. I didn't really notice until now just how dirty they both were. Sam glanced at the rubber bands hanging from my gearshift. "You mind?"

"Help yourself."

She pulled her hair back, and did that thing that women do with their hair and a rubber band. Then she helped Hope do the same. I reached in the back and handed her a box of baby wipes and a clean towel. Sam looked through the side window of the topper into the back of the truck. "You don't happen to have a hot shower back there, do you?"

"Give me a few minutes and I can probably rig one up."

They walked to the bathroom while I ordered breakfast. They were in there a while. I had a feeling they hadn't eaten much in a few days so I ordered five egg McMuffins, two orders of pancakes, three OJs, and two large coffees to go.

Then I pulled out my cell phone and dialed home.

Dumps answered. "You all right?"

"Yeah…long story. How's Brodie?"

"Sleeping." I could hear the percolator chugging in the background. "You want me to wake him?"

"No, let him sleep."

A pause followed. "You got an answer to his question?"

"Which one?"

"Any of them."

"Not yet."

He laughed. "When will you be here?"

I watched Sam and Hope walk out of the McDonald's. "I'm making a bit of a detour."

"Where?"

"New Orleans."

"Some detour."

"It's part of that long story."

"You in trouble?"

"Not yet."

"She pretty?"

"Depends."

"On what?"

"Which one you're talking about."

I heard him smack his thigh. " 'Bout time you jumped back in with both spurs."

"It ain't that. Got to go. I'll call later."

I was right. They hadn't eaten.

I drove, ate one egg McMuffin and drank a coffee. They ate the rest. All of it. Midway through breakfast, Hope pulled Turbo from his cage, set him on her lap, and began feeding him pieces of grass she pulled from her pocket along with little pieces of pancake and hash brown that he mostly sniffed and licked.

"What is that?" I asked.

Sam answered. "A guinea pig."

"Oh." While they were gaunt and perhaps skinnier than they should've been, he seemed rather plump. "What you been feeding him?"

Sam rubbed his head between the ears and smiled. "Just about everything."

She put him on the console where he promptly started making funny faces, walking in slow circles, and dropping little black turds.

Sam pointed our way through town, which got us lost so I pulled over and unfolded the map. To her credit, she was close. A few streets off. We ended up on the outskirts of the Garden District. While Hope had not coughed, she also hadn't spoken. She had a journal she wrote in a few times, but I'd not heard her speak since she'd shouted "Turbo," in the parking lot. The only thing she'd done to let me know she was in the car was scratch her arms and legs. A lot.

We pulled up in front of the house. "This is it?" Sam nodded. I admit, I was impressed. Her sister kept a tight ship. A beautiful two-story with manicured shrubs and blooming flowers everywhere. Fresh paint. Wrought-iron railings. Wraparound porch. The grass was mowed in straight strips angled toward the road. Polished brass lion's head door knocker. Even the weather vane atop one of the three chimneys had been polished and turned without squeaking.

Sam sat staring at the front door. Hope, shrouded in her dirty blanket, said not a word. I asked, "You want me to knock?"

She shook her head, stepped out, then stepped back in and sat down, nodded once and looked straight ahead.

I pulled on my hat. "What's her name?"

"Mercy."

"What's her last name?"

"DuVane, I think. She's . . . changed it a few times."

I walked to the door and knocked. The maid answered. I tipped my hat. "Ma'am, my name's Tyler Steele. Does a Ms. Mercy DuVane live here?"

She shook her head and inched the door closed. "No."

I had a feeling that was coming. I showed her my ID to make her more comfortable. She read it and handed it back. "Do you know if she used to?"

"Sir, I work for the McTinneys. They bought this house about a year or so ago." She leaned forward and whispered, "They bought it at auction." Her eyes darted left, then right. "Off the courthouse steps."

I stepped back. "Sorry to bother you, ma'am. Thank you for your time." She nodded and shut the door.

I pulled down my hat and walked back to the truck. When I got there, Samantha's eyes were watery and her knee was bouncing up and down. I opened the door as she was pulling Hope out. She grabbed Turbo, never looked at me and said, "We'll be going. I'm sorry. I've got— We, we're going . . ." She chewed on her lip, then looked left, then right. "This way." And began walking left. Hope carried Turbo and looked over her shoulder, dragging her blanket. I followed them about a block in the truck. She was frantic but what I knew about women—which wasn't much and was usually wrong—told me she needed to get whatever this was, out. After two blocks, she stopped, walked to the curb, crumpled, and hung her head in her hands. I put it in park and left it running. Hope stood holding the cage looking at me. I knelt in front of Samantha.

Last year, I was driving down a dirt road checking on some cows when I came up on a dog. Or, what was left of one. Mange had eaten off most of its hair, every rib stuck out, sores covered it. It was lying in a pile on the side of the road, licking its blistered feet. Its mouth was foamy and a hundred flies were crawling across its muzzle. I stopped and rolled down the window. It was too tired to lift its head so it just raised its eyes. I lifted my .22 and stared at it. Its breathing was slow. Death's door. No medicine in the world would bring it back. I thought long about it, but I didn't shoot that dog. I should have—it would have been merciful—but I did not. I left it right there, licking itself. I returned the next day and a buzzard was eating what remained of its eyes. I thought about shooting the buzzard but it wouldn't bring back the dog. I thought about that dog for several days, wondering what was the turning point. Did someone throw it out? Quit feeding it? Was it a mean dog? What made it mean? How'd it get like that? How in the world did it get like that? That dog wasn't always like that. It had a tipping point. Where was it?

I studied the cut above her eye and the picture of that dog came to mind. If I left them, would the buzzards circle and start eating tomorrow?

I stood and held out my hand. "Come on."

She looked at it but didn't move. I spoke softly. "Ma'am, please let me help you."

She looked up, disbelief coloring the image of me. "Why?" Hope crowded behind her. "Why would you do that?"

"Let's just say I watched too many Westerns as a kid."

She shook her head. "You'll have to do better than that."

"I don't know that I can."

She stood, rubbing her hands together, rolling one thumb over the other. She began nodding. She couldn't see past the next fifteen minutes. "A hotel maybe. To, let us think through things." She was cracking. I'd seen it before.

I set the overfed rat and his cage in the car, got them buckled in the backseat, and the three of us drove off in search of a hotel.

I had one in mind.

The Big Easy is one of the dirtier cities I've ever visited. I'd been there a dozen or so times on business. Years back, I worked for the state and the man that was my boss always stayed in the same place. Hence, I did. I drove straight there: 921 Canal Street. It'd been a few years. Well, okay, more than a few. I wondered if they'd remember me. Funny thing about the Ritz-Carlton, their people have amazing memories.

I drove around back, inside a covered driveway, and left it running. "You two sit tight. I'll be right back." Sam's eyes were big as half dollars. Hope's mouth hung half open.

The doorman held the door, and I made my way to a help desk of sorts—the one with little traffic. I waited until a guest had cleared out and the hall was empty. I wanted to know who was working the desk. She shuffled some papers and scratched her scalp with the tip of a pencil.

Jackpot.

Marleena saw me, screamed, slapped her desktop, and came running, arms wide. Told you they had good memories.

Miss Marleena is about five-foot-five and she's stacked in there pretty good. She's got some pretty severe arthritis so she sits behind that desk and does what she can. Which is mostly smile and hug people. She likes to tell people that "she's a whole lotta woman with a whole lotta love." She grabbed me, pressed her big bosom to my chest, and pulled me down to her, kissing me on the cheek. "Tyler Steele...Good Lord!" One of the porters pushed a cart toward an elevator. She hollered, "Look who's here!"

"Let me look at you." She turned my face, studying my neck. She ran her finger along the scar, the tightened skin, her lips tight. She noted my hearing aid. "I heard about that. We all heard. How you doing?"

I held my hat in my hand. "I feel like my side's winning."

She pressed her meaty palms to my cheeks. "I love it when you say that. Always have."

"Well, I'm better than I deserve. You?"

She thumbed over her shoulder. "Seventeen years in that chair and I'm just great. Can't complain. So long as Katrina don't come back." She held my hand in hers. "You back working? You need me to set you up with the same rooms?"

I shook my head. "No, not working. Retired. But I need a favor."

"Baby, just ask. You got it. I don't care if I got to kick Bono his'self out of the seventh floor. You name it."

"I need a room."

"One or two?"

"Just one. For them. A night. Maybe two. Nothing fancy. Just whatever you got."

She glanced at the truck. "Done. What else you need?"

"Well, are those girls still working at that clothing store a few doors down? The one with the expensive faded jeans that already got the holes in them?"

She nodded. "Every day."

"Can you get them to bring a few things upstairs?"

"Just tell me the size and color."

"And, one last thing, how about that doctor? The one who made room calls?"

"Got him on speed dial."

"Can you send him up first?"

Her face changed. Game time. "You need help with bags?"

I shook my head. "No, ma'am. They don't have any."

"Is the state picking up the tab on this?"

"No, ma'am."

I walked to the truck, opened the doors, grabbed the cage, and led Sam and Hope back to the desk. Marleena's face changed again when she saw us coming. She grabbed Hope's hand and said, "Baby doll, you just come right up here with Momma Marleena and— Good Lord, child!" She studied Hope's face and arms and then turned to the doorman. "George, run down and get Miss Vicky for me, will you, sweetie? Tell her I'm on the sixth and it's a rush." George nodded and disappeared.

Marleena herded us onto the elevator, used her key to get us on the club floor, and started humming. Sam and Hope looked shell-shocked. We exited the elevator and Marleena led us to the end of the hall. She inserted a key card, pushed open the door and said, "You all come right in here." The door read, Travis Suite.

Sam walked like she'd just stepped foot on Mars. Hope stopped at the door and ran her finger along the doorbell. Marleena noticed. "It's okay, honey. You can ring it." Hope mashed the button and an electronic version of the first few notes of Canon in D sang out. They walked in and Marleena promptly dialed the phone. "Doc Micheaux, please." She paused. "This Miss Marleena." Another pause. "Hey Doc, how you?" She began nodding. "Wondered if you'd make a house call. Yep. How about—" she studied Sam and Hope "an hour. Yes, sir, I'll meet you at the elevator. Thanks, Doc." She hung up and turned to Sam and Hope. "You two make yourselves at home. Get cleaned up, I'll be back in an hour. If you need anything, dial zero and it rings in this phone in my pocket." Sam and Hope nodded in unison. Marleena disappeared while the two of them walked around the room staring at everything but touching nothing. Marble floors, mahogany furniture, three types of curtains, original oil paintings, a stocked refrigerator, king-size bed, a large flat-screen TV, Bose stereo. After a moment, Hope made it to the bathroom and screamed, "Momma!"

Sam ran to the bathroom and found Hope pointing in the corner. Sam eyed the tub. It was big enough for four people. Sam turned slowly toward me, waving her hand across the suite. "Is this legal?"

I laughed. "Yes. It's legal."

"Do you deal drugs?"

Another laugh. "No. I don't deal drugs. Not yet anyway. Though I have had my opportunities." I opened the door. Behind me sat a chair in the hall where I'd spent many an hour. "You two get cleaned up and holler if you need me. I'll be right there. Oh, and hand me your clothes when you step out of them and I'll get them cleaned."

She frowned. "You're going to do my laundry?"

"Well, no. But, I'm going to give it to some people who will wash, dry, and fold it for you and then wrap it in paper and tie it with a little bow."

"Let me get this straight—the laundry fairy is going to wash my clothes and then wrap them in paper and tie them up with a little bow, just because you ask?"

Her disbelief was palpable. "Yes, ma'am."

"What do you want?"

"Nothing."

"Look, we're both adults. There's a price for everything."

I sat in the chair. "I'll be sitting right here."

She shut the door but I don't think I'd convinced her.

Five minutes later, sitting in the chair, scratching my head, Sam cracked the door and passed me their clothes. They were wadded up and stuffed in a plastic bag. "If we didn't have to put them back on, I'd tell you to burn them." Beyond the door, I heard Hope splashing around in the tub. I rode the elevator down to the first floor and Marleena's desk. On the way down, I dug through the bag and found Samantha Dyson's driver's license in the back pocket of her jeans. What's more, I found Hope's little journal in the front pocket of the dirty, hoodie sweatshirt she'd been wearing.

Dr. Jean Paul Micheaux shook my hand and smiled. "Good to see you, son. How you been?"

"Fine, sir, and you?"

"Can't complain. Tell me about these two."

I told him what I knew and we knocked on the door. Hope answered the door wearing the white terry cloth robe, which was dragging on the floor. Sam stood behind her, wet hair, same robe, except hers hung at knee level. A cut above her heel told me she'd shaved her legs.

"Doc, this is Sam and her daughter, Hope." I led him in. "Sam, Hope... this is Dr. Jean Paul Micheaux. I been knowing him a long time. He's sewed me up a time or two. He'll take care of you. I'll be outside."

Fifteen minutes passed, the elevator bell rang, a woman stepped off wearing a white jacket, a stethoscope, and carrying a bag. She knocked on the door and the doc let her in. Another fifteen and the woman left. A few minutes after that Jean Paul opened the door and walked out. He said, "I put three stitches above Sam's eye and wrote her a scrip for the pain. She took a pretty good hit to the head. Probably a mild concussion."

"I saw it. It was a good hit."

He sucked through his teeth and shook his head. "As for Hope, I wrote her several scrips. First, she's got scabies."

"Scabies, sir?"

"Mites. Comes from living in dirty conditions. Got her a topical cream that she will need to basically bathe in for a few days and she'll be fine. Second, I'm putting her on a steroid for a few days, which will open up her airways. Get rid of that cough."

"Any idea what's causing it?"

"Yeah... cats. She's allergic. Sam told me she was trying to get the money to buy the steroid at the truck stop but ran into some trouble. That's when they met you."

"Yes, sir, but I didn't know anything about the steroid."

"I'll bet that's not all you didn't know." He paused. "The girl... Hope... she's got some... well that's why I brought in Dr. Greene. She was the woman. We needed to catalog what evidence remained."

"Evidence, sir?" I had a bad feeling I didn't want to know where this was going.

He turned his reading glasses in his hands. "She's got some tears in her, well, in a place where a little girl don't want tears."

"Sir?"

He stared at me. "Forced entry."

Something in me felt real bad real quick. I stared at the floor. "That explains the blood on the blanket."

He nodded. "It does. There wasn't much, if any, evidence and it's better to have a woman do that kind of thing. The girl wasn't too keen on letting anybody have a look. Dr. Greene was a big help."

"I'll call down and have Marleena put a halt on their laundry. Might be some evidence left in there."

"Be a good idea although I doubt we'll find much."

"What can you do?"

He shook his head. "I'm putting her on a preventative antibiotic but I can't write a scrip for what really hurts."

I nodded, turning my hat in my hands.

He paused. "Ms. Dyson asked me to tell you... when she heard about the... the tearing... well, she's taken it pretty hard."

I shook his hand. "Can't thank you enough."

He pulled down on my collar exposing my neck. He tapped my earlobe with his finger. "I heard about your trouble. Read about it. It was in all the papers. You call me if you need anything. Anything at all. And Tyler?"

"Yes, sir?"

"That's good people in there. You do what you can."

"I will. Thanks again."

He stepped on the elevator and I paced the hallway asking myself just what I'd gotten into and how exactly I was supposed to go about knocking on the door. After a few minutes, the door cracked and Sam's hand waved me in. We stood at the far end of the room in front of a marble-topped sink, while Hope frolicked in the tub behind a shut door. New Orleans shone through the window.

Sam rubbed her palms, glancing over her shoulder. "She loves that tub. Says it's like a swimming pool. Got two feet of bubbles in there." Bourbon Street lay two blocks away. People crisscrossed like large ants.

"Tell her to swim all she wants. There's no limit to the hot water up here and we can get more bubbles."

She turned, fists at her side. She was shaking. Speaking to her own reflection in the glass. "What kind of a man—?" She faded. Veins along her wrists popped out. She turned. "You must wonder what kind of a mother—"

I cut her off. "Ma'am, I'm not judging you."

"Would you stop that?"

"What?"

"Calling me 'ma'am.'"

"Okay."

"I feel like I need to tell you..."

Part of me wondered if it'd be better if she had an attorney present but the other part of me chastised the first part for having the thought. Decades of law enforcement can jade a fellow. Twist the way you see the world. Also makes you a pretty quick reader of people and my read told me she had no idea. "You don't need to tell me anything."

"What if I want to? What if I need—"

I waited.

"He was...handsome in a uniform. Clean, for a change. Said all the right words." She laughed. "Didn't have a criminal record. No parole officer." A shrug. "Had a little money. I thought, 'How bad could he be?' He bought me nice things. Had a little house. A mother-in-law suite connected by a covered walkway. Offered it to us. It was like our own little world. He'd built it for his mother before she passed. What kind of a grown man still loves his mother? I didn't know he, until...I was working late, the cash register. Called to check on Hope. She didn't answer, which was strange. She always answered. Then I called Billy and he didn't answer and I knew he had to be there 'cause I don't leave her without…" She trailed off. "So, I asked my boss if I could cut out early and he said yes, and so I drove home and Hope wasn't in the little mother-in-law suite. She was inside." Her voice slowed and the events replayed across her mind's eye. "I called to her but she didn't answer. I called again and still she didn't answer. And then I found her, sitting on the bed. Naked. With her knees tucked up into her chest with—my baby—" She turned and wiped away the tears. "I saw the blood. How she was sitting. The tremble. The grimace." Sam's eyes filled. "I grabbed her, we stole the car and—" She was shaking. "I swear I didn't know."

A pause. I probed. "What's his name?"

She stared out the window. Across Bourbon Street. Over the Mississippi. "Billy-freaking-Simmons."

Just then, a knock on the door. A voice sounded on the other side. "Miss Sam, it's Marleena." I handed Sam a towel off the mini bar and she wiped her eyes.

Marleena marched in with two girls in tow who were rolling two racks of clothes. I turned to them, "Thanks, ladies." Noise echoed from the bathroom. "Whatever they want. Give me the bill."

I let myself out, walked down the hall to the window and dialed my cell phone. She picked up after two rings. "Deborah Vinings."

"Hey, how you?"

"Well…if it isn't Clark Kent himself. Been wondering when you were going to come ringing back into my life."

"Was wondering if you'd let me trouble you."

Her voice warmed. "You know better than that. What you need?"

"I need whatever you can tell me about a lawman southeast of us. Somewhere around San Antone…Billy Simmons. Might run a SWAT or narcotics unit."

"Anything else?"

I paused. "Yeah, let me give you a driver's license number."

"Who's it belong to?"

"I was hoping you could tell me that."

"Go ahead."

I read her the number.

"Give me a few hours."

"I will."

"You got the same cell?"

"Number? Yes. Phone? No."

She laughed. "I heard that. I doubt Motorola makes a fireproof phone."

"Not yet. Maybe I should write a letter. Thanks, Debbie."

"You don't have to thank me."

"Well...thanks anyway."

# CHAPTER EIGHT

Outside the suite I listened to Marleena laughing inside it. I set there turning that girl's notebook in my fingers. She had stuck a few of the Tinker Bell stickers on the cover. I know I shouldn't have, but I did. I opened it. The first page read:

Dear God,

My flashlight is dying making it harder to see beneath the sheets, but I like it in here. It's like my own tent. It's quiet now. Momma's at work. Second shift. Gets off at midnight. 2:00 a.m. if they give her some overtime. I like to wait up for her 'cause she's tired and not sleeping much. I know 'cause I sit up and watch her. Sometimes I scratch her back and she falls to sleep. But, during the day, she rubs her hands together, and she's always pressing her palm to her forehead or rubbing her neck.

I can breathe okay most of the time. Haven't been to the hospital in a while. Not since that one in Georgia when my throat all swolled up. Momma makes payments to the hospital when she can. Says she'll be paying that down for a long time. I told her I'm going to buy a lottery ticket when I get some money.

My cough is better. Well…to be honest, 'cause you'd know if I was lying, I don't think it's getting any better. Momma thinks it's getting worse. We ran out of the medicine again. Momma says she'll have enough money in her next paycheck to buy some more. I told her I don't need it but I can breathe better when we have it.

The good news is that I think Momma really likes Billy and I think I like him, too. He's real clean, he's good at his job. Momma says he's real involved in the community and he's even received some awards for doing good stuff for people and kids. Momma says he looks good in a coat and tie. And he has lots of them. Says he's a "looker." There's a picture of him with the mayor out there on the wall by the TV. Even some newspaper articles. Momma says she thinks he's a good man. He's real kind to her. Lets us stay in this little cottage for free. It sits right behind his house with a little stone walk to the back door. And we've been here a couple of weeks.

Last night, Billy got home before Momma and he knocked on the door and asked me if he could come in and I said sure. So, he sat me on the bed with him and put his arm around me and he's real strong. He works out a lot. He's got this big vein on his right arm that looks like a piece of yarn or cord. Anyway, we just talked like grown-ups do. He asked me questions and then listened. And I mean he really listened. And I don't think a grown-up man has ever listened to me before. Then he told me that I'd be a beautiful woman one day, which nobody has ever told me.

You know all the other men that Momma's gone out with never talked to me like that. They never asked me what I thought and nobody ever told me I was or would be beautiful. He was nice. Didn't treat me like I was in the way. We even had ice cream at the kitchen table. He let me have three scoops and I covered it in gummy bears and chocolate sprinkles. And he said not to tell Momma. That it would be our secret. That sometimes secrets are good and it was okay if we had a secret and he asked me to promise. And I did. 'Cause I like ice cream. And I like the way he puts his hand on my back. It makes me feel good. Makes me feel wanted. Like he's hugging me. And he smells good. Momma says she likes the way he smells.

I finished reading the entry and had to force myself to quit gritting my teeth. I skimmed through to another entry.

Dear God,

Last night, while Momma was working and me and Billy were sneaking some ice cream, Billy asked me if I'd ever been told how women become women. I told him no so then he whispered how that happens. Said, if I wanted, when I was ready, that he would help me. That it was up to me. No pressure. Said it would be our secret. Like the ice cream. Said a couple of times is all it takes. Said every girl does it. Said it doesn't hurt and it's real natural. Like, it's the way our bodies are supposed to work. Said for me to think about it and we'd talk more tomorrow, which is now today. I was thinking maybe I should talk to Momma about it but then I got to tell her about the ice cream, too. And she's not gonna be happy if I tell her that. Plus, I promised him I wouldn't and he's a real good man. Even Momma said so.

I turned the page. I was not ready for what I found.

Dear God,

He lied. It hurts. I didn't like it. If that's how you become a woman, I don't want to be one.

I closed the book and cussed myself for opening it.

# CHAPTER NINE

Thirty minutes later, the two girls and their carts walked out, followed by Marleena. She ushered them onto the elevator then returned to me. "Baby, you sure I can't get you a room?"

"No, I've asked too much as it is. Will you make sure I get the bill?"

Her head tilted sideways. "You taking them to dinner?"

"Hadn't really thought about it."

She raised her eyebrows. "Their ribs are sticking out."

I stared at the door. "They do look hungry."

"You want me to make you a reservation?"

"I'm not sure they're gonna feel like going much of anywhere. They've been...doing a lot of that."

She scratched her chin. "You want me to have Chef Cleo cook up something special?"

"I think they'd like that. You still got that little room..."

She nodded and started walking toward the elevator. "About seven then?"

Marleena was the kind of woman that made you want to climb

up in her lap and just set a while. The cradle of her bosom could deflect a nuclear blast. "Yes, ma'am."

Marleena disappeared and the door opened. Turbo came scurrying out, checking every corner and dropping turds on the carpet. Hope followed. She was wearing her robe, crawling behind him on her knees. She still hadn't said a word to me. She stopped, lifted Turbo to her shoulder, avoided eye contact, and nodded toward the open door.

Sam was standing against the window again. I walked in, feeling like a cat caught with his hand in the fish bowl. I handed her the driver's license. "You left this in your jeans." Then the notebook. "This was wrapped up in the laundry. I figure she'll want it."

She nodded. Set it on the bed. I could tell she wanted to know if I'd read it, the window into their lives, but to ask me might open a can of worms she didn't want opened at the moment. Maybe I should have told her that I did, but I still had too many questions.

She was fidgeting with her hands. Chewing on her lip. "When I get someplace with an address, I think I've got one more check coming from Walmart, I'll send money. For all this. They were good to me. They should send it." She shook her head. Her voice dropped—lowered by the shame. "I wasn't always like this."

I checked my watch. It was nearly four. "Why don't you two get a nap and—"

"Do you always do that?"

"What's that?"

"Ignore people who are trying to thank you."

"I'm not doing it for the thanks. Lady…Sam, why don't you try and not look past the next few hours. We'll figure out tomorrow, tomorrow. Take a nap, get some rest." The television was a flat-screen and looked forty-five to fifty inches across. "Watch a movie, let me fill the prescriptions, and we'll eat about seven p.m. Okay with you?" I grabbed the scrips off the tabletop. "You two hunker down. Kick your feet up. Raid the mini bar. Have a drink. Have two. You look like you could use one. I'll be back at a few minutes to seven."

# CHAPTER TEN

I needed some air so I went and got it. Sucked in all I could. I walked down to the Mississippi and watched the water roll past. Imagined Huck and Jim paddling in the distance. Maybe Tom Sawyer close behind. The thought took me away for a minute. It was one of my favorite books. One of the few I'd read more than once.

I ran by the drugstore and picked up $407 worth of prescriptions. A number that made me want to get in my truck and drive away. I was standing in the checkout line trying to figure out if I had enough room on my credit card and noticed a neatly stacked pile of fleece blankets. The label called them "Cuddlies." All rolled up and waiting on opportunistic buyers—like me. They had a light blue one printed with little angels. One light pink with Tinker Bell. I thought she'd like it.

I walked around the corner and stepped inside a bookstore. Found a pocket-sized American Heritage Dictionary for five dollars. It was about three inches thick so I figured she could most nearly find any word she needed. I threw the dictionary in the bag with the drugs and headed back. Slower this time.

I counted the cracks in the sidewalk while thinking about tomorrow. I won't lie. I was starting to wonder what I'd gotten myself into. To be honest, I wanted somebody else to be in this place and not me. My plate was already full. I made it into the parking garage and around the backside of my truck where I started getting ready for dinner. I'd parked in the corner which gave me some privacy. Besides, there wasn't anybody in here but the valets. I was starting to smell a bit ripe so I stripped off my shirt, and baby-wiped my pits and whatnot.

I put on some deodorant, shaved in my side mirror, slapped on some aftershave, then sat in a folding chair next to my truck and rolled a cigarette. Linus had his blanket. I have my truck and rolling papers.

At 6:30 p.m., I heard a pair of slippers shuffling across the parking lot. Hurried. Purposeful. I poked my head around and found Sam walking at me in her robe and wet hair. Still dripping.

I stood up, snapped up my shirt, and started tucking it in.

She walked right up to me, totally invading my personal space. She held her finger in the air and then her eyebrows sort of leaned in toward one another, then one lifted slightly higher than the other. She looked around my truck, stepped back, and pursed her lips. She had taken my advice and had a drink. "You're not actually staying down here, are you?"

A deep breath. "Look, I'm tempted to lie so you don't feel bad but me and this truck have a history. I've spent many a night right here and I'm just as comfortable down here as you'll be up there."

"But Marleena said she could get you a room."

"And she offered, but I'm fine right here."

Her shoulders sunk even further. "Ours is costing too much, isn't it?"

"This place, normally, is real expensive, yes. But I used to work down here a lot and Marleena's giving me the same rate."

"Which is?"

"Ninety-nine dollars."

She frowned. Hands on her hips. "You're paying a hundred dollars for that palace in the sky? That room probably sells for six or seven hundred dollars a night." She paused. "I didn't always have nothing."

"No kidding. I wouldn't lie to you. Besides, if your friend Billy comes looking for you my guess is that this would be one of the last places he would look."

The sight of me here and not in some opulent room upstairs took the wind out of her sails. She regrouped, stepping back into my personal space, and crossed her arms. Water from the shower still rested on her chest and the lobes of her ears. She smelled clean and fresh. "I need to know something."

"Okay."

"Do you want out?"

"Not sure I follow you."

She wrapped her robe tighter about her. Doing so gave me a flash of what lay covered on the inside. I'll admit, my eyes were drawn. She tied her belt. "Come on, we're both adults. I'm a big girl. You can leave now, we'll slip out early tomorrow morning and nobody is the worse for wear. I'll send you some money—"

"Have you got any other option?"

"Other than?"

"Me. If I leave here, what other option do you have?"

Her lips grew tight. She looked toward the light of the entrance to the garage. "I'll figure something."

"Okay, then what are you figuring between?"

She crossed her arms. "I'm trying to give you an out. If I were you, I'd want it. If I were you, I'd take it."

"Yeah, well...you're not me."

"Don't tell me you haven't thought about it."

" 'Course I've thought about it. Every few seconds. But every time I walk through what it looks like, I see some bad things."

"Like what?"

"Things I've seen before."

"But you don't even know me."

"You're right. But what I've seen has told me you need a break. Now, I can't offer you much but I can drive you back west, back home, which is where I was headed when all this business started. It'd give you some space. You could regroup. Look at some options. Go from there."

Both eyebrows raised. "You'd do that?"

"It's a small town. One of those places where everybody knows everybody's business but they mean well. Mostly."

"Why?"

"Well, they just do, I mean—"

"No, not them. You. Why?"

I sat down, checked my watch, and began rolling a cigarette. "I watched the soul of a woman crack in half one time. Not a"—I licked the paper—"pretty sight. Rather not see it again. I'm not the best judge of souls, 'specially when it comes to women. Matter of fact, I'm right horrible. But best I can tell, yours is close to doing the same. The fact that I just met you really doesn't matter much." I shrugged. "A soul is a soul."

She stood, arms folded, studying me. Her left leg showed through the slit of her robe. I tried not to notice but it was tough to miss. My wife and I had not slept in the same bed in about three years. I'm a man. Not an idiot.

She stepped closer, eyeing my cigarette. "Why do you do that?"

"It reminds me of my father."

"How so?"

"He did it whenever he was thinking or about to say something meaningful. It usually marked a moment of importance."

"Are you about to say something real important?"

"He also did it when he was facing a tough decision with no easy answer and he didn't quite know what to do."

"Did he smoke them?"

"Yes."

"Do you?"

"No."

"Why not?"

"It ain't about the smoking."

"Is he alive?"

"No."

"Did he die of lung cancer?"

"No."

"What then?"

A pause. "Lead poisoning."

"I'm sorry. Was it something he ate?"

"Sort of." I paused. Turned toward her. "I was just wondering whether or not this Billy Simmons will try to find you. I mean, how motivated is he?"

She looked at the floor and chewed on one side of her mouth. "Real." I told you there was more the second and third time around.

"What makes you say that?"

"When I came home and found Hope on his bed, naked and shaking, I heard the water running, which told me that Billy was in the shower and I didn't know how long he'd be there. The only thing I could think of was getting Hope out of there. But then I saw the screen. Off to the side, on his desk, a computer screen was lit up and Hope was staring at it. The one he worked on. We never messed with it. Anyway, when I looked closer I found a screen full of files. Videos mostly." She paused. "They were saved by date so I clicked on one of the more recent." She shook her head. "It was a video of him and me. I didn't know he had a camera set up. I'd have never..." She trailed off. "The last video was dated that day. Last Thursday. It had been modified, or saved, about ten minutes before I arrived." She broke off again, rubbing her hands together. "It was him with Hope. You can hear her...so...he had this thumb drive and the light was flashing. I guessed he was saving video onto the thumb drive. I grabbed it, wrapped her up in her blanket, carried her out back to our little place to grab whatever I could find and then we heard the water cut off. We had to pass back through the house to get out so we crept in and hid in the front room while he was getting out of the shower. I heard his electric razor cut on, which told me I had a few minutes. Or so I thought. I had a lot going on, I was scared. I was holding Hope, and I dropped the thumb drive on the hardwood floor behind the sofa. You know those A/C vents that come up through the floor?"

I nodded.

"It fell in one of those. I could feel the top of it with my finger, but couldn't lift it up. I needed pliers or something. We didn't have time. When we heard his bathroom door squeak open, we snuck out the front door, across the street, and I stole that old woman's car." She shook her head and tried to laugh. "I imagine he found us gone, went to his computer, found the thumb drive missing, and, here we are." I considered this. Her eyes narrowed. There was fear behind them. "You think he'll find us?"

"If he's any kind of lawman, he'll get his hands on the surveillance tapes from the truck stop. He'll see my truck drive in, fill up, then drive off with you in it. While I covered the tags on the drive out, he'll be able to identify us from when we drove in." I nodded. "Yes, I think he will look." We were quiet a minute. I turned to her. "Is Hope...okay? I mean..."

"Physically, yes."

"She need anything?"

She shook her head. She continued, "When I left, I wasn't thinking too clearly. I just knew I had to get out and I didn't want pictures of me and my daughter broadcast, or sold, over the Internet. But...can the authorities help me? I mean, if we went and talked to them, like right now, do you think they'd, I realize it's all hearsay, my word against his, but if I told them about the drive. Better yet, if they saw it."

I nodded. "I think it'd be a good idea. I know some folks. Let me make some calls. You all have been through enough for one day. Let's tackle tomorrow's trouble, tomorrow."

She turned. I could hear her stomach growl. "You still want to take us to dinner?"

I handed her the prescriptions and she tucked them under her arm. "Yes, ma'am."

"And would you please stop doing that?"

"What?"

"Calling me 'ma'am.' I'm not your mother."

I nodded. "Yes, ma'am." I gestured toward the bag. "I got her a new dictionary. That other one is sort of worn out."

She tried to smile, turned, and walked away.

"Ma'am?"

She stopped but didn't turn around.

"Sam?"

She turned. I took one step toward her and turned my hat in my hand. "I should have told you earlier, but—well, I read a few pages of Hope's journal."

This sunk in, as did the unspoken admission that I'd been suspicious of her when I gave it back.

"You might hold on to it. It could be used as evidence."

"Why tell me now?"

"Because not to feels like lying."

She nodded and looked away. "Yes, it does."

I watched her go and I was pretty sure she knew I was watching. Most women do. I was about to ask myself what my father would do in this situation, but he gave me that answer a long time ago.

She disappeared and my phone rang. It was Debbie. "Hey, honey, you got a second?"

"Sure."

"Billy Simmons is a decorated lawman out of San Antone. Pictures in all the local papers. You're right, he runs the SWAT unit.

Evidently he's a pretty good softball player, too. Coaches both boys and girls. Took his girls team to a few championships."

"And the license number?"

"Samantha Dyson. Female. Nothing. No outstanding warrants, parking tickets. Nothing. Thirty-three-year-old female from Cordele, Georgia. Model citizen far as I can tell."

Figured as much. That decided a few things for me. "Is he in tomorrow?"

She checked his calendar. "No appointments that I can see but you know him...he'll find any reason to get out of here."

"Ask him to meet me at my house, tomorrow night. Will you?"

"Sure thing. He'll be there."

"Thanks, Debbie."

"Oh, and Cowboy?"

"Yeah."

"You okay?"

Seconds passed. I stared through the glass as Sam stepped into the elevator and the doors closed. "I'll be in touch. Thanks again." I clicked the phone off and scratched my head. I'd never understood how people worked their whole life, or part of it, retired, and then—for no reason that was apparent to the rest of us—came out of retirement.

Until now.

# CHAPTER ELEVEN

*Somewhere back in my childhood.*

The second hand rounded past the six. Thirty seconds and counting. I double-knotted my Converse, tucked my books under my arm, and scooted to the edge of my seat. If I got out the door, down the hall, and past the lockers, I had a chance. I felt eyes over my shoulder. Some laughter. A spitball hit me in the neck. Three . . . two . . .

The bell sounded and I shot from the classroom, weaving through the kids pouring out the doors. First one out, I bounded off the steps, sprinted the sidewalk, and turned alongside the line of buses. I climbed onto the second, and chose my seat in the front row. I rode the bus after school to my grandmother's where I'd stay until my dad picked me up and took me home to the Bar S. If he was working nights, then I just spent the night. Ms. Webster, the bus driver, lowered her paper, eyeing me over the top of her glasses. "Well . . . good afternoon, Tyler."

My knees were bouncy. Eyes darting left and right. "Ma'am."

The four of them loaded a few minutes later, each popping me in the ear or smacking me in the back of the head. Ms. Webster watched them in the rearview mirror above her head. Sitting up front meant they got their licks in when they got on, rather than at random throughout the ride. Last week, my teacher asked me to take out the trash. The Dumpster was behind the school. The buses lined up in front. That put me last on the bus. Didn't take a genius to know they had me.

They'd saved me a seat in the middle. Of them.

There were four and most all had nicknames. The nickname thing started in school. Last summer, they'd made us read *The Outsiders* for summer reading and after that, everybody in school had a nickname, like it or not. A fat kid nicknamed "Knuckles." A skinny kid who wore Coke-bottle glasses, we called him "Eyes." An eighth-grade scrapper named Stacey, which probably explained why he was called "Scrapper." And the fourth kid was known as "Holes," because he was big, like a black hole. He was a foot and a half taller than every other kid in fifth grade and he wore a size eleven shoe.

Ms. Webster hadn't even shifted into second when Scrapper reached over and grabbed the top of my underwear while Holes turned around and pushed down on my shoulders. Scrapper pulled so hard it tore the elastic band off my shorts and caused my underwear to cut into the skin at the top of my crack. Throughout the ride, he kept holding up his prize. Once he hung it around my neck. When I teared up, the taunting grew worse.

I'd become a lot wiser since then, but it wasn't enough.

The bus stopped, door swung open, I tucked both my books under my arm and bounded off, washed in a wave of spent diesel and West Texas dust. The shuffling grew louder behind me. So did the footsteps. I knew better than to turn around. I took off. My Converse high-tops were a white blur. One block. Then two. A third and I was out of breath with a cramp in my stomach. I stopped, pinched my side, caught my breath, crossed the street, and glanced over my shoulder.

Ten days ago, I'd walked into the bathroom and found the four of them surrounding a stall. They were giggling like hyenas. Ginny Prater stood against the far wall, no skirt, no panties. She was crying, knees together and trying to pull her sweater down over her privates. Sunlight reflected off her glasses, which were lying on the ground across the bathroom.

Scrapper had turned, held out his palm and said, "Get out. Ain't no affair of yours."

I didn't want any part of Scrapper. Nor did I want to take on all four of them. So, to Ginny's great dismay, I simply nodded, shut the door, and yanked down hard on the fire alarm. Then I casually walked down the hallway while Mr. Turner ran from his empty class and began checking all the rooms between his and the exit—the first being the bathroom. Each boy got two weeks after-school detention and a phone call home. The detention was no big deal. The calls home were. Each boy got blistered.

I was about to pay for the blistering.

I learned later that Ginny had been a willing participant in a "you-show-me-I'll-show-you" sort of deal. It turned sour when the guys wanted to see more than she wanted to show and add the element of touch.

I turned the last corner and saw my grandmother's house in the distance. I sprinted past the last few driveways gasping for air, turned into my garage and pushed on the garage door. It didn't budge. I leaned hard. It was locked.

Our back door was never locked.

I banged on the door. "Grandma! Grandma!"

Beyond the door, I heard slow footsteps, felt her hand turn the doorknob. Behind me, heavy feet pounded the sidewalk. She cracked open the door. Fresh coffee wafted from inside. I heard the percolator gurgling on the stove. I could see her nose and lips. "Tyler...I'm not letting you in this door."

"What!" I heard an evil giggle just outside the garage. I pushed on the door but the chain held it fast. My voice rose. "Why?"

She stood back, looking down at me. "Sooner or later, you got to face what's facing you." With that, she shut the door and thumbed the bolt across.

I turned slowly. I was scared and starting to cry. I wanted to throw up. I peed a little bit. Scrapper mocked me, "Look at the crybaby. Mommy can't help him 'cause he ain't got no mommy."

Scrapper was the first kid I knew to shave and I didn't want any part of him but he had just said the wrong thing. And something in the way he said it dislodged something in me. More than that, it made me forget that I was afraid. I came off the concrete step and nailed Scrapper with a wild hook. Blood shot across the garage like an exploding balloon. Scrapper hit his knees and started shaking his head and blowing tomato puree from his nose. Holes and Eyes were momentarily stunned by the sight but Knuckles came at me so I kicked him as hard as I could in the gut. That brought him to his knees. He started making noises like he was about to blow chunks. Holes made some loud noise letting me know I was about to get it. I picked up my granddaddy's anvil, the one he used to beat bent plows and sharpen knives. I could only lift it about a foot off the ground. Holes stepped in, and I let go. The tip of the anvil caught the top of Holes's foot and he screamed like a girl.

Scrapper recovered, jumped on me, put me in a headlock, and rushed me toward the wall. Just before my face hit the two-by-four stud, I squirted loose and kicked backward with my foot. That sent Scrapper flying like Superman into his own target. If his nose wasn't broken before, it was now. He lay on the floor screaming.

Eyes had bolted, leaving his glasses, splattered with Scrapper's blood, on the garage floor. I picked them up and set them on my granddaddy's worktable so they wouldn't get crushed. I took a few deep breaths, stepped over Holes and knocked on the back door. I was shaking so I hooked my thumbs in the belt loops of my jeans. My voice quivered. "Granny…"

The dead bolt clicked and the door swung open. She stood, a cup of coffee in her hands. "Can I come in now?" She raised an eyebrow and stared around me into the garage. Knuckles was retching; Holes was holding his foot, crying; Scrapper was a soaking red mess.

She stepped aside.

I walked to the fridge and pulled out the milk. My hand was shaking as I poured it.

Granny stared out into the garage, focusing first on Holes. "Get your lazy butt up off the ground. You ain't hurt. Big ole boy like you." She looked at Knuckles. "You better get to cleaning that mess up off my floor. The Pine-Sol is behind you. Stacey…" She stared at him. "I better call your mom. Doc Pipson might need to set that."

I walked out back, trying to breathe, trying not to cry. My adrenaline was about played out. I went around the house, where nobody could see me, and threw up from my toes. Mostly milk. White specks splattered my jeans and high-tops. When I looked up, my dad stood across from me. He was leaning against the house, next to the window. Two cigarette butts stamped at his feet.

He was forty. Sun-spotted hands, callused palms, big fingers. Tall, skinny, tanned. The Marlboro man. He smoothed my hair. "You okay?"

I wiped my mouth on my shirtsleeve. "Yes, sir."

He nodded, and pulled his tobacco bag from his shirt pocket, opening it with his teeth. He fingered out a roll paper with his left hand, quickly poured with his right, then while balancing the Carter Hall on the paper, he cinched the bag tight with his teeth, dropped it in his pocket and rolled a cigarette. His fingers were steady. Then he flipped the paper together, rolled it with a quick twist, and licked it. Tight and cylindrical, he dropped it on the end of his lips. He slipped his Zippo from his front pocket, lit the tip of his cigarette, then slammed the Zippo shut on his thigh.

I'd seen him do that a couple hundred times and to this day, it's one of the noises that reminds me of my father. He drew deeply, the end glowing bright red. He exhaled, talking through a sheet of smoke. "What'd you learn?"

The smell showered me. I filled my lungs. "Hit the toughest first, and hit him with everything you got."

He nodded, squinting one eye. "Then get ready to hit him again in case that didn't work. Whatever you do, plan on it not working. That way you're always one step ahead of them. Then, if it does work"—he smiled—"be thankful." Another deep draw. A glowing ruby between his teeth. "What else?"

"Just 'cause they're big, don't make them tough."

"Sometimes that's right. And…" He smiled again. "Sometimes, they're big and tough. Each time is different." He exhaled. "Anything else?"

I stared through the glass at Knuckles and Holes still sitting on the garage floor. Granny had Scrapper sitting on the back steps with ice on his face. She had his face tilted back. He was coughing and hacking and spitting blood. I looked at my dad out of the corner of my eye. Polished boots made by a man named Dumps he'd put in prison, starched jeans, double-thick belt, button-up white shirt, white hat. His .45, a custom-made Les Baer, sat holstered on his right hip in a black Milt Sparks holster. His star hung on his left shirt pocket. Polished to a shine. The edges were worn. I whispered and could not look at him. "Dad, I was scared."

He laughed, flicked ashes and ground them into the dirt with his toe. He knelt, looking up at me. On Fridays he'd take me to the drive-in and we'd watch John Wayne reruns. We could quote entire scenes. He smiled. "Remember, courage is being scared to death—"

I finished it. "And saddling up anyway."

He pushed the hair out of my eyes. "Being scared is okay. It's better than not being scared. If you're not scared, you're probably cocky and about to get in a whole mess of hurt. Trust me…scared is good."

"You ever get scared?"

"All the time."

"But…you're a Texas Ranger."

We sat, leaning our backs against the garage. "Rangers get scared, too."

"Really?"

"Really."

"What do you do?"

He smiled "Keep swinging." He nodded over his shoulder. "Or, if need be, focus on the front site."

I nodded like I knew. Like I understood.

He put his arm around me. Dad didn't talk much. I discovered after he was gone that when he did, it was worth listening to. "Sometimes, we're the only one to stand against bad people." He looked out across the fence, out across the pasture. "If we don't... who will? Who's gonna stand up for someone who can't stand up for themself, or those they love?" He shook his head and spat. "I won't stand for that. I wasn't put here to tuck my tail and run." Several hundred acres of flat Texas ground lay around us. Nothing but rows as far as the eye could see. A tree line on the far side. "Like it or not..." He traced a line in the dirt with his toe. "This is a battlefield. Has been since Cain killed Abel. And don't let it get complicated. Gray it ain't. It's black and white. Good versus evil. You might as well choose sides right now." He nodded back over his shoulder. "Thanks to you..." He lifted my hand and stared at the center knuckle. The cut had spread open. "...those boys in there are reconsidering their choice."

I nodded, trying not to cry.

I stared at his .45. He picked up on it.

"The gun don't make you right. You're either right or wrong long before you pick this thing up. Matter of fact, if you're wrong, it'll only get you in trouble. But, if you're right...this can help even the odds. They say God made man, but Sam Colt made them equal." He patted his hip. "Then John Browning came along and made some better than others." He paused. "Oh, and, just so's you'll know, the odds ain't usually in our favor. Bad stuff happens to good people. Happens all the time. Remember that."

He paused, staring out across the field. Then he turned, took off his white hat and placed it on my head. "You keep going the way you're going, and there may well come a day when that choice involves more than just you. When on the other side, is someone who can't defend themself, maybe himself or herself, and all that stands between them and some real bad stuff is you. Some folks don't care. Some walk away. Some lie down and cower. And, some of us, well..."

The sun was going down. Setting on the edge of Texas. We studied it. He spoke through the air in front of us. "When I joined the Rangers, your grandfather walked me out to that fence yonder and we leaned against it a long time. He said he'd been infantry in World War II. Stormed a beach or two. Said he was at the Bulge when things got real bad. Cold. Snow. Nearly surrounded. They got in a fight that lasted all night. Come morning, he looked down the line and saw a lot of his buddies lying alone, exposed. Half blowed up. Germans just picking them off. Said his lieutenant crawled up and ordered him to pick up a stretcher. He did. That night they had to pry his hands off the handles." He paused, nodding. "Sometimes the most courageous thing a man can do is run back across the battlefield and rescue the wounded." He shook his head and spat. "But don't fool yourself. It ain't glamorous. Ain't at all. It's simply a choice."

I looked up at him. "You ever had to make it?"

I could tell he didn't want to answer. It would take me years to understand the answer once he did. Finally, he whispered. "Every day."

# CHAPTER TWELVE

Dear God,

You're not gonna believe this. I'm not sure I do.

We were at the truck stop, trying to get some money or something when Billy showed up and tried to kidnap us. It scared me real bad and I peed in his van.

Then, just when I thought Billy was about to do what Billy done, this man…the one that helped us…his name's "Tyler," I guess you already knowed that. His nickname is "Cowboy." He's the guy that wears the hat. Anyway, he thumped Billy in the head, tied him up, threw him in the bushes. Then he carried Momma all the way to his truck. He must be real strong. And then he gave Momma a gun and told her to shoot anyone that ain't him.

I didn't know what Momma was gonna do. When he walked off, she got out of the car, and stood there, pacing back and forth and she just didn't know what to do. She was clutching that gun and waving it around and muttering to herself and, I just didn't know what she might do. But, after a few minutes, she climbed back in the car, put her arm around me and told me everything was gonna be all right. That all we had to do was get away from Billy and this man was our ticket out of here. And then she looked at me and told me, "Baby, if that man gets in this truck and puts one hand on you, I'm gonna shoot him in the face."

I think sometimes that Momma's had a rough go. Like maybe things is harder on her than they are on me. That maybe sometimes she feels all the bad that happens to both of us. Like, she feels the bad that happens to her and then on top of that she feels the bad that happens to me so all that bad is just piled on Momma. That's why I believed her when she said that bit about shooting him in the face. 'Cause I think she's had about enough of all the bad stuff.

Then Momma told me when he got back I had to hush and not say nothing, which I wasn't planning to anyway. But then she told me she was finished trusting men and she'd be danged, well—that ain't what she really said but I can't say that word to you, but she said she'd be that if she told him our real names so she didn't. She made up a couple. She told him her name was Virginia and my name was Emma. And she told me to go along with it like it was true. Now we both know that ain't my name and it ain't her name but we didn't know nothing much 'bout this man and we ain't having too much luck with men right now and I was just wondering if you were okay with us lying to him, even though she told the truth later. I mean, when Momma said it, I didn't disagree with her. Which makes me an accessory—I saw that on TV and then looked it up which means I didn't do it but knew about it which is just like doing it—which is why I'm bringing it up.

When the man came back, he gave Momma the chance to keep the gun. Told her she could. Told her right there,

"Ma'am, if you want, you can keep that as long as you're with me. If it makes you feel better. Safer." But Momma didn't. She gave it right back. Handed it back like it was a hot potato. And then he gave her another chance and he said, "You sure?" And Momma just nodded. And I can't tell you why other than I think it had something to do with his voice. His voice just makes you want to believe him. It ain't like other voices. It's like one of them voices that when you hear it, everything in you wants to believe that what he's saying is true and if it's not, then, well, something's not just wrong with him, but something's wrong with the whole wide world.

I know I'm rattling. I tend to do that when I'm scared. But, I ain't as scared as I was. I ain't peeing myself no more.

Dear God,

Cowboy drove us to Momma's sister's house in New Orleans but she was gone. Like, she didn't even own the house anymore so Momma freaks out and starts walking down the sidewalk and Cowboy lets her get about two blocks away and then he stops her, puts Turbo in the car, puts us in the car and carries us to this hotel where like kings and princes and presidents would stay. It's a palace. They got marble everywhere. And in the bathrooms, like the ones in the lobby, they got real towels. Not paper. And they got free perfume in little spray bottles. The bed in the room is huge and it has a tent over the top. We got our own coffeemaker and stereo with speakers in the ceiling and the TV is real thin and bigger than I can reach across. Cowboy even had a doctor come to the room and sew up Momma's eye and then he had a woman doctor come and look at me and she said I'd be fine. And, to be honest, it don't really hurt no more. Well, maybe a little, but not much.

Then they let us swim in the bathtub. Which we did. Momma and I got in, dumped in two bottles of bubbles and we soaked and sang and played like dolphins. She shaved her legs and armpits 'cause she said they were " 'bout long enough to braid" and then I put the plastic cover on the razor and pretended 'cause I ain't got nothing to shave. Then we got out and we started laughing 'cause we were all pruny. Our skin was drawed up like raisins so we put on these robes. I ain't never had a robe before. It smells like flowers. I felt like a movie star. All I need now is some wet concrete and a sidewalk.

You remember that woman I was telling you about downstairs? The big woman? Well, she came back up and brought these two women pushing racks of clothes—all our sizes. And we got to shop with no one else around. They made us try on everything. And we did. I got new jeans, new T-shirts, new panties, a new gown, and everything was still new and never been worn 'cause it still had a price tag. And you know what? Those jeans...they cost a hundred dollars. A hundred dollars! Can you believe that? He must be real rich 'cause he bought us all this stuff.

A little while later, Cowboy knocked on the door and when Momma opened it, he held his hat in his hand and cussed. But I don't think he meant to 'cause he apologized to me but I think it's okay 'cause he just don't know that most men say lots of other stuff when Momma gets all prettied up. So, we went to dinner and sat down to a white tablecloth and candlelight— just like you see on the soap operas. We ate for an hour. They had this cheese, the lady said it was like a breeze, whatever that is. It was creamy. Momma spread it on a cracker and then talked with her mouth full. She rolled her eyes and said, "Oh my...oh my...that's good." She shook her head and took another bite. "That's like sex on a cracker." But I don't think she was being ugly. I just think it was really good cheese.

And Cowboy laughed. His face even turned a little red but I noticed he never drank a sip of wine or nothing. Just water.

We had more to eat than I've ever seen on one table and then we had dessert and the chef rolled out this table and did something with bananas and poured something like gasoline over the top and then lit it on fire and it burned blue and I've never eaten gasoline but it was yummy. Didn't upset my stomach or nothing. Cowboy let me have three helpings. Three helpings! Momma said I couldn't have any more or I'd be bouncing off the walls. But Momma didn't eat much dessert 'cause her stomach is having a hard time. Stuff ain't staying in her very long. I think it's 'cause she don't know what to do. She's been to the bathroom fifteen times today. The doc says it's her nerves. She said it's like "crap through a goose" but I've never seen a goose crap. Me? I've only been to the bathroom like twice. Which they said is good.

After dessert, they ordered coffee and the man in the white jacket brought me some milk in a little cup with a spout which I thought was real cute so I sipped it straight from the spout but when I tasted it, it wasn't milk. Well, not exactly. It was milk but it was sweet and thick. Momma said it was cream. I told her I liked it and asked her if I could drink it and she looked at Cowboy and then at me and shook her head but he just sipped his coffee and said that if I wasn't going to drink it that he was gonna and he don't know why we even bother with that other stuff so Momma smiled and nodded, which meant I could drink it so I did. Every bit. The man in the white jacket even brought me some more. It was the best milk I ever drunk. I don't know why we don't drink that all the time. I mean, Cowboy is right. Why do we even mess with that other stuff?

After dinner, Cowboy took us back to our room and showed us how to watch movies and he gave us his phone number. Put on his reading glasses, and wrote it down for Momma on a napkin.

We found a movie, which cost us $14.99—for one movie—and I guess it's worth it 'cause we didn't have to go to the theater. It's like they called the theater and brought the movie to us. I'm sort of watching it right now while I write, and I'm eating out of the refrigerator in our room. Momma's over there with her eyebrows scrunched together thumbs twitching. Rolling one over the other. I think she's thinking about tomorrow. I asked her if we could stay here another night and she shook her head. But, I don't know where we'll go. And she don't neither. Funny thing is, we're up here in this nice room and I don't know where Cowboy is. I asked Momma and she shook her head. I think she's worried that Billy is gonna find us and come knocking on the door and she don't know what she'll do when he does. Wait—

Things are all upside down here. Just as the movie was getting good Momma threw her robe back on and said we're going to find Cowboy. So, we rode the elevator in our slippers down to the parking garage and walked out to his truck where we found him sleeping and I felt real bad being up there in that palace and him down here in this old truck but he said it weren't no problem at all and he slept there many a night so I felt a little better but not much. Then Momma curled her finger like she does when she wants you to do something right now and he got up and pulled on his boots, put in his hearing aid and turned it up and grabbed his hat, which he don't never go nowheres without and when we got back up here Momma pulled out the sleeper sofa, straightened the sheets and made him sleep right there. He's over there now. Sleeping. I thought all men snored but he don't. He's quiet as a church mouse. I can tell Momma ain't asleep yet 'cause she ain't breathing like she does when she's sleeping. Like she's holding part of her breath. Which is most of the time.

One thing you should know about Cowboy...he carries a gun all the time. Actually, two guns. One on his hip and one on his ankle. I been thinking. I think Momma needs to learn to shoot and she needs to carry a gun. That way she could shoot Billy. And you know what...I think Momma's starting to think that, too, 'cause she keeps looking at his gun. One of them is resting right there in a holster on his hip. I can't see the other but I can sort of see the bulge around his ankle through the bend in his jeans.

I got one more question. Cowboy seems like a good guy, but Billy seemed like a good guy, too. Saw his picture with the mayor. He helped kids. But he turned out to be bad. How do you know? I mean, what's the secret? What if Cowboy turns out to be like Billy? Just what do we do then? I asked Momma that and she shook her head and said, We're screwed. I think Momma's having a tough time.

I'm glad he sleeps with that gun on. I like that. I hope he shoots Billy. I hope that's okay to say. Oh, and if you're wondering what those two things are below here, one is a Tinker Bell sticker and the other is a lottery ticket but we didn't win nothing. Least ways not no money. At first I threw it away, but then I went back and got it 'cause no one ever got me one before. I taped it in here so I wouldn't forget.

# CHAPTER THIRTEEN

I woke up and something wasn't right. Not wrong in the universe but wrong as in something was warm next to me. My hand told me it was a person. A small person. I rubbed my eyes and sat up. I was right. Hope was lying next to me. Crashed out. Sprawled like a snow angel. I scratched my head and then looked at the end of the bed where Sam was staring at me. Wide-eyed. Tears welling up. I shook my head. "Ma'am, I didn't. I swear I didn't have nothing to do—"

She wasn't listening. "I saw it. With my own eyes. She crawled out after you went to sleep and got in with you. Said nothing to me. But—" She swallowed back the tears. "She slept...through the night."

"She doesn't normally do that?"

She shook her head. "She's never done that."

"Since when?"

"Since forever."

I had slept in my clothes so I pulled the covers back up her shoulders, slid on my boots, and checked the condition of my weapons—making sure they were both loaded and safe. Then I went into the bathroom to splash some water on my face, and used a washcloth to wipe down my pits—wishing I had a baby wipe. I unlocked the door and whispered to Sam, "See you at breakfast. You two come on down when you get dressed. Breakfast around here is a real...experience. You don't want to miss it."

It didn't take a Rhodes Scholar to realize that if I left them here—as in drove off without saying good-bye, which is what one half of me wanted to do—they'd be on the street before nightfall. Probably sleeping in a public bathroom or bus station. Like Will Smith in that movie with his son. The only difference between yesterday and tomorrow would be new clothes, a shower, and a full stomach. None of which would last very long. The conversation I was having with myself over coffee wasn't much of a discussion but it was one I needed to have.

The breakfast buffet on the club floor of the Ritz-Carlton is the stuff of an Audrey Hepburn movie. It's a sea of white table-cloths filled with exotic fruits, world-class pastries, omelets made to order, three-inch-thick waffles, boutique bacon and sausage, fifty different types of cheese, several types of yogurt and cereal, fresh-squeezed juices, imported coffee. And all of this is blanketed in classical music that for some reason makes food taste better. Every time I eat here it reminds me of Templeton the rat at the fair in *Charlotte's Web*.

Sam appeared first, followed by Hope who had her notebook tucked under her arm, her new blanket around her shoulders, and crusty little sleepers hanging in the corners of her eyes. They turned the corner and Hope's jaw dropped. Sam's did, too.

Sam led Hope down the buffet tables, helping her fill her plate. I watched them out of the corner of my eye. I had thought, because I am guilty of judging a book by its cover, that two filthy, down-on-their-luck, penniless loners wouldn't know how to navigate a place like this—that maybe they'd clash with the social graces required to fit in here. Not that I'm the guru of social graces. It's just that I've been here before and while here I had pretty good training so I can pass for a talented counterfeit. But, as I watched Sam quietly educate Hope, I got the feeling she was not new to all this. And the more I studied how she carried herself, how she spoke, how she lifted the spoon, the portions she took, how she stepped, the way she held her shoulders, how her chin never seemed to dip, her entire demeanor, I wondered if she'd had far more practice in this world than I. The kind you're born into. Maybe, in truth, I was the poser. Maybe survival trumps class and once surviving is no longer an issue, the class creeps back in. I sat back, sipped my coffee, and realized that knowing this was the first good feeling I'd had about them since we met. Somehow, the thought that life hadn't always been this bad was a comfort. 'Course, as I looked at the future, discomfort wasn't far behind.

They sat and Sam nodded at Hope. Hope folded her hands in her lap and looked up at me. Then she looked down. I asked her, "How's the itching? The little red bumps?"

She nodded, looked away, then picked up her fork and began eating in small bites looking everywhere but at my face.

I tried again. "Is your cough better?"

She covered her mouth and coughed once. Whatever doc had given her was working. The mucus had cleared.

I wanted to ask her about the rest of her, and tell her that she'd be okay, and that the world isn't all like that, and tell her that I'd thought a good bit about how to deal with the man that did it, but figured it was none of my business.

Least not yet.

I turned to Sam thinking maybe Hope needed to hear the conversation she and I had in the parking garage yesterday. I said, "I really need to get home. Got an eleven-year-old boy there that's missing me." Hope looked up at me. "If you all are game, I thought I'd take you with me and, because I've been there most my life, I know a good many people in town. I think we can get you settled, maybe get you a job, that is if you don't mind relocating to West Texas."

Sam exhaled. From the sound of it, she'd been holding that breath for about a week. "That'd be great."

Hope made eye contact and held it, slowly forking eggs in her mouth while she studied me. Milk covered her top lip.

I spoke softly. "You got a mustache."

Hope licked it off but never took her eyes off me. Sam dabbed the edges of her mouth with a napkin.

I stood, folded my napkin and laid it on the table. "You two take your time. I'm going to go clear things with Marleena. I'll meet you at the truck in just a bit."

I walked around the corner and rode the elevator down to the parking garage. I walked to the edge, where the cell signal improved enough to give me four bars and dialed. Dumps answered after the first ring. I said, "Hey...how you two holding up?"

"Great. He's got a teacher planning day so he's home from school. I'm making him a bologna sandwich. How you?"

"I need you to do me a favor."

"Name it."

"Pick up a bit. Make sure the sheets are clean."

"Which bed?" A pause. "The one you sleeping in now, or the one you used to sleep in?"

"Used to."

He sucked through his teeth. His tone changed. "Cowboy...you okay? Sounds like you're carrying a bit of weight."

"Yes, sir. But, it's part of that story that's getting longer all the time. I'll tell you when I get there, but it's gonna piss you off, so pour the bourbon and I'll see you when I get home."

"When's that?"

"Barring any more surprises...tonight."

"Hold on, somebody wants to talk to you."

The phone rustled as it switched hands. "Hey, Dad. When you coming home?"

"Today, big guy. How are you?" I tried to steer the conversation away from where it was going. "How's school?"

"Good. I got a hundred on a history test." His voice rose. "Hey, Dad...?"

Here it came—the runaway train. "Yeah?"

"You get to see Momma?"

Sometimes all the pain in life can be summed up in one question. I leaned against the edge, steadying myself. "Yeah...I saw her."

"She getting better?"

"She's doing well. Misses you. Said to give you a hug."

"Still thirty-two days and counting?"

A pause. "Yep, she's finished up there in a month."

"I'm taking Mr. B to the river. See you when you get home."

"Hey, Brodie?"

"Yes, sir."

"I need to ask your permission about something."

"Yes, sir."

"I want to know if it's okay with you if I bring home a woman and her daughter."

"Why?"

" 'Cause they don't have a place to stay."

"Are they in trouble?"

"That's one way to put it."

"Where'd you meet them?"

"At a truck stop. Some guy tried to kidnap them."

"What happened?"

I rubbed my forehead. "I didn't let him."

"Would it be for very long?"

"Couple of weeks I should think. Just until they get on their feet and I can find them a place to stay. You know we've got that extra room and..."

"What about Mom?"

I dodged it. "I think they'll be gone before your mom starts thinking about coming home."

He thought for a moment. "It's okay with me. Here's Dumps."

"Hey, Brodie?"

"Sir?"

"Keep a watch out for snakes. And don't trample the blue-bonnets."

"Yes, sir."

He laid down the phone and I heard him running across the kitchen and flinging open the screen door.

A kid on a horse in Texas. All was right in the world.

Dumps spoke again. "You know...you're running out of 'X's."

"Tell me about it."

"It ain't like you can just buy him another calendar."

I spoke as much to me, as him. "I know that."

"That's a good boy. You need to talk with him."

"And just how do you expect me to explain all this to a fifth-grader?"

"Look, I ain't said it was easy. He's your son. She's your wife—"

"Was."

"Whatever. You need to—"

"Dumps."

He was quiet a minute. He scratched the whiskers on his chin. "I'll get the sheets cleaned. Tidy up a bit. You need me to run to the store? We ain't got much around here."

"Yeah, whatever you think. Thanks."

"Drive careful."

I hung up but the thought that kept going through my head was a question: If someone had hog-tied me, stolen something from me and put me to sleep in the far corner of a truck stop, leaving me face down in the mud and grass with no keys, what would I be doing right now? Fact is, it wasn't the question that was bothering me, but the answer.

# CHAPTER FOURTEEN

Dear God,

We're driving out of here today with our new friend, Cowboy. Momma got onto me about sleeping next to him, said we don't know him that well, and then asked me why I did it. I told her that he had the gun and she got real quiet. That told me that she'd been thinking about getting down there, too. At breakfast he told us about where he lives. He said he lives in West Texas. He owns a little place. Says it's not much but it's his. Least, for now. He said it's safe and best yet, Billy won't find us. He said there's a good school and he thought he could help Momma get a job. When he said that, Momma stood and walked to the bathroom. I guessed her stomach was still acting up, but when she came back, her eyes were red. I think for so long she's been trying to protect me that to finally find someone to help her, well she just broke down.

We finished breakfast and found him waiting on us at the truck. That woman, Miss Marleena, let us keep all the clothes we tried on. I got two pairs of jeans. I've never owned two pairs of new designer jeans. And Cowboy paid for all of it. He must be really rich. Miss Marleena also told us to keep the robes and the slippers. So we did, along with every shampoo and piece of soap in that place. She even brought us more.

She was real sweet. Said we were lucky and that Cowboy had gotten her out of a real bad spot one time. Things have been real good since.

When we got to the truck, Cowboy was rolling a cigarette. He does that sometimes, when he's thinking, I guess. He's always quiet when he's doing it. But he doesn't talk much anyway. He loaded up our stuff, then lit that cigarette and laid it on the concrete ledge next to the truck. It lay there, and the smoke looked like string climbing up. He's funny. He rolls cigarettes but don't smoke them. I guess when you're rich you can do that.

I been trying to think of a way to tell you what I'm feeling but even with this nice new dictionary that Cowboy got me I can't find the words so, you know how sometimes you walk outside, like out of a cold room, and the sun is coming up and it feels warm on your face? And all you want to do is stand there and soak it up? Well, that's kind of how I feel. I want to stand here and soak in this a while.

# CHAPTER FIFTEEN

*Thirteen years ago.*

I wasn't looking for it. Not hardly. And I certainly wasn't looking for her. Love was the farthest thing from my mind. I was twenty-eight and had one thing on my mind and, believe it or not, it wasn't a woman. I'd just pulled a double—twenty hours straight. Dead on my feet. I needed to wash some clothes and get a few hours sleep before my next shift, which started in eight hours.

The Fluff and Fold was twenty-four hours. Worn tile floors, buzzing neon showering down, dead flies on the windowsill. Cobwebs stretched high in the corners. Four machines spinning. Thursday nights were low traffic—easy to get a machine. I walked in, basket on my hip. She was lying on the ground in the back, a bloody lip, one leg folded and tucked under the other, three guys standing over her, a bad look in their eyes. She was breathing. The vein in her neck was rose-vine thick and beating fast. They motioned with the knife and told me to get lost.

I didn't.

When she woke, I bought her a coffee and a piece of cherry pie at

an all-night diner. Told me her name was Andie. A small-time barrel racer making the Texas circuit. She stared at the gun on my hip.
"What do you do?"

"I'm a narcotics agent with DPS."

She was attracted to the excitement. The strength it represents.
Over my third cup, I'd asked her out. She'd raised an eyebrow and
smirked, "You always pick up girls at the Fluff and Fold?"

I looked around. Smiled. "Evidently."

Our first date was the drive-in. A Tom Hanks movie, *Turner &
Hooch.* At her doorstep, I was fumbling with my hat, too afraid to
try and kiss her when she asked me to come watch her race.

Our second date was a rodeo in Fort Worth where she was
competing in the barrel racing. Lord, that woman could ride a
horse. Second place but her horse stumbled. She lost by three one-
thousandths of a second. She was staying at the Stockyards hotel.
I picked her up and took her out for a steak dinner. That's when
she let me hear her laugh. Easy. Gentle. A laughter you could see
through. Or, into. It hid nothing. Deflected nothing.

Months passed. I fell fast, hard, and you know how I told you I
had a one-track mind and a woman wasn't part of that? Well, forget
I ever told you that.

We had gone "looking." I knew better. In truth, it was shopping.
She came alive. Every girl's dream. Glisten and glitter at every turn.
She tried on ten or twelve different ones, different sizes, different
prices. I had nothing. I couldn't really afford to buy anything she
tried on. 'Course, I didn't tell her that. I had secured a line of credit
with the bank for two thousand dollars. Another thousand I could
put on a credit card. A few dollars in the bank. Figured I could pay
it off in a year or two. She held it up, asking without asking. I told
her that I liked them all—I wanted what she wanted. She smiled.
Stared through the case at all the glitter—all the hope staring back.
It was dark outside, dim inside. Lights danced around her face. She
turned away. In the mirror's reflection, I saw the tear. What'd I say?
She pointed and the salesman pulled out one last item. She slipped

it on, turning it. I edged in closer, afraid I didn't have enough credit. The band was platinum. Simple. Round and plain. Not too thin. Not too wide. Not a diamond in sight. She held it close. Eyes glassy, she looked at me and nodded.

I whispered, "But, honey..."

The salesman stepped aside, gave us room. I shrugged. "You... you need...every girl needs a diamond."

She shook her head.

I paid the man. We drove to the river. She waded in. Barefoot and leading me. The river spread around a small island. About as big as a master bedroom. A canopy of scrub oaks, bunch of rocks, soft sand, an old fire pit. We'd picnicked there. She climbed up. Laid the blanket down. Pulled me to her. Placed her hand flat across my chest. "I want two things." Starlight blanketed us. She was trembling. She was all in. Her life had come to this. She tapped her finger just above my heart. "I want...this."

"Already gave it to you."

The side of her mouth twitched while her finger traced her name across my skin. "And I want you to promise me something with it."

"I promise."

"You don't even know what it is."

"Doesn't matter."

"Are all cowboys as headstrong and stubborn as you?"

"Some are worse."

"I want you to promise me that, no matter what, you will—"

"Done."

"I'm not finished."

I waited.

She blinked, bit her lip. "Come for me. If I lose my way... you'll...come back for me."

"I will."

"Always?"

"Always."

"How do you know?"
"I just do."

My great-grandparents, grandparents, and my mom and dad had married out beneath a sprawling oak up on a hill on a piece of property that had later become our ranch. None of the Steele men had enough money to buy the land until my dad. For good reason, we called it "the marrying tree." Limbs grew parallel to the earth, dipped down, then rose back up like angel's wings. The tree was a good bit wider than it was tall. Dad thought the tree tied us to the ground. Something permanent. I think he had it right.

Andie and I stood there eight months later.

I remember the wind tugging at a white dress. How the sun fell off her bare shoulders. Wide and round brown eyes. Long fingers wrapped around fresh-picked bluebonnets. Light brown hair in a ponytail that bounced when she turned her head. Boots that smelled of horses. Wispy hair at her temples. A small mole at the corner of her mouth like that cover girl on all the magazines. We said, "I do." She stood on her tiptoes to let me kiss her and then I lifted her onto May, her wedding gift, and walked her out across a sea of blue.

We spent our honeymoon driving the Big Bend pulling a borrowed horse trailer with a built-in sleeper cabin for two. The second night, we were parked down by this creek. Clear, cold water. Moon high. A house-sized boulder above us. A soft rain on the roof. When the rain quit, the clouds cleared and the brightest night I'd ever seen came up out of the edge of the earth. Bright as day. We climbed up on that boulder, wrapped ourselves in a blanket, and watched the world turn beneath the holes in the colander where the light of heaven shone through the darkness.

A year and a half later, the doctor placed Brodie on her chest while she lay there too exhausted to lift her arms. Sweat pouring off her. Some blood, too. She was so excited, so tired. She laid her head back. We listened as she breathed and he swallowed and fought the absence of fluid. Moments later, summoning what remained, she cradled him and lifted him to me. "Your son."

Words don't come easy. They didn't then. They don't now.

I'd never cried as an adult, but then she passed that child—moments old—into my arms and, from some place I'd never felt, never known, never sensed, a well broke loose, burst forth, and poured out of me. I couldn't stop them. Didn't want to.

I know this: At the risk of her life, she opened up, and gave me a gift for which there is no equal. No reciprocity. No barter. In return, she only asked for one thing. An offering. It cost me nothing and it was all she ever wanted.

And yet, for reasons I cannot understand, I did not give it.

Ever.

# CHAPTER SIXTEEN

We'd been on the interstate an hour when I realized that Sam had been quiet since she got in the car. Guess she was waiting on me to talk. I didn't pick up on this. I seldom do. Sam spoke quietly, "Tell me about Marleena."

"Several years back, I was working a good bit in the Big Easy. We stayed at her hotel. She had some trouble and I helped her out of it."

"What kind of trouble?"

"One of the guests said she'd stolen something from his room. A piece of jewelry. Valuable. Along with a bunch of money and a Rolex. He presented himself as a respectable man and had a pretty good story cooked up. Anyway, I'd known her a while and she's as honest as the day is long so I did some looking around and asked a few questions on my own. Turns out he was lying. And that lie was just the tip of the iceberg. Which is usually the case in my experience."

"What happened?"

"He'd given the jewelry to his girlfriend. The one he kept in a condo here in town. The one he didn't tell his wife about."

"Oooh."

"Yeah. Anyway, ever since Marleena has been a friend of mine."

"How much do I owe you?" The question was abrupt and almost stiff.

I laughed. "I'll bet you have a pretty high credit score."

"What do you mean?"

"You don't like owing people money do you?"

She shook her head. "Not if I can help it."

"Marleena comped the rooms and food. I asked her not to, but she insisted. Said that after seventeen years running that desk that she's management now and she can do stuff like that and for me not to give her no lip about it. The women at the boutique charged me cost for the clothes, which Marleena also paid. I gave her three hundred dollars but she said that was too much and gave me a hundred back."

Sam wedged her hands between her knees and whispered, "Thank you."

I nodded. "Marleena is good people."

Sam spoke, staring out through the windshield. "It takes good people to know good people." She turned toward me, tucking one leg under the other. "Can I ask you something?"

"You know, you can ask without asking me if you can ask."

"So, can I?"

"Sure."

"I noticed when you meet people, say hello, and they ask you how you're doing, you often say you feel like your side's winning."

"I do."

"Where's that come from? You make that up or get it somewhere else?"

"My dad used to say it. I picked it up from him."

She turned back toward the dash. "I like it."

\*　　\*　　\*

Two hours into the ride, Hope stretched out across the backseat with Turbo under her arm and fell asleep. Four stacks of Ritz-Carlton pancakes, a cup of powdered sugar, and a pint of syrup will do that to anyone. I pulled down my sunglasses and stared at her. "Speaking of good people, and since we've got about eight hours, why don't you tell me about you."

"What do you want to know?"

"How'd you get from where you were, to where you are."

"Oh...that story."

She took a deep breath. "I'm thirty-three. Born in Cordele. My dad was a...peanut farmer." She smiled. "And if I never see another peanut that'd be okay with me. We had a great big farm, lots of hands, even hired help in the house. They did all the cooking, even cleaned my room." She shook her head. "I had no idea what we had. My momma trained me to be a lady." Told you she had class. "Anyway...I graduated high school...number three in a class of over four hundred. Had big dreams. But, Daddy had leveraged himself to the hilt. We lost everything. I remember standing in our front yard watching them carry out my bed. My bed! There ought to be a law against a bank taking the place where you sleep. Take the house but not the bed." She pushed the hair out of her eyes. "Anyway, Daddy tried hard to get it back, had a massive heart attack and that left me alone with Mom. So, I gave up college to take care of her. I took one job, then another, then her medical bills piled up, so I took another, and I been working ever since."

"Where is she now?"

"Buried right alongside Daddy."

"Sorry."

She nodded and watched the trees pass. "Me, too."

"And, Hope?"

She turned sideways, tucking her left heel under her right leg and glanced in the backseat. "I was twenty-two, alone, he was a few years older. Owned a night club. Always had lots of cash. He would come in late at night and eat at the diner where I was working. Always left good tips. Asked me out." She shrugged. "I thought he'd...thought he was...well, he was nothing like I thought. He liked to gamble and he liked strip bars and he liked to drink. He left me standing at the altar wearing jeans and a white linen shirt—which was the only thing I could find that would fit over my stomach. So, we been on our own since she started pooching my belly out. My choice in men hasn't been too good. I tend to go for the flashy and promising. Most promise the moon, then deliver a scrubbed launch."

"And Billy?"

"I'd saved up some money. Thought we'd travel west. Maybe California. I don't know. I just knew I didn't want to be anywhere I'd been. So, we were sitting in a sandwich shop in San Antonio when this guy walked in wearing a black SWAT uniform. Just took my breath away. He looked strong and safe and secure, and to be honest, I needed strength and safety and security. So, next thing you know he'd offered us a room at his place—which we promptly accepted 'cause I had eleven dollars left in my pocket. He helped get me on at Walmart. Before long he was bringing me flowers and Hope ice cream." She paused. "I had no idea he would, well, I just didn't see it coming. I didn't see any signals. I mean, you'd think that a highly decorated cop who runs a freaking SWAT unit wouldn't be a sick, perverted son of a—" She caught herself. "Sorry." She slowed down. Controlled her tone. "That he wouldn't be the sick miscreant that he is. That if—" She rubbed her hands together and palmed her forehead. "If you can't trust him, then just who can you trust? I mean what is the world coming to? Anyway, he"—she shrugged—"and I grabbed Hope and we took off. You found us a few days later on the highway praying that the front end of a seventy-mile-an-hour Peterbilt would just end it all." A pause. "That's the short version without all the drama." Another pause and this time, she changed the subject. "What's your son's name? Or, do you mind my asking?"

"Brodie, and no I don't mind."

"How old is he?"

"Eleven."

"What's he like?"

"Well, he's a little like me in that he is more quiet than not. He's a thinker, not a talker. And, he's more like his momma in that once he gets stuck on something he wants to do or see or...fix, he has a tough time letting it go." I laughed. "He's dogged in his determination."

She looked at my left hand and the absence of a ring. "And his momma?"

"We're divorced." The word came out of my mouth and sounded new and strange and like a description of someone else.

"How long?"

"She's been gone about three years. Give or take."

She weighed her words. "What happened?"

"Life."

"Was it you? Were you...unfaithful?"

"No." I shook my head. "Least not with another woman if that's what you're asking."

"Is that one of those questions I shouldn't ask?"

"No. Not in my book."

"Did she find another man?"

I paused, glanced in the backseat and lowered my voice. "Yes."

She grimaced. "Ouch. What, are you bad in bed or something?"

I saw the joke as a good sign, even though it was at my expense. I chuckled. "Evidently." I looked at her. "You ask tough questions."

"Sorry. I do that so others won't ask the same of me. One of my...friends, a psychiatrist, told me—just before he kicked us out, changed the locks, and threw our clothes out the second-story window—that it's a defense mechanism. I do it to defer attention from my own baggage."

"He sounds like a real winner."

"He was right, I had and have baggage but that doesn't explain the naked coed in the closet."

"Sounds like you've earned the right to ask a few questions."

She stared out the windshield. "Maybe a few."

We small talked for the next several hours. We crossed into Texas, skirted around Dallas and Fort Worth, hopped on Highway 180 and drove through Mineral Wells, Palo Pinto, and Caddo, crossing into the city limits of Rock Basin late in the afternoon. My little place, the Bar S, lay on the other side of town, a few miles outside the limits. When Dad bought it, it was farther outside of town but like people, the town's waistline had bulged. I turned off the paved road and began winding my way around the potholes in the clay-packed road. My house lay a half mile ahead down a single lane dirt road lined with cottonwoods that rose like sentinels over the barbed wire fence. Dumps was mending the split rail with help from Brodie. Sam saw him and squinted. I said, "That's Dumps."

"Dumps?"

"Yeah. He's sort of like an uncle."

"Sort of?"

"He's not blood, but he is family."

She smiled. "And that one?"

Brodie climbed atop his pony—Mr. Bojangles. He galloped the fence line toward us. "That'd be Brodie."

Hope leaned forward between the two seats, Turbo nibbling on her shoulder. I drove slowly toward the house, careful not to kick up too much dust. Brodie met us halfway, turned, spurred Mr. B and then cantered alongside. When I stopped, he stuck his spurs hard into Mr. B's flank, who raised up on two hind legs, stood momentarily, and then rocketed back to the house. Sam's eyes grew big as Oreos. Hope's jaw fell. Turbo dropped a turd.

I watched the dust swirl behind him. "That's Mr. B. I bought him when he was two and gave him to Brodie on his second birthday. A two-year-old for a two-year-old. They've grown up together. In a sense, Brodie doesn't know life without Mr. B. He's one helluva..."

I glanced in the rearview. "I mean, heckuva horse. Gentle as Jesus."
I smiled. "Where Brodie goes, so goes Mr. B."

I parked the truck and turned to Sam. "You better give me a
minute. You're not the woman he was hoping I'd bring home." She
nodded. Brodie sat at a distance staring inside the truck. I walked
toward the fence, grabbed Mr. B's reins and rubbed his muzzle. I
stared up at Brodie. He sat, stoic. Just like he thought he was supposed to. The way all his silver screen heroes did. All "our" heroes
did. He was the picture of everything John Ford ever tried to do
with John Wayne. I patted his leg. "How you doing?"

He nodded, not taking his eyes off the car but his Adam's apple
rose, paused, and fell.

"I need you to help me with something."

He looked at me.

"Remember those people I told you about?" He nodded. "Well,
they're in the truck. Running from a bad man. They need a safe
place for a while. The girl is named Hope. She's ten. And she's had
a rough go. I need you—I was wondering if you'd help me make a
safe place for them. They don't have any place else to go. Can you
do that?"

"What about Mom?"

His world was a chasm. Ripped in two. He lived in the middle.
The dry riverbed between. Trying to figure out how to bridge the
gap between two cliffs that he couldn't climb or move or stretch a
cable between.

My voice rose a bit. Maybe my tone changed. "Son, they're not
replacing your mom. I just couldn't leave them in the middle of the
highway with the rain pouring down and no gas. And when the bad
man thumped them on the head and shoved them in the back of his
van with socks in their mouths, I couldn't let him do that." I turned
and stared at the truck. "They needed a break. I didn't know where
else they were gonna get it."

He looked at me. "What'd you do? With the man?"

"I didn't let him do what he wanted."

"Is he coming after them?"

I scratched my chin. "I'm not sure. I need to find out how motivated he is. I would if I were him."

"I thought you were retired."

"I am, so I got to ask permission. Captain's coming by tonight."

"And after that?"

"After that, we'll talk about your mom."

He hopped off Mr. B and stared up at me. "Promise?"

I nodded.

He started toward the truck, then stopped, looking up at me. "You can tell me the truth, you know."

I swallowed. He was the best of both of us. I tipped his hat back so I could see his eyes. "Son, the truth hurts me to tell it." I shook my head. "And I don't want it to hurt you, too."

He tugged on the brim of his hat, hiding his eyes. Looked like *The Man from Snowy River*. "Dad, not knowing hurts worse."

Brodie led Mr. B to the truck. Wrangler jeans. Boots. T-shirt tucked in. Buck knife on his belt. Hat sweaty around the band. He was me, he was my father, he was my grandfather, wrapped in an eleven-year-old package. His shoulders were getting broader and he was getting taller. His momma would cry if she saw him. If she said it once, she said it a hundred times. "That right there is the best to ever come out of Texas." She was right then. And she'd be right now.

He stood back from the truck about three feet and then opened the back door. He held his hat in his hand. "Hi, I'm Brodie."

Hope recoiled and clutched Turbo.

He turned Mr. B and held the stirrup. "Wanna ride? Mr. B's real gentle. Ain't gonna hurt you none."

Sam patted Hope on the leg. "Go ahead, baby. I'll be right here."

Brodie shook the reins. "I'll hold the reins. We can just walk if you like." He eyed the animal on Hope's shoulder. "You can bring him if you want. Mr. B won't care none."

I held out my hand and, to my surprise, Hope took it. She scooted across the seat and I steered her foot into the stirrup. She hopped up, swung her leg over, and Brodie turned them toward the cottonwoods. I spoke over his shoulder. "Go easy, son. Nothing fast. Nothing sudden." He nodded and started the walking tour of the Bar S—a picture of Texas a hundred years ago.

Dumps walked around to Sam's window and pointed at me. "Since he ain't got no dang manners—" He rubbed his dirty hand on his dirtier jeans. "I'm Pat Dalton, ex-con and boot maker extraordinaire, but most folks just call me 'Dumps.' "

Sam talked with Dumps while I watched my son lead a scared young girl through the trees on his horse. Maybe it's me, but boys in Texas become men sooner than most. I was watching it happen right before my eyes.

He'd started early.

# PART TWO

*He was despised and rejected by men, a man of sorrows, and familiar with suffering. Like one from whom men hide their faces he was despised, and we esteemed him not. Surely he took up our infirmities and carried our sorrows, yet we considered him stricken by God, smitten by him, and afflicted.*

*—Isaiah 53:3*

# CHAPTER SEVENTEEN

*Five years ago.*

He sat in my lap. Hands on the wheel. Almost seven. Oblivious. Bouncing to the rhythm of the song coming out his mouth. The light turned. "Light's green. Look left-right-left." His head swung on a swivel. Large, exaggerated movements.

Satisfied, he nodded. "All clear."

I pressed the accelerator. "Here we go." He bounced faster. The house faded, growing smaller in the rearview. White picket framed in cottonwood barbed wire, and weeping willow. A black squirrel scurried across the road. She stood on the porch. Faded jeans. Bare feet. Arms crossed. Hair blowing across her face. Swaying slightly.

Objects in mirror are not closer than they appear.

We rattled across the railroad tracks. "Push that down." He did. The left signal started blinking and clicking. "Give me some left turn." He inched the car leftward, afraid to turn it and afraid to let go of it. On our current path, we'd take out the light pole. I laughed. "You're not milking a cow. Turn the wheel. Give me some left in that rudder." In one large motion, he overcorrected and we rolled out into the left lane. "Good. Now straighten out." We snaked our way to town, bouncing between the lines. He was oblivious to the conversation sitting on the tip of my tongue.

Fifteen minutes later, the ice cream dripped off his chin. His tongue made the circuit around his face but smeared more than it mopped up. He looked like a puppy chasing peanut butter around his muzzle. Light blue and pink coated his fingers.

"You saving that for later?"

He was licking the rim of the cone, but it was dripping faster than he could keep up. "Uh-huh." He stared at me out of the corner of his eyes, nodding at my chest. He spoke while looking at his cone. "You wearing it?"

I pulled on a snap in the center of my shirt exposing the giant blue and red "S" beneath. He smiled. He'd given it to me. He liked it when I wore it. His mom thought it ridiculous.

He dropped the paper from his cone in the trash. I pulled a wipe from my pocket and bathed his hands and face. He squirmed. "You ready?"

"Yes, sir."

I handed him my hat and he put it on his head where it swiveled loosely on the crown. I lifted him, raising him above my head and rested him on my shoulders. He locked his hands around my head, covering up my eyes. I laughed. "Hey, big guy..." I groped like a man in the dark. "I need those things if we're going anywhere other than right here." He locked them under my neck, nearly choking me. "Much better." He rested his chin on my head and we walked down the street. I'm six-two, which made him about eight feet atop me. We walked a block and when I purposefully missed the turn, he pulled on my right ear and then "spurred" me with his right heel. I turned, staring at our shadow. Him wearing my hat and towering over everyone in town. We walked straight down the sidewalk so he held his arms out and made propeller sounds with his mouth. Mornings with him made all the world right.

We passed a lady carrying a shopping bag and shuffling on flat feet. She was short, stocky, black as night, and had purple eyes. He tipped my hat and spoke. " 'Day, ma'am."

She smiled. Stopped. Tugged on my arm. "You're that boy. The one I been reading about."

I held out my hand. "Tyler Steele, ma'am."

She nodded. "Thought that was you. Recognized you from your picture. You caught that murdering killer. Put him in jail. Glad you did. Hope he stays there. Hope they hang him for what he did." She shaded her eyes. "That's a handsome boy you're carrying up there."

He held his hand down. "I'm Brodie."

She stood on her toes and shook his hand. "You gonna grow up and be like your daddy?"

He nodded. The shift in weight told me he stuck his chest out. "Yes, ma'am." Another shift told me he sat up straight and lifted his chin. "Planning on it."

She patted his legs. "You do that."

She gritted her teeth and patted my arm. "You keep doing what you're doing. We need more just like you."

"Thank you, ma'am."

She turned and waddled down the street.

He spoke down over me. "Daddy?"

"Yeah, big guy."

"How come you and Momma don't sleep in the same bed?"

"Well, we do it's just that you been sleeping in there and there's just not room for all three of us."

"That's not what Mom says."

"Yeah? What's Mom say?"

"She says with you working late, you don't want to wake anybody up so you just sleep on the couch. Is that it?"

How is it that someone so young can pick up on pain so deep? I tried to sound convincing. "Yep."

"You can wake us up, you know. I asked her. We'll snuggle with you, too."

I didn't answer. He was tugging on both ears. "Hey, big guy, left or right. Not both at once."

He tugged left, spurred me twice. Three blocks to go.

Rock Basin, Texas, sits north of Abilene. Wide expanse, big skies, rolling dust clouds, it is everything West Texas. On a clear day, from most anywhere in town, we can look due west and see the Llano Estacado. We call it the Cap Rock. It's a tabletop place of earth that rises up several hundred feet like the Great Wall of China and runs north, to Canada. It marks the end of the Great Plains and was, at one time, covered with over a million buffalo. Now, it's covered with nearly a thousand windmills taller than many buildings. If you stop the truck and roll down the window, you can hear the propellers whipping through the air. Rain and snow up on the Cap Rock drains down into the Brazos, then runs eight hundred miles to the Gulf of Mexico. That's tricky, too, 'cause rain up there don't necessarily mean rain down here. No, sir. Not at all. So, flash floods aren't uncommon.

Rock Basin was once an oil-boom town. Brick-lined streets, gas lamps, oil derricks on every corner, three restaurants, two banks, and a railway station. In some parts of town, folks drilled so many wells that the derricks crossed neighbors' fences like they do east of here over in Kilgore. The mayor used to brag that a squirrel could scurry across town jumping from derrick to derrick and never touch the ground.

An old Ford F-100 rattled down Main pulling an empty cattle trailer. Closed shops, FOR LEASE signs, empty factories, broken glass, boarded-up windows, faded signs, tumbleweeds, and unmoving derricks tell the story of a boomtown that dried up. Across the street, a clothesline stretched between the rusty legs of two unmoving derricks. I stopped before the bank window and stared at our reflection. I watched him. Pure promise, boundless possibility, limitless hope.

George Vickers ran the five-and-dime. His son, George Jr., got kicked in the head by a mule when he was young. Scrambled him.

He's thirty now. Acts like he's five or six. Happiest kid I've ever known. Stepped out of the store, aimed his Polaroid at us, clicked the picture. Handed it to us. A voice sounded above me. "Thanks, George Jr." Brodie looked at the Polaroid, then stuffed it in his shirt pocket. He loved that picture. He was so proud. "Look, Daddy, I'm taller than you."

I glanced down the street to the beauty parlor. I could see her shadow moving in the window. She was getting her hair done. Wanted to look nice for another weekend out with the girls. Vegas this time. Last month was New York. Or was it San Francisco? He tugged on my left ear. Dumbo wearing boots and jeans. Another glance at the beauty parlor, then him in the window's reflection. She was right. He was the glue. Or, had been. Sometimes when the earth quakes, it's the tectonic plates several thousand feet down causing the damage on the surface.

I slipped on my Costas. Four blocks up, a Monte Carlo turned onto the street. Tinted windows. Riding low. Shiny chrome wheels and spinners gave the impression of forward movement when it had little. I'd seen it before. Seeing it here surprised me. It crept toward us. Deep bass from the speakers rattled the license tag. The passenger was looking through binoculars, pointing. I jogged slightly. Brodie tugged on my right ear, laughing, unaware.

I reached the far side of the street and the bed of my truck. I lifted him off my shoulders and set him in the bed. "Hey, big guy, I want you to lie down." I patted the bed and kept my eyes trained up the street. "Out of sight. Right now."

"But—"

"Nope, lie down." I pulled my hat down tight. "Now."

He did. Three blocks up, she appeared on the porch, shading her eyes from the sun. I needed distance between me and the truck. I climbed up the curb, walked four stores down and stood in the shadows. The car approached. Smoke wafted from inside. Shiny black hair. Shoulder-length ponytails. Hands covered in tattoos. Beady black eyes sat perched atop blue bandanas that covered their faces. One of them tossed an empty malt liquor bottle into the back of my truck, then spotted me and pulled ahead. There were five of them. Twelve feet separated us.

The FBI will tell you that gunfights are statistically short in time. But, that's little consolation when you're in one. The first round entered my right leg, spun me and knocked me against the brick wall of the five-and-dime. The next four rounds impacted my vest, slamming me through the glass and spreading my body across what was once the display window. I glanced at the car and something shiny came spinning out. A flame twirling on one end. It spun slowly. Like a punted football, tumbling end over end. I knew what was coming next. The adrenaline dump was total. Tunnel vision. Auditory exclusion. Gross motor movement took the place of fine. The blast occurred about the time the bottle hit the ground, not too far from me, showering me in flaming goo and slivers. The pain in my ears was intense but then the whole world went mute.

When I looked up, a man stood over me holding my Smith & Wesson model 327. The eight-round .357 I carried on my ankle. Just before he squeezed the trigger I remember thinking, "This is going to hurt." He said, "Cowboy, this is from José Juan." Then he calmly placed five rounds into the "S" on my chest.

Standing there beneath that kid, I had three distinct thoughts that I can't explain. Maybe four. The first was, "I hope this vest holds." Second, my skin was on fire and I did not like it. Third, despite the emotional distance and the angry shouts and the months that had passed since we'd touched—I didn't want her to see this. I'd tried so hard to protect her from this side of me but this was one mental picture that would not fade. Pictures like this are seared into the backs of eyelids. Lastly, I remember hearing his voice, afraid and alone, screaming my name over and over and over.

I don't remember much after that.

# CHAPTER EIGHTEEN

I woke naked on the table.

I blinked. My eyes fought to focus. I stretched my fingers. They curled. The skin felt raw and taut across the knuckles. I wiggled my toes. The right side wiggled back. The left was slow to respond. I tried lifting my head. A wave of nausea followed.

Fluorescent white showered down. Clear fluid dripped from a bag above my head. A plastic line led from the bag to my right arm. Voices were muted. Mouths moved but noise was sporadic. My eyes detected motion. Shadows crossed me. A woman in white hovered above me. Sweat dotted the fuzz above her lip. She was squeezing the bag and barking at other people.

The right side of my face and chest was on fire. My left leg felt heavy and numb. I was sweating and cold. I touched my right cheek and felt slivers of something sticking into my skin.

I pulled up onto one elbow. There was a hole in my left thigh. I looked down at my arm. Liquid dripping in. The bag above me was almost empty. I looked at my leg. Liquid dripping out.

Strange.

The area around the hole in my leg was that weird yellow iodine color. Evidently, they were prepping me for surgery. The memory returned. I wanted off that table.

The nurse pressed me back down. I managed a broken whisper. "Brodie?"

"Sir, please lie back down."

I pulled myself up on an elbow. "Where's my son?"

More hands appeared pressing me down. It was Andie. Tears streaked the black soot on her face. Like she'd been fighting a fire. She pressed her palms on my chest. She was crying. "Ty. Ty, lay down."

"Where—?" She broke, pounding my chest with her fist. "Did they take him?"

She was screaming. "They took him. Those—! They took him. They—"

I sat up. The nurse cradled me. Urgent voices sounded over the intercom. Shuffling footsteps in the hall. I dropped one leg off the bed. The doctor appeared in the doorway, his hands wet and held above his heart. He looked at me. Surprised. He spoke from behind a mask. "Where you going?"

I steadied myself. There were two of him. "To get my son?"

He shook his head. "I don't recommend that."

One ear was not working. I turned my head. "Say again?"

"That's not a real good idea."

"I know, but—" I looked at him. A wedding ring on his left hand. I tugged on the plastic line leading into my arm but it was taped. I asked, "You got kids?" He nodded. "Would you?"

Andie lay in a pile on the floor. Stomach-deep sobs cut the air. I'd never heard that sound. Her head swayed slightly. Her hair brushed the floor.

He pulled down on his mask, wanting the truth. "Have you got it left in you?"

I nodded.

He wiped his hands on his pants, and helped me up. The world was spinning. I leaned on him. "Doc, I need you to help me make it through the next hour."

The nurse held a wad of gauze to my leg while he wrapped it in twenty circles of tape. He slid the IV from my arm and spoke to the nurse. She walked to a counter and started loading a syringe.

The tattered and burnt remains of my clothes were in a heap on the counter. My vest sat upright, five slugs embedded in the plate in the center. That would explain the problem I was having taking a deep breath. I lifted the remains of my shirt, found my belt, and hung it around me.

My boots lay on the floor. Burnt leather. Slit down the side. Crusty with blood. I sized up the doctor. Then his feet. He was wearing Crocs. "You mind?"

He kicked them off, slid the syringe into my arm, and shot me full of something.

The full-length mirror, opposite the nurses' station, showed my reflection. I was not a pretty sight. Charred skin, much of it cracked and peeling, boxer shorts, green Crocs, black leather belt, holster, magazine carrier, tape and gauze the size of a VW, blood trickling down my leg and out both ears. The doc handed me a water bottle. "Drink this while you drive."

"Thanks."

My truck sat just outside the door. The driver's side window was blown out. Evidently, Andie had followed the ambulance. "My keys?"

She tossed them at me. Something smelled like lemon and Pine-Sol. I caught the keys and walked toward the parking lot. When the automatic doors opened, the sunlight blinded me.

I let my eyes adjust, and cranked the engine. Mashing the clutch was excruciating and I almost passed out. When I got it to the floor, I threw the stick into first and shoved the accelerator as far as it would go. The diesel wound up and whined. By the time I exited the parking lot, I was in third gear. I ran three stoplights, slid sideways onto the highway, and when I looked down, the needle was pegged somewhere above a hundred.

I kept it there and fought the desire to close my eyes.

I had a hunch that they'd make one stop before they disappeared. A dog always returns to its vomit. I had put their boss in jail and I felt certain they'd make a visit to their clubhouse before they slipped back across the border. I parked in the trees, grabbed what I needed out of the back of my truck, and bled my way through the pasture, the planted pines, and down the bank to the river. Whatever the doc had shot into me had started to work. Good stuff, too, but if it played out I'd be in trouble. Waist deep, shotgun above my head, I waded across. I walked up the bank, pulled back on the slide of the 870, inserted a Brenneke slug into the chamber, slammed the slide forward, pressed the muzzle of the shotgun against the lock, and pressed the trigger. Brenneke slugs have been known to shoot through engine blocks. The lock disappeared. I didn't bother with earplugs. They were still ringing from the last explosion. I stepped inside two tractor-trailers welded together end to end. A laboratory, of sorts. I pulled the door behind me, stuffed a piece of paper in the clean shotgun hole, and stood in the dark. I knew if I sat down, I wouldn't get up so I leaned against the wall, pressed up on my eyelids, and counted the drops on my foot. Blood was puddling inside my left Croc so I took them off and stood barefoot. I trained my eyes on daylight breaking through the crack at the far end.

There have been a multitude of changes in handguns since John Browning created what became known as the "1911." Many good. Glock. Springfield. A host of others. But, nobody yet has made a weapons platform better than the 1911. Many have tried. None succeeded. In the annals of weapon craft, it's known as the perfect fusion of function and form.

I unholstered, depressed the magazine release button, and dropped the magazine into my left hand, feeling the top with my fingers and pressing down. Eight rounds. Capacity. Chances were good I'd need it. I replaced it, clicking it shut, then press-checked the chamber—letting my index finger tell me the same thing it told me when I put it on this morning. A total of nine. An extra magazine on my belt. Plus six rounds in the shotgun. I didn't know how long the fight would last—nobody every does—but I doubted it'd last much longer than those twenty-three rounds.

My chest was tender. Any expansion was painful.

I heard the hum of the motor, the sound of tires on gravel. The pounding of deep bass from the speakers. When the Monte Carlo came to a stop just outside the door, I'd venture that no one in the car was thinking of me. I was counting on that. It might have been my only advantage. The car door shut and I told myself, *Slow is fast . . . shoot slow.* My adrenaline was playing out. The world was a tunnel and the sides were closing in. I shook my head.

I don't remember all that happened next. Most shootouts take less than seven seconds in a space smaller than the average bedroom and I suppose all that was true here. I remember them shuffling in. Cocky and carefree. I remember letting the third get through the door before I pressed the trigger on the shotgun. I don't remember it running empty but it did. I do remember that the third guy was fast but not faster than the last round in the shotgun. I remember men shouting, I remember seeing a flash, feeling searing pain in my right rib cage, falling backward and then getting up. I remember walking out the front door—sort of—dragging my leg. The fourth man turned and tripped trying to get out the door. Oddly, all the world was quiet. He tumbled down the steps and ran toward the river. The shotgun empty, I dropped it, drew the 1911, dropped the safety with my thumb, and pressed the trigger when the front site settled on the naked woman in the center of the tattoo on his back. He was knee deep in the river when the bullet did what bullets do. The fifth man turned to me, a dog I'd backed in a corner. He came fast, too, and while the .45 ACP is a subsonic round flying at best 950 feet per second, it is still faster than any man that ever lived.

But none of that is really important.

\*     \*     \*

The smoke cleared. Muffled cries rose from the car trunk. I punched the latch and he cowered, whimpering, covering his head with an arm. I reached in. He fought me, then opened his eyes, climbed into my arms, and latched hold. I needed a place to lie down so I stumbled a few feet into the river. Shin-deep, I set us down next to a tire-sized boulder. The water soothed my skin. My strength was gone.

He was a mess. We both were. Downstream the river was red. I leaned against the rock and hugged him. The Cap Rock rose up out of the corner of my eye. Windmills spun slowly in the distance. Cottony clouds floated above. Blue everywhere. My eyes wandered upriver. A mile from here, we used to camp, fish, spend the day swimming and checking our trotlines.

Distant sirens were getting closer. The river rolled across us. A whisper of red snaked from my leg with the current. Washing me to the Gulf. The sand beneath me sifted. Just hold on a few moments longer.

I held him to my chest. "You okay?"

He was crying, shaking, rocking in the water.

I asked him again.

He buried his head in my chest. The pain took my breath away. He was in shock.

He pressed his cheek to mine and cried in my ear. The left one was working better than the right. His voice sounded like a thousand angels echoing off the clouds. He pulled on me, "I thought, thought you were—" He shook his head. I nodded. "But I thought you were—"

My skin was on fire. Mourning doves sped overhead. F-18s headed to Mexico. The pain was making me nauseous. Sleep was heavy. If I could just close my eyes.

I pulled him closer, resting him on my chest. Somebody was slapping my cheeks. I snapped my eyes open. He pressed his head to mine. I heard voices in the distance. My throat was dry. I think he was holding my head above water.

How can my throat be dry if I'm lying in a river?

I wanted to take his mind off all of this. Take him someplace safe. Where the fear wouldn't follow. I spread his palm flat over the surface of the river. The current gentle beneath. My voice was hoarse, broken. He was bleeding from the nose. I whispered, "You know how the Brazos got its name?"

He shook his head.

Images of my father flashed before my eyes. "Spanish explorers. South of here. Lost. Dying of thirst. When they found it, they jumped in. Swam around a while. Kind of like us." I palmed his face. His cheek was sticky. Tears had streaked down the smoke residue that had painted his face. Drippy, sidewalk ice cream seemed like another lifetime. I took a breath. "They called it—" My Spanish wasn't too good. I dug up the words. *"Río de los Brazos de Dios."* Clouds sped overhead. More doves cut streaks in the air above. I coughed.

He shook his head. Tears were puddling along his lips. He closed his eyes. "I'm cold." The ambulance skidded to a stop, slinging gravel into the river. She climbed out of the police car. Began running toward us.

This would be the straw. Everything would change.

I pulled him close. "It means—" Water splashed my face. The paramedics reached in. I pressed his ear to my lips. "It means the 'Arms of God.' "

I was right. Everything did change.

# CHAPTER NINETEEN

We got Sam and Hope settled in the house, showed them their room and gave them time to get cleaned up. An hour later, Sam walked to the fence and leaned on it. She scanned the horizon. The sun was going down. Hiding behind the mesquite. Blood red hanging on shades of gray. The river shone like molten silver rolling out of the smelting pot in the distance. "This is yours?"

"All that doesn't belong to the bank. Goes that way about a mile down to the river—where you see those treetops, then each direction about a mile. Give or take, it's 640 acres."

"That's a lot."

"In Texas, it's very little."

A shrug. "When you got nothing, it's something." Her attention turned to my cows. "Those yours?"

"That's Brodie's college tuition and my retirement. Ninety-eight head."

"What are they?"

"'Round here we call them 'F1.' Which means 'first cross,'

or the first generation when you cross different animal lines. Maybe the best example is a mule, which is an F1 resulting from the cross of a horse and a donkey. These cows here are Brahman crossed with Herefords. We call them Tigerstripes for obvious reasons. Those there are Hereford and Angus. They're called Black Baldies."

"Why do you do that?"

It was a good question. "It gives us all the vigor of both breeds without the weakness. More milk. Better brains. Bigger cows. More framey. No pinkeye. More of the good. Less of the bad."

"You sound like you know cows."

"I know a little. Learning more all the time."

"You always had cows?"

"No." I shook my head. My Angus bull stood silhouetted on the hill. "My dad gave me his grandfather along with three Hereford cows when I was eighteen."

"You started all this with four cows?"

"Yep."

"You've done well."

I smiled. "They're resilient. Feed them. Get a good vet. Treat foot rot when you get it. Trade actively. Pull calves when the mothers need help. Be honest about a cow that won't calve. It works out."

We walked toward the house. "Tell me about the Bar S."

"My dad bought it for my mom before I was born. She left him before he finished the house so we moved in. The house is right at forty years old. A two-bedroom. Simple. Front porch. Front door and back door in the same line so you can see straight through the house and catch a cross breeze coming off the river. In August, there's little difference between hell and Texas so any moving air is welcome. Dad liked to watch the sun rise and fall so he built a porch front and rear." We walked around the side. "The barn is tattered, the wind rattles the tin on the roof but she's sturdy and there's a cellar beneath if Dorothy's twister returns."

A small adobe, brick-looking building canopied by scrub oaks with bars over the windows sat beyond the barn next to the wind-mill. "And that?"

I smiled. "That's the oldest building in and around Rock Basin. The jail."

"Jail?"

"Rock Basin was once a stop on the Pony Express. Given the river, people gathered, a town grew up and when people grow a town they need a jail. Bad always follows good. Fire burned the town, but those walls are three feet of brick. It scorched the walls a bit, but little else."

"Looks lived in."

"That'd be Dumps."

"Dumps lives in the jail?"

I laughed. "It's grown on him."

Dinner was quiet with all of us watching each other. Trying to get used to one another. After dinner, Dumps shuffled in wearing his reading glasses and carrying a cloth measuring tape and a small notebook. He looked at Hope, pulled up a stool in front of her, and patted his lap. "Little lady, I need to measure your feet."

Hope recoiled. Sam looked at me. I whispered, "It's okay."

Sam sat behind Hope and whispered. "Go ahead, baby."

Hope slowly extended her foot toward Dumps. He held it in his hand, studying the curve, size, arch, instep, length of toes, some-thing I've seen him do several times. Using the cloth tape, he mea-sured Hope's foot: across the ball, the arch, the top of the arch where that bone is on the top of the foot, the ankle around the heel, and three places up the calf. After each measurement he scribbled in his pad. His glasses hung off his nose. His big, gnarled hands swallowed her foot. He tried to tickle the bottom but she wasn't having any and didn't laugh. He checked his measurements then remeasured around her instep and followed that same procedure on the other foot. When finished, he patted her foot. "Okay, you're done." He looked at Sam. "Ma'am?"

Sam shook her head. "Oh, my feet are really dirty and I haven't done my nails and—"

"Trust me, I've seen worse."

Sam pulled off her socks and extended her leg to Dumps. He cradled her foot in his hands, performing the same series of measurements. I watched him thinking of the prince holding Cinderella's foot.

He turned to Hope. "What's your favorite color?"

She said nothing. Sam spoke for her. "Pink."

His laughter came from way down deep. A belly laugh. I asked him one time about it. He said, "Prison does that." He nodded to Sam. "Well then, by God, we'll put some pink in them."

Sam spoke. "In what?"

"Your boots." He raised his eyebrows. "And you, young lady?"

Sam said, "I like turquoise."

He nodded. "Good call. I'll see what I can do."

He made notes, then looked up from his book. "You two like brown or black?"

"Black."

Dumps folded his notebook, stuck his glasses in his pocket, and walked off toward the barn. "Then black it is."

The wrinkle that had been sitting between Hope's eyes disappeared as she watched him leave.

The screen door squeaked, Sam sat on the swing. The breeze tugged on the ends of her hair. "She asleep?"

"I think so. She had a pretty big day. Told me she wants a horse. 'One just like Mr. B.'"

I laughed. We could hear Dumps rattling around in the barn.

"How long have you known him?"

"He's been here about eight years, but I've known him most my life."

"How'd you meet him?"

"He was the first man my dad arrested forty-five years ago. Put him in jail. A jury put him in prison."

"What'd he do?"

"Shot a man." Her eyes widened. "He was eighteen, with a bunch of drunk kids. He wasn't the triggerman, but by his own admission, he didn't do anything to stop it. He got out of prison about nine years ago and I found him sitting on the curb in town. Had the clothes on his back."

"Sounds familiar."

"I stopped and asked him what he was doing. He was staring up at the clock tower and said he was thinking about jumping out of it. He didn't have anybody or anything. Nowhere to go. No options. He said he'd have gone back to prison but he was pretty sure they wouldn't let him in. Asked me if I had any ideas how he could get his old cell back. I drove him to a diner, bought him coffee and eggs and asked him if he minded living with a Ranger and his family. He gave it some thought and said no, he didn't mind. Least not with me. We gave him 'the jail,' which he was real happy about. He's been there ever since."

"And the boots?"

"He learned to make them in prison. And in thirty-five years, he had a lot of practice. The warden gave him a shop, locked him in there during the day, frisked him at night to make sure the tools stayed inside the cage. He made boots for the warden, all the guards, my dad, me. Once we got him set up in the barn, he started making the rodeo circuit, fitting cowboys. Now, a lot of cowboys come from a long way to get him to make them a pair of boots. He's not Paul Bond, but he's close. Makes a good working pair of boots."

She looked at my feet. "He make those?"

I nodded.

"How long will it take to do whatever he's doing?"

"There are about two hundred steps involved in making a pair of boots, but if he keeps his head down and shortcuts a few of the custom items...a couple of days."

She looked at me out of the corner of her eye. "I'll bet when you were young, that you were the kid in the neighborhood that cared for all the stray cats."

I shook my head. "I hate cats...but I've cared for my fair share of calves and horses."

She studied me. "That's a wicked scar on your neck."

"Yep."

"You don't offer much do you?"

"What do you mean?"

"I said, 'that's a nasty scar.' You should've said, 'Yep...' and then told me how you got it. But, you only answer what you're asked."

I nodded. "It is a fault in my person."

"Everybody's allowed one." She leaned forward. "So...?"

"You know...sometimes people don't answer a question 'cause the answer is painful."

"In the last forty-eight hours, I've told you that my daughter was sexually abused by a man I was dating and that he's got naked videos of both of us. You think any part of that is not painful?"

She had me there. "I was in an explosion."

"Explosion?"

"A man threw a flaming bottle at me, it blew up, splintered me with glass slivers, set much of my right side on fire."

"You look like you're doing okay."

"A good doctor and lots of skin grafts."

"And the limp?"

"The man that threw the bottle then jumped out of the car, and shot me with my own gun."

"That had to feel good."

"Yep. But not quite as good as the five times right here." I tapped my chest.

Her eyes grew. "What were you doing?"

"Taking Brodie to get some ice cream."

"Why'd they do it?"

"Four kids jacked up on crystal meth don't need a reason to do much of anything."

She shook her head. "How come you're not dead?"

"I've asked that question many a time."

"Seriously."

"I was wearing a vest."

She looked surprised. "You always wear a vest when you eat ice cream?"

It was time to come clean. Put my cards on the table. I stood. "You feel like going for a walk?" I glanced at the house. "She'll be fine. We're not going very far."

She stood, and I led her through the moonlight and cottonwoods to the pasture out back. We skirted cow patties, one of our seven rusted oil derricks that had long ago quit pumping, and up the hill dusted with live oaks. From there we could look south toward the river. North down toward the house. It was my father's favorite spot. Even in the moonlight, you could make out the shade of blue. "What is that?" A large, charred tree that had been struck by lightning a decade ago stood barren and alone. The cows now used it to scratch their hides.

"That's 'the marrying tree.'"

A smirk. "The what?"

"Marrying tree. My dad bought this place as a wedding gift for my mom. My grandparents, my folks, and Andie and me, got married out there." I laughed. "But, the tree must be cursed 'cause my mom left my dad, and you know about me and Andie, so if you're looking to get hitched, I'd steer clear of that tree."

"And those?"

"Bluebonnets."

Her voice softened. "They're beautiful."

We didn't speak several minutes. "Speaking of beautiful, how's she doing? I mean with the...?"

She shoved her hands in her jeans pockets, elbows close to her sides. "She's okay. The physical discomfort has passed."

"How's the rest of her?"

"She's afraid."

"Of?"

"Billy Simmons."

Somewhere a whip-poor-will spoke. "I thought you were going to say me."

She looked surprised. Shook her head. "What makes you say that?"

"Sometimes, when evil stuff happens to kids, they associate that across a broad spectrum. One bad man soon becomes all men are bad."

"If she was afraid of you, she'd never have gotten on Mr. B, or for that matter, gotten on the couch with you in New Orleans."

"When you two get up in the morning, I won't be here."

She crossed her arms, sort of holding herself. "Can I ask where you're going?"

I stood. "I'll be back late tomorrow night or the next morn, if all goes as I'm hoping."

"You didn't answer my question."

"I asked Brodie to show you around. Maybe take you down to the river. I think it's best if you all stay around here. Lay low. I don't really expect him to find you here, but—"

"You did it again."

I didn't look at her. "Yes, I did."

She put her hands on her hips. "If it involves me, I'd like to know."

"I'm going to San Antone."

"He's not going to let you just walk into his house and put his hands behind his back while his buddies arrest him."

"It won't come to that if things go as I hope."

"So, what? You're just gonna march down there and tell the San Antonio's chief that one of his best officers isn't who he thinks he is."

"Stranger things have happened."

"Would you please answer my question?"

"Yes, I am."

"And you think he's going to believe you?"

"The word of a Texas Ranger still means a lot in this state."

She looked confused. "You play baseball?"

I laughed. It wasn't the first time that'd happened. "I'm not that kind of Ranger."

Her expression changed. "You're a Ranger-ranger?"

I made no response.

Her eyes darted back and forth and her mouth slowly fell open. She was starting to put the pieces together. When they settled somewhere in her brain, she sat back, crossed her arms, leaned her head against the chain of the swing and stared at me. "That explains the vest."

I nodded. "It does."

"And New Orleans. You were there working as a Ranger?"

"I was working security detail for the governor. It's a crap detail, but he liked me and it seems governors like to conference in the Big Easy. So, we were there a lot. Several times a year over two terms."

"The explosion—is that part of this, too?"

"I'd tracked a man a few years. José Juan Chuarez. Finally caught up with him, put him in prison. He and his minions didn't like that."

She nodded. "You really are a cowboy."

"I grew up loving everything about them. The romance. Ethic. The code—most of which is unwritten. Marshall, sheriff, Ranger. They were the Titans of Texas. I even admired their shadows." I smiled. Remembering. "I dressed like them. Mimicked their walk and the cadence of their spurs. The way they spoke. Their measured response. I spent long hours out back of my house where I, alongside Jim Bowie, Davie Crockett, and William Travis, turned the tide at the Alamo screaming, 'Victory or death!' I carried the mail for the Pony Express. Rode shotgun atop a stagecoach filled with people and payroll. Tracked down ruthless rustlers and hung the horse thieves. Turned the stampede with a shot from my Colt. Foiled the bank robbery. Rode at full gallop with the reins in my teeth and a Winchester 94 in each hand. Tipped my hat to the ladies. Never spit on the sidewalk. I cried like a baby when John Wayne died in *The Shootist*." I laughed. "At night, my father would read to me. Great stories about great men. My favorite was a little book called *The Brave Cowboy* by Joan Walsh Anglund." I shook my head. "How I dreamed of being one." I tapped my chest. "A man who wore the star." The sum of the last thirty seconds was more unsolicited words than I'd spoken to a woman in a long time.

Moments passed. "You really going to San Antonio?"

"Yes."

She crossed her arms, sort of hugging herself. "You'd do that? Risk that for me? For us?"

I stared west. "A man I knew once withheld from me what I deserved, and gave me what I didn't. Doing that changed the way I think about me and other people."

"Who was that man?"

"My father."

"Was he a Ranger, too?"

"One of the best."

"Wish I could have met him."

"A few more feet that way and you'll be standing on his head."

She jumped like she'd stepped on a snake. Dad's grave lay behind her. She stepped around it, knelt and brushed her hands over the stone. An iron cross, with a cinco peso badge in the center, stood at the head. Below it, a marble stone read:

Dalton Steele
Texas Ranger. Company F.
He did not fear the terror of night,
nor the arrow that flies by day.
1949–1989

When she looked at me, a lightbulb clicked on. "When you said that he died of lead poisoning, you didn't mean from something he ate, did you?"

"No."

"What happened?"

I told her.

# CHAPTER TWENTY

I was a junior in high school. The five of us—Scrapper, Holes, Knuckles, Eyes, and me—had become friends. Given my dad's occupation, we fell into the idea that we could do what we wanted. So long as we didn't get caught. Holes had a thing with cars—could hot-wire anything. Stacey had an uncle who bought bootleg tequila off some Mexicans a good bit south. We'd steal a car, drive south on back roads never dipping below a hundred, fill the trunk with booze, then return to little towns along the way and sell it out of the back for a profit putting the car back where we got it before the owner knew it was missing. I didn't drink the tequila but I soaked up the adventure. The rush. You might say I enjoyed the Kool-Aid. And they all knew I was pretty good in a scrap.

Harmless, right?

Wrong.

Saturday night, Dad was out all night, working a case.

Holes had found his dream car—a *Smokey and the Bandit* Pontiac Trans Am with a supercharged 400-cubic-inch engine. He quipped, "It'll burn rubber in all four gears." We broke into the man's garage, pushed it out silently, and headed south. At one point in our drive, the dotted yellow line in the middle of the highway had become solid. Holes grinned and said calmly. "One forty." We filled the trunk, sold most of it on the way home, and sold the rest when we got into town an hour before daylight. The trick was getting the car back where we'd found it before the owner discovered it missing. We filled it up, cut the engine and pushed it two blocks and back into the man's drive and garage—only with a little less rubber. We left him a gallon of bootleg on the front seat to thank him for the use of his car. We didn't normally do that but that car was something special.

What I didn't know was that the Pontiac belonged to a judge who worked long hours. When he woke at two, let out his dog, and saw an empty spot in his garage where his car once sat, he called my dad.

The rest of this story doesn't get any better.

My friends disappeared out the garage door, I laid the bottle on the front seat, and began making my way out when I heard his voice crack from the shadows. I nearly crapped in my shorts.

He said, "You 'bout done?"

I turned. "Sir?"

"I said are you about done?"

I figured the less I said the better. "With?"

He struck his Zippo. The flame cast a shadow across his face I did not like. He lit a cigarette. "With being an idiot."

I was never very good at playing dumb but I had little choice. The fading sound of hurried footsteps and quick whispers told me the guys had vamoosed. I would face this one alone. "Sir?"

Until that point, my father had never hit me and never cussed at me. That night, all that would change. Although he did not hit me, I wished he would have. It would have been better than what he said, and the tone in which he said it.

He reached in the car, pulled out the bottle, and handed it to the judge who was staring down at me over my shoulder. "Your Honor." The judge nodded and tucked the bottle under an arm. Dad continued, "He'll start Monday, soon as school lets out. He's yours for the rest of the school year." I tried to swallow but couldn't.

Dad walked up to me and raised his hand to backhand me but stopped midair. By then, I'd grown as tall as him so we were eye to eye. Spit had gathered in the corner of his mouth. His bottom lip was quivering and his right eye was twitching. "Get in the truck."

He drove me to the morgue. Walked me in. The smell made me gag and I threw up a little in the back of my throat. Two tables lay in the center. Both covered with sheets. He walked around one and pulled the sheet off. A kid. An odd shade of pale bluish-white. I'd seen him before. Looked like Swiss cheese. Five holes center mass. Dad then turned around and pulled the second sheet off. A big, bearded man. Same shade of blue. Swollen. Bloated. A tag tied around his toe. I recognized him.

He had bought booze from us on more than one occasion.

My dad said, "Come stand here." I walked between the two tables and he rolled each up next to my hip. One of the boy's eyes was half cocked. Part of the man's head was missing. Dad said, "Give me your right hand." I did and he laid it on the chest of the boy. My index finger landed in one of the holes. "Now give me your left." I hesitated. A strong combination of hurt and anger were blocking the words. He managed, "Give it." I held it out and Dad laid it atop the man's chest, spreading my fingers wide and pressing my palm flat.

He walked around the tables. His heels echoing on the concrete floor.

"Frank Jones." He nodded. "A drunk." He paused. "Came home yesterday morning, heard something rustling in his closet. A burglar breaking into his house. Frank grabbed his Smith and went to work. Emptied the cylinder. What he didn't know was that"—he glanced at the boy—"Justin was home, skipping school. Went to a movie with some friends. A new Disney movie. Had the Jujubes in his back pocket to prove it." Dad paused, swallowed, stared at the man. "With the gun still smoking, Frank opened the closet door and found this. So, he swallowed the end of his twelve-gauge, which explains why the top of his head is missing."

Dad stood staring at me. "Frank was drunk on...tequila." He drew deeply on his cigarette—the end glowing like a ruby, or the eye of Satan. When he'd reduced it to a stub, he dropped it and twisted it beneath his toe. I could feel blood on my hands. He stared at me. His eyes red and wet. The Marlboro man incarnate. He spoke through gritted teeth. "I been telling you my whole life that there are consequences to the choices you make, now you're gonna see what they look like." His finger was shaking as he told me to get in the truck. It was the first time he'd ever cussed at me. " 'Cause I've got to go find Roberta and tell her how her husband shot their son."

I can still see that lady's face.

Dad didn't speak to me for a week. That following weekend, he took a rare day off. I can count the few on one hand. He walked me out back of the house to two saddled horses. His and mine. It was Easter weekend. Bluebonnets everywhere. The pasture was a sea of blue. We mounted and rode several hours, giving rein to the horses. Next to me, the Bar S was the thing that meant the most to him in this world. It was where he found peace and it was the only home I'd ever known. Toward evening, we circled back and stared at our house from a half mile off. The wedding tree was a sprawling cottonwood that sat alone, its branches falling over the river.

He hooked his right leg around the saddle horn. "Your mother left us when you were quite young. I know you have few memories of her." He fiddled with the end of his reins. "I have not...I know I have not been the best of fathers. I've been married to the law and you have often, rather most all of the time, played second fiddle to my being a lawman. In truth, I haven't known how to be anything else." He glanced downriver. "I taught you to shoot down there and, well, you shoot better than most. Maybe better than me. Certainly with a long gun. But, I do regret things." He swallowed. "Me and Frank aren't...weren't all that different. He was addicted to liquor. Me to this." He tapped his chest. Ranger tradition holds that after 1947 or 1948, Rangers had their stars cut from Mexican cinco pesos, which were 99.9 percent pure silver. Dad's was one such peso. "Being a lawman was all I ever wanted. A Ranger. A dream come true." His voice rose. "To be a part of, counted as a member of, the most storied law enforcement agency this country's ever known. Maybe ever. To be one of a hundred men chosen to guard Texas." He shook his head. "I dove in. Gave Texas all of me—and God knows I do love her. Gave her the parts you never got. I learned right quick that to do this job and do it well, and hopefully not die in the doing, I had to be 'on' all the time. Never let my guard down. Never, for one second, clock out because if I did, I give the upper hand to the bad guys...the evil I am, was, chasing." He nodded. "That meant that I never gave you me. Not really. Not like I should." He shook his head. Stared a long way away. "I've lived my life looking for something worth dying for." He looked at me. "I just forgot to look at home."

For the first time in my life, my father was crying. Tears pouring down off his cheeks. He took his hat off, turning it in his hands. "I have been angry about Frank and his son and am disappointed, but not at you. For the record, Frank was not drunk on your tequila. We confirmed that with the bartender who sold him somewhere north of a dozen shots of pure agave." He spit. "I have spent the last week realizing that if I'm not careful, I will do the same to you that Frank did to Justin." He shook his head. "Not with a wheel gun. Not shooting blindly through a closet. But, with the absence of time. With alienation." He trailed off, shook his head. "I've done that to you enough already. So, I thought I'd tell you before I told anyone else. I'm resigning the force next week." My jaw cracked open. "Was wondering if maybe you'd like to go into business with me. Maybe we'd—" He ranged his hand again across the sea of blue. "Raise cattle together." I couldn't swallow. My heart was stuck in my throat. He turned in the saddle, and wiped his eyes on his shirtsleeve. "Was wondering if maybe you'd like that, too."

A breeze washed over us. It was the conversation I'd been wanting to have with my dad for most of my life. I squeaked out a broken and cracked, "Yes, sir."

We sat a long time. The river rolling beneath us. He was about to start toward home when he stopped. Spent several minutes staring down across the water. Finally, he rolled a cigarette, got off Blue, and laid that cigarette on the limb of a tree then saddled up and pulled down on the brim of his hat. He said, "Want you to promise me something."

"Sir?"

"When I'm old, and, I leave this earth, I want you to bury me in the Brazos."

It was a good wish.

"Right there." He rested his hands on the pommel. "Right there, in the arms of God."

"Yes, sir."

He spurred old Blue, turned toward the house and said over his shoulder, "You've got a birthday coming up. Right?"

"Yes, sir."

I followed. His tone of voice told me he was smiling. "Seventeen, I believe."

I rode up alongside. "Eighteen."

He nodded and led me to the barn. "Rangers never make much money. It's not why we do what we do. You know that. But, I saved up a little and..." He stepped down off Blue and slung open the door. He pulled the sheet off the most beautiful rusted old car I'd ever seen. Torn ragtop, a dented quarter panel, missing left rear hubcap, cracked tires, sagging tail pipe. "It's a 'sixty-seven. Needs a little work but I thought maybe at night, you and me, we'd fix her together. Put her back together." He weighed his head side to side. "Maybe a bit faster than she once was."

It was a convertible Corvette SS. I ran my fingers along the back of the fender wells. I could barely speak. I managed, "Didn't know you had a thing for fast cars."

"Son." He smiled. "Every man has a thing for fast cars."

I laughed. "Didn't know you knew how to do all this."

"There's a lot you don't know about me. Thought maybe this car could change that." He stuck the key in the ignition. "Go ahead." She cranked on the first turn. Rough. Timing was off. Plugs misfired. Needed work. "Give it some gas." I did and the engine revved, popping and backfiring but the revolutions climbed. "Want to go for a spin?"

I shut the door, pushed the clutch to the floor. "Thought you'd never ask."

It was one of the best hours we ever spent together.

That night, sitting at the dinner table, a call came in over the radio. A bank robbery gone bad. Dispatch said, "Dalton, the robbers shot Mr. Langston and they're holding Betty Sue. They're all jacked up on some Mexican hash and doing all sorts of bad stuff to her. You can hear screaming out the bank windows from down in the street. One of the witnesses escaped and he says she's bleeding a good bit. Maybe don't have long." The bank sat in the center of town, just opposite the courthouse. Dad hopped up, gulped down his last sip of coffee, and said, "Be back directly." I watched him sling gravel out the drive and head to town. One more call amidst the hundreds I'd witnessed in my life.

I sat there a few minutes. Then I hopped in that Corvette and broke the speed limit to town, parking alongside the courthouse. I heard the gunshots as soon as I stepped out of the car. People would later tell me at the burial that my father ran up the bank steps with his Remington 870 and shot it off the hinges. They were upstairs, looking down on him. The gunfight lasted several minutes.

I crept around the courthouse and knew Dad would be measured in his response, not just blasting away. I could see the reflection of the powder flash off the marble steps' reflection. I listened as he methodically emptied all five rounds in the 870. I could see him in my mind's eye running it empty, loading two more in the tube, running it empty again, then laying it down and going to work with his secondary. His .45.

A .45 has a distinctive sound. A sharp quick report. Different than a shotgun or rifle. I listened as he emptied a magazine—eight rounds. Back then, magazines carried seven rounds. The eighth sat in the chamber. A pregnant pause followed, which meant he was reloading. And most definitely moving. Another seven followed. I heard myself whispering, "Front site. Front site. Front site. Presssssss." Another pause. Followed by two more. Then silence. The fight was over.

He'd finished it.

Flashing lights were everywhere. People standing around. They tried to stop me. "Don't go in there." When I got to him, he was fading. His face ghostly. Shotgun blast to the right side of his chest. Not much left. His body was lying over hers. The blast had been intended for her. He was sucking air through the hole. I took his hand. The tears coming down. I was shaking my head. He reached up, thumbed them away, and winked. "The price we pay." The blood pooled on the marble. Circling my feet. Dark red. Almost black. The sucking sound stopped. Three men lay like pickup sticks at his feet—their legs folded at unnatural angles. Two more upstairs. One writhing on the stairwell. Another hanging over the banister. He eyed the seven bodies. Then the woman. He tried to breathe but couldn't so he grabbed my hand and placed his badge into the center of it, closing my fingers around the edges. It was slippery. He nodded. "Something worth dying for." He tried to say more but couldn't and exhaled.

The girl lived.

The governor laid a wreath on his casket and flew the capitol flag at half mast.

I cried like a baby.

# CHAPTER TWENTY-ONE

Sam and I walked back to the house as headlights pulled down our road. She jumped again, grew rigid, started nervously looking at the house where Hope slept. She rose up on her toes, ready to pounce. I touched her arm. It was the first time I touched her in comfort, and not out of necessity. "It's my captain. I asked him to come."

She exhaled. "Think I'd better get some sleep. Long day." She turned, walked away. When she spoke, she wasn't looking at me. "Don't take him lightly. He prides himself at being very good at what he does."

"I'm planning on that." Captain Packer turned and parked. "I'll see you tomorrow night."

She still wasn't looking at me. She spoke low, fear had crept back in. "You promise?"

I walked around in front of her, lifting her chin. "Yes."

She walked inside and I met Captain Packer in the drive. He measured me, then pushed his cigar to the other side of his mouth. The end glowed a dull red reflecting off the wrinkles that made up the war map that was his face.

Captain John Packer Jr. had entered the Ranger service with my dad. He'd been at it some forty-plus years. One of the longest serving Rangers in existence. Highly decorated. An icon. Revered by every man that served with and under him. If he asked us to go to battle, every man in Company B would be standing in front of him.

Texas had changed a lot in his tenure. He'd pinned my dad's badge on my chest after I'd been appointed to the Ranger service and sworn the oath. When he did, he said, "Cowboy, I've only known one chest big enough to carry this piece of silver." He smiled. "But, I imagine yours will, too."

I'd nodded and felt the weight of it pulling down on my shirt.

He stepped toward me. I shook his hand. "Captain."

"Son. How're you doing?"

"Fine, sir."

He measured me under the moon. "You're thinner."

He looked older. More tired. "I 'spect. A few pounds maybe."

"How long's it been?"

I shrugged.

He squeezed my arms. "Little over a year?"

We both knew. "A little."

He smiled and nodded. The ice had been broken. He let go. "Heard you've been traveling."

I turned my hat in my hands. "I've seen some country."

"Dumps says you been burning through tires like, well—"

"Been keeping them warm."

He sucked through his teeth, then spat out a piece of his cigar. "You are a rare breed, Cowboy."

"I believe you've told me that before, sir."

The years had aged him. More wrinkles. Hair whiter. More silver. Still magnificent. Broad-shouldered. Taller than most men. Still commanded a presence. Still polished his boots and wore double-starched shirts. His Wranglers were ironed, the creases showing down the front. But he was now sixty-two—no, sixty-three. None of us really knew. Had he softened, or was it just me? Time has a way of knocking the edges off. Pain does, too. He lifted his chin. "How's the leg?"

"Don't feel it much."

A fake smile. "You lie."

His lips grew tight while his eyes walked up me, then split: half frown, half smirk. He did that when he didn't want you to know what he was thinking. Only problem was, we could all read him like a book. He walked to the front of his Ford and leaned against it, took off his hat and lay it on the hood. His belly had grown. Sort of pushed out over his belt. "Now, why don't you tell me why you've got me out here this time of night."

"I need to go hunt a man and I need your permission to do it."

"That's not all you need."

I kicked at the dirt with my toe, then looked at him. "Yes, sir."

"Who is he?"

I told him.

He scratched his chin, thinking. That meant he was going to let me do what I wanted but that he'd worry about it until I got back. "I'm going to call his boss, let him know what's about to happen."

"If you'd wait 'til after lunch, it'd let me know whether this is going to be easy or..."

"Or...?"

I laughed. "Or not."

He dug in his shirt pocket. "A while back, you walked in my office and laid this on my desk. Said something about me finding another chest to pin it on." He blew on it and then polished it on his shirtsleeve. "I been keeping it till... till you wanted it back."

"I just need it this one time."

"You sure?"

"Yes, sir."

"And what about the next time?"

"There won't be a next time." I stared at the house. Brodie's room.

He stuck his finger in my chest. "No heroics. You get in, get out, get the evidence to his boss. Let them take it from there."

"That's my plan."

I had a long drive in front of me and if I left right now, I could get an hour or two's worth of sleep at a rest area before I ended up at his place.

He pulled a toothpick out of his shirt pocket and peeled off the plastic. "Something you need to know. There's talk that your buddy José Juan Chuarez is going to be released on a technicality."

"I heard."

"Seems he's hired some pretty good lawyers. Paid them a lot of money. Thought you'd want to know."

I nodded.

He looked around me. "You're kind of isolated out here. If he starts giving orders, you might find you need help."

I tapped my cell phone. "Don't worry. Still got you on speed dial."

He shook his head once. "By the time I got here, it'd be too late. Even the smoke would have cleared."

I laughed. "I doubt it. He shows up, there'll be a good bit of smoke."

He smiled. Nodded. Pushed the toothpick to the other side of his mouth. "I got a question I been meaning to ask you." He ran his fingers through his graying hair. He took his time. A breeze washed over us. "Do you blame you?"

"Blame me, sir?"

"Do you blame yourself for"—he eyed the Bar S—"what's happened to you?"

My voice softened. "The night my dad was killed, we'd spent the day together. Dreaming. He told me he was retiring that next week. Going into the cattle business with me. Just him and me. He realized he'd given his life to Texas and not Mom and me. Didn't want to live a life of regrets." I stared at Captain. "I was going down the same track. Gonna be just like him. Took me a while to see that. So, in answer to your question, yes, I blame me." I shook my head once. "Every day."

We stood in the dark. Listening to an evening in Texas. He poked at the dirt with the toe of his boot. A breeze pushed through. "Son?"

"Sir?"

His eyes shone a deep, brilliant ebony. "You want me to go with you?"

"Sir, if it goes the way I'm planning, I won't even see the guy until after I've got the evidence and handed it to his captain. I've got her house key. I intend to let myself in, find what I'm looking for, and leave. I don't want to mess with this guy. I wear an 'S' on my chest because it makes my son happy. Not 'cause I think it's got anything to do with me."

He laughed. "Just don't let it go to your head. And be careful."

It'd been almost three years since I'd worn my father's cinco peso. A feeling I'd missed. I cranked the truck and the needle on the gas gauge pointed through the "F" at Brodie who was still smiling at me. Just above it, on the dash, sat the legal-sized manila folder that would change his world forever. The papers requiring my action lay stacked inside.

I scratched my head. One thing at a time.

I was driving to San Antonio to help a woman I'd known for less than three days, while severing ties with a woman I'd known for thirteen years. A woman who gave me a son. Who used to wait up for me. Whose crow's-feet showed up in the corners of her eyes after we got married. Whose tomato garden now lies covered in weeds out back of the house. I know the number of freckles on her back, the length she likes her stirrups, how she likes her feet rubbed when they're tired, and how she breathes when she's sleeping.

I circled out of the drive and nearly ran over Sam. For the second time. She shone white in the headlights. Barefoot. I rolled down the window. She slid her hands in her pockets, walked up next to the window. "You don't need to do this."

"You got a better idea?"

An unconvincing shrug. "What if we just lie low? Disappear. Start over. We're a long way from there and he's not going to find us. You said so yourself."

I chuckled. "If you believe that then why can't you sleep?"

She nodded. Picked at the sand with her toe. "You still don't have to do this."

"I know that."

"Why then?"

"Because bad men who have a lot to lose, like him, are rather motivated."

"But"—and this time she looked right at me—"you don't even know me."

"In my line of work, that really has little bearing on whether I go or not."

"What if—?" She shook her head. Swallowed what she'd hoped to say. "So, we're just supposed to wait here until you get back?"

I glanced at my watch. "You could get some sleep."

She stepped back, and nodded. "Right. I'm sure that'll happen."

"Listen, there are some things about my life that I regret, but, this"—I tapped my badge and let my eyes roll down the drive—"is what I do. Telling me not to go is like telling Brodie he can't ride Mr. B. It's all he's ever known. He don't know nothing different. Life for him is life with Mr. B."

She smirked. Spoke slowly, enunciating her words. " 'Doesn't know anything different.' "

"And you understood me, didn't you?"

She tried not to smile. "Yep." She hung her hands on the side of the door. She'd bitten her fingernails. Her expression changed. She reached out and placed her hand on my arm. Eye contact again. More words she didn't speak. Or maybe, the same ones. It was a plea. She left it there, stared out across the pasture, nodded, and hung her head.

I rolled up the window, slid off the clutch, and idled out the drive. The rearview showed her, standing, arms crossed. Maybe a wrinkle between her eyes. When I neared the hard road, Dumps appeared off the front porch, put his arm around her, and led her back in the house.

In my experience, it's those words on the tip of the tongue that we most need to hear. They are the key. The thing that's missing. But you can't pull them out. They have to be offered. Freely. And they won't be offered until the owner trusts you with them. And to do that means they've got to break through a world of hurt and pain just to get them out of their mouth.

I caught my reflection in the mirror. I was shaking my head. If I was a running mother trying to protect my daughter, I wouldn't trust anyone. No matter what they wore on their chest.

# CHAPTER TWENTY-TWO

Dear God,

This place is big. Me and Brodie rode around today for an hour and he said we didn't see hardly none of it. He said he'd take me to the river tomorrow. Maybe we could swim if Momma would let me. She said she would but it's probably too cold. Oh, and there's cows here, too. Lots of them. Brodie said they're Black Baldies, but they're not bald. They got hair. And they're big, too. The bull, that's the male. You know, the one with the, well, you know. He's a Brahma and he's twice the size of the females and his you-know-whats hang down to his knees. It looks funny. Momma says I shouldn't talk about that stuff but how can you not? I mean, they're hanging down to his knees. Don't that hurt when he walks? I guess you'd know. Did you do that on purpose? Did the first Brahma do something to make you mad? He's got a big hump on his back like a camel but Brodie says it don't hold water.

Wait...

There's people talking outside.

It's Momma and Cowboy. They went for a walk. I think Momma likes Cowboy. I can hear it in her voice when she talks to him. She's like a candle. He lit her and now parts of her are just melting down her sides.

Momma's in the bathtub now. Cowboy's walking around out in the hall. I asked Momma what he's doing and she didn't answer me.

Cowboy's gone. He just left. I watched his taillights disappear like two bright-red eyes down the drive. Momma wouldn't tell me where he's going but I think I know. When he walked out of the house, he was carrying a rifle like the soldiers use. It was black and looked like the kind you see in the movies. I think he's going to Billy's.

I hope he gets it. And I hope he shoots Billy. Is it a sin to say that? Even if it is, I hope he does. I hope he shoots him in the you-know-whats.

---

Dear God,

It's morning. Brodie's at school. Mr. Dumps is in the barn. Momma's on the porch sipping coffee staring down the road with her knees tucked up into her chest. And I'm in the bathroom sitting on something called a bu-day. It's kind of like a toilet but only you don't poop in it. If you did, you'd have to poke it through the little holes with a stick or something 'cause otherwise it'd never flush. I saw it last night and then asked Momma this morning what it was and she said it's a thing for girls to wash their bottoms. Front and back. Women use it sometimes when they don't want to take a shower. I asked Momma if I could use it and at first she shook her head. Then she chewed on her fingernail like she does when she's thinking and she changed her mind and said I could. It's weird but I like it. Momma said it probably wasn't here when the house was first built and that Cowboy put it in here for his wife. Momma said his wife must have been a real lady 'cause ladies use these things. I figured I'd sit here a while and let that sink in.

Oh and God, Cowboy should be in San Antonio by now. Are you watching? You should be. Not that I'm telling you how to be God, but well, you should be. And you need to make sure Cowboy knows about the security system. The one that don't make no noise but calls Billy and his friends on his cell phone. And about all the guns. And about how Billy knows how to shoot them real good. Cowboy needs to know that, 'cause Cowboy's just a cowboy.

Well. I got to get off this thing 'cause it's starting to feel weird. I guess it done did whatever it's supposed to do 'cause it's made my butt pucker. I don't know why women don't just take a shower 'cause your backside's all wet anyway. You need a towel to get dried off. I won't bother you none the rest of the day so you can help Cowboy. Okay?

If you said yes, you need to speak up . . . but I'll take that as a yes.

---

Dear God,

I've left you alone almost all day and not said a word, but it's after dinner, Cowboy's been gone all day and we haven't heard a thing. Momma hasn't said much. She's about rubbed blisters on her hands. She's done drunk so much coffee she's peed fifteen times. She keeps getting up off the porch, walking to the railing, staring a while at the drive, then sitting back down on the swing and fidgeting. Then she starts it all over again. Except when she puts on another pot of coffee.

Today, Momma and me were being nosy and rummaging through the bottom of his closet and found this shoebox at the bottom. We opened it and found all these articles about Cowboy. About how he shot a man who was holding a kid hostage on a bridge. The bad man would hold the baby out over the water so the police couldn't grab him. If they tried, he said he'd let go. Cowboy's boss knew he could shoot real good at long distance 'cause Cowboy grew up shooting whistle pigs at out to six hundred yards. I don't know what a whistle pig is but I don't think it's a pig that whistles. Momma says she thinks it's something like a rat. Anyway, Cowboy had been shooting these things since he was little so he was real good at shooting small things a long way off, so his boss told him to lie down on the opposite bridge, about eight hundred yards away, and shoot the man. And that man died but that girl didn't. 'Cause Cowboy shot him in the head when he pulled the little kid back over the bridge and then the bullet hit him and he fell down dead and Momma said the baby probably just fell on his chest where it was soft rather than the concrete so it didn't get hurt none. The article showed Cowboy standing with the governor who gave him a honor medal. We found other stuff in that box, too. An old article about his daddy. It was yellowed and real thin. Said he was shot here in town in some bank during a robbery. He saved some lady's life. I guess Cowboy and his daddy, they just go around saving women from bad men. 'Cause he did it for us.

After that picture of Cowboy with the governor, I got to thinking. I think Cowboy and Billy are a lot alike but they're a lot different, too. They both got pictures with famous people where they did stuff good, but Billy puts his on the wall where everybody can see it and know all about him and think one way about him when he's not really that way, but Cowboy, he stuffs his in the closet down in a dusty shoebox with tape on it where nobody can see it. Where nobody don't know nothing about him. Where only nosey people who shouldn't be looking were looking and found it. Why is that? Is that 'cause maybe sometimes people hide the good in them and others around them got to go digging to find it?

Momma read an article about an explosion and how Cowboy got blowed up and then some kid shot him with his own gun. Momma says that's how Cowboy got that burn on his neck and it probably goes all the way down his side, too. The boys that did it were working for some drug lord from Mexico. Cowboy had hunted that man down and put him in prison. Said it was one of the biggest arrests in a long time. The article said that Cowboy retired after that for "personal reasons." The article made it sound like Texas had lost something 'cause he was born to be a Ranger but retired at the pinnacle of his career. The captain's secretary said he walked into his captain's office and laid down his badge and said, "Cap'n, I can't wear this no more." When the Captain asked him why, Cowboy just shook his head and said, " 'Cause it's killing me." Said Cowboy was crying when he did it. But that don't really make sense, 'cause when he walked out of here last night, he was wearing it. I could see it shining in the moonlight. Does that mean he ain't retired no more? I know I'm hitting you with a lot of questions but there's a lot going on and I figure you can handle it. Right? You're supposed to say yes. Maybe you said it and I didn't hear you. If that's the case then you need to speak up.

The end of the article said Cowboy now lives on a small farm called the Bar S that belonged to his father. That's where we are now. That's where I'm writing from. He lives there with his wife, their son Brodie, and an old boot maker named Dumps. Said Cowboy raises cows and runs a private shooting school for people who want to learn how to defend themselves. Momma says he teaches normal folks. I told her she should ask him to teach her and she started chewing on her lip. That means she was thinking that, too.

I thought maybe if I talked long enough that you'd get Cowboy back here safely. Like maybe it'd help burn the time away. But, it didn't. He ain't here. What are you doing about that?

I don't mean to be disrespectful, but...what are you doing about that?

Oh, and one more thing. Brodie took me down to the river today and said that's one of your arms. I told him I don't think so. When he asked why, I told him you'd be stronger than that wimpy little river.

Dear God,

It's midnight and Cowboy ain't back. Momma's worried. I asked Brodie if his dad had called and he said no. I asked him if he was scared and he said no but I think he was lying. Mr. Dumps said we don't have anything to worry about, that Cowboy ain't no dummy, but neither is Billy. And Billy's mean. While Cowboy's not. And sometimes, I think mean beats not. It just does.

Just look at all the bad stuff that happens to good people. If good beat bad, then all that stuff wouldn't be happening. I don't get it. I mean, if you're who everybody says you are, and you can do all the stuff you can do, then why is it like that? Momma tells me all the time that I ask too many questions and that makes me pernishus. I don't really know what that means yet 'cause I can't find it in the dictionary either but I do ask a lot of questions. But what do you want me to do? I got all this stuff swirling around my head and what am I supposed to do with it? Some of those questions have got to be answered. They're like those itchy bumps on my skin. The doctor calls them "scay-bees." Little bugs crawling all over me. Making me itch. My questions are like that. They crawl all over and make me want to scratch my skin off. But you, you're like that cream the doc prescribed and Cowboy bought. Maybe that's how you beat the bad. Maybe you use people like the doc and Cowboy to put cream on kids whose skin is itching and who hurt down there 'cause some man stuck something in there he shouldn'tve stuck in there.

I'm just being honest... I hope Cowboy shoots Billy.

---

Dear God,

Momma just shook me awake. Headlights in the drive...

---

Dear God,

Thank you.

# CHAPTER TWENTY-THREE

The house was lit up like a runway when I drove back into the drive. I could almost hear the meter spinning. Dumps and Sam were standing on the porch. Sam was barefooted, arms crossed. She met me at the truck, her eyes sunk in dark shadows, and asked without asking. I stepped down, rubbed the stiffness out of my thigh and answered her. "When I got there, he was gone. I let myself in and found the house in a bit of disarray. The sofa had been moved and the vent ripped up and out of the floor. There was no thumb drive. Nothing. Some smeared blood on the floor but that's about it." She stood stone-faced. "Best I can figure is that Hope's blanket made a faint trail down the floor. He followed it and it led him to the vent."

This information did not satisfy her. "So, what now?"

I shrugged. "You certain it was in the vent?"

"Yeah, I could see it. Hope could, too."

"Then, he got what he was looking for. Case closed. He's proba-bly glad to have you running. He's got nothing to worry about. The absence of any evidence on Hope—" I shrugged a second time trying to soften the blow. "We—you don't have much of a case. Your word against his. And he's decorated."

She nodded. "And I'm not, I know."

"I didn't mean that."

"I know. I'm sorry. So, what do we do?"

"First, we get some sleep. All of us. Then, over some coffee and a hot breakfast, we figure out tomorrow—tomorrow. You probably ought to spend some time figuring out if you want to start over in Rock Basin. If you do, I can help you. You want to do it someplace else, I'll help you get there."

She nodded. Smiled. But the smile did not erase the wrinkle between her eyes.

Hope met me on the steps, stared up at me with sleep in her eyes. "Hi, Hope."

She squinted against the porch light. "Did you really shoot a man eight hundred yards away?"

Sam put her hand over Hope's mouth and said, "Shhh."

I laughed. "You two are nosey."

Sam started apologizing. "We were—I'm sorry."

I knelt down in front of Hope. "Yes, I did."

"And is that why they gave you the honor medal? For killing that man?"

I shook my head. "No, they gave me that medal because that little girl got a chance to grow up. She's in Brodie's school now. Her name is Chelsey."

"Did your daddy die trying to stop a bank robbery?"

"I think when Dad got there, they were finished robbing the bank."

"Then, why'd he have to die?"

" 'Cause they, the men robbing the bank, were hurting a woman who worked there."

She reached up and touched my neck, touched me for the first time. Ran her fingers along the ripples of the burn. "Is Brodie going to be like you and your dad?"

I shook my head. "No. He'll be better than us."

"Is he going to be a Ranger?"

"That's up to Brodie. But he's got a few years to figure it out."

I stood and started walking to Brodie's room. She spoke from behind me. I turned. "Brodie told me today that the people who discovered that river down there call it 'The arms of God.' Is that right?"

"Yes, they do."

"Well is it?"

"If it's not—" I shook my head once—"then, I don't know what is."

I pushed open Brodie's door and found him lying sprawled across the bed like his mom. Taking up every square inch of the mattress. Sleeping with him was like snuggling with an octopus. "Hey, big guy."

He rolled toward me. "Hey, Dad."

I knelt next to his bed. "You okay?"

"Yes, sir."

I brushed his face with the back of my palm.

"Dad?"

"Yes."

"Are you a Ranger again?"

"Son, I'll always be a Ranger." I slid off my father's badge, laid it on his chest and kissed him on the forehead. "Get some sleep. Morning'll be here 'fore you know it."

"Dad?" His hand closed across my badge. "Can we get ice cream in the morning?"

"Yes, on one condition."

He sat up, rubbed his eyes. "What's that?"

I smiled. "Nobody sets me on fire."

"Hah. Like the Scarecrow?"

"Yes, like him."

He rolled over, curled up, closed his eyes, then stuck his arm straight in the air and showed me my father's badge buried in the hollow of his hand. "I got your back."

The house quieted. Everybody went to bed. My adrenaline had yet to play out so I grabbed a towel, a bar of soap, and walked down to the river. Above me, ten trillion stars shined down. The Big Dipper was scooping up West Texas above the Cap Rock. I got to the bank, slipped off my boots, then my clothes, and walked down into the water in my birthday suit. When it got knee deep, I sat down, leaned into it, and let the water roll over my shoulders. That's the second time I'd taken off that badge and I still had no idea who to be without it. It had created a lot of good, but a lot of bad had happened, too. I lay in the river and tried to make sense of that.

I could not.

# CHAPTER TWENTY-FOUR

When Andie moved out, I quit sleeping in our bed. Too many smells that brought back too many memories and surfaced too many questions. I threw a twin in the room with Brodie and we bunked together when I didn't crash on the couch or sleep in the hammock on the front porch. Dumps had taken to calling me a bed nomad and he was right. Sleeping alone, after having not done it for twelve years, didn't set well with me. Neither did the waking alone. Many a morning I woke to the sound of her breathing in my ear, drooling on my pillow, her left leg anchored over mine, her hand laid flat across my chest. I've seen vines do the same thing around the columns on our porch. And in my experience, if you pull one away from the other, both die.

I woke to the smell and sound of breakfast so I dressed and assumed, wrongly, that Dumps was cooking. Thought I'd help him out. It wasn't so much that it had become his job as he was an early riser and liked it. I let him. I was surprised to walk in and find Sam creating a breakfast fit for the club floor at the Ritz. I don't know where she got it all but we had eggs, grits, sausage, handmade biscuits, orange juice, coffee. It'd been a long time since that table had seen a spread like that.

"Hi."

Sam was flipping pancakes in an iron skillet on the stove. "Help yourself." I stared at the mountain of food. Flour dotted her nose and cheek. "Dumps offered to go to the store yesterday. Hope you don't mind."

I poured myself a cup and blew off the steam. "Not at all."

Brodie walked in with bed head, sat down, and started eating.

I turned to Sam.

"I thought that maybe after breakfast, if you feel up to it, that I'd take you to town."

She wiped her nose with her sleeve, smearing flour further across her face. "That'd be great."

"I know Brodie's principal if you want to talk to them about school. It's public, so, it's free and they're good people."

She nodded but didn't take her eyes off the skillet.

"Speaking of, how's she doing?"

"Good. She's...she's been using the bidet. Hope you don't mind. She'd never seen one and—"

I half laughed. "Well, take my word for it, ain't none of us using it."

"I told her real ladies use them and that your, well, your wife must be a real lady."

I nodded. "She is—one of a kind."

I piled butter on a biscuit, smothered it in raspberry preserves, and shoved it in my mouth. By the time Hope joined us and we finished eating, Brodie and I could barely move. I pushed back. "Why don't you two let me and Brodie do the dishes and then we'll take you two to town."

Rock Basin, Texas, is little more than an old brownstone courthouse surrounded on four sides by several buildings that house a drugstore, pharmacist, attorneys, a barbershop, land surveyors, a bail bondsman, and others needing to be close to the courts. There's only three other noteworthy structures in town. The bell tower stands 127 feet in the air. Bill and Jason's Bar-B-Que is run by two overall-clad bubbas that dress out somewhere north of 300 apiece. They sweat grease rather than salt, and cook possibly the best brisket and smoked sausage this side of eternity. And the federal prison, a steely gray world surrounded in double fences, concertina wire, hardened guards with rifles, and roaming German shepherds.

Rock Basin's public school isn't what you'd call college prep but it's K–12 and run by good people, many of whom I went to school with. I introduced Sam and Hope to the principal—a girl named Beth that I'd known all my life—and gave the short version of their story. She listened, picked up the intercom, and called one of her teachers. Next thing we knew, Brodie was showing Hope to her new classroom. It was a neat picture, but not nearly as neat as watching Hope grab Brodie's hand as they walked down the hall. Sam stood there shaking her head, dabbing her eyes with a tissue that Beth gave her. We thanked Beth, walked out in the sunshine, and Sam turned to me.

"Do you always cut through red tape like that?"

"What do you mean?"

"That. That right there."

"Oh. Folks around here think rather highly of Rangers. It's a Texas thing."

I slipped on my Costa Del Mars and she shook her head. "There's more, isn't there? You're not telling me everything."

"I caught Beth's eighteen-year-old son, Pete, dealing marijuana. I cuffed him, took him to jail, and put him behind bars. Mainly, to scare him. Before I told him he 'had the right to remain silent,' I called her, let her come down, and watched her read him the riot act between the bars. By the time she finished, he was begging me to let him stay there. We released him and he's been clean ever since. Some kids need a wake-up call." I nodded. "I did. He's no different."

"And she's always remembered that."

"She wants the same thing I do. The best for the kids we bump into. Hers. Mine. Yours. Kids today are growing up in a dark world." I shrugged.

A Super Walmart sat on the outskirts of town where the interstate intersected the state highway. I drove Sam out there where she talked with management and arranged to pick up her last check. Several hundred dollars. She inquired about a job and they said they wanted to call her former boss first and see if he'd recommend her. It made sense.

Walking out, we passed the optical center. I said, "You think they have your prescription on file?"

"Probably."

"Why don't we get you some glasses?"

"You don't mind?"

"No." A chuckle. "I don't mind."

She checked with the lady at the counter, who did have Sam's prescription in her computer. The lady said, "Pick out a pair of frames and I can have them ready in maybe thirty minutes."

Sam began shopping frames while I tried to act like I wasn't paying attention but when she started looking at the bargain frames under twenty dollars, I inched forward and handed her one of the designer styles. She shook her head. "Too expensive."

"Look, I realize I am not a fashion consultant but you can't go around wearing"—I blocked her view of the bargain rack—"those. They look—"

One side of her lip raised. "That bad, huh?"

"Pretty bad." I offered the designer frames again.

She shook her head. "Those will take close to my whole paycheck when it comes in."

"I'll put it on your tab." Slowly, she began looking at the nicer frames. I pulled down a pair of titanium frames that drilled directly into the glass so that the lenses were free of any metal. Somewhat rectangular, they were really attractive. She stared in the mirror. I nodded. "Get those."

She handed them back and shook her head. "I can't. Hope needs—"

I walked to the lady at the cashier who was listening to us talk while trying to act like she wasn't. I handed her the frames. "Can you put her prescription in these frames?"

She smiled. "Give me half an hour."

Sam and I walked to the in-house McDonald's and she bought us both a cup of coffee with my three dollars. She was quiet and I was afraid I'd embarrassed, or worse yet, shamed her. I made eye contact. "Did I goof? Do you not like those? You can get some others if you—"

"No, I like them very much. The most. I've just never spent two hundred dollars on glasses."

"Well, if the advertisements are true about titanium, those can be wrapped into a pretzel, then hit with a hammer and they'll retake their shape, which will be helpful if you keep hanging out around truck stops."

She smiled, sipped her coffee, then spoke softly. "Thanks."

Thirty minutes later, the lady walked out of the optical center and flagged us out of the McDonald's. Including a scratch-free guarantee, and a free replacement if they break, the lady said, "Two hundred and seventeen dollars."

I turned to Sam. "Do you wear contacts?"

The lady behind the cash register broke in. "Yes, she does. I have her contacts over there on the wall. Boxes of ten. She can wear each one for about a week."

I nodded and she added them to the bill. Sam slid on her glasses, the lady made sure they fit her face and we walked out. Sam hung her head slightly. I realized it wasn't like that when we walked in there. Then I realized I was the reason it was hanging. We stepped into the sunshine. "Sam?"

"Yes." She spoke without looking at me. Her glasses complemented her face and looked really good on her.

"I didn't mean to shame you. Please don't hang your head around me."

She looked at me. Crossed her arms. "I don't know how to...I already owe you so much right now. I'll be months paying it off and Hope needs—"

"Sam?"

She looked away.

"Sam, please."

She turned toward me. "What if I can't repay you?"

"I told you once that a man once gave me what I didn't deserve and withheld from me what I did. When I told you it changed the way I see people, I wasn't kidding."

She squinted and shook her head slightly. "I still intend to pay you back."

"Okay, but we're going to a job interview and you can't go in there with your head hanging. I know these women and—"

"Job interview?"

"Yep. And—"

"What am I interviewing for?"

I laughed. "You grown particular in the few days I've known you?"

"No." She smiled. "I'm just afraid by the way you said it that it's marginal or illegal...or involves me doing something I'm not going to want to do."

I pulled my hat down. "Well, looks like you'll have to trust me on this one."

She crossed her arms. "I'm not real good at that."

I nodded. "I don't blame you."

We drove back into town, walked two blocks to a building with a giant peach as its marquee, and I led her up the sidewalk. The

Georgia Peach is the only salon in town. It's a full-service place where they pride themselves on being able to set, cut, color, and gossip with the best of them. I don't know about the set, cut, and color, but they've got a corner on the market when it comes to knowing everything about everybody. Georgia owns and runs it. She's midfifties, well endowed, maybe on the bigger side of plus-sized, wears enough red lipstick to keep Revlon in business, and loves everybody. Hence, everybody loves her. Something of a Texas version of Marleena come to think of it. She employs four stylists, a lady who washes hair, and a receptionist, and they are always busy. Georgia has got somewhat of a monopoly on the market, as women drive a hundred miles just to spend three hours in there.

I pushed open the door and she screamed from across the room. "Tyler Steele! You big, good-looking hunk of a man, come here! I need to kiss you on the mouth." She doesn't really walk as much as levitates. When she moves around it reminds me of that land scooter thing that Luke Skywalker rode in *Star Wars*. She floated across the room, I removed my hat, and she threw herself at me—something she did with the few men who dared walk into her shop. Oh, and every time I see her she's colored her hair a different color. Right now, the color of the week seems to be fire-engine red with streaks of blond and black thrown in for accent. She kissed me with a big wet slobbering kiss that made me blush. She sized me up. "You look thinner. You look like you could use a chicken fried steak or two. Where you been? Were your ears ringing?" Hands on her hips. "We were just talking about you."

"Good or bad?"

"You know better than that. Now"—she turned to Sam—"who is this dear, good-looking thing?"

"Sam Dyson meet Georgia."

Georgia pursed her lips and eyed her. "Honey, do you like feet?"

Sam looked confused.

"Can you give a pedicure?"

Sam nodded. "I can do most anything if you show me one time."

"Oh, it ain't difficult. Just rub their feet with something that smells exotic, tell them a few lies about how they look skinny, agree with them that their husband is a no good goat roper, and the tips will come rolling in." Sam laughed. Georgia winked, "Honey, with your looks, a low-cut shirt with one too many buttons unbuttoned, I'll have a line of men out the door who had never once given thought to a pedicure until they saw you. You're hired."

Sam turned to me. "Is that okay with—"

I shrugged. "I called ahead. Told her about you."

Sam looked at Georgia. "Thank you. That'd be great. When can I—?"

Georgia said, "Wait right here."

She disappeared in the back and Sam whispered in my ear. "How do you know her?"

I shrugged. "Long story."

"Give me the short version."

"Her husband was trying to kill her, so I helped her get a start here."

"And her husband?"

I turned my hat in my hand. "He can't hurt her anymore."

Georgia reappeared with an apron and a basket full of small metal instruments. "Victoria here will show you how to get started." Georgia then ran her fingers through my hair. "Good Lord, honey. What did you do to your hair?" She shoved me toward her chair. "Sit."

"No, really, I—"

She pressed the tip of her scissors gently against one of the buttons on my chest. "Don't even think about it. I have already cut one man in my life and don't think I'll hesitate to do it again."

"Yes, ma'am." Georgia spread that sheet thing over me and started massaging my head.

She skinned me like a peach but she's got such gentle hands I didn't say anything. In truth, I love sitting in that chair. I spent half my time like a bobblehead doll, 'cause I was dozing off.

# CHAPTER TWENTY-FIVE

I told Sam I'd be back at five to pick her up. I walked across the street, down a block toward the square and into First Federal Bank and Trust. The receptionist said, "Hey, Cowboy. How you been?"

"Good, Mira. Thanks. He in?"

"I'll check." She dialed a number, told Jean I was standing down-stairs, and then nodded. "Go on up."

The bank president was a fellow name Mike Merkett. The bank my father defended had been sold a year later to the Baldwins. The Baldwins sold it to the Langstons who sold it to the Merketts. So while the building had not changed, the owners had. Mike Merkett was not a bad fellow, born and raised in Dallas, and had ambition of growing this bank as large as he could and selling it to one of the national chains, then starting over and doing it again, and again. He loved banking. To each his own. Despite my history with the bank and the stain on the tile floor below which they'd never been able to really clean, Mike had no loyalty to me or my business. He knew there had been a shooting in the building at one time but that could be said for a lot of the older banks in Texas. To Mike, I was an account number on a ledger and my account was causing him trouble—despite the fact that I'd never missed a payment. His problem came in an opportunity. One of the national banks had come calling. They liked Mike and the book of business he'd built but they wanted some of the bad loans off the books before they sealed the deal. And Mike was anxious to seal the deal.

Their auditors saw me as a bad loan.

Jean stood, and hugged me. Mike walked around the desk, shook my hand and said, "Tyler, how are you?"

"Good, Mike. Thanks."

He leaned against his desk. His was a good-sized man. Tall as me. About as broad, but bigger around the middle. I, on the other hand, created my own occupational hazard if I started getting too heavy so I stayed pretty lean. His size was an asset. People associated it with authority, or power, or his command of the business. In part, that was true. To be honest, Mike was a good banker. I just hated what he was doing to me. He crossed his hands. "How's things?" Mike wasn't one to beat around the bush. I appreciated that, too. When he said "how's things," he was really asking, "You made any progress since the last time we talked and can you pay off your loan before I foreclose on your farm?"

"I've got a hundred head of cattle. Forty-eight are about to calve. In six months, with conservative numbers, I can get you twenty thousand. Three payments like that will get me almost to zero."

He took a deep breath. Stared at the ceiling. That meant he didn't like my answer. "And if you sold the whole herd right now."

"Mike, I've never missed a payment. Each of my three credit scores is above 800. I'm not going anywhere."

"The auditors are concerned that between your mortgage and the amount on your home equity line of credit, mixed with the fact that you are now retired, technically living on less pay, that you're overextended and if you were to default—"

"I won't default, and between my retirement pay, the cows, and my instruction, I'm making more money now than when I worked with the DPS."

"I know that and you know that, but the auditors from Massachusetts see a different picture." He paused. "Can you make any other arrangements?"

Mike was getting pressured and had made up his mind. He was going to close my loan off his books so there was no chance it would interfere with this sale, or the next, and he could get another ten cents a share. I don't begrudge him that, but I'd prefer it not be at my expense. I stared out the window of his office that overlooked the tellers and lobby below. The flag of Texas had been inlaid in the marble of the floor. Dad died lying sideways on the star. I remember kneeling next to him, empty brass shell casings scattered about the floor. I stood. "How long do I have?"

"Tyler, we've been talking about this for almost three years. We've been more than understanding. It's not new."

"And in those three years, have I ever missed an interest payment?"

"No, but you've paid down very little principal, too."

"Andie's treatment has not been cheap."

"I can empathize. Honest. But . . . my hands are tied."

"Can you show me anything that I signed, ever, that said I would decrease principal in the last three years?"

"That's not the point."

I raised an eyebrow. "Then what is?"

He folded his hands. "Six months ago, we met. I told you that you had six months. They won't let me push it back any further."

"So, when do they intend to kick me out of my own farm on which I've never missed a payment?"

"You have three weeks before they post the auction notice. They'll sell it seven days after that in a live auction. You're welcome to attend if you can find financing elsewhere."

"So, I can buy my own farm?"

"Tyler...I'm sorry." The star below looked dirty. Sullen, I stood and walked out.

My attorney's office stood a block away. Small towns are like that. I grabbed the paperwork off my dash and walked to his office. I wasn't in a very good mood. George Eddy was divorced, an alcoholic, and an unfaithful man, but he was one heck of an attorney. Besides, given our history—which meant I caught and arrested a man who was trying to kill him before he did it—George liked me and worked for free. Which, obviously, I needed. He'd been after me for nearly a year to sign the papers and he'd file them with the court. Simple as that.

His assistant smiled and hollered, "Come on in," when I knocked.

I walked in, laid the folder on his desk and he smiled. He opened it, examined the three copies, and said, "One for you, one for her, and one for the court. Great. I'll file today and you'll be done." He smiled again. "And free, in short order."

"When will you notify her?"

"Soon as the court stamps it and notifies me."

"I'd appreciate it if you'd let me do that."

He laughed. "I'd advise against that."

"I know."

He nodded and checked his watch. "I'll get Delilah on this right away. File it this afternoon. Should be just a few days."

"Thanks, George."

He shook my hand and I walked out. I stood in the sun, set my hat on my head, and rolled a cigarette, taking my time. Seems like getting divorced ought to be more difficult. Seems like I ought to sense some vague notion of finality. The storefront two doors down caught my eye. It was where the four Mexican gang members had set me on fire and shot me. I shook my head. I stared back up the street toward the Georgia Peach where Andie had gone to get her hair done, heard the car rumble past, and had come running out.

Screaming. Tires squealed. When she got to me, she couldn't touch me. Shock set in.

All this had started there.

I laid the cigarette on the window ledge of George's office and thought through the process. The court will receive the paperwork, stamp it, file it, and declare me divorced. And while that takes care of the legal technicality, it did nothing to erase the signature across my heart.

I set my sunglasses on my face and walked three blocks toward the garage apartment I kept in town.

# CHAPTER TWENTY-SIX

It was after dinner. Brodie got ready for bed and I was tucking him in. "Dad?"

"Yeah, son."

He stared up at me. "Momma's not really coming home when she gets out, is she?"

I was tired of lying. "No. She's not."

His eyes welled up. He swallowed. "Where will she live?"

I shook my head. "I don't know, son."

"Will I see her?"

"Yes."

"Is she going to live in town?"

"I don't know. We haven't talked about it."

"How will I see her?"

"I don't know."

"Do you love Momma?"

"I don't know, son."

"Did you used to?"

"Very much."

He paused, his eyes scanning the ceiling. "What happened?" The truth was that she became an addict, wrecked me financially, started sleeping with another man, and then tried to kill herself. I figured I'd skip that part of the truth.

"Son, I—"

"Couldn't you just bring her back here and—"

I ran my fingers through his hair. "No, son."

"I don't understand."

"I know. I don't really either. I know you hurt. I hurt, too. I just don't know how to—" He rolled over, closed his eyes, and pushed out the tears where they spilled onto his pillow. I kissed him on the cheek, turned out the light, and told Dumps I was walking to the river. I had imagined that conversation differently. It had taken me by surprise and I was pretty sure I hadn't handled it too well.

I sat on the bank, my toes digging into the sand. Behind me, I heard footsteps. She walked quietly up beside me. "Mind if I sit?"

I slid over. "Sure."

Sam and I sat staring out across the river. She tucked her knees into her chest, chewing on her words. After a few minutes, she spoke. "Thank you for today."

I nodded.

She bumped me with her shoulder. "I learned a lot about you."

"Yeah?"

She smiled. "You did that on purpose, didn't you?"

"What's that?"

"Put me in there with all those gabbing women."

I skipped a small, smooth stone across the water. "I had an idea it would happen and it doesn't bother me that it did."

"Is your wife really in detox?"

"Yes."

"Is it really her third time?"

"Yes."

"And you've actually paid for each one?"

I rolled a pebble between my fingers. "Yes."

Her voice lowered. "What happened?"

"Andie had a tough time with me being a Ranger. Not initially. But, as the years dragged on and she put herself to sleep more nights than not, she got tired. The worry got to her. We grew distant, argued some—or rather, she yelled at me and I listened to her, and then the thing happened in town."

She touched the burns on my neck. "You mean—?"

"Yeah, that was the straw. She couldn't take it anymore. Wanted out. So, I got her an apartment in town and we separated. She kept Brodie some during the week, which helped 'cause I wasn't home much anyway, and I got him on the weekends." I skipped another rock. "I thought if we just let the dust settle, she'd come back."

"What then?"

"She fell in with some girls, started making systematic withdrawals from our HELOC and intercepted the bills for about six months."

"How much did she take?"

"Sixty-nine thousand four hundred seventeen dollars and twenty-seven cents."

"Ouch." She smiled and tried not to laugh. "What did she spend it on?"

"What did she not spend it on? She and her girlfriends, all divorced or separated, took to the casinos or weekend shopping trips to Manhattan. Best I can figure, she 'spent' it on designer clothes or wasted it at the craps tables."

She fell quiet a minute. "Where is she now?"

"A few hours east of where I bumped into you on the highway."

"Think she'll come back?"

"She can leave anytime, but if she doesn't want to go to jail, then she's got to stay where she is for now."

"Spending money on a line of credit doesn't land you in jail."

"Four or five years ago, she was having trouble sleeping and got a local doctor to give her prescription meds."

"What for?"

"She told him 'depression.'" I nodded. "And that'd be true. She was depressed."

"A lot of people take prescription meds who don't land in jail."

"Once she'd tapped out our HELOC, she started selling. That put her in league with the good doctor."

She nodded. "Earl Johnson?"

"Yep."

"Georgia said he was interested in more than just prescribing medication."

I nodded. "I'd gotten her this apartment in town. It was relatively safe. I could check on her from time to time. Anyway, I checked on her one afternoon and her doctor friend was making a house call. I caught them." I shrugged. "She was real mad, embarrassed."

"Where's the doctor?"

"Working every day in his practice in town."

"And he's married, right."

"If you call that a marriage."

"Why didn't you do anything?"

"What? Like tell his wife?"

"Yeah."

"Would it help?"

She shook her head. "No, but it might make you feel better."

"I doubt it."

"How'd she end up in the hospital?"

"Boy, they really gave you the long version, didn't they?"

"They talk a lot."

"After that, she spent about a week showing up at the house, medicated out of her mind, saying all kinds of crazy stuff. I shut the door, wouldn't talk to her, wouldn't let her see Brodie, filed a restraining order, which kept her away from me and Brodie and then did the thing I thought I'd never do."

"Which was?"

"File for divorce. A few days later, I took the papers by her place to drop them off. The door was cracked, I stepped in. She was lying on the bathroom floor, a pale shade of blue, an empty pill bottle next to her. I got her to the hospital. Pumped her stomach. Once we got her awake and coherent, we Baker Acted her. The handcuffs were precautionary but I felt like she was a danger to herself. Since then, she's been in and out of programs."

"When's she get out?"

"Little less than a month."

"What then?"

"I have no idea."

"Do you care?"

"Sure. She's the mother of my son, a woman I've been married to for twelve years. We shared . . . a lot. More than any other person. But, in another weird sort of way, I couldn't care less."

She didn't look at me. "Word is you filed those papers today."

I shook my head. "Got to love a small town."

She nodded. "Word spread pretty fast. Your attorney's secretary came into the shop after she left the courthouse."

"So much for confidentiality."

She laughed. "She never said any names but everybody knew who she was talking about." She shook her head. "Those women really think you're something."

"Oh, I'm something all right."

"How's Brodie with all this?"

"He's hurting."

"He's a great kid. Real tender with Hope. Really looked after her at school. Sat with her at lunch. Made a point of finding her in the cafeteria." She looked at me out of the corner of her eye. "Rather protective."

"It comes with the Steele DNA." I skipped another flat pebble. "He's the best part of both of us poured into an innocent, hopeful, sweaty, eleven-year-old package."

She dipped her toes in the water, sending out ripples. We didn't say anything for several minutes. When she spoke, her voice was soft. "Georgia said she'd pay me Friday. With that and a few tips, I can pay you back."

"No hurry."

"Sounds like you could use the money."

"It won't really make a difference."

She chose her words. "Is that apartment in town...for rent?"

"No."

"You saving it for your wife when she—?"

"No. I didn't mean you couldn't rent it. You can, just...I don't own it. It's owned by a lady in town. She lets me have it for nothing."

"Is that the same lady your dad—?"

"You really did get the long version, didn't you?"

"Took most of the day."

"I went by there today. Cleaned it up. You're welcome to move in anytime. I just didn't know how to bring it up. Didn't want you to think I was kicking you out. It's a nice apartment. Furnished. Full kitchen. Nice tub. I call it an apartment, but it's a good home. Spacious. Clean. Got a porch. Swing. 'Course, most porches around here got one of those. Flat-screen. Cable. If it wasn't built above a garage, you'd think it was a house. You can walk to work and you can walk Hope to school. Everything's pretty close."

She leaned in, pressed her face to my cheek, and kissed me. It was warm, soft, and earth-shattering. She touched my face. "Thank you."

"Well..." I blushed. Beets were a lighter shade than my face. "You're welcome."

She placed her palm on my cheek, pulled closer to me, kissed me a second time. This time on the side of my mouth. "For everything."

In all the ups and downs with Andie, even after her and the doctor, I'd never been unfaithful. Never strayed. But, I will admit that second kiss tugged on me in places that, well, let's just say it tugged on me. I said nothing, which was good, 'cause I'd have never gotten the words out my mouth.

She sat next to me, staring up at me, rocking back and forth with her arms wrapped around her knees. "Were you ever unfaithful to your wife?"

I looked at her. "Good night, lady!"

"What?"

"You don't mess around when it comes to asking tough questions, do you?"

"I don't have much patience for games."

"I gather that."

"Well? Seriously."

"No. Never unfaithful."

"Not even in your mind?"

"Well, I got a pretty good imagination, but I've never let it go very far."

"What about me?"

"What about you?"

"Have you seen me in your imagination?"

I laughed. "Well, that's the funny thing. I've never needed much imagination when it comes to you. Between that truck driver's cab and the parking lot of the Ritz, I've seen a good bit."

"You saw that?"

"Tough to miss."

She smiled. "Good. I was hoping so."

The conversation in my mind was loud. Technically, I was no longer married. The formality with the court would take a few days. For all practical purposes, Andie thought we'd been divorced since she signed the papers nearly a year ago. I carried them around in a coffee-stained folder not because I needed her signature, but because I needed mine. We'd been separated more than three years. And three years is a long time to go without a woman when you've been used to having one.

She stood. I stopped her. "The apartment, tomorrow?"

"Tomorrow."

"You sure you're okay with it?"

She put her hand on her hip. The curve of her body in the moonlight did not escape me. "Let me put this in perspective for you. Anything's better than Billy's, or that station wagon, or the last half dozen crap holes I've put my daughter in." She looked around. "This is the first time, maybe in her life, that we've had a start. A life. A clean one. With good people. And I'm not saying that to put more pressure on you. I'm just saying, that we think it's great. A boy, a good boy, held my daughter's hand and walked her to class today. Made her feel like somebody. Life here is . . . better than I've known in a long time. You know, I actually heard her laugh today. My baby laughed. You know what that did to me?"

I waited. Let her talk.

She knelt behind me, placing her hands on my shoulders. She spoke over me. "You know who made her laugh?"

"Is this a trick question?"

She chuckled. "No. It was Brodie."

I nodded. "He gets that from his momma. She could always laugh at most anything."

"Well, wherever he gets it, you need to bottle it up and sell it. Your money woes would disappear overnight." I was learning that she was real touchy, feely. She liked to have her hands on me. Which, to be honest, didn't bother me a bit. She squeezed my shoulder. "See you in the morning."

She walked off and I was pretty sure she knew I was watching. Again.

# CHAPTER TWENTY-SEVEN

We dropped Brodie and Hope at school. He walked her in, carrying her bag. Sam crossed her arms and shook her head. "You done good with that one."

We walked to the truck, stepped in, and began driving. I was in no hurry. She picked up on it as the streets rolled by. "This is a quiet town. Real Mayberryish."

"We have our moments."

"Such as?"

We passed a church on the left. I looked at it as I spoke. "Few years back, a man walked in there Sunday morning. Place was packed. Marquee out front said, REVIVAL. Singing. Dancing. People smiling. Anyway, man walks in and starts shooting people. Kills eight before the ushers rush him. He kills two of them. When I got there, the man was DRT."

"DRT?"

"Dead right there."

She shook her head.

"Like I said, we have our moments."

"You'd think church would be a safe place."

I laughed.

"What's so funny?"

I turned, drove a few blocks, pulled out onto a wider street, passed a few farms, a tractor supply store, and finally stopped in front of a large white church that set back off the street. I studied the grounds and church building. "Twenty years ago, I was a newbie patrol officer. Hadn't even made my way up to narcotics yet. Still wet behind the ears. We got a little elementary school down the street. Closer to town. During recess one day, two boys in a Chevrolet—Carl Trudeau and Kyle Becker—been drinking since the night before, drove by the schoolyard and picked out the only kid on a swing and shot him through the chest. The kid was seven. The boys in the car drove off. We tracked that car and those boys for the better part of three days. Knew if we kept the pressure up, they'd either slip up or go to sleep. We found them passed out in an abandoned barn. We arrested them, separated them, and started our interrogation. Since I'd known that little boy, I was more than a little interested in their answers. Few hours later, we had confessions out of both of them. Detailed, too. Couple of singing canaries. Wrote them out in their own hand. They did a pretty good job, too. But since it was after midnight and the secretary was gone, we just figured we'd wait till the next morning to get them typed and signed. I went home and went to sleep.

"Next morning, when I showed back up, I grabbed a cup of coffee and found a man waiting on me in a shiny brown suit. Alligator boots. Handed me his card. Said he was the attorney for the two. Big smile on his face. The court threw out our 'unsigned' confessions. Carl and Kyle walked. Told the judge that we coerced them. Showed them their bruises and black eyes. Said they wanted to press charges against us." I shook my head. "If I'd have hit that boy, he'd have had more than a black eye. Carl went to California. Never seen again. Kyle disappeared a few years, only to resurface here." A new white Cadillac sat in front of the church. "Shiny suit. Shiny car. Dapper-Dan hair. He started a church. Pastor Kyle now spends his days talking about 'the ways of a sinner' and 'the Love of the Lord.'" I nodded. "I went in there one time. Heard him preach. Lots of people. He's good. Convincing, too."

"You're not serious?"

"Yep. Been in there almost fifteen years. Drives by me and doesn't even wave. I see him in a restaurant and he acts like we never met. But, we met." I pulled out my wallet, unfolded his handwritten confession. "I keep thinking one day, I'll walk into his church, lay this down, and ask him if he remembers that little black boy on the swing. 'Cause I do. I had to take the lollipop out of his mouth and close his eyes."

She stared through the glass. Spoke softly. "So much for 'quiet little town.'" She paused a moment. "What can you do? It's been a long time and while your word is good, it's yours against his. Plus, you're retired."

"Whenever somebody reminds me that I'm retired, I think of Frank Hamer."

"Who?"

"Captain Frank Hamer. Retired lawman. Pretty distinguished career back in the Roaring Twenties. Kept law and order when there was none. Wounded seventeen times himself. Left for dead four times. He was tenacious and once he started something, he didn't quit on it."

"I hear a punch line coming."

"The governor brought him in, asked him to lead the posse tasked with capturing public enemy number one, Bonnie and Clyde. Frank hunted them for months. Hounded them. Never let up. There were thousands of lawmen looking for the duo but he was the only one who found them. Set up an ambush. Waiting with Browning automatic rifles. Caught them on a deserted country road. All alone. Clyde was shot over fifty times when they pulled him out of the car. Bonnie about thirty." I did the windshield wiper–thing with my finger. "Never underestimate retired Rangers. Not getting a pay-check doesn't mean we're off duty."

"I'm gathering that."

I drove her to the apartment, unlocked the door, and let her in. Two bedrooms, kitchen, den. "Given that Andie had a limitless bank account, it's well decorated."

"I'll say."

"She didn't spare much expense. Both rooms are furnished. Kitchen has everything you need. TV is HD, which means football games look like you're in them, and the bathroom looks like something out of a designer magazine."

She walked into the bathroom. "That's a big tub."

"Andie's always been a big fan of bathing. She'd sit in there till her toes turned to raisins, empty the water, fill it up, and do it again."

She ran her fingers along the ledge. "I like her."

I walked to the fridge. "Peterson's is our local grocery. I have an account, which thank goodness she didn't wreck 'cause eating just wasn't on her radar, and John, the guy that owns it, I called him and told him you could charge whatever you needed to get going. Just introduce yourself when you walk in." She had that look on her face. The one that made me think I'd shamed her 'cause I'd done too much. I tried to dodge it.

"You keep a pretty tight record of accounts, don't you?"

"What do you mean?"

"Accounts payable versus receivable."

She nodded, then shrugged. "Not sure how else to do it."

"It's a good way to live, I think. Means you're honest."

She fought to make eye contact. "I'm not always."

"I imagine you want to get settled. Buy some groceries. Make yourself at home. Phone works. The number is scribbled on the paper, inside the handset. Speed dial number one is my cell phone." A set of keys hung on the wall. "I had to sell Andie's Honda to pay for one of her treatment centers, but below you is an old Ford.

Pretty good truck, too. It's the widow's but she can't drive 'cause her cataracts are too bad and she's asked me to drive it every now and then. Keep it running. You're welcome to it. No A/C but"— I smiled—"if you drive fast enough with the windows down, you can hardly tell the difference."

I may be thick sometimes but I'm not stupid. I knew I was doing more than just leaving her to get settled. I'd brought her here, and I was, whether I like it or not, responsible. I'd figured that out in New Orleans. There is an emotional thing that occurs after you've been protecting someone. It happens in both the protected, and the protector. Cutting that tie is a purposeful act. I'd done it many times. And rightly so, but this one, for reasons I couldn't quite nail down, was different. Tougher. And I had helped protect folks who were equally as needy so the degree to which Sam and Hope needed help wasn't the issue. It was something else and I was afraid of it.

She saw it on my face. "Go ahead. You can leave. I'm a big girl."

"You sure?"

She smirked and traced her belly with both hands. "I have stretch marks. I earned them. So, yes. I'm sure."

"That's probably more information than I needed."

Ever spunky, she smiled. "And you got the picture, didn't you?"

"Good point."

"Besides." She stopped me. "Hope and I are cooking you guys spaghetti soon as I get paid. And I'm paying for the groceries."

"Sounds good." And, it did, too. Not because of the food, although I'm a fan of spaghetti, but rather because there would be an end to the me-not-seeing-her part of the week.

# CHAPTER TWENTY-EIGHT

A week passed. George called. Said he had some papers for me. I dropped Brodie at school, told him I'd be gone all day, and then stopped by the Peach and asked Sam if she could watch him until I got home later tonight. She said she would.

I stopped by George's and then drove east. No radio. No noise. No nothing. I was lost in the once Technicolor, now black-and-white, memories of something I'd never get back.

I wanted her to know she was free and we were finished. And I wanted her to know it from my hand. Or, maybe I was wondering if we were. Maybe I was looking for a reason. When I got there, what I found did not give me what I was looking for.

I walked to the counter, envelope tucked under my arm, and said, "I'd like to see Andie Steele."

"Well, she's just right popular today." The receptionist stood and turned a clipboard around. "Sign here, please."

I did.

"Are you carrying any narcotics or anything that could be used as a weapon."

I supposed a pocketknife and two handguns qualified. I nodded. "Yes."

"Sir, I can't let you in unless you return them to your vehicle or place them with my supervisor."

I showed her my identification. She pulled another sheet out of her desk and said, "Sign here." I did and then she clicked a button that unlocked a door. "Her room is that way, room 116, but I think she's outside near the tables."

"Thank you."

I walked the halls. People sat in their rooms staring blankly out windows, read paperbacks, played checkers, or drank coffee. A big glass window overlooked the lawn and tables. Andie sat at one. Still thin. Long hair. Frayed ends. The veins on the backs of her hands were showing. A steaming mug in her hand, the tag of the tea bag fluttering just outside the rim.

It would be a lie to tell you that this was the first time I'd been there. In truth, I'd been there a good bit. 'Course, Andie didn't know that. The last time was the night I bumped into Sam and Hope on the highway. Having been there was probably the reason I hit them since my mind wasn't concentrating on the road in front of me but rather the one behind me.

It was the first Sunday in April. I had driven all night and turned off I-10 at an exit with nothing. No gas, no food, no bathroom, no roach motel. Simply the intersection of two roads. They hid this place in the sticks on purpose. A white-clapboard church rose up on the hill surrounded by grass and a dirty parking lot. The marquee read, HAPPY EASTER. A man in a blue suit was setting up orange cones to steer traffic. I wound eight miles through a series of back roads, ending on a red clay one lane. Another mile and I unlatched the gate and drove down the narrow lane to the clearing.

I tugged down on the brim of my hat, pulled up my collar, and eyed a low-hanging, gray sky. The world around me had begun to bloom but winter wasn't letting go just yet. I threw my pack over my shoulder and shoved my hands deep in the pockets.

East Texas is more piney woods. Some Louisiana swamp. The half-mile trail bordered a cypress swamp, wound along an old hand-dug ditch, through a pocket of towering oaks, around a few acres of ten-year-old planted pines and into a dried-up part of the cypress swamp. Stiff from sitting, I rubbed the ache in my thigh, pushing my thumb into the unnatural knot.

I checked my watch. I had time. I crept along, watching and listening—something I'd learned as a kid. Dad had seen to that. Some of the cypress trees looked seventy feet tall. I skirted some standing water and walked to the far edge, rimmed by a split rail fence. Winter rye, emerald green, stretched from the fence to a cluster of buildings some half mile away.

My trail ended at the ruins of a large cypress tree. It had been cut four feet off the ground and the stump had rotted itself hollow. Big enough to sit in—a good place to hide. A holly tree grew up alongside it. The limbs draped toward the ground and the waxy leaves offered concealment. On previous trips, I'd trimmed a few of the limbs for a better view. The fence was a visual barrier and not designed to keep people either in or out. The people here, like Andie, could leave if they wanted. Where they went was another issue. As was what happened to them once the court caught up with them. Most had more reasons for staying than they did leaving.

I climbed inside my stump, brushed off my seat, and poured myself a cup of black coffee from a dented and scuffed green thermos. Leaning back against the trunk of the tree, I stared out through the limbs and blew off the steam. Wouldn't be long now.

A few minutes to six I set up my tripod and attached the spotting scope to it—a 12-40X Leupold. In practice, it allowed me to see the color of someone's eyes at half a mile. I checked my watch, adjusted my face to the eyepiece of the spotting scope, and began turning the focus ring. The picnic table, a little over 800 yards away, came into focus. One eye staring through the spotting scope, one eye on my watch face, I waited.

A male cardinal perched above me. I replaced the battery in my hearing aid with a spare from my shirt pocket and slid it back into my left ear. The cardinal's song grew louder. The rocket-red male hopped to another limb and the brownish-red female appeared just below him. Calling upward. Wooing. The two chased each other, a flurry of aerial acrobatics, then they disappeared dancing over the tree line. I sipped, watched the picnic table, breathing deeply and exhaling slowly.

Frankenstein behind the woodpile.

At 6:01 a.m. Andie appeared. Gray sweatpants, light blue hooded sweatshirt, and a steaming mug. Motion lights detected her movement and turned on, lighting the patio in fluorescent orange. She walked to the picnic table and sat on top, her feet on the bench, the mug between her hands wedged between her knees. She hovered, sipping occasionally. The string from the tea bag dangled across the outside of her hand. The breeze rattled and spun it. Her hair was pulled back. A single ponytail. Maybe not as bouncy. Single strands fell across her eyes. The blond highlights had grown out. A few of the other guests woke, stepped outside, and stretched. One or two waved at her and then disappeared back inside to shower and find the courage to face another day. Breakfast started at eight. The programs at nine. The monitoring was 24/7. Urine tests random and often.

At 6:18, she stood, arched her back, walked inside and returned with more steam rising off her mug. At 6:40 a man ambled up with a mug of his own and a cigarette dangling. He spoke briefly and smiled, resting one foot on the bench, scratching himself. Lizards do the same thing when they perch on a windowsill and blow out that orange thing below their chin. She brushed him off. At 6:58 a.m., she stood, took a deep breath, and walked inside only to reappear a few minutes later wearing her running shoes. She did not stretch—she never did—but set off at a light jog along the perimeter, following the trail out across the lawn where it met and paralleled the fence.

The circle brought her closer. Her pants were baggy. Her face was more drawn, cheeks thin. Not anorexic, just disinterested. I could hear her now.

Halfway around the loop, she passed me for the first time. The sweat was beading across her forehead and top lip. A distance of twenty-two feet.

She passed, I closed my eyes and waited. Seconds later, it arrived. The fragrance was different but the aroma the same. It lingered a moment, then the same tea-bag breeze pushed through. My eyes followed her. About eight minutes later, she passed again. Another wake. Another breeze. I followed her. She circled, slowing, returning a final time.

A Japanese magnolia towered above the fence. Its limbs, which spread and fell half on her side, half on mine, were covered with a hundred or more, palm-sized blooms that looked something like a tulip. Depending upon soil conditions, which I don't pretend to understand, the blooms will vary in color from snow white to deep purple and every shade in between. These were blood red, trimmed in white.

She slowed beneath the limbs, stopping below the umbrella of blooms, a few scattered on the ground. She stepped around them. Thunder in the distance spoke of rain. She stared over her shoulder, then turned and faced the fence. Surveillance cameras hung scattered in the trees around her. They were controlled by joysticks in a room on the other side of the buildings. The eyes monitoring the video screens cared little about the movements of people outside the fence, but they cared a good bit about what people inside the fence put in their mouths, or arms, or...

She spread her arms, reached high, grabbed a limb a foot above her head and hung there. No nail polish. No manicure. Nails were trimmed short. She closed her eyes and hung her head. Sweat trickled off her head and dripped onto a leaf below. I didn't need the spotting scope. She didn't see me because she wasn't looking and I know how to hide. Circles shadowed her eyes. No makeup, and the ends of her hair were tired and frayed.

Like her.

Her breathing was deep, rhythmic. Sweat rolled down her. I counted the pulse beating on the side of her neck.

Her breathing slowed—each inhale deeper. She put her hands together, resting her head in the bend of her elbow. She swayed.

We had this tree out in front of the house. A live oak—it spread like an octopus across our yard. You could stand on the porch, reach out and hang on the limb, stretching. I'd had a long day. A bad day. A friend had been killed. I wasn't with him. Not there to help him. A senseless act. I'd had to inform his wife. I couldn't count the number of times we'd had dinner or drunk coffee. I pulled off the hard road, a half mile home. I was still holding it together. I could see her standing on the front porch, arms hanging from that limb, resting her head in her elbow. Swaying. Waiting. Needing me to need her. I parked, walked out into the pasture, crumpled amongst the prickly pears and cried a long time. When I looked up, she was kneeling, too. She pressed her head to mine. She walked me to the house, then around back by the barn. We stood beneath the wind-mill. She turned on the shower and that sweet water spilled over me, soaking my clothes but it could not wash out the sorrow.

The sweat drained off her face, around her lips, and into the base of her neck. Something flashed and caught my eye. Something new. I eased back in front of the spotting scope and turned the ring.

I sat back.

The ring hung on a tight necklace just big enough to fit around the base of her neck. A single band. Scuffed. Thin edges. Slightly bent where she'd slammed the door on it.

The bell sounded. Fifteen minutes to breakfast. She wiped her face on her shirtsleeve, pulled her hood up over her head, and walked across the lawn.

I rolled a cigarette and watched her grow smaller. She disappeared inside the door. I walked to the limb and gently ran my fingers across the wood. It was warm. Sweat moist. The smell of her hung in the air. I laid the cigarette in the elbow of the branch and walked away.

She reappeared briefly at 10:30—alone. Again at noon with a tray where she returned to her picnic table and pushed her green beans around. She ate two bites of turkey and turned the applesauce container in her hands for several minutes. She pressed it to her forehead, closed her eyes and finally peeled off the top and ate one bite. At four, she appeared again. A bottle of water. The same guy trailed her but she said nothing to whatever he asked so he took the hint and started sniffing another woman four houses down. At 6:00 p.m., she returned to her condo. I stared through the windows as she passed from room to room. She walked straight to her bedroom, and lay down. I was sipping cold coffee and eating a peanut butter and jelly sandwich. She'd survived another day. I checked my watch.

Time to move.

I skirted the fence line and walked nearly a mile down another trail. I made my way to the water's edge, cupped my hand and drank. I circled the spring, pulled aside the brush I'd stowed there, dropped to my belly, and began elbow-crawling through the granite. The rock outcropping was an anomaly the size of a semitrailer that bordered the water. The tunnel had been created when the rock split a hundred million years or so ago creating a man-sized space that ended in the shadows of the shelf that overhung the water. The tunnel was my vantage point. The shelf, her launching point. The tunnel ended and I propped myself on the smooth rock. An arm's length away, the blue spring bubbled up, clear rolling glass for sixty feet where it overflowed its bowl, turned into a creek and flowed southeast.

I lay there, staring through a six-inch crack.

She appeared two hours later. Quietly. I smiled. I'd taught her that. Her hair fell across her shoulders, a towel hung around her neck. Barefoot, she tiptoed to the edge and stepped onto the shelf. Her back to me, she undressed, laid her sweats in a pile, then ran her index fingers along the lines of her hips, slipped off her panties— the Jockey athletic kind that were all function and no form—and set them on the pile. Naked against the backdrop of the night, she folded her hands atop her head and breathed deeply. Some three feet away, she stood staring up through the trees while the moon rose on the other side.

The baggy pants had not lied. She was thinner. There was less of her.

She did not dip her toe and test the water. She never did. Not in swimming. Not in horses. Not in life. In one fluid motion, she swung her arms, kicked with her calves and Peter Pan'd out into the water where she rolled, floated, and swam for the better part of an hour. Tiring, she climbed back up on the rock and sat there, dripping dry. Her hair lay flat across her back, sending the water down her skin in thin lines. Warming herself, she pulled her knees up, tucked them against her chest, and laid her head upon her arms. Goose bumps rose up on her back and shoulders. I could feel the heat rising off her. Separated by inches...plus a million miles.

Dry, she spread the towel and lay flat on her back, and rested her head on the pile of clothes. I did not move. Did not breathe.

She had weaned Brodie. I could give him a bottle. One morning I caught her looking in the mirror, her hands cupped beneath her breasts. Lifting. Worry on her face. She asked, "Can you tell?" If my wife had started to sag, I wasn't going to be the idiot to agree with her. I shook my head. She frowned. "You're lying." My wife's beauty did not lie in her perkiness. It lay in the sum of her. Convincing her of that was another matter.

Her chest rose and fell. I shook my head slightly. I still didn't agree. The light reflected off her neck.

On nights when I couldn't sleep, I'd raise the blinds, shower her with moonlight and watch her heart beat in her neck while her eyes flipped like wipers beneath her lids. She was multilayered. Complex. Sleeping didn't slow her mind. Sometimes she'd wake more tired than when she went to sleep. Some nights she'd sweat through her gown so she'd pull it off, throw aside the sheet and lie there, glistening, letting the ceiling fan dry her skin.

The breeze washed over her. More bumps on her skin. Her white skin pale in the light. The water dried. Except for a puddle in her belly button.

Ticklish would be an understatement. But she also hated losing. A fiery combination. I'd bet her dinner that she couldn't keep a straight face while I traced a circle around her belly button. She'd lie there, resolute, biting her lip. I'd start slowly... one o'clock, two, drawing it out, taking my time. She'd squirm—a worm in hot ashes. 'Course, anywhere straight out from there was fair game so I really did take my time. By three o'clock, she was losing her grip. By nine she was screaming and kicking her feet against the mattress. By ten thirty she was throwing blows and laughing.

Her pulse slowed. Maybe she dozed. The ring glistened.

Toward midnight, she dressed, dried the ends of her hair with the towel, wrapped it around her neck, and disappeared through the trees, taking my longing with her. Within minutes, even the smell of her was gone. When the midnight bell sounded in the distance, declaring lights out, I clicked on my headlamp, and sat as upright as the rock would let me. I sunk my thumb deep into the knot in my thigh, working it back and forth, then bent my knee, pulling it into my chest, stretching. The blood rushed in and pushed out the ache. Having spent the day like Frankenstein, I'd be stiff tomorrow. I pulled the legal papers out of my backpack and laid them across my lap.

The words "Steele vs. Steele" and "irreconcilable differences" jumped off the page—as did her illegible signature on the last page. She'd signed it nearly a year ago when I shoved them in front of her as she walked out of the judge's chambers toward the van that brought her here. Her handcuffs had rattled atop the clipboard with the jerking movement of her hand. I leaned against the rock, my hand—and pen—hovering above the blank signature line.

The pictures returned.

Flashes mostly. Moments outside of time…watching the wind bend and dance through the bluebonnets as we stood under the wedding tree, Sunday afternoons on the island, skinny-dipping in the river, feeding Mr. B out of our hands, counting her ribs, feeling the muscles flex in the small of her back, cutting the cord and setting Brodie on her exhausted chest, sitting at the coffee table—her knees pressed against mine, watching the corner of her mouth lift and twitch just before she smiled, finding her in the kitchen wearing an apron, a fun smile, and then swinging on the porch wrapped up in a blanket, showers under the windmill, mucking the stalls and then ducking for cover when she threw a shovelful at me, pulling the calves when the cows got tired on nights so cold we could see our breath, branding and cutting weeks later, waking nights to find her back pressed to my stomach, her feet tucked beneath mine, my arm around her and tucked beneath her, the smell of her alongside me, and long lazy afternoons spent in the saddle ambling down the middle of the river, her hat tilted, shading her eyes, heels deep in the stirrups, staring over her shoulder…

That's my favorite. That one right there. Her, horseback. I'm riding behind her. It's late in the afternoon. She's turned in the saddle, a tank top. Her hat angled down low over her eyes. Sweat has soaked through her headband, the centerline of her back, her waistline. She's lean, suntanned, the muscles showing in her arms and back. Her jeans are tucked in the boots that Dumps made her, she's staring back over her shoulder, waiting on me, smiling with that little I'm-up-to-no-good-and-you-should-be-too thing in her eyes. I used to kid her that somewhere way back in her family tree, somebody married a Comanche 'cause she was good on a horse. Always better than me. And I've spent a lot of time in the saddle.

I've heard West Coast people remark to East Coast people how they prefer earthquakes to hurricanes. "Least we don't have to evacuate." I'm not so sure. You can see a hurricane coming. Read the storm warning and the level. Category 1. Category 2. Category 5. You can prepare: buy candles, water, gas for the generator, more shotgun shells. An earthquake arrives unannounced, splits the world in two, and sends a tsunami some two thousand miles away where folks didn't feel the tremors.

The pleasant pictures in my head come to an end. The next set shows a jagged and scarred earth. Tumbleweeds roll through. Things that once stood, now lie toppled. A desk covered in bills I can't pay. Mike Merkett telling me he's sorry and I've got ninety days. Brodie asking questions about his mom that I can't answer. Finding Andie on the bathroom floor, pale and blue, an empty pill bottle next to her. Flying to the hospital and screaming my way through the ER with her in my arms. Watching them pump her stomach and fighting the guilt as ninety pills come back up. The judge's chambers, her sitting across from me—handcuffed, screaming at me. An attorney asking me for a signature. And while these are playing, some giant hand pushes the mute button and drains the color. The images are silent, black-and-white and grainy. Only subtitles and closed-captioning. Monochrome.

An owl hooted over my shoulder. The hour passed. The moon climbed casting the pen's shadow across the page. I brushed my fingers over the dried water spots. The same questions returned. Nearly thirteen years ago, I walked into the Laundromat.

How'd we get from there to here? Where'd it all unravel?

The film of our life ended. She turned, rode away, and did not look back. Her shoulders fell. The slope betrayed her.

My hand dangled above the line. I'd been coming here for the better part of twelve months trying to find a reason not to sign on the dotted line. The process was simple. Sign. File. Move on. People did it every day. Multiple times a day. Half of all married couples did it at one time or another. Why couldn't I? If that one don't work, find one that does.

When I was a kid, I was playing around an old abandoned barn. I climbed down a ladder into an underground storage area. The wind blew the door shut above me, locked itself from the outside. No matter how loud I screamed nobody rescued me—because no one but my horse knew I was there. That was a long night. My horse stood outside a long time, but finally figured I wasn't coming up, so he ambled home and a day later, my dad lifted the latch. "You hungry?" I remember the feeling of sun on my face, of clean air in my lungs, but more than anything I remember walking out.

The owl sounded again. This time one answered a mile away. A lonely echo.

I scratched my head, wiped my eyes, pressed the pen to paper, and made the letters that spelled my name. I crossed the "T" and crawled out of the rock but it felt nothing like walking out of that cellar.

Later that night, in a downpour, I bumped into a stalled car on the highway.

Andie sat at the table, cupping her mug with both hands. I pulled my hat down, tucked the folder up under my arm and exhaled. About the time I was to step outside and speak to her, Dr. Earl Johnson stepped into view. He was carrying flowers.

My immediate reaction was difficult to control. I stepped back into the shadows and stared through the glass. He reached down to kiss her and she gave him her cheek.

That a girl.

Then he sat and they began talking. He reached across and held her right hand in both of his. Five minutes was all I could take. I figured I'd better do what I came to do before Earl ended up shot in the head and they put me in prison for the rest of my life.

Cowboy boots make a distinctive sound on concrete. Andie knew the sound. I stepped onto the patio. She turned and disbelief was soon followed by shame and discomfort. I walked to the table, set the court-sealed envelope in front of her that contained her court-certified copy of our court-ended marriage. Her eyes, surrounded in dark circles and sunk in her head, showed hurt. I turned, walked out, and the words of my father echoed: If you're riding a dead horse...dismount.

# CHAPTER TWENTY-NINE

It was Saturday. The sun was not yet up. I sat on the porch huddled over a steaming mug, smelling the smell of cows knowing neither it, nor they, would be here much longer.

It was no secret around town that I took good care of my herd. In truth, I raised two separate herds. One Angus. One Hereford. Doing so allowed me to crossbreed for Black Baldies, or F1s. And my cattle were registered. More important, they were registered-to-registered. To cattle people, that's important. I put the word out, along with my price, and it didn't take but a few days to find a private treaty buyer. I'd heard of him. Art Bissell. He owned and operated a couple of ranches. One up in Tyler. Another out west. He drove down to see me, spent some time looking over my cows and agreed to a premium market price given the condition and makeup of my herd. He brought his trailers in the next morning. Sunday. I thought about having him come a day later—Monday, when Brodie would have been at school—but Brodie had raised a bunch of these cows, birthed and nursed them. He'd even pulled a few of the calves when the cows got too tired to push. He needed closure and I felt the only way for him to get it was to help drive and load them. So, we did.

I finished my coffee and woke him at daylight. When the trailers pulled into the drive, we were saddled and moving cows through the pasture. We bunched them, eased them toward the fence, and used the fence to route them to the corral. Then we combed back through the mesquite and picked up a few stragglers. I watched Brodie, working his way through the brush and trees. Cutting cows. Cinch and I held back, letting him work. He was a natural on a horse and more cowboy than many of the men I knew.

By midmorning, we had them loaded. Art paid me with a certified check, then he and his two cowboys drove off with my and Brodie's herd in three gooseneck trailers. It'd taken me twenty-three years to build it up from a bull and three cows. It was more than half my life's work. Dust swirled behind the trailers as they rattled away.

Brodie mounted up and spent the rest of the morning with Mr. B. I walked Cinch to the barn, pulled off his saddle, and brushed him down. An hour later, Dumps poked his head around the corner. "You brush him any more and he won't have no hair left."

I'd lost track of time. I nodded. He said, "What's got you so tied up?"

An empty pasture spread out before us. "That's a lot of hard work that got pissed away at the craps table, shopping trips, and wherever else she blew the money."

"Yeah, it is." He nodded, then spat. "Question you got to answer is 'Do those circumstances dictate your attitude?' "

I looked at him out of the corner of my eye. "You learn that in prison?"

"Yep."

"Sounds like something my father would have said."

He patted me on the back and walked off. "That's 'cause he's the one that first said it to me."

"Figures."

\*　　\*　　\*

I scratched my head most of the afternoon trying to figure out what kind of cowboy doesn't own cows. It was like a pair of boots that did not fit. When I finally landed on the answer, it did not soothe me. I knew the rest of this equation was going to hurt almost as much so I decided to get it all over with at once. Sort of like pulling off a Band-Aid. Without giving myself time to chicken-out, I called Mike Merkett at home. He answered. I asked him to meet me at the Bar S. When he stepped out of his Escalade, I handed him the check. He nodded, approvingly. I said, "Mike, I still owe your bank seventy-nine thousand dollars."

I knew more about Mike than I let on. I knew he liked old cars. Even kept a warehouse where he spit and polished about twenty or so rotating beauties depending upon what he'd bought or sold at the latest Barrett's auction. I also knew he had a weakness for Corvettes, and of the seven he'd bought, he'd never sold a one. That meant something to me. I may have owed Mike money, and a lot of money, but that didn't make him a bad guy. He didn't drive a truck, he didn't wear a hat, he didn't look like what I thought a banker in Texas ought to look like. He was just different. But different ain't wrong. It's just different. I tried to remember that as I walked to the barn.

I pulled open the barn door and let the sunshine fall inside. Mike's eyes caught the dustcover and the shape underneath. I pulled it off slowly. "My father gave this to me a few days shy of my eighteenth birthday. After he was shot in your bank..." I paused and let that sink in. "I set it up on blocks and it gathered dust for a few years. Then, slowly, I began taking it apart. Every bolt. Every nut. Every speck of paint. Took me four years. The odometer is true. Twenty-seven thousand original miles." He walked in a circle, his fingers tracing the lines. "To the right buyer, this is worth somewhere between fifty-five and sixty-two." He nodded in agreement. "At the right auction, maybe a bit more."

He nodded again. This time the smile growing.

"You know how you hear stories about guys who meet some old widow with a car she ain't driven in twenty years and then how they buy it and bring it home and show it off to all their buddies who can't believe what he found and stand googly-eyed in lustful, covetous amazement at their friend's good fortune?" He knew where this was going. He was no dummy. "Well, this is your day and I'm that old woman."

I lifted the hood and his jaw dropped. He managed, "It's beautiful." He sat in the front seat, his hands rubbing the wheel. After several minutes, he stepped out and clicked the door shut. "Sold, and I'll take good care of her. It's obvious she means a lot to you. If I ever sell her, you get first right of refusal."

"I'd appreciate that."

When he climbed back into his Escalade, he asked, "Am I mistaken or are you now completely out of debt?"

I stared across an empty pasture. Cow patties dotting the trails beneath the mesquite. Paths to the river where I'd picnicked with my wife. Where Brodie was conceived. "Mike, I may not owe your bank, may not owe any man, but that don't mean I don't owe nothing."

Mike promised to return that night with his wife and drive it home. I handed him the keys. "Whenever it suits you."

I walked out across the sea of blue, beneath the gnarly scrub oaks, and stood over Dad's grave. Ringneck doves were working their way north. A few scurried across the ground or lit in the trees. Their wings whistling with each flap. The river shone silver below me. One of the oil derricks sat rusty and unmoving down the hill to my left. A scrub oak grew up a few feet from Dad's marker. I sat next to it and leaned back, staring west across the river. For the first time in my life, I owned, outright, a piece of land. It had no oil, no cows, and I had no wife to share it with.

It was a wide stretch of dust set down behind the sun.

I rolled a cigarette, lit it with Dad's brass Zippo, and inhaled deeply. I turned and exhaled into the breeze. I did that several times. The smoke exited my mouth, hung suspended before me, was caught by the breeze and returned, washing my face.

And while it filled my lungs and senses, it did not dry the tears.

And there were a lot of them.

# CHAPTER THIRTY

I pushed back from the table. Stuffed. Not even Al Pacino, Robert De Niro, or Marlon Brando had eaten spaghetti that good. Brodie had liked it, too. Had sauce all over his face. I turned to Sam. "Don't know when I've had better." She smiled. Hope, too. "I need to check some fence." Obviously, I didn't 'cause I had nothing to contain but that didn't seem relevant. I needed an excuse. "You want to go?"

Sam lit. "Sure."

"Can you ride?"

"Don't know. Never done it."

I shook my head. "What is the world coming to?" Hope chuckled, which I thought was a good sign.

Andie liked her stirrups long. Hole number seven. While their legs were close to the same length, Sam wanted the feeling of more control. I shortened it to the sixth hole. I ran my fingers across the worn leather around the seventh hole. I'm not sure if they'd ever been at any other length in the ten years we owned the saddle.

I walked us out of the barn, leading her by the reins. Brodie had spent three years here without his mom. Prior to that she wasn't in all that great shape emotionally. For that matter, neither were we. It'd been a while since he'd lived in a healthy home. While he hoped to have her back, he had gotten used to her not being here. In the same way I had gotten used to it with my dad. His problem, and it was the same problem I would have had, was the introduction of a woman into this equation that was not his mom. And while he liked Sam, and was in a small sense becoming a big brother to Hope, he didn't like the picture of Sam and me riding down toward the river. Especially since Sam was riding May. I turned, saw him standing next to the barn door. When I waved my hat, he disappeared into the barn.

Sam picked up on it. "Is this okay?"

"Yeah."

The best way to see Texas is on the back of a horse. It's also a good place to do some thinking. I pushed open the gate and locked it out of habit. Sam spoke. "Since you don't own any cows, do you really need to check fence?"

"No."

"Then, is this a date?"

I laughed. "No."

Hands on the saddle horn, she said, "Tell me what you love about Texas."

"Everything, I suppose."

She shook her head. "Nope. You've got to do better than that. Use words."

I thought about that. Finally, I gave her what I could, pointing at what my eye could see. "I love the 183 men who died at the Alamo; the fact that we fly the Texas flag the same height as the American; the Brazos that flows from the Great Plains and the Llano Estacado to the Gulf of Mexico some eight hundred miles later; the hill country that's rolling and green and covered in deer; farm-to-market roads where men pull to the side to let others pass; men who tip their hats at ladies and boys who tuck in their shirts; brisket that falls off the bone; the Fort Worth stockyards; Black Baldies; Santa Gertrudis; sunset skies blackened by a million ringneck doves headed south to Mexico; Wrangler-clad boys who value a farmer's tan and a crew cut; the fact that we have our own power grid; that we were first a republic and could be again; handmade boots; the way the sun sets over there and...I guess you get the point."

"Those are some impressive words."

"I'm one little piece of a great big ole piece called Texas."

"I like the way you say that. How'd you become a Ranger?"

Good question. I tipped my hat back and wiped my forehead with the sleeve of my shirt. "I don't ever remember not being one. Even when I was little. I mean in my heart, and in my thinking. Growing up, all my heroes were lawmen. That they happened to be cowboys didn't hurt either. John Wayne topped the list. Still does, I guess. Around my house, we took seriously the ideas of right and wrong. I remember carving my own cinco peso out of wood. I remember seeing my dad dress every day for work. Starched jeans, starched shirt, shiny buckle, shined boots, white or gray Stetson. He used to tell me that he knew he'd put enough starch in his clothes when they could stand up on their own. For a long time he told me the department didn't issue bulletproof vests 'cause no bullet made could make it through all the starch." I shrugged. "That upbringing bred in me a strong sense of justice." I paused, rested my hands on the saddle horn, and pushed my hat back.

"High school was tough for me. With little female influence in my life, I was unsure of girls and how to interact. I skipped my senior prom 'cause I was afraid to ask anyone and I knew sure as shooting I didn't want to have to dance." She laughed again. "I avoided love in high school by keeping to sports. Did some rodeoing, and lettered four years on the shooting team. I finished local college in three years with a degree in criminology and then attended the academy. I spent seven years in local law enforcement from sheriff's office to highway patrol, did a stint in narcotics, then, on the second best day of my life, I received an appointment to serve as a Texas Ranger joining Company C making me one of, at the time, 104 Rangers. My territory covered a sizable piece of West Texas."

"What was the best day?"

"The day Andie gave me Brodie."

"Tell me about her."

"Still not shying away from the tough stuff, are you?"

"Well, I want to know what kind of girl you like."

"Andie was, is, a pretty girl. Big, round eyes. Medium height. Freckles on her upturned nose. Loved jeans that had been worn—maybe frayed at the edges and a good pair of boots. I can't tell you how many times I saw her cook breakfast in boots and a nightgown. She liked the smell of a horse, reading stories to Brodie, didn't mind mucking the stalls, liked a good sweat, didn't worry about her nails but liked getting them done when she could. A good momma. At one time, she was a good wife. Tender, but not afraid to tell me what she thought. There was a time when she fought for me...that passed. Always good on a horse. Probably better than me when it comes down to it."

"Do you value that in a woman?"

"I do, although, it's not like it's a deal breaker."

A few minutes passed. She turned to me abruptly. "Are you ever scared?"

"Of what?"

"Being shot. Dying."

I shrugged. "Every man dies."

"Yeah, but not every man gets shot."

"Maybe not with bullets, but we all get holes poked in us." I turned around, looked at our trail, then laughed at the two of us. "We went from superficial to not-so-superficial in a rather short distance."

Moments passed. She pressed me. "You don't seem like the kind of guy to quit on anything so, what happened? Why'd you stop being a Ranger?"

"My wife would argue I've never stopped being a Ranger."

"Would you?"

I sucked through my teeth. "Yes."

"So—?"

"Some folks have a hard time with the way I think and talk. I see black and white and few to no shades of gray. 'Course, those critics grow silent when the man on the bridge is holding their kid two hundred feet above the water or wrapping duct tape around their mouth."

She waited. I pulled back on the reins, turned Cinch. Folded my hands across the pommel. Unfolded my handkerchief and wiped my face. "I'm no scholar. No expert. But, I'm told that every culture has the stories they tell their young. We call them fairy tales. Whether they admit it or not, every girl grows up dreaming of Cinderella. Dancing at the ball with a handsome prince wearing silver slippers."

"They're glass."

"See what I mean?"

She smiled. I continued. "Other day I was driving somewhere, song came on the radio. Pretty good beat. Girl singing. Something about Romeo and Juliet and some guy throwing pebbles. I started singing along. I liked it."

She burst out laughing. "You were singing, 'Love Story'?"

"I don't know what it's called but I walked in the door singing it and Brodie listened about two seconds, then revoked my man card."

She started laughing. "He revoked your what?"

"My man card. Brodie said any man caught singing that song—I think the girl's name was Tyler Fast or—"

Sam was doubled over. Barely got the words out. "Taylor Swift."

"Yeah, that's it. Anyway, he said any man caught singing that song suffered a mandatory revocation of his man card and that I could reapply in ninety days but I'd be on mandatory probation for at least a year. Any further infraction would result in a year-long suspension."

She still couldn't talk. "Anyway, the point is that we still buy into the fairy tale. We love them. They are the stories that feed us and thank God they do. Lord knows we need something to feed on 'cause the nightly news sure ain't doing the trick." I gently bumped the pommel with my fist. "Cinderella ain't wrong to want to dance, to be swept off her feet, live inside the castle. I just think she ought to be able to do so without being raped or murdered or made to fear." I spat and shook my head. She was listening now.

"Greatest trick ever played on mankind is that somewhere, somebody sold us a bill of goods convincing us that evil ain't real." I nodded. "Evil's got a face. I've seen it. Many a time." I pointed south toward Abilene, and west toward the Cap Rock. "It's walking around—wearing white collars and tattoos, SWAT vests, badges, standing behind pulpits, hiding behind every manner of disguise. Evil is as real as that cactus right there and it wants your head on a platter. My daddy described it as a roaring lion, prowling around looking for someone to devour, and in my experience, that is true." I fell quiet a minute. "But, no matter how it dresses, and no matter what disguise it takes, it's still evil." My tone of voice dropped. "And there's only one way to deal with it. It ain't by playing defense. You can only play defense for so long. My father told me that when I was a kid, but it didn't start sinking in until I held his head in my hands. So, when I got my chance, I went on offense. I pulled on my boots, cinched down my hat, clocked in and never clocked out." I nodded, staring at her. "I was always 'on.' I arrested a lot of people, put many a man in prison, confiscated truckloads of drugs. That made me a very good Ranger. Decorated. Then somewhere in there I met my Cinderella, we married and she gave me a son." I paused and shook my head. The admission painful. "But, in my experience, marriage and law enforcement aren't all that compatible. Oil and water. That part of the fairy tale didn't make the finished book. Didn't end up in the song." She watched me. Studying me. I took off my hat and wiped my brow. "That made me a bad, even incomplete, husband. So, when you ask 'What happened?' Well"—I waved my hand back across the story I'd just told—"that happened." I folded my handkerchief and set my hat back on my head. "Now, I haven't spoke this many words to a woman in I don't know how long."

"I like hearing you talk." She stood up in the stirrups, staring out and down, stretching. The saddle creaked. A familiar sound made by an unfamiliar rider. "Your voice is soothing." She rolled one thumb over the other.

"Can I ask you something?"

"Ask away."

"What do you dream?"

She chuckled. "That's easy. To live with and alongside...rather than without and alone."

I nodded. "A good dream."

"Yeah, well, I'm not really holding my breath."

We rode up a small hill and stopped on a high bluff some thirty feet above the river. A chuckle. She ran her hand through the ponytail bobbing on the back of her head.

"Why's that?"

She looked surprised. "You serious?"

"Yeah."

"We must not be looking at the same me."

"Well, what 'me' are you looking at?"

"The one in the mirror."

"Which one is that?"

"The one that looks like a walking disaster. The one who's made a string of bad choices followed by another and another. I'm the poster child for 'don't do this.' I see a high-mileage woman who chased dreams, got close, but got passed over. Whose dreams got shattered. Then 'cause it hurt too much, she forgot how, or worse yet, quit trying and buried them. And now she's resigned to settling for less and living that way 'cause anything else is too painful. And whenever she thinks that maybe she can put the past behind her, she remembers that there are awful images of her daughter that have probably circulated the globe by now. Let's face it, I'm a mess." She turned the question on me. The crow's-feet had returned. "What do you see?" There was a lot embedded in her question.

"I see a strong, beautiful woman who's struggled a lot and come out the other side still smiling, still laughing, still fighting. I judge a tree by its fruit and your daughter is about the...well, she's good fruit."

She turned away. A whip-poor-will whistled off to my left. "If you ask Hope what she's dreaming, she can't answer you." Several seconds passed. "That's the toughest thing of all." I clicked my mouth twice and Cinch headed down the bank. May followed. Sam brought her up alongside me. Our thighs touching every few seconds with the amble of the horses.

The horses made the river and sunk their muzzles in, sucking deeply. I let them drink. I hopped down, helped Sam off May and we walked along the bank beneath the scrub oaks and weeping willows. A few cottonwoods spiraled above us. I looked at her, letting my eyes walk up and down her. "I've seen what a train wreck looks like and you're not."

She leaned against me. "Thank you." We walked a while. She looped her arm inside mine. It was casual, comfortable. "Any regrets?"

"Sure. Lots."

"Like?"

A shrug. "By the time I clued in to the fact that Andie had spiraled downward, it was too late. She'd tried to get my attention and I hadn't given it. So, she found it first in an activity that gave her a sense of value, i.e., spending money like it grew on trees, and then someone." I tried to laugh. "Every now and then I get a notice telling me I owe money someplace else. Someplace I knew nothing about. Got one last month for a hotel, limo, and bar tab in Manhattan.

It's been two years and they tracked me down. Three thousand and twenty-three dollars. That must have been one heck of a martini." I shook my head. "Nowadays, I look at the mailbox through one eye, never quite sure what's inside."

She was wearing a button-up white oxford—unbuttoned to the second button. Sweat trickled down. She glanced at my 1911. "Have you shot men with that?"

"Yes."

"Are they dead?"

"Yes."

"Do you regret that?"

"No. They were trying to kill me. A few were trying to kill Brodie."

"Do you only shoot people to kill them?"

"No. I shoot them to stop them from threatening me or others. If they die, that's their problem. If they don't want to die...well, they should have thought about that before they started being a threat."

"It's simple for you, isn't it?"

"Some things."

She put her hands on her hips and raised one eyebrow. Her shoulders often moved in unison with the corner of her mouth. A puppeteer controlled both. "Georgia told me you taught her how to shoot."

"Yes, I did."

"Why?"

"Well, a single woman. Rough past. Running her own business, leaving at night with cash on her. Spending a lot of time afraid. Lots of reasons, I guess."

"Will you teach me?"

I scratched my chin and tried to make light of it. "Given your choice of male companionship, it might be a good idea."

She laughed and punched me in the shoulder. "I thought you said you weren't judging me."

"My dad taught me a long time ago that there's a big difference between being judgmental, and making a judgment."

She nodded and tried not to smile. "True." Her wall was crumbling. "So, you'll teach me?"

I turned to her. She was smiling. Sort of bouncing on her toes. "Yes, I'll teach you."

She smiled. "Good."

And while I believed she would do well to learn, that it would give her peace of mind and help her take care of herself and protect her daughter, I cannot say with all honesty that is the sole reason I agreed.

When we got back to the house, Brodie and Hope were sacked out on the couch. Shoulders touching. *Finding Nemo* was finishing up in the DVD player. I carried Hope to the truck and Sam drove out the drive while I struggled to carry Brodie to his bed. I was tucking the covers around his shoulders when he said, "Daddy?"

"Yeah, big guy."

"Momma called."

That would have been the first time in almost a month. I swallowed. "What'd she say?"

"She was real quiet at first. I think she was crying. She wanted to know how I'd been. Wanted to know how I was doing in school and if I'd grown." I pushed the hair off his forehead. "Daddy?"

"Yeah..."

"I told her you sold the herd and...the Corvette." He swallowed. "She started crying real hard then. And...I cried, too."

"Nothing wrong with crying."

He sat up. "I asked her if she was coming home and she said she was moving back to Rock Basin at the end of the month but didn't know where. Daddy?"

My voice cracked. "Yes."

"Do you cry?" A tear puddled in the corner of my eye, trickled down alongside my nose, around my lips, and hung on my chin. I tried to stop it, but—

He reached up and it fell into the palm of his hand. He stared at it. Hurt was written all over him. I gritted my teeth. I can protect total strangers from would-be abductors but not my own son. His voice cracked. "You don't always talk about it but I was wondering if sometimes your insides hurt 'cause sometimes I think they do and you don't say nothing 'cause you don't want me to be sad, but if they do then, you can tell me. Okay?"

I nodded, kissed him and turned out the light. He stopped me at the door. "Daddy?"

"Yeah, big guy."

"I think Momma hurts, too. I heard it in her voice."

"I know, son. I know."

I walked outside, letting the air fill me and reminded myself how his mother was an addict, that she'd wrecked me financially, that she'd slept with the town doctor, taken from me most everything I held dear, and never once said she was sorry.

It didn't help much.

# PART THREE

*Él es muy bueno para cabalgar el río.*
　　　　　　—One Texas Ranger describing another

# CHAPTER THIRTY-ONE

Daylight found me outside, hovering over a steaming mug, and staring at the wind vane. I needed to grease it. The wind was coming out of the east, but the vane was angling north. The barn doors were open. A grease spot stared back at me. My car was gone. Goodyear tire tracks were all that remained. I scratched my chest but it didn't satisfy me.

Andie was never much of a gardener save one thing: tomatoes. She grew them, and lots of them, with a vengeance. They were an addiction. Out behind the barn, I helped her till an area of ground that was ten rows wide. In it, she staked a hundred tomato plants. I ran PVC pipe from the water tank and put an individual sprayer on each plant. A hundred heads. We even put four plastic owls on stakes at each corner to scare off the crows. For about nine years, we had tomatoes coming out our ears. She gave them to everybody and everybody wanted them. They were sweet, tasted like fruit, and I cannot count on both hands and feet the number of time I've seen her pick one, bite into it, and then smile as the juice ran off her chin.

I walked through the garden. The weeds had taken over. The plants were long gone. The owls had fallen off the stakes. I scratched my head. Scanned what once had been so healthy.

It was a good picture of us.

By 9:00 a.m. I'd worked up a pretty good sweat so I did one of the things I love most in this world. I took a shower beneath the windmill. The windmill stands some forty feet in the air and draws water up from over six hundred feet. It's cold, sweet, and clear. It pumps it up into a holding tank where we use it for irrigation and to water the horses. We used to water cows with it. It stands out from the barn, surrounded in scrub mesquite and shrubs that conceal it. You have to walk around the back to get in through the trees. If you do, and someone is standing under the water, you get a pretty good view of them. Which is exactly what Sam did just moments after I stripped down to my birthday suit and stood below the water. She walked around the corner, put her hand to her chuckling mouth, and stood there staring—the other hand on her hip, a big smile across her face. I was rinsing the soap out of my eyes. When I opened them, I found her enjoying the picture of me. Which, incidentally, is not something a woman had done with me for some time. I started looking for my hat. I tried to get a few words out of my mouth but stuttered and stumbled my way through nothing. She crossed her arms and laughed. "I'll wait. Take your time."

I grabbed my hat and held it over my privates. "Don't you know—"

"Know what?"

The water dripped off me. "That you're not supposed to spy on people when they're showering."

"I'm here for my lesson but this is better, so go ahead. I'll wait."

"Get! Go! I'll be 'long directly."

She eyed the scar on my left leg, leaned in, looked closer. She stood maybe five feet away. "Is that where the guy shot you?"

I pointed toward the house.

She turned, took two steps, then looked back over her shoulder with a sneaky grin. "I'm glad to know that the fire didn't burn everything."

She saw my embarrassment, walked right up to me, and patted my shoulder, the water splattering us both. "It's okay. I know the water's cold."

I shook my head. "You are killing me."

She walked off laughing. I shook the water off my hat and found myself mumbling, "Well, it is cold."

The range is a few acres on the backside of my property where a dry riverbed runs between two bluffs some twenty feet high. Thirty to forty yards stand between them and they make good berms for a pistol range. I parked the truck, grabbed my bags, and we walked into the middle. I helped her thread a Milt Sparks belt through the loops of her jeans then a BN55, which may be the best holster ever made. I pulled a Les Baer 1911 out of my bag, press-checked it to make sure it was clear, and held it so she could eyeball the empty chamber. "If you ever do this with anyone else, if you ever pick up a weapon, make sure you visually confirm the condition of it. If it's dark, use your finger." I lifted her arm out of the way, and slid the pistol into the holster. Then I snapped a magazine holster on her left hip. To her credit, she had quit cracking jokes, which is needed when you start working with guns. I pushed my hat back. "A couple of rules before we get started." She nodded. "They govern how we do what we do and keep us safe." She nodded again. The weapon hung high on her hip. "This thing breathes fire, and the second we take it for granted or treat it with less respect than it deserves, it'll change our lives and not for the better. The two worst sounds in the world are 'click' when we're expecting 'boom,' and 'boom' when we're expecting 'click.'" She thought about that and smiled. "So, first, set it in your mind right now that you will treat all guns as if they're loaded. And I mean all of them. Even if you know they're not."

"Got it."

"Two. Never point it at anything you aren't willing to destroy."

She considered this, then another nod.

I held her hand, separating her index finger from the others. "Three. Do not put your finger on that trigger until you're on target and ready to fire. In short—on target, on trigger. Off target, off trigger."

"Got it."

"Lastly, make sure of your target and backstop. Meaning, bullets are made to go through stuff, so if Hope is standing behind the bad man, don't shoot the bad man. Least, not yet."

A final nod.

"Now, you repeat those back to me." She did, not word for word, but she got the general idea.

"What I'm about to teach you are the fundamentals, and fundamentals win fights. 'Cause that's what you're doing. You're learning to fight for your life. These are the 'X's and 'O's. I operate on the fundamental assumption that if a bad man down the hall has your daughter with a knife to her throat, you're going to fight. And you'll fight with a spoon if you have to, but that's why we're here. So you don't have to. If you choose to fight back—and you will— you better do so with more than just a pencil sharpener. A handgun is not the best fighting tool, but it works. So, we'll learn it. If I know I'm going to a fight, I'm taking a rifle, or a grenade, or a tank, or a nuclear bomb, or a…you get the picture, but for now, let's stick with handguns. And, lastly, all of this is not a license to become someone else. It's simply an equipping. But, and here's where the rubber meets the road, if you do have to use it, then you get mad-dog mean and fight with all you've got. Clear?"

"Clear."

"Let's start with the basics." I pulled a magazine out of my back pocket and thumbed off a .45 ACP round. "This is what's called a .45. There are dissertations written about what cartridge is best: 9 millimeter, .40 caliber." I shook my head. "I'm not getting into all that. This is what you're shooting today. When you leave here you can choose for yourself. This is what I use." I explained to her how a cartridge works. Percussion. Combustion. And what happens when the bullet cuts into the rifling of the barrel. Then I explained how the weapon worked. The safety. Trigger. The magazine. Recoil. How the recoil expelled an empty cartridge then loaded a new one off the top of the magazine. She listened intently. Finally, I explained the sights, sight picture—what it should look like, trigger control, and trigger reset.

I stood next to her, waving my hands over her getup. "I don't expect you to walk down the hall at three a.m. looking like this but since we're on a range and we've got to figure out how to run a safe range, I have you wearing a holster. That means I've got to teach you how to get from holstered to on target." So, I took her through stance, then the draw stroke. How it works. What it looks like. What a firm final firing grip feels like. How much of her finger actually touches the trigger. Where her left hand should fall in relation to the right.

Once she'd come to understand, we practiced dry firing several times. I let her draw to the ready, acquire a sight picture, press the trigger, acquire a follow-up sight picture, then I'd cycle the slide— mimicking recoil—then she'd return to ready. She did this several times. With an empty magazine and chamber, the weapon didn't recoil when she pulled the trigger so I stood to her right, perpendicular to her, put my left hand on her right shoulder and racked the slide with my right hand to simulate recoil.

An hour in and she began to get comfortable. I gave her a set of ear muffs, loaded several magazines, then taught her how to load and make ready. "Keeping the barrel pointed in a safe direction, which is downrange, and with your trigger finger straight, insert a magazine with your left hand. Flat of the magazine against the flat of the magazine well. Insert vigorously. Roll your left hand over, grabbing the slide between the meet of your thumb and three fingers, careful not to cover up the ejection port, then rack the slide.

And this thing is not your friend. Tenderness will get you nowhere here. Rack that thing. Throw it in the parking lot behind you. Then, because your elbow is designed to work in a circular motion, roll your hand back under, reacquire a shooting grip and click the safety up with your right thumb." She did this. And, as she was not afraid of it, she manipulated it well.

"Now..." I pointed at the target seven yards away. "Acquire a good sight picture, focus on your front sight, and press the trigger. And listen to me carefully...this is not the movies and neither you nor I are what we see on the movies so don't slap this thing. Press it. Think about squeezing one drop from an eye dropper. Recoil should be a surprise." She did. The bullet cut a hole two inches from the center, high left. "Do it again." She did. An inch from the first, still two inches from the bull. We did this nine times until the slide locked back.

When it did, she squeezed the trigger but when it didn't go bang, she spoke out of the corner of her mouth, "What do I do now?"

"All weapons, no matter how they are fed, will go empty at some point. It's not bad luck. It's a function of having been in a fight. So, don't crap a brick." She smiled. "Depress the magazine release button right there with your right thumb." She did. "The old magazine will fall to the ground. Let it. It's empty." It did. "With your left hand, insert a magazine out of your pocket, careful to index the top bullet with your left index finger. That way you know which way the magazine is oriented, and since sixty percent of all altercations occur in low, altered, or failing light, you might have to do this in the dark. So, don't look. Not to mention the fact that you may be in a dog-stomping fight which means you've got something to look at so keep your eyes downrange and chin up so you don't block off your airway." She took her eyes off it, lifted her chin and stared downrange at the target. She was sweating now and I could smell both her and her perfume. "Then replicate how I taught you to load. Insert it vigorously. Roll your left hand over. Rack it. Then reacquire your grip and get back to work. In short, that sequence is called 'tap, rack, and attempt to fire.' " This she did.

We ran through seven magazines that way. Not fast, but slow. Focusing each round, each sight picture, each trigger pull independent of the last. After almost a hundred rounds, I told her, "Finger straight, safety on, and return to holster." She did. "Now shake it out and take a bunch of deep breaths." She smiled and let out a deep breath that she'd seemed to have been holding since she stepped out of the truck.

We continued this way throughout the morning. Soon, her target had one giant hole in the center with several strays peppered within a few inches of what was once the center. "Don't get lazy. Focus each round. It may be your last. You have no guarantee of the next. The last visual control you have is that front sight. Take your time. Focus on it. The last physical control you have is the trigger. Say it out loud if you have to: 'Front sight. Front sight. Preeeeeesssssss.' Once you send this thing downrange, you can't take it back. It's a lot like a word spoken—you better make sure it's what you want the receiver to hear 'cause once it's out of your mouth—" I smiled and shook my head.

Toward lunch, I introduced the idea of multiple targets. I stopped her. She held the gun at the ready, arms extended, finger straight, just below the target. "Most altercations involve more than one assailant. Why? Because wolves travel in—?" I prompted her.

"Packs," she said.

"Right. So, stop the threat in front of you, then search and scan. Be looking for what you can't see."

The morning brought us in close proximity to each other. It demanded that I learn to trust her and she me. Multiple times, I adjusted her grip, placing my hand on hers, brushed shoulders, placed my hand on her back. Or, maybe it didn't demand it. Maybe I brought myself into proximity with her. Maybe.

She wasn't bashful and when she'd learned that I'd forgotten the paper cups, she didn't mind drinking out of the large Gatorade cooler on the back of my truck by sticking her mouth to the spigot.

We each ate a bologna sandwich, two MoonPies, and polished it off with an RC Cola. She toasted me. "The lunch of champions. You shouldn't have."

"I got a can of sardines in hot sauce if you'd prefer that."

After lunch, I introduced the three types of malfunctions that can occur—a failure to feed, a failure to eject, and a double-feed—and how to clear them not so that she'd master them but just to bring it to her attention and let her know that we'd revisit it in lesson number two.

Finally, I stepped alongside her, shoulder to shoulder, and drew to the ready. "If you're fighting for your life, it's best to do it with someone else at your side. A partner is a good thing to have. Texas is a big state and there aren't nearly enough of us Rangers so we don't often get a partner, but when we do, we know the value in it. Hence, learn to communicate."

She interrupted me with a smile. "Sounds like you should take your own advice."

I smiled. "Easy, Annie Oakley. Right now, I'm teacher. You're student."

She shrugged. "I'm just saying."

For the next hour, we ran drills simulating multiple threats. I acted as her partner. When I ran empty, I hollered, "Cover!" She fell silent and looked at me out of the corner of her eye. I leaned toward her and said, "You're supposed to say, 'Covering.'"

Sam yelled, "Covering!" She turned to my target and fired three rounds center while I loaded.

Seconds later, when she ran empty, she yelled, "Cover!"

I turned the turret of my shoulders and arms toward her target and responded, "Covering!"

She reached for a magazine but she was out. Seven empties lay at her feet. Her left thumb was cut and bleeding from racking the slide and she had smeared powder across her lip. Sweat trickled down the sides of her neck. Her focus surprised me. She shook her head without taking her eyes off the target and said, "I'm out."

Without looking at her, I reached in my back pocket, handed her a loaded magazine. She accepted it without moving her muzzle away from her target. She loaded without looking and fired three rounds.

If there was a moment when I felt something twinge inside me, it may have been there. That moment. When she took that magazine from my hand. When she took it without looking and then loaded without looking.

She returned to ready, checked over both shoulders, and said, "Clear."

I nodded, thumbed my safety up and "on" and holstered. She did likewise. I pulled off my earmuffs, nodding. "That's a good place to quit. Line's cold."

She slid off her muffs and looked up at me. "How'd I do?"

We walked toward her target. The ground was covered in hundreds of spent brass casings. She'd done well. She'd kept her head, learned much, shot well, and been safe—which meant using her brain. I ran my hand across the plate-sized hole that once represented the chest of her cardboard target. "I'd hate to be him, but more important, we're safe and not leaving here with any more holes than when we started."

She laughed.

I helped her loosen her belt and slide the holster and magazine carrier off. I confirmed the condition of it, which means I double- and triple-checked to make sure it was empty, then placed it inside my range bag on the tailgate and gave her a towel to wipe her face and hands. She wiped the back of her neck and arms. She said, "Some girls perspire. I sweat."

I nodded at her sweaty pits and the trail of sweat down her stomach. "I gather that."

I drove her back to the house and we stood next to the widow's truck. She handed the towel back. "Well, since you're not going to ask me, I'm asking you." This had a bad feeling to it. "How about a date?"

"What do you mean by 'date'?"

"You and me. Doing something fun."

"This is you and me and this was fun."

"Nope. No, sir. You're not getting off that easy. This is not a date. You didn't ask. And while this was fun, I 'bout pooped my pants ten times and I'm pretty sure I peed a little, so no...this doesn't count. Besides, you've taught me something. Now I want to teach you."

I scratched the back of my head. "Like what?"

"To dance?"

I shook my head. "H-e-double-L no."

She laughed. "Yes. I want to go dancing."

"I'm not going anywhere where other people are watching me make a fool of myself."

"Okay, how 'bout just you and me. Nobody's watching."

"Couldn't we just go for a walk or something? Maybe catch a movie."

"Nope. You need to dance. Those hips are so stiff. You walk like you been sitting on a horse your whole life. I want to teach you to dance."

I let out a deep breath. "I'm not going to win this, am I?"

"Nope."

I chewed on my bottom lip.

"What if we asked Georgia to watch the kids while I gave you a dancing lesson?"

"Where?"

She looked up, out of the corners of her eyes. "Your barn. There's room in there. And no one will be watching."

She had a point. "When?"

"This Friday is movie night at school." I could tell she'd already been scheming. "Maybe Georgia could take the kids to watch *Star*

*Wars* then keep them company a few hours. She's got an iPod with a little speaker I could borrow. You could cook me dinner."

I nodded. "Deal. What do you like to eat?"

"Anything. You pick it. *But...*" She stuck a finger in the air. "I get to pick the dancing and the music."

"I'm not going to like this, am I?"

"Sure you will. Once you loosen up. I think all that starch has sunk into your skin. Look at you, there's not a wrinkle anywhere and I look like I've been wadded up a week." She pulled on my shirt, reached up, kissed me. Then kissed me again. "Thank you for today. I'll see you tomorrow?"

"Yes, ma'am."

She climbed in, I shut the door and she raised both eyebrows. "It's okay. You can smile. It was a kiss. Lots of people do it. You should try it sometime."

"I know what it is. It's just I hadn't done it in a few years. I was hoping I hadn't just messed it up."

She licked her top lip. "There's room for improvement."

"Listen, since you now know what you're doing, Andie's got one of these in a hand safe bolted in the closet. Combination is four fingers in sequence." I demonstrated. "There's a flashlight and a couple of loaded magazines in there with it. I thought you'd feel safer, at night, given things being what they are."

"Thank you."

I walked to my truck, cranked it, and sat with the diesel idling. I stared through the windshield watching the dust settle. While it did and she disappeared, I licked my top lip and then tried to decide if I liked the taste.

It didn't take me very long.

# CHAPTER THIRTY-TWO

Dear God,

Momma's calling him "Tumbleweed" now. He limps and I saw
his leg. Got a big scar. I can tell Momma likes him. We saw
him naked. Actually, Momma saw more than I did. She told
me to go back to the house but I didn't. I stared through the
trees. He didn't see me. We were walking across his pasture
when we came around the corner and he was standing underneath the windmill rinsing in the shower. Naked as a jaybird.
Momma calls it his birthday suit but I don't know if it's his
birthday. He's got a big scar on his left leg. The one he limps
with. And he's burnt all up and down the left side of his body.
But, his privates weren't burnt. Not that I could tell. Not that
I was looking. Not really. But, when I asked Momma she said
no, they didn't look like they were burnt and then she started
blushing. So, I think Momma likes him. Seeing him naked
didn't scare me.

He taught her to shoot. Gave her a gun. She keeps it in a little black safe bolted in a drawer next to the bed. I'm glad, 'cause if Billy shows up, she can shoot him.

Oh, and I forgot to tell you one more thing. It's not that I hadn't wanted to tell you, it's just that I been thinking a lot about it and I hadn't been quite sure how I felt about it until maybe now and even now maybe I'm still a little fuzzy about it, but well, the other night, Cowboy took us to get ice cream. He knew it was kind of a bad memory for me and all so he sat me down with Momma and told me about this place in Brenham, Texas, called Blue Bell and how they make the best ice cream in the whole world and how they have this truck that delivers it to Rock Basin so we don't have to drive all the way to hell and gone. Sorry, his words. Not mine. Anyway, I said I'd go but that I really didn't want any, but then we went and Brodie got some and he gave me a bite and you know what it tasted like, it tasted like the cream at the Ritz-Carlton in New Orleans and I thought it was real good. So, Cowboy bought me some. First I had two scoops. Then I had two more. Then him and Brodie and me and Momma laughed till we about peed, well, we laughed a lot. And I liked the ice cream. He told us we could go back anytime. That ice cream was so good, it got me to thinking the same thought I had back in New Orleans. Why do we even mess with the other stuff when we got Blue Bell?

Turbo's doing good. I think he likes it here. He's growing. I think we're feeding him too much and I think Brodie is worried about his mom. I asked about her but he wouldn't talk about her. Then he started talking about her and he didn't stop for a long time. He told me all about her. Told me about how they'd go riding together, how she made the best salsa in all Texas, how she breaks the speed limit when she drives, and how sometimes she'd let him stay up late and sit with her on the porch and wait for Cowboy to come home. He told me how she loves him. How she loves them both. How she still does.

That made me sad. I'm just being honest. Momma and Cowboy were off having fun, having a date, and there was Brodie talking about how he loves his mom and how she loves his dad. Well, if that's the case, then what's he doing with Momma?

# CHAPTER THIRTY-THREE

I drove Brodie to Georgia's salon and waited for Sam to finish her last pedicure before we walked in. He was quiet. "You okay, big guy?"

He looked down between his feet. "Dad, are you going on a date tonight with Miss Samantha? Hope said you two were going on a date."

"Is that what she said?"

He nodded.

"I suppose, in a way. Yes."

"You know Mom will be home in two weeks."

"I know." I had told him about the divorce. He'd taken it like the man he was becoming. His mom had been gone long enough that it wasn't a shock.

"You gonna ask her out on a date?"

"I don't think so, son."

"Why not?"

"I think maybe your mom and me...we've had our last date."

He nodded.

"I think your mom is dating another man here in town."

"So, Mom's not your"—he seemed to search for the right word—"girlfriend anymore?"

I shook my head.

"Is Miss Sam your girlfriend?"

"No, not yet. But, she might be." I put my hand on his shoulder. "Would that be okay with you?"

He stepped out of the truck and climbed the steps into the salon.

Sam eyed me as I led her to the barn. She raised her nose in the air. "You smell good. What is that...Brut 33?"

"Very funny."

"Stetson?"

"Old Spice."

"I knew I'd smelled that before. This'll be just like dancing with my dad." Her eyes climbed up and down me. "You always look like that when you go on a date?"

"What?"

"The starch, and the gun and the hat and the:...did you actually iron your jeans?"

I turned around, and started walking away from the barn. She ran around me, hooked her arm in mine, and kept walking me toward the barn. "Just a few steps further." She laughed. "It's like getting a shot. The worst part is thinking about it before you get it."

Sam set the iPod on the counter while I shut the barn door. My nearest neighbor was two miles away but I wasn't taking any chances. I clicked on all the lights and raked some of the straw out of the middle. The smell of horses, straw, and manure filled the air. Cinch leaned over his stall and looked at me like I was nuts. Sam was wearing the jeans I'd bought her, the boots Dumps had made her, a white designer T-shirt, and a straw hat one of the girls in the salon had loaned her. The edges of the brim were folded up like Tim McGraw or Kenny Chesney.

I met her in the middle as some song started that I'd never heard. I glanced at the white iPod. "What is that?"

"Celine Dion."

"Brodie told me if I listen to Tyler Fast anymore that he'd stamp my man card."

"Taylor Swift."

"Yeah, her, too. He said, if I dance to any of the stuff that sounds like that, he'll revoke it for a year and I can only reapply after a probationary period in which I must recite Merle Haggard, George Jones, and Willie Nelson backwards."

"Cowboy, you ever been to Hollywood Boulevard?"

I shook my head.

"Well, me, either, but I'm told they have stars on the concrete, like poured in, for the people that are permanent fixtures. It means something like, they are Hollywood."

"Your point?"

"I think you're a permanent member of the man card group thing. If ever a man earned one..." She shook her head. "Yours is not revocable."

"You don't know Brodie."

"Funny. Come here."

She held out her hands. I did likewise. She took my hands and commenced leading me in a few steps. She kept stepping on my toes. I said, "You walk on the tops and I'll walk on the bottoms."

After about sixty seconds of this, she stepped back, shook her head and chewed on a nail. "This won't do."

"What won't do?"

Her eyes climbed up and down me. "This."

"What's wrong with this?"

"Most everything." She paused, and then curled her finger with that "come hither" motion. I stood next to the counter. She took off my hat and set it down. Next, she said, "Pardon me," and unbuckled my belt, slid it out of my jeans while I caught the holster. "Put that on the table." I did. "Magazines, too." I emptied my back pocket of the two loaded magazines. She eyed my ankle. "What about little brother?"

I unvelcroed the holster and laid both holster and the S&W 327 on the table. She crossed one arm and tapped her chin. "Any more weapons of any kind?"

"Pocketknife."

"Lay it on the table."

"Lady, I ain't felt this naked since I was born. I'm keeping the knife."

She put her hands on her hips and pointed at the table. I slid the knife from my pocket and laid it on the table along with half a tube of ChapStick. Then she reached up and began unsnapping my shirt. Once unsnapped, she slid it off my arms, folded it, and laid it on the table. She stared at my blue undershirt. "Are you actually wearing a Superman T-shirt?"

"Brodie makes me wear it. Says it keeps me safe."

Her left eyebrow lifted slowly above the right. "You mean, you have more than one?"

"Got a drawer full. One for every day of the week."

She shook her head, untucked it, and began pulling it over my head. "I'm not dancing with the Ranger. Or Clark Kent. Or John Wayne. I'm dancing with Tyler."

I stood there, bare-chested, feeling like an idiot.

"Boots, too."

"Nope. Man's got to have his limits and the boots are mine. Boots stay on."

She raised both eyebrows and stuck a finger in my face. "Tyler Steele, put the blasted boots on the table."

I slid them off and stood sock-footed next to the table. She combed my hair with her fingers. "Much better." She pushed a button on the iPod and pulled me by the hand. "Now come here." We walked back to center and stood facing each other. I'd never felt so naked in my whole life. Not even under the windmill. She extended her hands. "Sam Dyson. Nice to meet you."

"Tyler Steele. I'm the town idiot."

"Well, just play along. You should fit right in."

The music started. I held my arms like I'd seen Patrick Swayze do in *Dirty Dancing.* She laughed. "You need to relax. You ain't Patrick Swayze." She adjusted me.

I eyed the iPod. "Who's singing now?"

"Josh Groban."

"You got any Don Williams? Waylon? Willie? Hank Jr.?"

"Hang in there. This won't kill you, but your beer-drinking, two-stepping, somebody-shot-Momma-who-was-drunk-when-she-picked-me-up-from-the-train music is killing me."

"But I've always liked David Allan Coe."

"Yeah, well, get over it."

"Then, at least, please tell me you have Emmylou Harris? Everybody knows she's an angel on loan. I've always thought if I was dying, I'd like her to sing over me while I passed from here to there."

She smirked. "Maybe."

We danced in the barn for the better part of an hour. To her credit, we really danced. And I don't mean bump and grind. I mean like real stuff. She twirled beneath my arm and smiled. "I sort of let it slip that you and I were doing this."

"Yeah, it slipped all right."

"And once the girls found out, they created a playlist and had a couple other ideas."

"Like?"

"Just wait. All in good time."

Georgia had apparently created most of the playlist and while I didn't know many of the songs—starting with Josh whatever-his-name-was, she'd added a few that I did. By about eight, Sam had danced me until I didn't want to dance anymore. She kissed me on the cheek and said, "That wasn't so bad, was it?"

"No."

"Good. Now, I'm hungry. Feed me."

"On one condition."

"What?"

"What happened in the barn...stays in the barn."

She laughed.

I walked to the table and stared at everything laid out across the boards. "Can I put me back on now?"

"Yes."

I'd packed a basket, an actual straw basket, and placed it in the truck. I opened her door, helped her up, and drove down along the river. On the southern end of my property, the river narrows. At times of low water, you can walk across and not get your shorts wet. Tonight was one such time.

In the middle sat a mound of rock and sand and trees. An island of sorts. Only the highest of floodwaters trickled over it. I parked the truck, grabbed the basket and a Coleman lantern. We slipped off our boots, left them on the bank, rolled up our jeans, and walked across the river. The moon was just climbing out of the west and an April breeze cooled us. We climbed up onto the island and beneath a thin canopy of four scrub oaks that thrived there. I lit the lantern, spread a wool blanket, laid out my spread of food, opened a bottle of Cabernet and motioned for her to sit.

"Wow. You think this up all by yourself?"

"Well, Dumps suggested the lantern."

"I am impressed."

She sat and poured Cabernet into plastic Solo cups. She offered one to me. I shook my head. "No."

"You're not having any?"

"I never drink when I'm carrying." And I didn't.

She sipped and shook her head. "You are so uptight. You wear that thing to bed?"

"Well, I don't exactly wear it."

She studied the river. "You think there are any bad guys out here?"

I shrugged, staring west. "That's the thing. You never know."

She offered the cup. "Drink the blasted wine, Cowboy."

"A sip or two."

I sat and offered her a plate. I'd fixed a spinach salad, cooked a piece of salmon in the oven, and made some rice. Being a bachelor had forced me to do a few things I'd not done before. Cooking salmon might be at the top of the list, followed closely by making a spinach salad. I offered her oil and vinegar dressing and she took it. Then the salt and pepper. She sat cross-legged, facing me, plate in her lap, smiling. She was enjoying this immensely. And, I suppose I was, too. I handed her a Tupperware filled with sliced strawberries. "The salad is better if you cover it with these."

A few miles off, coyotes cackled. Closer in, maybe a mile, a few answered.

She chewed. "I figured something out about you yesterday."

"You did?"

"Yep."

I waited.

"That..." She pointed her fork at the 1911. "It's an albatross."

I'd read "The Rime of the Ancient Mariner." I knew the metaphor. I nodded once in agreement. "At times. At others, not so much."

"But you have a hard time taking it off. Don't you? And I don't just mean physically."

"The tough part is not learning the skill, but what it does to your thought process after you learn it. They pin that badge on your chest, hang that on your hip, and you change the way you see the world. Always looking at every scenario you come across in terms of how you'd defend it. How you'd protect those around you. Others. Always sit in restaurants facing the door, checking the exits, making notes."

"And that's not the worst part, is it?"

"No. Although I wouldn't call it a 'worst part' as much as it is a calling."

She waited. Pushing her salad around her plate. Sipping occasionally. I continued, "Pretty soon, you lose your ability to engage in the midst of your life. You miss moments. You miss relationships. You miss a lot. Least, I did. But as bad as that is, and as undesirable as that is, if you're in a fight for your life at three a.m. with a bad man walking down the hall—maybe he's got your wife with a knife against her throat, or your daughter, maybe he's jacked up on speed, crystal meth, or maybe he's trying to stick something sharp in you, or even worse your wife or kid—you better go into that with the right mind-set. And, you'd better go with something other than a spoon. You may not believe this but I don't enjoy carrying this thing. Don't relish it. The cool factor played out a long time ago. It is designed to wreak destruction and havoc and if wielded well, it does so well. Trust me, mopping up blood, especially your own, is not a lot of fun. Worse yet, is mopping up that of those you love."

"Why then? I mean, really. You're retired. You could set it down. Let it go."

"I've thought about it, but doing so is like peeling off my skin. I'm not sure how long I'd live without it. I know, and have always known, that there will be people whose path I cross who will not be able to fight for themselves. The sheep need a sheepdog. They might not know it, might not ever thank me, but that ain't the reason I do it."

"So, you'd die for a total stranger."

"Well, I'd work to avoid it but any time you take this thing in your hand, dying is one possibility. It goes with it. The flip side of the coin. Listen, I'm not walking around with a messiah complex, but I've spent over twenty years in law enforcement and I know this—bad guys aren't dumb. They're not coming at you with fly swatters. They're coming at you with what will subdue you. Conquer you. Enslave you. Most folks, people out there in polite society, don't like to think about it, but that's a fact. So, there are people like me who think, 'Maybe if I'm prepared, and willing, and able, I can help someone who might not be able to help themselves. And, in doing so, maybe I can push back the tide.' 'Cause, at the end of the day, that's what it's about. It all boils down to good versus evil.

And while I don't hate many things, I do, with an absolute hatred, hate evil when it is played out on mankind."

She looked away. "Tyler Steele, I've never met anyone like you. You may be a dying breed."

"My father was."

We finished our plates. She said, "Got any dessert?"

"Sorry. Never big on sweets."

"Let me guess, they slow you down or something. Affect your shooting."

"No, most give me the wind."

"The what?"

"The wind."

She laughed. "Got it." She stared at the water, stood up suddenly, and slapped her thigh. "Let's go swimming."

"You want to do what?"

She kicked off her shoes, unbuttoned her jeans, and began slipping off one leg. "Go swimming."

"Well…"

"Oh come on. Stop being such a prude. Boxers are like a bathing suit."

This was not the way I'd seen this evening panning out in my mind.

The water was clear, cool, and flowing gently. She unhooked her bra, pulled it out the sides of her shirt sleeves like women do which I've never understood. I stripped down to my underwear and she held my hand as we walked into the water. We sat on the sandy bottom while the water climbed to the middle of my chest. She sunk her head and tucked her hair behind her ears.

We sat, talked, splashed each other and laughed for the better part of an hour. The moon was high as we rose to climb back up the bank. I sort of squeegeed the water off my arms and legs, slid my jeans on and then sat on the blanket. She stood in front of me squeezing the water out of her hair. The river had vacuum-sealed her shirt to her skin. The underwear was a new purchase and not the stuff we'd bought at the Ritz. I have two words for you: lace and not much of it.

She turned, sort of modeling. "You like?"

I nodded and swallowed. "Yes."

"I'm glad."

I smiled.

She sat next to me, tossing her hair from one shoulder to the other. She slipped off her T-shirt, laid it across a rock next to us, then sat next to me and pressed her back to my chest, wrapping my arms around her.

"Cowboy?"

I swallowed, the warmth of her warmed me. I whispered, "Yes."

"I'm falling for you."

I nodded. My hands were wrapped around her stomach. Her hands were wrapped over the tops of mine.

She looked over her shoulder. "I was just wondering if that was okay with you."

"Yes."

"You sure?"

"Yes."

"How about Brodie?"

"He's having a rough time with it."

"Are you having a rough time with it?"

"I'm having a rough time not letting my mind go places it shouldn't."

She turned, facing me. My hand in hers. "You don't have to."

When Andie and I had first married, and for many years after, our love had been tender. Fun. A shared longing. Never ashamed to find me in the dark, she would pursue me, take my hand. Brodie was conceived not too far from where we now sat.

Love like that lingers. Lace and a bikini wax don't diminish that.

I paused. Trying to figure out how to get the words out of my mouth. Her head tilted.

"Cowboy, I'm literally throwing myself at you. Is there something about this picture you don't like?"

"No, I—"

"Then speak, before you give me a complex."

I scratched my head. "Sam, trust me, this whole picture right here is intoxicating, but I need to get unmarried from Andie. Permanently. My divorce isn't final for another couple weeks."

She rolled her eyes. "You're kidding, right?"

"According to the law, I'm still married and until now, I've never been unfaithful. And as tempting as this is, and you are, I don't want to start now."

She flopped down, shaking her head. "Really?" She looked defeated. "Really. Really? Wow."

She was quiet a few minutes, then without saying a word, she reached forward, and kissed me. "It's not easy being you, is it?"

"Not right this minute." If ever I didn't want to be me, it was that moment.

She stood, and slipped off that underwear I was telling you about. "I can't stand sitting in wet underwear."

I heard myself say, "Lord have mercy."

She stuck both feet in her jeans and started shimmying them up her legs. "What? You thinking about changing your mind? Having a tough time being so resolute?"

I looked some place other than at her. "You're not making it any easier."

She smiled and buttoned her jeans. "I'm not trying to make it easy."

"I gathered that."

We dressed, which was a great relief, crossed the river, and rode beneath the moonlight back up to the house and then to town to pick up the kids. Both were asleep on Georgia's couch. I carried them to the truck. At the apartment, I stood on the front steps and turned my hat in my hands, trying to find the muster to kiss her good night. She stopped my hat from spinning and looked at me. I said, "At the end of the month, when things are final, I was wondering if we could have another date? Maybe go dancing someplace. Would that—"

"Yes." She shook her head. "The girls are never going to believe this."

"What about, 'What happens in the barn...'?"

She leaned forward, pulled on my shirt. "Cowboy, tonight I wanted you to be one man, but needed you to be another. Thank you for being what I needed and not what I wanted."

I nodded, walked to my truck, and drove off whispering, "It ain't easy."

Streetlights lit the cab every tenth of a mile until we got out of town. Brodie was awake. He rubbed his eyes. "What, Dad? What ain't easy?"

I patted his head. "Nothing, big guy. Go back to sleep." He drifted off. We pulled into the drive. I carried him to his bed and knew there was no way on earth I was going to be able to go to sleep. So, I grabbed a towel and walked out to the windmill. I opened the spigot to full and walked beneath it.

I stood there for a long time.

# CHAPTER THIRTY-FOUR

Dear God,

Things here are good. Mom's working a lot and she likes painting people's feet. She's practiced on me a couple of times and she's pretty good. My feet ain't never looked this pretty. And she's now working up to shampooing when the other women are too busy. She says she gets good tips 'cause she scrubs people's heads real good 'cause she's got strong nails and they really dig into people's scalps and they like that. They say it's relaxing.

I got some good news. I got my first grade today in school. It was an "A." That's real good. It's one mark shy of the best you can get. I got it for writing a story in my Language Arts class. We were asked to tell about something that had happened to us in the last few weeks. Just any old thing but start at the beginning and use detail. So, I wrote about us meeting Cowboy and how he saved us at the truck stop and then how he took us to the Ritz and then how he took us home, and how we met Brodie and Mr. Dumps and well, everything that's happened since then. It was a lot. She said she would have given me an "A+" but she had only asked for three pages and I gave her seventeen so she said she had to mark me down but I didn't mind none 'cause I got to tell it and it reminded me. It reminded me that good stuff has happened to us. That you ain't forgot us. That maybe we matter. I titled it, *Down Behind the Sun*. She said she liked my title. I said I got it from Cowboy 'cause it's how his daddy used to describe West Texas and the Bar S. It's a good description. I don't know if it's what Cowboy's daddy meant but to me it's like down behind the sun would be a good place to be. It'd be where you are. Where you hang out. And if we tried to get there without talking to you then we'd burn up 'cause we'd have to get past the sun and ain't nobody can do that 'cause it's hotter than a nuclear bomb. Least that's what I think.

And Momma's been talking to me about, you know, about the thing that happened. Been trying to get me to talk to her or somebody, anybody, about it all. Says I shouldn't bury it but go ahead and just tell what I feel and what I think. She asked me if I wanted to talk to a doctor about it. That we could find one and I said my body don't hurt no more but my heart does and I don't think the doctor can help the part of my heart that hurts and she started crying and didn't stop for a long time and I didn't mean to hurt her and I told her I was sorry and she just hugged me and then I asked her if I could talk to her about it and she sat up and said well of course. So, I asked her stuff I been needing to ask. And we talked a long time. When I finished asking all my questions and she finished trying to answer them all, she told me I didn't need to be ashamed. I said I didn't know what that meant and she told me it was that thing that made me want to look away when people looked at me 'cause I didn't want them to see what I saw when I looked at me. And I told her I do feel that and all that happened to me is my fault. And I told her it felt like it was 'cause I kept stuff secret from her. Like the ice cream and the gummy bears. Like maybe I got what I deserved. And she cried some more and said there ain't been a thing in this world that's happened to us that's been my fault or that I deserved. And when we finished she brushed my hair a long time, which is my favorite thing and while she did that I told her that I didn't need to talk to no doctor 'cause the part of my heart that hurt didn't hurt as much anymore. It was like the words she spoke were the words my heart needed to hear and when it heard them some of the pain left. I told her maybe if we talked about it some more that some or most of the rest of the pain would just up and fly away. And she cried some more and said we could talk about it every day if I wanted.

Listen, Momma's home. Gotta go. She had a date with Cowboy. Her face is all flush. She gets that way when she eats chocolate or drinks wine. Or oysters, but she don't eat them much 'cause they make her gassy.

Oh, and God, I know I've asked this a lot but please keep Billy away and don't let him find us. 'Cause you and I both know he's still looking for us. And we know why. I guess the thing I'm wondering is if we know that, and Cowboy don't, are we lying?

I guess I kind of know the answer to that.

# CHAPTER THIRTY-FIVE

Sam showed up Saturday with Hope. It was raining buckets. She splashed through the puddles from the truck, up to the porch. I ran to the passenger door, scooped up Hope and Turbo and carried them back to the porch. Sam wrung out her hair. "Now that's a rain."

I nodded. "Like a cow peeing on a flat rock."

"Like a what?"

"Cow peeing on a flat—"

She held up a hand. "I got it the first time. Boy, that really paints a picture."

"Well, it's just how we describe a—"

"What do you do around here for fun when it's raining like this?"

"We read a lot."

She studied my shelves. "These are all books about battles, generals, Indian chiefs, famous lawmen." She pulled one down and read the back jacket, "A collection of stories of common men performing great deeds." She shook her head. "Don't you have any fiction? Any love stories?"

" 'Fraid not."

"Let's watch a movie?"

"Sure."

She looked at the VCR tapes next to the books. "VCR?"

"What's wrong with that?"

"Nothing." She picked through them. "Nothing but cowboy movies."

"There are some good war movies in there."

"What's the difference? Don't you have anything like *Sweet Home Alabama, Notting Hill, New in Town,* or *The Proposal?* Maybe *Steel Magnolias* or *The Notebook?*

"Afraid I'm not familiar with those."

Over the next seven hours, as the rain continued to fall, she made me watch every tear-jerker she could find on TV. Each time the credits rolled, I asked her, "Why do you like that?"

Tears rolling down her face. Nose snotty. Wadded tissue in her hand. " 'Cause, they love each other."

Sometime after dinner, I found Hope sitting on the porch, writing in her book. When I walked out, she shut it real fast. Like I'd caught her with her hand in the cookie jar. "Can I sit with you?"

She nodded. When I sat on her left, she placed the book, closed, on her right side. "How're you doing?"

"Good."

"How's school going?"

"It's okay. I'm not too good at math. Sometimes all those numbers don't make much sense, but my English teacher says I write real good and I'm getting better all the time. She says when she reads it she thinks I'm a lot older. That only people who done some living write the way I do. I'm not all that sure, but I think that's a compliment."

"You making friends?"

"Yes...sir. A couple. I have the same lunch as Brodie and he sometimes sits with me. Well, every day that is except two 'cause I had some girls sitting there."

"He told me that."

She rubbed her hands between her knees. "Brodie has lots of friends. Everybody likes him. They look up to him. Mostly."

"He's a good kid." Turbo lay on her lap. Eyes closed. Unmoving. "How's Turbo?"

"He's not doing too good."

"What do you mean?"

"He's just not getting around as much and he's sleeping a lot. Sometimes he eats and sometimes he doesn't. Momma says he may just be real old." She stroked his tummy. "He may have a tumor 'cause his stomach is different. I think he'll be okay though 'cause when he's awake he still likes to sit on my shoulder."

I changed the subject. "How you feeling? I mean, the itching on your arms and all. I don't think I've heard you cough since we drove into Texas."

She nodded. "I'm good. Itching's gone. Not coughing any."

"And..." I was way out of my league here but I wanted her to know that I was concerned. "Everything else?" I searched for comforting words. "Your mom says you're doing great and you'll be fine."

She nodded. Recoiling a bit. "It don't hurt to pee anymore."

Maybe I shouldn't have said that.

She stared at the porch.

"You know," I tried to recover. "I...or, we, almost had a girl."

She looked up at me.

"Yep. My wife, Andie, she was pregnant once. Before Brodie was born. But she was only pregnant for about two months and then lost the baby. The doctors said that happens to a lot of women the first time they get pregnant. Me and her, we always thought for some reason that she was a girl. 'Course, we didn't never know. It's just a guess."

She thought about this. "How old would she be now?"

I counted. "Twelve or so."

"I'm sorry."

"It's okay. It was a long time ago." I glanced at her journal. "What you writing?"

"Just stuff."

I listened to the rain. It had lessened. Pattered the roof. "I've never been very good at that. Could never figure a way to get the words out. Sort of like my mouth ain't connected to my hand."

She stared down at the floor. "Sometimes I think my mouth's not connected to the part of me that makes words. So, they come out my pencil." I nodded and we swung. The spring squeaked. Her feet didn't reach the floor so I pushed us slightly. We sat in the quiet. She tapped her pencil against the cover of her notebook.

While I was trying to figure out some way to carry the conversation, Sam and Brodie walked out carrying either end of the card table upon which sat the Monopoly game now in its fifth night. They set it down in front of the swing, and dragged over a couple of old wooden rockers.

We decided to start a new game. At first we were all against each other, but when Brodie took me to the cleaners and left me with ten dollars, Hope had mercy on me, and made me a loan. When I got back on my feet, I repaid my loan, and she suggested we go into business together. Sort of a two-are-stronger-than-one kind of deal. That worked out pretty well for us, and soon, our pile of cash started growing while Sam and Brodie's individual piles started shrinking, which prompted them to circle the wagons and team up. I don't know if that's legal in the bylaws of Monopoly but in Rock Basin, Texas, we really don't care.

Soon, they had a bit of a cash edge over Hope and me but we owned more property and were buying hotels every chance we got. If either of them landed on Boardwalk or anything remotely near Tennessee, we could take them to the cleaners, foreclosing on everything they owned, down to the little silver train piece they were using to navigate the board.

You might say the competition was starting to heat up a bit.

Brodie started talking smack and feeling right proud of himself until he rolled a seven and landed on Pennsylvania where we had two hotels. Sam handed him the money and told him she was thinking about dissolving their partnership. Brodie then handed the money to Hope who counted it slowly, licking her thumb like a teller, displaying the dollars in the shape of a fan across one corner of the board. Three more turns, and Brodie and Sam were teetering on the edge of bankruptcy until I landed on Ventnor, then Hope landed on Illinois, and finally, I rolled a double deuce, which landed me on Chance. Ordinarily, that's not a big deal but we have this rule that if you roll a double anything and that roll lands you on Chance, then whatever happens to you must be increased by adding a zero onto the end. Depending on the card, it can be really good or really bad. So, I rolled a double deuce, picked up my card, and it said, "Give each player $500." Hope and I argued, to no avail, that because we were now working in teams that I should only have to give $5,000 to the team of Sam and Brodie, but Sam and Brodie, using the card as evidence and emphasizing the words "each player," said, "No way, José" and "fork it over." So, we shelled out $10,000, which totally cleaned out our cash leaving us with four lousy one-hundred-dollar bills. I looked at Sam and Brodie and told them I felt like they'd been taking classes from some of the local bankers I knew.

Once Brodie had counted our money, Sam recounted it "just to be sure." They each counted slowly, mimicking Hope by licking their thumbs like a teller, and then using both corners of the board to display their own money fans. I didn't think it was all that funny. They thought it riotous.

The game continued like this for another hour. And while fortunes changed hands several times and Hope and I fluctuated between flush and abject poverty, the one thing that didn't disappear was the laughter spilling off the porch. It was a good feeling and our house needed it. Like the boards themselves needed reminding. It'd been a while. I sat there listening, breathing it in. Flashes of a thunderclap in the distance. Cool air blowing off the warm. The slow easy sway of the swing. A perfect Texas night.

I was the first to see Dumps walk around the house. His face was somber, ashen. He held his hat in his hand but he was crushing it more than he was turning it.

"Ty," he said quietly.

The laughter stopped.

"You better come look at this."

All five of us walked around the house to the barn where the light was on. I heard a sound in the pasture beyond that I didn't like. Dumps turned, shook his head, looking a long second at Brodie, then stared at me. His eyes were red. "Just you."

Sam wrapped her arms around both Hope and Brodie inside the barn with Cinch and May while Dumps and I walked out into the pasture. A few hundred yards and the noise told me most everything I needed to know. So did the large dark figure on the ground that was trying to stand but could not.

I knelt next to Mr. B, whose foreleg was broken. Compound fracture. The bones were sticking through the skin. He'd half stand, put weight on a leg that wasn't there, then fall forward, his legs shooting out from beneath him, like a horse walking on ice. I grabbed his reins, laid him on the ground, and whispered, "Easy, boy. Easy." I turned to Dumps. "Bring me Brodie. But just Brodie. Take the girls inside."

I lay there, cradling Mr. B's head. He was afraid, nostrils flared, and he was in a lot of pain. The only thing holding his leg on was a dirty piece of hide. The air smelled of blood, dirt, and manure.

Brodie walked around the barn, then started running. By the time he got to me, he was screaming, "No! No! Mr. B!"

He landed on the ground next to me. He tried to hold Mr. B's leg but he wouldn't let him touch it. Mr. B was kicking it around. The sharp bones were gliding through the air like razors. I tried to speak softly. "Brodie?"

He didn't look at me. He was trying to figure out how to fix the leg.

"Brodie?"

Tears were streaming down his face. He turned, looked, and said nothing. The pain was too great. The rain started again.

I tried to speak but couldn't. The two of us sat holding Mr. B's head. His horse was finished and behind the sobs, I heard a part of my son dying.

Finally, Brodie turned to me. He wiped his nose and nodded. "Daddy, this time of night, Dr. Vale is an hour to two hours away."

I nodded. An hour was a long time for Mr. B to be in pain. Five minutes was too long.

"We got anything in the barn?"

Most cowboys play vet with their horses to a limited extent. We were no exception. But we didn't have what Brodie knew we needed. I shook my head.

He sat up on his knees in front of Mr. B. Wiped his palms on his jeans. Mr. B. was making a noise that rose the hair on the back of my neck. Brodie held out his hand. "I'll do it."

I shook my head. "No, son. You go on—"

He looked straight at me. "Dad, he's mine. I'll do it." He extended his hand again. I knelt behind him. Unholstered. Placed my 1911 in Brodie's hand. The webbing of his palm sank deep into the back strap, his finger went straight and he grasped it firmly with two hands. Mr. B had grown tired and lay his head on the ground. The mud around his nose moved every time he breathed out. Brodie placed the muzzle against the hide, just above his brain. He clicked off the safety with his right thumb and took a deep breath. For a long moment, he held the pistol pressed against Mr. B's head. He was crying, tears rolling off his chin and falling onto Mr. B's muzzle. He was talking to him softly. "You remember when we crossed the river the first time? And when we rode all the way to town to get bubble gum? And when you told me not to go by that rock cause you could smell the snake I couldn't see? And—" He kept talking but I couldn't hear the words. Brodie had walked inside himself.

Finally, his mouth quit moving, he placed his finger on the trigger, and began applying pressure. A second later, his finger went straight, he thumbed up the safety and he raised the pistol, allowing me to take it. He shook his head and closed his eyes.

"You want me to?"

He nodded.

"Brodie?"

"Sir?"

"Turn your head away."

He did, closing his eyes, trembling. The rain came in sheets. I laid my hand on Mr. B, kissed his face, and said, "Thanks, Mr. B. You're…Well, I never—" I pressed the muzzle to his forehead, thumbed off the safety and pressed the trigger.

Mr. B. was dead before the bullet exited the other side.

Brodie jerked, turned, and saw Mr. B lying lifeless and still. The picture hit him pretty hard. He stroked his mane, whispering gently. Crumbling. We sat there several minutes.

I found myself growing angry. Angry that I couldn't protect my son from the stuff that threatened to crack his soul in half. I shook my head and wrapped my arm around him. He melted. Crying. Sobbing deep, loud sobs. He hugged me tighter than he'd hugged me in a long time and cried for minutes on end. If the last three years had created a Hoover Dam inside Brodie, the hole in Mr. B's head broke it loose.

After a while, I said, "Run, crank the tractor. Let's bury him over there next to Daddy."

He looked up at me. "Dad?"

I ran my fingers through his hair. "Yeah, big guy."

"I'd like a few minutes with—"

I stood and walked toward the barn.

\*   \*   \*

We dug a hole not too far from my dad. He'd like that. Cowboys can be odd creatures but we put great stock in a good horse. Dad was no different. With the hole dug, I eased up behind Mr. B and we slid his body into the bucket. I lifted him slightly, Brodie tucked his legs under him so they didn't dangle and we drove slowly to the hole. Brodie walked alongside, holding his tail. When we got to the hole, Brodie stood back and I slowly lowered Mr. B into the ground. Brodie dropped down into the hole and folded his legs and straightened his tail. I stood over watching him. A boy shedding his shell. A man in bloom.

I said, "His tail—he'd want you to have it."

He wiped his eyes with his forearm and looked up at me. I nodded. He dropped to a knee, opened his knife and cut Mr. B's tail. Then he reached up and I pulled him out. The lights of the tractor shone across the hole, and Dad's iron marker, casting an odd shadow along the grass on the other side. Sam, Hope, and Dumps stood in the shadows beneath the barn, watching from a distance. Brodie turned to me, "Can I fill it?"

I nodded.

Brodie climbed up on the tractor and slowly filled the hole, packing it down with the bucket. With a fresh mound above where Mr. B's body lay, Brodie cut the engine and climbed down. He stood several minutes staring at the dirt. He looked up at me. "Dad?"

I put my arm around him.

"Does that—" The air smelled of dirt, spent diesel, and blood. "Am I a coward?"

"Does what?"

"The fact that I couldn't—"

I wrapped my arms around him. Tight. Us both staring out across a wet Texas night. My cheek pressed to his. "No son. It makes you a man. One helluva man."

I stood in the rain, shaking. A steady downfall. Easy. Gentle. Large egg-sized drops. I wanted to throw up. The death would hit

Brodie hard. The earth mounded swollen before us. More than Mr. B lay beneath it. "This time next year...he'll be covered in bluebonnets."

Brodie's stoic shell cracked and he broke. A limp rag doll. I caught him, hit my knees, and held him.

But it didn't do any good.

# CHAPTER THIRTY-SIX

Dear God,

Something horrible happened tonight. We were all on the porch playing Monopoly when Mr. Dumps came to get us. I could tell in his face that whatever he had to say wasn't good. And, it wasn't. We all walked to the barn, then he and Cowboy walked off into the pasture and he gave real clear instructions for Brodie not to follow. We heard a real weird sound coming from the darkness out beyond where we could see. It was Mr. B. He had broke his leg and he was trying to get up but he couldn't so he just kept spinning and falling out there in the mud. Cowboy got to him, wrestled him to the ground, and called Brodie. When Brodie got to him, he made a sound that I ain't never heard come out of a boy before. And it lasted a long time. Then they was quiet a while. And then we heard a gunshot that about jumped me out of my skin. And Mr. B quit moving. We were scared until Cowboy came to the barn but he had a look on his face like I ain't never seen. He told us what happened and then got the tractor. He went back and then he and Brodie dug a hole and laid Mr. B in it. We walked out there in the rain as they were starting to cover him up. Brodie was real torn up about it. Brodie said he tried to do the shooting but couldn't so his dad did it. I don't think that makes Cowboy a bad person though. I think he did it 'cause Brodie couldn't and he knew Mr. B. was in pain and somebody had to do it.

We had a funeral in the rain. I spoke some words over Mr. B and thanked him for being such a good horse and that I would sure miss him. And I will. Mr. Dumps said a few words, Momma was real quiet, and Cowboy just stood there staring at Brodie.

Cowboy and Brodie stood in the rain a long time. Cowboy just holding Brodie. After they'd been there a while, Brodie started clawing at the ground, trying to dig up Mr. B. He was screaming words I couldn't understand and Cowboy was trying to hold him back. Finally, Brodie quit and the two just sat out there in the dirt crying. Rocking. Shaking. Every now and then, Brodie would scream, "Nooooo!" and shake his head. Cowboy couldn't even talk. He just held him out there in the mud. Momma and me and Mr. Dumps stood in the barn watching cause we didn't know what else to do. Momma asked Mr. Dumps, "Is there anything we can—?" And he shook his head and said, "Pain is a lot like a volcano." He nodded. "I seen it afore. If you crack the mantle, best you can do is let it all out. And that boy there, he's known his share. More than most." I think Mr. Dumps was right 'cause after an hour, he quieted down and he and Cowboy walked back to the barn. Brodie's eyes were real red and his face was smeared with blood and dirt. We got him to the house, he got showered, then he went to bed and he was out pretty quick. I know, I checked.

Momma asked if we could stay here tonight and do anything to help. Cowboy nodded, said, "I'd be grateful," and walked out on the porch. Me and Momma laid in bed a long time, listening to Cowboy swing on the porch. The rusted springs made a lazy sound.

After a long while, the sound stopped, but I didn't hear the screen door open. Momma was asleep, so I snuck out, but Cowboy wasn't on the porch no more. He was walking out into the pasture. The rain had quit. Stars were shining. I guess you saw him. I followed him a little, but didn't get so close that he'd see me.

He stood out there next to his dad's grave. He just stood there. Every now and then he'd shift his feet. Cross his arms. Put his hands in his pockets. I don't know what he was doing. Then, kind of suddenly, he fell, hit his knees, and lay there like he was kissing the ground. At first I thought maybe he was hurt, and I should get help, but then I thought it wasn't that kind of hurt. I heard a sound come out of him that I never heard come out of a man before. It was deep and lasted a long time. Then he made it again. And again.

---

Dear God,

The sun is almost up now. Cowboy's walking back to the house. I don't think he ever went to sleep last night. His face looks pained. He's got big, broad shoulders but this morning they look like they're hanging off the sides. Like something pulling down on them.

I can see the mound out in the pasture that's covering up Mr. B. I guess he's laying out there in that dark, cold dirt. I guess he's gone now so he don't really know where he's laying, which is probably good. He might be scared if he woke up and found it all dark and black.

God...I need to ask you something. Something I been thinking about. Why did Mr. B have to step in that hole? Why didn't you stop him? Why didn't you nudge him off to one side? You could have, you know.

There's a part of me way down deep inside that wants to be good. Wants to see good. Wants to live good. But, every time I turn around, all I see is bad. It's like evil bubbles up out of the ground and all we can do is step around it and try not to get any on our feet.

My insides are hurting real bad. And, I'm tired.

---

Dear God,

We're back home now. Momma told me that she thought maybe we were imposing and that maybe we should give them some space, so we left real early, even before breakfast. I told her they didn't need no space and that we should go check on them but she said, "No baby," and patted me on the head. She's been pacing the floor and shaking her head ever since we got back. She didn't even notice that I hadn't gotten ready to go to school, which told me things were real bad 'cause she don't like me missing school. Now she's just staring out the window, toward town, arms crossed, talking to herself. I've tried talking to her but she's mainly just talking to herself. But, like I told you before, I think Momma feels other people's hurts. Like I think she's feeling Brodie's hurt right now. And Cowboy's, too. And I think Cowboy's feeling Brodie's hurt. 'Cause I know I'm feeling Brodie's hurt. And all that means that we're just a bunch of hurting people. And I can tell Momma wants to do something, wants to help, but she don't know her place. Or, maybe she does and maybe that place is that it ain't her place to do nothing. Maybe that's why she ain't said much and she's drunk like two pots of coffee and she's bit her nails down to the quick.

Sometimes, like now, when I write, I feel it's just words on a page. They don't mean nothing and they don't go nowhere. I guess what I'm saying is... Are you up there? Are you paying attention? What are you doing? Why can't you do anything? Maybe I shouldn't ask that. Maybe I shouldn't be so disrespectful but I want to know. I drank three sodas this morning to help me stay awake so I'm a little jumpy and my hand is shaking but I look around and I see bad stuff happening to good people and bad people getting away with doing bad. That don't make any sense. No sense at all. And I'm tired of it. I know I'm only ten but I seen a lot and what I seen ain't good. Ain't right. Shouldn't you be making it right? Shouldn't you be doing something? Isn't that your job?

I'm not writing any more today. I think my mouth is 'bout to get me in trouble. I'm going to bed now, but I don't think I'll be able to sleep. I can still hear Cowboy screaming and crying. Every time I try and close my eyes, it's still there. Echoing around my head. I see him holding Brodie in the rain. Rocking back and forth. I thought maybe if I wrote you a letter, that the sound and pictures'd go away but they ain't. I wish you'd get Brodie a new horse. He really loved Mr. B. He was a good horse.

Dear God,

It's only been five minutes since the last time when I said I wasn't going to write no more today but I just wanted to say that I was sorry. I went back and read over what I wrote, and... it was disrespecting you. I looked that word up. I would erase it, or tear it out, but I promised you when we started this thing that I wouldn't never erase nothing I wrote here. So, I'm sorry. Maybe you won't hold that against me and then let more bad stuff happen to us. Or to Cowboy. Or Brodie. If you let that stuff happen to Cowboy and his horses 'cause I said something wrong in some way I shouldn't, well...I'm real sorry. I'm going to try to think of something good now.

This new dictionary that Cowboy gave me is real nice and it's easy to find the words and it's got more words in it, not that I know them all. Momma says I'm filling up my vocabulary. That I know more words than her. I think she may be right 'cause sometimes I say stuff and she looks at me like I've plumb lost my mind. Then I explain it to her and she nods or shakes her head.

Oh, I almost forgot. Cowboy said his wife had a baby before Brodie. One that died before it got here. He said it was a girl but that they didn't know for sure. Whatever it was, would you tell her "Hi" and let her know that he thinks about her sometimes.

I like it when Cowboy talks to me. His voice is real kind. Like he means what he says. And his voice changes when he talks about his wife. Her name is Andie. She was his wife. But she's not dead. Momma says they're divorced but he don't sound like he's divorced. I've heard other people talk about the people they're divorced from and he don't sound like them. He ain't angry. Ain't calling her bad names or nothing.

I been trying to figure a way to describe Cowboy to you. So you'll know he's good people and you should stop the bad people. Cowboy is like, well, when I think of what you're like, Cowboy comes to mind. I hope you don't mind. I'm just telling you so's you'll know. I think you done good with him.

---

Dear God,

Momma took a nap, even though she was twitching a little. I know. I watched her. I even heard her cry a little in her sleep.

She didn't know I heard her, but when she did, I just put my hand on her back and she quieted down and quit crying. I don't think she ever woke up.

Now Momma's pacing around the apartment again. She's had like eight more cups of coffee. She keeps walking to the window and staring out, tapping her teeth, and talking to herself. She don't know it but she's spitting little pieces of skin against the window. One or two of them stuck to the window but she can't see it 'cause she's looking way down the road. I think she's worried about Cowboy.

I hope you're not upset about what I said about him being what I think of when I think of you. Is that confusing? Oh, and one more thing. I told a lie. I told Momma that my stomach hurt so I could skip school again today. She let me. But, it don't hurt like normal. It was a different kind of hurt. The kind of hurt you have when other people you know are hurting and you hurt 'cause they're hurting. So, I'm sorry about that.

I just called Brodie to ask him how he was feeling but the phone just rang and rang and rang and right when I was about to hang up, he answered. His voice was real quiet. He sounded like he'd been crying. I told him I hoped he felt better and I was real sorry about Mr. B. He couldn't talk no more so he just hung up.

Momma just ran in here and dressed real quick, told me she was running down to the store and for me to stay here but I think Momma told a lie, too, 'cause she ran down the street but she didn't turn toward the store. She went straight down the street and turned in to the bell tower.

Sometimes I think this world is a mess and it ain't nothing but a whole lot of hurt.

# CHAPTER THIRTY-SEVEN

I didn't wake Brodie for school. Figured he needed the rest. I drank coffee until ten. Dumps just nodded at me as I stepped out the door. "I'll watch him," he said. I was walking out the door as he shook his head, mumbling, "I shoulda seen that hole. Shoulda filled it in."

I turned, kissed Dumps on top of the head, and drove to town.

I parked at the courthouse and walked down the street to the bell tower. Andie's—or Sam's—apartment sat two blocks away. I could see it when I parked but I wasn't in the mood for conversation. I walked behind the tower, used my key to get through the gate, used my other key to get in the door, and climbed the eighty-seven stairs to the top where the seven bells hung. I walked the platform around the bells and then shimmied up the vertical ladder to the small ledge above, about the size of a sheet of plywood. I used another key to unlock the padlock, flipped up the trap door, and crawled up. I slid across on my belly, coughing in the dust, shooing the pigeons, and stared out the small hole.

Eight hundred and twenty-seven yards to the south sat the first fence of the high security federal prison. Another ten yards sat the second. Both topped in razor wire. German shepherds patrolled the no-man's-land between. I got comfortable, slid into position, and eyed my watch.

At 10:57, José Juan Chuarez, walked out of cell block B and into the yard. A minute later, he walked to "his" section of the fence from where he ran most of the activities inside the prison, and many out. I pressed my face against the cheek weld of the rifle, turned the scope to 14X, dialed 32 MOA into the gun, gauged the wind as one-two left to right, and held half of one mil-dot left on the center of his neck. Eight hundred thirty-eight to target. I lay there, measuring my breathing, watching José direct the prisoners. I pressed off the safety, took a deep breath, let out half, and began depressing the trigger. At two and a quarter pounds of pull, it didn't take much. Halfway through my trigger pull, I heard the muted words, "Is that a real gun?"

Finger straight, I pulled the safety on, but I didn't take my eye off the target. "Yes."

"What are you shooting?" Sam asked.

My tone of voice told her I was not in the mood for conversation. "Better question is 'who?'"

I glanced back as more of her climbed through the trap door. "Who?"

"José Juan Chuarez. Forty-seven-year-old male, convicted murderer, and dope dealer. Not to mention Mexican gang leader. I put him in prison a few years back."

"Oh, you mean"—she ran her fingers along her neck and then gestured at mine—"him."

I nodded and checked my watch again.

"You're going to shoot a man in prison?"

"Thinking about it."

"Why?"

"Because a federal judge just reduced his sentence to time served based on a technicality."

She gently pulled my hand away from the trigger. "You want to talk about it?"

Oddly, I did.

I sat up. Leaned against the wall. Wiped the sweat off my forehead. "About nine years ago, we started getting intel about a new kingpin running drugs through Rock Basin. We tracked him south, started monitoring his movements, and charted his organization. Pretty sophisticated, too. He even bought his own local cell network. We took our time. Did our homework. Took us four years to figure out he'd systematically planted GPS tracking devices on all our vehicles so his people knew where we were at all times. After we found them, we sent all our cars one way while we drove in rented vans to his clubhouse. A late night thing. We caught him with enough evidence to put him away for several lifetimes."

"Like?"

"Drugs, dead bodies, and his fingerprints on both." I stared across the distance between José Juan and me. "I arrested him. Walked him to jail myself. The pictures made all the papers. Lot of people around here were real proud. Proud of all of us. Even stopped me on the street. The next morning, I took Brodie to get some ice cream. What we didn't know was how deep José Juan's tentacles stretched. Even in prison, he's still powerful. So, he told his boys to light up my life. They did."

I swallowed and closed my eyes. "I look back on my life and that's the day. The moment." I shook my head. "In the four years leading up to that, I spent so many nights away. So...committed. I gave all of me to getting"—I nodded through the window toward where I knew José still stood alone—"him. Nothing but a piece of garbage." Sam was staring at me. "So many times I swore to Andie, 'Just as soon as I catch him, we'll take a vacation, be a family.' I didn't know it but all the nights I wasn't there, all the days I missed with Brodie, all the times…it took its toll. She hid her pain pretty good. I didn't know she was taking prescription drugs for a long time. By the time I did know, it was too late."

The rifle drew her attention. "Can I see?"

I shifted. She lay down and squinted through the scope. "He looks so little. How could you hit him from here?"

"A little practice is all."

"Anyone ever told you that you might have an unhealthy attraction to weapons?"

I chewed on that. "In 1867, nineteen soldiers northwest of here were guarding six civilian hay cutters near Fort C. F. Smith up along the Bozeman Trail near the Bighorn River in Montana. About mid-morning, somewhere close to 800 Cheyenne and Sioux warriors showed up. The fight lasted all day. The soldiers were armed with breech-loading Sharps but Al Colvin, a civilian and Civil War veteran, owned a sixteen-shot Henry Rifle—something seldom seen on the frontier and probably never seen by those Indians. The Indians had been fighting muskets so long that they'd been trained to wait for a volley of fire, then charge while some redcoat reloaded. That changed that day. Several accounts record that by nightfall, the pile of empty brass casings at Colvin's feet numbered over three hundred—as did the number of dead Indians lying in the field out in front of him. That night, those civilians and all but a few of the soldiers went home to their families."

"So, what are you saying?"

"A man with the right weapon can change the course of history for the better."

"So, you're really lying up here about to shoot him?"

I slid open the bolt to reveal the chamber and magazine. She said, "Where are the bullets?"

"None in there."

"So, you're up here trying to shoot a man with a gun that has no bullets?"

"Sometimes, things get cloudy. Looking through this changes that. Lets me see clearly. Like putting blinders on a horse."

"Are you afraid of him?"

"I don't know that I've ever been afraid of any man, but I am concerned with what I know he'll do when he gets out."

"Like what?"

"I put a lot of people in that prison. All of them deserved it but not all of them are bad people. Some just made bad choices. They're paying for that. A few of them tell me things from time to time. They tell me that he talks about me, and my family, a good bit."

She wiped dust off the top of the rifle. "How long has this been up here?"

"Couple of years."

"You been coming up here and doing this for a couple of years?"

"Yes."

I pulled a .308 Winchester cartridge from my pocket and turned it in my hand. She said, "Does that fit that?"

"Black Hills Sierra match; 175-gram boat tail hollow point; 2620 feet per second. Flight time from here to there is about one-point-three seconds. And yes, it fits it perfectly."

We sat a long time. An hour or better. Pigeons fluttered around us. She didn't press me with a bunch of conversation. Just sat with me when that's what I needed. Somewhere in there, I spoke.

"People been killing people since Cain slit his brother's throat, or bashed his head in. I don't know how he did it, just that he did. I always found it strange...the idea of one family member pressing the delete button on a member of its own. People have accused me of being over the top. Say I own too many guns. Take this star too seriously." I spat. "I don't give a flying flip what they think. Evil is as real as this bell tower. And like it or not, we're all in this. We're all in a fight for our lives. Evil wants to rip off our heads, post it on a stake outside our front door, then stack the bodies like cordwood and sit on the pile. People who don't think so weren't born Jewish in Germany in the 1930s. Have never seen the Killing Fields in Cambodia. Never walked through the halls at Columbine or Virginia Tech. I have. Flew to all those places because I wanted to know what history felt like. Smelled like. Looked like. And the thing I've learned is that evil is a chameleon." I stared at her. "You want to know what evil looks like? Want to see its face? Take a look. Doesn't get any clearer than José Juan." I paused. "His nickname is 'The Machete.' " I leaned back. Shook my head. "Some say the world's changed. That these bad people have changed. I've actually heard that one before. Mostly from defense attorneys speaking before juries. They say their client is not the man the prosecution details. I've heard José Juan himself tell that to his jury during his trial. They called me back on the stand and I looked at him square, " 'José Juan, that bs might fly with your jury but it won't fly with those four dead women. Especially the one that got her baby cut out of her stomach by your knife.' " I paused. "They struck that from the record, but that don't make it not true. It's true as the day is long. He wanted his drugs and his drugs were in little bags in her stomach."

I was talking as much to myself as her. "You ever seen those videos of the wildebeest migration? Ever noticed who's hanging out near the back, trailing the weak? Lions aren't stupid. That's you, me, all of us—the naïve, unsuspecting folks minding our own business, trying to get through the day, at the back of the pack." I nodded. "Dad was right: a prowling lion, looking for someone to devour."

I offered the rifle cartridge. "Killing people ain't all that tough. Put the bullet in the right place and it does all the work. He's 838 yards away. I grew up shooting whistle pigs at six hundred yards. His head is four times bigger than one of them. 'Well,' you say, 'if you shoot him then you're no better than him. That badge doesn't make you right.' And I'd agree, but it would make us all feel better and it would rid the earth of him. Others say, 'Well…he's just misunderstood. Too many drugs. Bad upbringing. Too much time in prison where he learned to think like a bad man.' All that may be true, but does it excuse him?" I sucked through my teeth. The anger growing. "I love being a lawman. It's all I ever wanted to be. But, the only problem with being one is that we are constantly responding to evil that has either already happened or is in the process of happening. Rarely, if ever, do we get to intervene before it happens. I don't care what your religion is, or where you land on the mercy meter, but that man right there needs to be shot. Because he will commit evil as soon as he walks out. 'Well,' you say, 'that's cold-hearted.' Maybe. I admit the job can jade you after twenty years, but, whatever happened to fighting back? Fighting for your life. Fighting back doesn't make you evil. You can both fight and be good. They are not mutually exclusive."

I was talking a lot and I knew it. Maybe scaring her a bit, but if I'm honest, I wanted her to hear the real me. The one I don't share with everyone 'cause it hurts too much. "Women want that fairy tale. They love the picture of the knight who breaks down the castle gate, charges the tower, slays the guard, and carries off the maiden on a white horse. But, what about the next picture? What about five years down the road? The knight is designed and trained for battle. It's his life. It's him. Men die at his hand. It's messy. His armor is seldom shiny. It is caked with other men's blood and guts. He is wounded and scarred but he still spends his nights sharpening his sword because every morning when he rides out the gate, his life may well depend on it."

I leaned back, resting on the brick wall. "The thing is this...if being a knight is what he was made to do, then how does he live with the maiden in his castle—after the rescue. How does he live as a lover set in a time of terrible war?" I paused. "Every time he leaves the safety of his castle, he fights—both the going out and the return. If he doesn't, then he is conquered, his wife is raped and tortured while he watches, and his head is cut off and stuck on a stake outside the city walls to dissuade other want-to-be conquerors." I wiped my eyes. "We live in a world on the other side of the rescue. We are living out the fairy tale and it is different than we thought."

Tears streaked her face. "Can I have the bullet?"

I handed it to her. She slid it in her jeans. I pulled a second out of my shirt pocket. She held out her hand. I said, "I have more."

"How many?"

"More than you have pockets."

She handed the bullet back.

My eyes returned to the prison. "That son of a . . . well, he needs to die a painful death, but I got a boy at home whose world is crumbling all around him and I can't do a thing to rebuild it. He's just a kid and life has punched a bunch of holes in him. I try to pour into him, plug them, but he's draining out faster than I can fill him up." I motioned to José Juan. "If I poke a hole in that man, I'll never get the chance to plug the ones in Brodie."

She brushed her palm across my cheek. Her whisper was slow in coming. "Maybe he's not the only one with holes."

We could see out the slats for miles. The landscape beyond was dotted with unmoving oil derricks. Some tall. Some yellow. Some rust brown. Some oil-sludge black. The heat mirage hazed the backdrop. "The holes in me ran dry a long time ago."

She curled up alongside me, I slung my arm around her, tucked her shoulder up under mine and pulled her knees into her chest. A pretty good fit. We sat there a while, during which she didn't say a word. After another hour, she lay down next to the rifle and stared at the fence where José Juan no longer stood. She said, "He's gone."

I nodded.

"If you shot him, could you get away with it?"

"I imagine they'd figure it out eventually."

"But the best thing for the world we live in is for you to shoot him?"

"I think so, but the moment I do that—absent orders from my boss—I put myself in God's shoes."

She smiled. "If you could . . . stand in His shoes for one moment, even one second, what would you do?"

"I'd raise Mr. B, feed him a big bag of oats, and apologize for letting him die in the first place." I paused. "And, I'd stop Billy Simmons from doing what he done."

"Nothing for yourself?"

I shook my head. "I don't want nothing."

"Would you cure your wife from wanting pain pills?"

"No, I'd fix the reason she took them in the first place."

She was quiet. Finally, she turned. Sat cross-legged. Back straight. Tapped me in the chest. "What do you want?"

"I don't understand."

"What do you want in a woman? In life?"

I thought a moment and stared out my pigeon hole toward the jail. "In the mid-1800s, the Rangers were tasked with, among other things, guarding the border. We'd had a little dispute with the Mexicans at a little place called the Alamo, which we later settled at San Jacinto. As a result, the border, or the Rio Grande River, became a violent and wild place. It was one of the places we 'ranged.' We rode in pairs because there weren't enough of us to ride in threes or hundreds. The choice of weapon, horse, and partner mattered. Who you chose often determined whether you lived or died—and more important, how. Out of that, we began to describe one another by a few simple words: *Él es muy bueno para cabalgar el río.* Meaning, 'He'll do to ride the river with.' In Texan, it means, 'I'd trust him with my life.'" I scratched my head. "I want someone to ride the river with."

Tears had streaked her face and were dripping off her chin. She cried easily. Evidence that she felt much, and most often for other people. A rare and beauty-filled gift.

Moments before the noon bells, she took me by the hand and we climbed down.

# CHAPTER THIRTY-EIGHT

A tough week passed. Brodie said little. Knowing they'd come back every year, we planted amaryllis atop the grave and then drove a white cross in the ground. We stood there, the wind tugging at us. There was always a breeze up on the hill. He stared down over the river. "Dad?"

"Yes, son."

"Can I ask you something?"

"Sure."

"And you won't get mad?"

"No."

"Do you like Miss Sam?"

"I think she's a good woman."

He shoved his hands in his pockets and looked up at me. "That's not what I asked you."

I didn't look at him. "I'm not sure. I might."

"What about Mom?"

"Son, I'll always love your mom. I just can't be married to her anymore."

"But, that don't make any sense."

"I don't expect you to understand."

"What's to understand?"

"Son, your mom is an addict. She fell in love with another man. She left us. Remember?"

"I know all that. But, it still don't make sense." He turned to me. "Do you love Miss Sam?"

"I don't know, son."

"You just said you love Mom and if you do then it ain't right for you to be kissing Miss Sam."

"Son, I don't expect you to understand, but I do expect you to give me freedom and to respect my wishes."

"Dad, I'm not disrespecting you. I'm just telling you what I see."

I tried to put my arm around him, but he walked down to the river. I walked with him, but he turned. "Dad, I'd like to be alone."

I watched him and scratched my head. Is this what my life has come to? Has it all led to this?

Two hours later, he walked up from the river. A wrinkle creased the space between his eyes. "Dad, I need to go to town."

"Right now?"

"Yes, sir."

"What do you need?"

"I just need something."

"Can you tell me what it is?"

"I'd rather not."

He got this from me. I knew that. I also knew that the bur under his saddle wouldn't go away simply 'cause I told him no. "Okay."

We drove to town. His arm resting on the open window. We crossed the city limits and he rolled up his sleeves. They were two rolls above his elbows. "Where we going?" He looked at me out of the corner of his eye, then pointed at the drugstore. I parked and put the stick in neutral. We sat listening to the Cummins idle.

He pulled on the door handle, but paused before he stepped out. "I'd like to do this alone."

"Okay."

He stepped out. His shoulders looked broader. He'd grown taller. He walked toward the drugstore, stopped at the entrance, pulled down hard on his hat, then turned and started running down the street at full go. I hopped out of the truck and started walking after him. He looked over his shoulder, saw me, crossed the street, ran two more blocks and turned into the front door of the professional office of Earl Johnson, MD.

I swore.

When I pushed open the door, Brodie wasn't in the waiting room. Neither was anyone else. I heard a commotion in the back so I walked past the receptionist's desk toward the noise. I turned the corner and two female nurses had him cornered. He was shaking his head. "No, I don't have an appointment and I'd like to see him right now." I stepped into the small waiting area about the time Earl Johnson rushed out of his office. All five of us stood in a circle. I extended my hand to Brodie. "Brodie...come on."

The nurses stood aside. Brodie was breathing heavy and looking up at all of us. His face was wet, tears were puddling. He was on the verge. Earl had yet to say a word. Brodie caught his breath, looked at me, then back at Earl. He spoke clearly. "Dr. Johnson, do you love my mom?"

Earl looked baffled. Tried to shrug it off with a laugh. "Excuse me, son?"

Brodie stepped toward him. "Do you love my momma, Andie Steele?"

"Son, I don't know what you're talking about."

"But the kids at my school said you made house calls to my momma's apartment and that you were lucky my dad didn't shoot you when he found you naked in her room."

Earl shook his head, more uncomfortable laughter. "Your father never found me naked—"

I took two steps and hit him square in the mouth. Something crunched in his face and he crumpled. Both nurses screamed. Blood ran from his mouth and nose and he spit out several pieces of teeth. He lay on the floor, one eye staring up at me, the other rolling back in his head. I stood over him. Blood trickling down my hand where I'd cut my middle knuckle. "That's for lying. And if you get up off that floor, I'll give the one you ought to get for sleeping with my wife." I put my hand on Brodie's shoulder and led him toward the door. He was looking over his shoulder as we walked out.

We got into the truck, I cranked it, and we drove out of town. The blood drying on my hand and arm. When the hard road turned to dirt, I pulled off to the side, pushed in the clutch, and slid the stick into neutral. I sat there, staring at my life on the other side of the glass. "Brodie?"

His eyes were wide. "Yes, sir?"

I shook my head. "I know we got problems. A lot seems to be going wrong. I can't quite get my hands around it. I see you growing up and I couldn't be more proud. You're... you're everything I ever hoped a son would be. And I know you're hurting way down deep. I know we both are." I swallowed. "But, all I've got is you." Two tears rolled down my face. Dripped onto my jeans. "It won't always be like this, but right now... I need you. And you need me. And—" I stared down at my hands. "That man in there, Dr. Johnson, he did wrong. Real wrong. I don't like him. I pretty much hate him. But he's not the one you should be mad it. You... you should be mad at me." His eyes grew wider. "Not for what I did. But for what I didn't do."

"But Dad, I don't under—"

"Your mom needed something I never gave her."

He scooted into the middle seat. I put my arm around him and he grabbed the stick with two hands. I pushed in the clutch, he shoved it into first and we eased toward home. We wouldn't be able to do this much longer. His knees were getting in the way. After he shifted into third, he sat back, looked up at me, and said, "I know, Dad. I know. I just needed to know if you knew."

He gets that from his mom.

# CHAPTER THIRTY-NINE

I was sipping coffee when I heard the truck rumbling down the road, hitting every pothole. I glanced out the window. Sam skidded to a stop in front of the house, nearly turning the truck sideways. She got out and left the truck running and walked quickly toward the door, an open shoebox in her hand.

I opened the door. She looked tired. Worried. She offered the box. "Help."

Turbo lay unmoving in the box. His stomach was real swollen and he looked to be having some sort of spasm. Hope stared at me through the passenger's side window. This recipe had disaster written all over it.

Brodie walked up behind me, rubbing his eyes. I told him, "Get in the truck."

He took one look at Turbo and did exactly what I told him. Sam followed me to town and the only vet within thirty miles. There were lots of veterinarians who served the area of Rock Basin but they drove from all over. Only one lived in town.

Sarah Glover was a local girl done good. She'd put herself through veterinary school, come back home, and built a good reputation. Only problem was, she tended to care for large animals: like cows. Our chances were slim, but I didn't tell Sam or Hope that.

I took the box and told Brodie to stay with Hope while Sam and I walked up and knocked on Sarah's door. Moments later, she unlocked it and looked up at me through Coke-bottle glasses. "Hey, Cowboy. How you doing?"

I offered the shoebox. "Sarah"—I looked over my shoulder then held up the box—"this is Turbo, and I need some help and even if you can't help me I need you to act like you can." She eyed the box, then the girl watching us from the front seat. "Roger that."

We walked in her office. All five of us stood in a circle around a silver gurney. Sarah clicked on an overhead light and began asking questions. "Tell me about this guy."

Hope spoke. "Well, he's not moving around much. Not really eating. Sleeping a lot. He had a seizure a little while ago where he stretched out real straight and stiff and stayed that way for a few minutes. And his stomach is weird in places. Like he's growing a tumor." Sarah pulled on a stethoscope and began listening to Turbo's heartbeat. She gently probed around his body, listening. She opened his mouth, stared into his eyes, then moved the stethoscope down around his tummy. After about five seconds, she said, "Has Turbo been around any other guinea pigs?"

Sam shook her head. "No. Just us."

"How long have you had him?"

"A little over two months."

"Where'd you get him?"

"Pet store in the mall."

Sarah pulled off her stethoscope. She was trying not to smile. "Well, couple of things. First, Turbo isn't a he. He's a she. And she—" Sarah's smile grew wide—"is about to give birth." She held out a hand to Hope. "Congratulations. You're going to be a mommy."

Hope's eyes grew saucer-wide. "Really?"

"Yep."

Hope got bouncy. "Well, how'd that happen?"

Sarah smiled. "In my experience, if you put guinea pigs around each other long enough, you end up with more guinea pigs. Usually something in the water."

Hope was jumping up and down. "What do we do? What do we do?"

Sarah shook her head. "Nothing. Let her do her thing. Probably have four or five when it's all said and done."

Sam laughed and sat down, hanging her head between her hands. "I thought he was dying."

I said, "You mean 'she.' "

She smiled. The relief painted across her face was palpable. Her eyes were teary. "Yes, she."

We walked out and Sarah patted me on the shoulder. "Nice job, Cowboy."

"I didn't know. It's not like it's a cow."

When she shut the door, she was laughing pretty hard.

By eight o'clock that night, Sam called with the news that Turbo had birthed three babies and didn't seem finished. Thursday morning, she called again. She sounded sleep-deprived and caffeine-infused. "Hey, I need your address."

"What for?"

"Hope would like you to know that she and Turbo are the proud mother of five healthy and suckling babies and they need your address to send you a birth announcement."

"That'd be a first."

"Yep, me, too." I heard Hope giggling on the other end. Sam's voice quieted. "You haven't forgotten have you?"

"Forgotten what?"

"I knew it. You forgot already."

"But I don't know what I've forgotten if you don't tell me."

"Tomorrow is the last day of the month, and when we were in the river you said—"

"Oh, no. I hadn't forgotten that. I'll be there at six."

"Good. Oh, and Cowboy?"

"Yeah?"

"I got you a surprise."

"What is it?"

"If I told you, then it wouldn't be a surprise now would it? You'll just have to wait and see."

To be honest, I was already thinking about that.

# CHAPTER FORTY

Dumps looked at me and said, "He gets out in about thirty minutes."

I nodded. "We better get going."

We drove to the prison, the guard waved us through the main gate, and we wound around to the admin building just outside the main walls where they process the inmates who are being released. We waited.

At 4:00 p.m., the gate opened and Mike "Jumpy" Silvers, now seventy-seven, walked out. Just fifty-seven years after he walked in. Dumps walked toward him. The two stared at each other several minutes. Finally, Mike shook his head. "I don't know what to say."

Dumps said, "Me neither." He led him to the truck. I extended my hand. "Hey, Mike. How you doing?"

"Ranger Steele."

"Mike, you can call me Tyler or Cowboy."

"Yes, sir."

We drove to Myrlene's, a diner in town. Mike sat across from us as we sipped coffee. He was quiet and kept staring at the walls and the space between them. Occasionally, he looked at the door and the fact that it was not locked. He ate a steak, five eggs, some biscuits, and drank a pot of coffee. Then he ordered ice cream. They brought him five scoops. He laughed. "One for each decade."

He looked at Dumps. "Been lonely since you got out."

Dumps nodded.

Mike smiled. "All the rest of my cell mates snored. But, not you. You never uttered a peep."

I asked him, "Mike, you got any plans?"

He laughed. "Hadn't planned on getting out, so no, sir, I don't really have any."

"Got any family?"

"Yes, sir. Got a brother in California. He sent me a bus ticket. Asked me to come live with him. He owns a vineyard. Thought I might spend some time growing grapes."

I asked him, "You got any money?"

He shook his head. "They wanted to give me a few dollars for my time served and hours worked but I asked them to send it to the widow of the man I shot." He fell quiet. "So, no. I ain't got none."

Dumps handed him five hundred dollars in cash. Jumpy eyed the money. He didn't say nothing for a long time. Finally, he swallowed and said, "Thanks, Pat. I'm grateful." Dumps passed him a box. Mike lifted the lid. Inside he found a new pair of boots. He nodded again, slipped them on his feet and smiled like a Cheshire cat.

We ate a few more minutes, then walked across the street to the bus station. As the bus pulled up, he said, "Ranger?"

I turned to him.

"There's word in the prison that Machete"—he cleared his throat—"I mean, Chuarez, well, he didn't get his release like he was hoping. He's downright mad. There's talk he aims to manufacture his own release. And, if'n you're asking me, he's got the means to do just that. You best be on the lookout."

I extended my hand. "Thanks, Mike. You take care. And"—I smiled—"stay out of trouble."

He nodded. "I aim to do just that."

Dumps hugged him and he hopped on the bus.

Dumps looked at me as the bus pulled away. "You know he's telling the truth about Chuarez. He's got no reason to lie."

"I know."

"What're you going to do?" He glanced at the bell tower, then back at me.

I raised an eyebrow and gritted my teeth.

"Oh, don't look so surprised. I'm not as old and dumb as I look."

I scratched my chin. "I don't know what I'm going to do."

We walked back to where I'd parked the truck, and Myrlene came out of the diner and stopped me. She'd run that diner for as long as I can remember and always wore the same light blue dress and white apron. Sort of like Richie Rich but in a poorer, female version. She tugged on my sleeve and motioned me out of earshot of any passersby. She whispered, "That girl you brought into town, the one down at Georgia's, what's her story?"

"Just a woman needing a break."

"Well"—she looked at me over the top of her reading glasses—"there was a man here this morning." The skin started crawling up the back of my neck. "Big, muscular guy. Never seen him before. He had breakfast, showed me his badge and then a picture of the woman, asked me if I knew her. I didn't tell him anything."

I turned quickly. "Thanks, Myrlene."

I had two thoughts. Hope and Sam and in that order. Dumps and I jumped in the truck and drove back alleys to school. Beth was in her office when I ran around the corner. She said, "Cowboy, you okay?"

"I need Hope Dyson and I need her right now."

She flipped through a notebook on her desk, then said, "Follow me." We walk-jogged down a hall, turned left, then down another. Hope was sitting at her desk. I felt myself exhale slightly. She saw me, smiled and then the smile left her face. I reached down, scooped her up and started walking toward my truck. Dumps followed close behind. She clung to my neck, looking at me. "Cowboy?"

"Honey, I need you to hang on to me and keep your eyes peeled. You understand?"

She started trembling and wet her pants.

"Did he find us?"

"I think so."

She started crying. "I knew he would. I knew it."

I placed her on the seat and Dumps and I jumped in. Dumps put his arm around her. We wound through the older brick streets of town coming up to the back of the Georgia Peach. I stopped two blocks away and turned to Dumps. "Drive her to my old office. I'll call in, tell them you're coming. She'll be safe there."

Hope clung to me. "Cowboy, I don't want to—"

I peeled her off me. "Hope." I looked at her in the eyes. "I need you to go with Dumps. I'll be along with your mom directly. You understand?"

She nodded.

"All right, go along then."

Dumps walked around to the driver's side while I grabbed my AR-15 and black tactical vest out of the box in the back of my truck. He drove off and I began the two-block walk down the alley that ran behind the storefront. While I walked I dialed. Debbie picked up after one ring. "DPS. Ranger Company C."

"Debbie, it's Cowboy."

"Hey, Cow—"

I cut her off. "Dumps is bringing in a little girl. I need you to keep an eye on her. Officially. And I need you to send whoever is close to the Georgia Peach. Right now. And tell them to come heavy."

"Roger that."

"I am en route. Walking up the back alley behind Smith's Antiques. I don't want to get shot by my own people so tell them to keep an eye out."

I clicked the phone shut just as a portly man I did not know walked backwards out of Smith's. He was moving what looked like a bed. I cleared my throat. He saw my badge and rifle, set down the bed, and walked back inside.

The Georgia Peach sat in a stand-alone brick building surrounded by grass and a parking lot out back. I crept up to the corner of the closest building, set my hat on the sidewalk behind me and slowly glanced at the back door which sat some forty yards away. All was quiet.

Through a window I could see Georgia, but her posture told me something wasn't right. She never stood still. At the moment, she looked to be barely breathing. She was quartering away from me. As was the lady in her chair. Neither looked very happy. I slid up the side wall in the shadows.

About midway, the gunshot rang out.

A second and a half later, I reached the door.

TV shows often depict guys like me flying through doors in moments like this. And sometimes that's needed. But so was a cool head. I didn't know who'd shot or at whom. And flying through a door may mean they'd turn that same gun on me and shoot without thinking. I stood off to one side, turned the knob, and firmly pushed the door open. Using the muzzle as an extension of my hands, I peered around the door.

Billy knelt in the middle of the room, blood streaming down the side of his face and neck, hands in the air. Most of his left ear was gone. Sam stood in front of him, holding Andie's Les Baer just inches from Billy's nose. The muzzle was shaking, Sam was crying, and her finger sat on the trigger. At that distance, I doubted she'd miss. Georgia stood over her shoulder pointing a Smith & Wesson

.357 at the side of Billy's face. She was calm, collected, and half of her face hung in an upturned smile. He may be one heckuva lawman in San Antone, but up here, he didn't stand a chance.

Four women sat in chairs to my left, flanked by stylists. Most of them were in some degree of shock and most were crying. All except Georgia who was whispering, "Pull the trigger, Sam. We're all witnesses. You were just defending yourself."

I stepped into the doorway and Billy glanced at me. He looked like he wished he was anywhere but right there. He'd definitely gotten more than he bargained for. He'd clearly not been expecting Sam to be carrying Andie's .45. Sam never glanced at me. She was telling him what she thought of him and doing a pretty good job of it, too. I didn't figure I had long before she torched that thing off again. If I set a hand on her, I was pretty sure she'd flinch and yank on the trigger, leaving Billy with little more than a canoe for a head. Yes, that's what he deserved and yes I hoped he'd rot in hell for what he did to Hope but Sam didn't need that on her conscience. Killing a man changes you. Even one that deserves it.

I whispered. "Sam?"

She didn't answer.

I leaned in closer. "Sam?"

Still no answer.

I brought the muzzle of my rifle up alongside her .45 and said, "Samantha?"

Billy was dripping blood onto the floor. His eyes were bouncing between Sam's muzzle, Georgia's, and mine. Sam looked at me. I spoke softly. "You have every right to do what you're wanting to do, and he deserves it. I won't stop you. But it won't help you sleep any better. Won't take the hurt away. Won't fix all this."

She spoke through gritted teeth. "What will? Permanently."

I couldn't blame her. She knew now he'd never have stopped until he found them.

I'd had a pretty good feeling she'd had it all along. If I were her I wouldn't want folks looking at pictures of me or my child doing stuff, or having stuff done to them, that shouldn't be on video. Ever. And she didn't need to explain that. Didn't need to justify it. She was—she thought—protecting Hope. She had reasoned that if she could get away, disappear, brush it under the rug, that the problem would disappear, too. But motivated men like Billy don't brush away easily. Especially when their entire life is at stake. I said, "The thumb drive."

She shook her head, pressed the muzzle to his forehead, and held it there, thinking. After a few seconds, she thumbed the safety up and on and then swung it as hard as she could across his face, sending him to the floor. When he rolled over, his nose had been spread horizontally across his face. Sam returned Andie's Les Baer to her backpack—the backpack she never let get very far from her. She unzipped the front pocket, pulled out a thumb drive and a small, portable hard drive. Billy's one unswollen eye grew Oreo big. She set both on the table next to me and then sat down at her pedicure station and started crying. I turned to Billy. "On your stomach. Keep your hands where I can see them—behind you."

He did as instructed. I pulled a Glock 23 off his hip and a 27 off his ankle about the time three officers came in through the front door and two more through the back followed by my captain who looked curious to see what kind of trouble I'd gotten myself into. He looked at me, assessed the situation, and said, "So, this is what retirement looks like?" He nodded. "I like it. Maybe I'll retire, too." He tipped his hat to Georgia who was still standing over Billy. "Georgia, how you doing this fine afternoon?"

She never took her eyes off Billy. "Just fine and, no"—the silver weapon flashed in her hand—"I'm not putting this back where it belongs till Cowboy tells me I can."

Captain nodded. "Good call."

Twenty minutes later, Billy sat handcuffed in the back of an unmarked car after having been read his rights. He was quiet as a church mouse and bleeding into a towel. I leaned against the car and explained the situation to my captain. He glanced inside the car. "She dang near shot off the side of his head."

"Yeah, a hearing aid won't fix that."

He shook his head and laughed. "I'm not sure anything'll fix that. That looks like it hurts." He tapped on the window. "Does that hurt? It looks right painful." He edged closer to the window, squinted and pointed to Billy's face. "I think your nose may be broken." Captain has a strange sense of humor.

About then, Sam stepped out of the Peach, backpack over her shoulder. She walked up to me, and captain tipped his hat, "I'll be in touch."

"Yes, sir."

She looked up at me, arms crossed. Tapping one foot, she looked like she had something she wanted to say. I tried to break the ice. "You shot most of his ear off."

"I was trying to hit his face but I was shaking so much…" She trailed off, crossed her arms, looked away. "I owe you an explanation."

"You don't owe me any—"

She jerked her head toward me. "Would you just—I want to."

I listened.

"I did lose the thumb drive in the A/C vent, but once I got the car started I got so angry that I ran back and about tore the place apart trying to get it out. I knew we had to have it and I wasn't about to leave it for that sick son of a—." She glanced at him in the car. "Then I stole the hard drive for good measure just as he was coming out of the bathroom. I didn't tell you I had it because, firstly, I don't want pictures of me, of my little girl, used as evidence. We are not evidence. We are women, or Hope will be one day, and I don't want people studying us in a courtroom. We're not circus freaks. It's painful enough without all that." She looked away. "And secondly, I was gonna tell you at the Ritz, honest, but, I—" Her foot began tapping faster. "After you, well, I wanted you to have a reason to keep us around. A reason to not just drop us off at some police station. Thought if you didn't, you'd, well, drive off into the damned sunset and leave us. Leave me." She put her hands on her hips. "I never, in a million years, thought you'd drive down there. All the way back to Billy's. What kind of a man does that?" She shook her head, pushed the hair out of her eyes and pursed her lips. The tears were coming again. "I know it was selfish, but I'm *not* sorry." Another glance in the car. "Not one bit." She turned, and walked back into the Peach as Dumps and Hope walked through the front door.

About then Georgia walked up to the car. She was wearing her apron. I could see the bulge of her revolver in the front pocket. She looked at me square. "Cowboy?" It was posed as a question but she was only getting my attention to tell me something.

"Yes, ma'am."

She glanced in the car, judging the distance. "Is he going to prison?"

"I believe so."

She stepped closer, looking in the car. Her tone changed. "You believe so... or you know so?"

She slipped her hand into the pocket of her apron. I stepped between her and the car. "Georgia?"

She looked up at me.

"We got this."

She raised her chin, stared at me, not backing off an inch. "You promise?"

I nodded. "I can promise you that what is about to happen to this man in prison is a lot worse than being shot by you."

She nodded, half smiled, and walked back into her salon.

Three hours later, we'd finished the mountain of paperwork required in an incident involving a shooting. The captain cut me loose and I drove to town. To the apartment.

I knocked on the door. Hope and Sam were packing. Or rather, Hope was watching Sam pack. I poked my head inside. Hope eyed me from the couch. Turbo, with all her youngins, lay in a shoebox on her lap. They were nursing. Turbo looked tired. I whispered, "What're you all doing?"

She glanced toward the sound of loud noises in the bedroom. "Packing."

I nodded and knocked on the bedroom door. She called from inside. "What!"

I pushed it open. She saw me. "Oh." Her face was flush. Mascara had smeared. "Where you going?"

She didn't answer.

"You don't know, do you?"

She plopped down on the bed, started rolling one thumb over the other and shook her head once.

"You can't leave."

She turned quickly. "Why? They don't expect me to stay here so they can put Hope on the witness stand? I'm not about to subject her to—"

"I'd never let them do that and you know it, so why the pack and dash?"

She threw some clothes down on the bed and crossed her arms. Shielding herself. "I thought maybe it was just best if we left. That we'd overstayed our welcome, that you were ready to be rid of us. That you were tired of women lying to you about stuff that matters and maybe it was best if I closed the last page on this fairy tale I been living here with you and Brodie and Georgia and Dumps and this Mayberry town. That maybe it'd be best if I just woke me up from the dream I been dreaming. That maybe this train wreck of a woman would just do you a favor and—"

She was rambling. She needed reeling in. I tapped the face of my watch. "Twenty-six hours."

She looked confused. Exasperated. "What?"

Another tap. "Twenty-six hours, and counting."

She threw up her hands. "I'm not staying here another twenty-six minutes—"

I interrupted her. "Two important things happen in twenty-six hours: my divorce will be final and we have a date. Remember? The river? And, I don't mean to put words in your mouth, but you said something about a surprise."

She took a deep breath, tried not to smile, and said, "You still want to take me out? Even after the—" She ran her finger in a curli-cue circle.

"Ummm, yes, but you might want to wash some of that black stuff off your eyes. You look like a raccoon."

She laughed. Palmed the tears away from her face, smearing it worse. "You're sure?"

Now she looked like a member of an eighties rock and roll band. I stepped across and kissed her on the forehead. "Yes."

She hooked her index finger inside my belt loop, pulling me toward her and resting her forehead against my chest. "Thank you for today."

I kissed her again. "I told you, it's what I do." I walked toward the door, turned, and tapped my watch. "Twenty-five hours, fifty-eight minutes and thirty seconds."

# CHAPTER FORTY-ONE ·

Dumps took Brodie to a local rodeo, which gave me about an hour to get ready. I shaved, ironed my clothes, polished my boots, and combed my hair, twice. Which I don't ever remember doing. I even stole some of Brodie's hair gel. It wasn't Dapper Dan but it'd do in a pinch.

It'd been six weeks since I bumped into Sam and Hope on the highway. On one hand it had passed quickly. The blink of an eye. On the other, a lifetime. For all of us, the range of emotions had swung the arc of the pendulum.

I stood at the mirror, my face half shaven, and took a deep breath. My divorce had been official at noon and I was a free man. Legally. Andie had been released that morning but I did not know where she went or how she got wherever she was going. The tether had been cut and I was no longer responsible. I knew she had no money, no transportation, and none of that was my problem. I figured at some point in the next few days she'd contact me and come by and get her things and we'd work out a schedule for her to see Brodie, but I wasn't too focused on that at the moment. I had full custody so it would be on my terms. I'd made up my mind to move on. Turn a new page. And I was doing just that.

I pulled on my sport coat, brushed my hat, grabbed my keys, and walked out the door.

Straight into Andie.

She stood on the porch, staring out across an empty pasture. Faded jeans, flip-flops, tank top. I pushed open the screen door and she turned, tried to smile. "Hey."

Every strong resolution I'd just made shattered. I nodded and spoke softly. "Hey."

She held out her hands. "I won't stay, I just—" She paused. "How's Brodie?"

"He's good. Mostly. He's doing okay. Dumps took him to the rodeo. He'll be back in a bit. Just let me know when you want to see him. I know he wants to spend time with you. We'll work something out."

She backed up, crossed her arms, looked away.

"Your things, you can get them whenever. Your key still works." Another nod. "You got a place to stay?"

"Jill's going to let me stay with her a while. Until I can get settled."

Jill Sievert was her oldest friend. "She was always good to you."

A pause. "The best." A Ford Bronco sat in the drive. "That's hers. She let me borrow it." She looked up at me. "You? You look good." She moved aside and spoke as I took a step toward my truck. "Brodie said you sold the 'vette."

I took another step. "I did."

She glanced out across the pasture. "Where's the herd?"

She knew the answer but I guess she needed to ask the question. "The bank... I paid off some debts."

"You sold the herd?"

"It was either the herd or the Bar S."

I wanted very much to leave. I glanced at my watch. "I've got to—"

"Ty? Please." I stopped and turned around. She took a deep breath but it only went in halfway. She gave a slight shake of her head. Tried to laugh. "I've had so long to rehearse this, now I can't remember."

Another glance at my watch. "Really, Andie...I'm late."

She looked down toward the river. Cinch and May were feeding together. Mr. B was noticeably absent. "Where's Mr. B?"

I eyed the cross on the hill.

"What! What happened?"

"Stepped in a hole. Nothing we could do."

"And Brodie?"

I shook my head. "He's taking it pretty tough."

A tear trickled down alongside her nose.

I stared at her. "Andie, you slept with another man. Remember? I never did that. Never shared us with anybody else. So, it's a little late to be wondering who here is crushed."

She nodded and stepped back. "I deserve that. And more." I climbed into the truck and shut the door. She stood until I rolled down the window. "Can I please say one thing?"

I waited. She bit her lip. More tears. No makeup. No running mascara. I'd seen it all before. I turned off the truck. Stared down at her. I said, "I drove down there...ten times. Eleven if you count the last. I sat in a hollowed out stump and watched you drink coffee. Jog laps. Lose weight. Smile with Earl. Then, after dark, I crept through the woods, crawled into a large rock, and watched you swim at night. Lie close enough to touch you. Count the freckles. Ten times. You know why?" Her tears were streaming now. Bottom lip quivering. She had hit bottom. The realization had come home. The weight heavy. Her shoulders bowed. I read the body language yet I could not get past the pain. The anger. "I wanted a reason, just one, not to sign those papers. Any reason at all." I shook my head. "I sat there looking back on the story of us and I could look past single events, each one. I could. Even Earl. 'Cause I could see my role in them. How who I'd become had created the woman you were. Are. But each time they all came flooding back and when hit with the sum of you, no reason remained. All I had to show for my time in that stump or rock was a cigarette I had not smoked. Then I'd climb back into my truck and drive home where I found that to hold on to this—" I scanned the boundaries of the Bar S—"I had to give up everything I ever cared for. 'Cause you pissed it away at some craps table. And no matter how I tried, I couldn't explain all that to a boy whose life was turned upside down and who can't understand why his dad doesn't want to live with his mom. And every time I looked in his eyes, I saw yours—'cause you gave them to him. For three years, I been holding on, hoping, but my hope is played out." I tapped my chest. "I wear this T-shirt for my son because he thinks it protects me from the stuff that's trying to kill me, but…it doesn't even slow it down."

I cranked the truck, the diesel idled. When I eased off the clutch, she held out her hand. Palm down. She was holding something. "Andie, really. I don't want anything from you."

"Please."

I shook my head.

"Tyler, please."

I extended my hand, palm up. She uncurled her fingers and ten tightly rolled and unsmoked cigarettes fell into it.

She stepped back, crossed her arms, and stared at the ground. I looked at each one. They were sweaty from her palm. Some more brittle than others. I swallowed. I stared through the windshield. "Andie, I have loved you a long time. I still do. But I hurt, too. I hurt a lot. This, you and me"—I looked at her—"is not easy."

"Tyler, I'm sorry. For everything." She looked away. "And for some things, more than others."

I wanted to be angry. To lash out. To hurt her like she'd hurt me, but what would it do? What good would come? She was once my wife. My best friend. The mother of my son. Would it ease the hurt? Lessen the pain?

I nodded, and cranked the truck. "Me, too."

* * *

I drove slowly. Trying to make sense of what made no sense. A few minutes after six, I knocked on the apartment door and heard the hair dryer blowing. I sat and waited until it quit. When it did, I knocked again. Sam ran to the door, swung it open, smiled, and then twirled, holding onto the sides of her sun dress. "How do I look?" The dress was black, thin straps, and fell just above the knee. When she twirled, light shone through highlighting her curves. It wasn't see through as much as thin. I whispered, "Lord a'mighty."

She smiled. "Good answer." She'd gotten comfortable kissing me, so she stepped forward, leaned onto her toes, and kissed the side of my mouth. She smelled my neck. "Mmmm, you smell good."

"For what they charge, it ought to."

"What is it?"

"Something Georgia ordered off the Internet and told me that if I wore it you'd melt like butter in my hand."

"What's it called?"

"Crabtree and..."

"Evelyn."

"Yeah, that's it."

"I like it."

She sniffed my neck again then twirled a second time, this time slower. The turquoise star on the front of her boots matched the jewelry hanging around her neck. She touched it. "Georgia let me borrow it."

"It looks real nice on you."

She stopped twirling, a smirk across her face, and slowly raised the hem of her dress a little more than halfway up her right thigh. Her legs were tan. Shaven. The skin smooth. "You like my new dress?"

"It's..."

The dress inched higher. "Yes?"

I blushed. Scratched my head. "It's very pretty."

She let go, and hooked her arm in mine. "Good. Then it was worth what I paid, which was stupid-crazy expensive."

I helped her into my truck and we drove to dinner. She was excited, talkative, and she'd grown comfortable with me. Shifting into second, listening to her talk about a lady with real smelly feet and nasty nails, it struck me that in the six weeks I'd known her, we'd become friends. I knew this because I'd never before in my life cared one iota about the intricate details of a pedicure, but there in that truck, I found myself actually listening and engaged.

I adjusted the rearview and stared at her profile while she talked. She'd pulled her hair up and back, and wore some earrings that matched the necklace. They swung with the animated movement of her head. And when she sat and crossed her legs, the dress climbed above her knee and draped across her thigh. One spaghetti strap from her dress had slid slightly off her shoulder exposing the tan line.

I was nearly drunk with the sight and smell of a woman. I felt like a sixteen-year-old kid. And, it wasn't just lust. Sure, I had a good bit of that, I admit. My thoughts were going places they hadn't gone in a while. But it was something else. It was beauty. In the presence of it. Witnessing it. Real beauty. And not just for beauty's sake but beauty shared. Offered. She'd done all this for me. And she was sharing it, herself, with me.

I'd made a reservation at Rock Basin's only white-tablecloth restaurant, Steve's. We were already ten minutes late but I didn't care. I just could not wait any longer. I drove us four blocks out of the way, out behind a deserted and rusty manufacturing plant alongside the railroad. I pulled up alongside a loading dock, pushed in the parking brake, set my hat on the dash, and turned toward her. She was in midsentence, lost in her own conversation, when I leaned over, wrapped my arms around her, and pulled her toward me.

She melted.

When I finished, she blinked, wiped the lipstick off my lips and said, "Wow, can we do that again?"

We did.

When I sat up, her face was flush. She said, "Oh my."

I put on my hat and shifted into first. "I been wanting to do that for about six weeks."

"Took you long enough."

They sat us at a table in the back. Candlelight. White napkins. I pushed in her chair and we ate and talked for nearly two hours during which she hooked her heel around my calf. She drank red wine, I sipped tea, and after dinner we split a piece of key lime pie and two cappuccinos. When we stood and I walked her toward the door, it hit me. I had fallen. Hard, fast, and devoid of a parachute.

We drove through town. I stopped at a light. "We can catch a movie. It's a love story about a couple lost in the mountains. *The Mountain* something or other. Supposed to be pretty good. You'll probably love it. Or—"

She lit. "Oh, all the girls were talking about it today. Let's go."

"Or..." I really didn't want to sit in a movie. "We could go swimming." Emmylou Harris and Don Williams were singing a duet on the radio. *If you needed me, I would come to you—*

She sat back. Shrugged. "No bathing suit."

I turned and started driving toward the river. "Me neither." She moved to the middle of the seat and pulled my arm around her shoulders. The song continued. *I would swim the seas, for to ease your pain.*

I drove back roads. Dirt mostly. Slow. Windows down. It was a cool night. We rolled off the road onto the hard pack alongside the river. I drove a mile and parked up on a bluff where the cottonwoods grew up over a spring-fed pool that bubbled up and joined the river. The water was clear and always bath-temperature warm this time of year for reasons I can't begin to explain. A moon rose outside my windshield and glistened across the water. Blooming amaryllis rose up along the water's edge. She whispered, "It's beautiful."

And she was.

I stepped out of the truck when the cell phone rang. I was in the process of turning it off when I saw the caller ID read, "Captain."

"Yes, sir."

I heard gunshots in the background. Too many to count. He whispered. "Come a running! Prison! Riot! Can't hold them. Down to my last magazine. Bring everybody." He said something else garbled. Then he screamed two words, "Come heavy!" And the line went dead.

I clicked the phone shut, climbed back up into the truck, and turned to Sam, "Put on your seatbelt and hold on." In the distance, I could see the lights from the prison reflecting off the clouds. An orangish glow.

They'd set it on fire.

# CHAPTER FORTY-TWO

There is an old fable that goes something like: A local sheriff was dealing with a town riot. He called the Rangers and stood on the train platform waiting for the train and the posse. After all the passengers departed, a single man wearing a badge unloaded his horse and walked toward the sheriff. The sheriff looked around him and said, "Where is everybody?" The Ranger replied, "One riot. One Ranger."

The truth is there are only about 130 Rangers. Total. We cover a large area. That means we are used to not counting on backup for we seldom get it in time. By the time it gets there, whatever was going to happen, has already happened. It's not that we don't want to back each other up, but rather that Texas is too big. Or, maybe we are too few. I have great respect for anyone who wears a badge, and this country has some world-class units—LA SWAT comes to mind—but the Rangers have been, are, and always will be the most storied law enforcement unit on the planet. There's a reason for that. And if there's respect tied to it, we earned it.

I placed four calls and had law enforcement coming from as far away as Dallas but even with helicopters and supercharged engines, it'd take time. On a straightway, I glanced at the speedometer. Brodie's face in the picture smiled up at me. The needle bounced somewhere above a hundred. Sam sat white-knuckled, sheet pale. I didn't want her to see this.

Eight minutes after I hung up the phone, we arrived. A local boy—just out of the academy, think traffic cop—his sheriff's badge still shiny and unscratched, sat outside the perimeter gate. Lights flashing. He was close to hyperventilating. A small crowd had gathered. I stopped. He had been speaking into his shoulder-mounted microphone when I stepped out. He saw my cinco peso. He let out, "Sure glad to see you, sir." He shook his head. "Word is that Chuarez feller didn't get let out like the papers was saying he was so he called for a riot and I guess we got us one."

He followed me around the back of my truck and briefed me while I unloaded my duffel bag and strapped on my vest. Word had spread. Cars appeared. Behind me, Dumps and Georgia stood at a distance. Hope clutched her notebook. Brodie blinked under the lights. Sam stood with one arm around Brodie, the other clutching Hope. "Get them out of here," I called to Sam.

The deputy continued, "Captain Packer is bottled up in the admin building just through the main gate but outside the primary fence. He was escorting a prisoner." Flames rose up on the other side. Smoke was pouring out the second story window. "But you've got men up in the towers where the guards used to be. And, they've got rifles. Dallas SWAT said to hold and that they're bringing the tank. It'll allow us to get to him."

I tried the captain on his phone. No answer. He didn't have ten minutes. Maybe didn't have five. As the sound of gunfire erupted from the admin building, I slung my rifle, checked magazines, press-checked my 1911, and pulled a mobile radio out of my duffel and turned it on, checking the frequency, and running the earpiece to my good ear. I turned to the boy. "Stay here. Guard them. Talk to me on"—I pointed at the mike on his shoulder—"that, and let me know when anybody else arrives."

"But, sir, you can't stop the riot."

I cranked the truck. "Son, I'm not trying to stop the riot. I'm trying to get to my captain before they do."

Sam grabbed me, shaking her head. "Ty, you could die in there."

I shook my head. "It's a hell of a thing."

She wouldn't let go. "But why?"

Time was wasting. "If you have to ask me, then you won't understand." I glanced at Brodie. The distant firelight flickered off his face, highlighting the tear cascading down.

I kissed her, climbed up, eased off the clutch, and glanced in the rearview. Brodie had hid his face against Sam. The prison flickered. Flashes of orange. Black smoke billowing. Concertina wire glistening. Some sort of acid rock blaring from the loudspeakers. Sporadic gunfire. Rumblings in the belly of hell. The river flowed off to my right, outside the fence, passing into the shadow beyond the spotlights. Not so long ago, and not too far south of here, horse-mounted Rangers riding into Mexico would glance back over their shoulder at the Rio Grande and do so with longing.

If we could but make it back to the river.

I drove a half mile, passed through the main gate, ripped the rearview mirror off the glass, and pressed the accelerator to the floor.

A second later, the first round passed through the windshield.

# CHAPTER FORTY-THREE

Dear God,

Cowboy just drove off. He's driving really fast. The prisoners are shooting at him. He just drove his truck through the front door of that building. I hear shooting coming from inside. There was an explosion.

God, if you're not here, you need to because some real bad evil is coming up out of the earth.

# CHAPTER FORTY-FOUR

We've seen ten thousand on television, from the O.K. Corral to the *Matrix*. We all have our favorites. They flash across the screen with slow motion and Hollywood, high-def results, but once they're over, nobody can remember much about them. Nor do they want to. Your adrenaline pumps, auditory exclusion blocks out much of the noise, peripheral vision becomes a tunnel, fine motor gives way to gross. Many men lose control of their bowels or bladder. And whatever the outcome, it's never pretty. Bullets don't just knock you down and kill you quietly or painlessly. They poke large holes, tear away flesh, and often kill you slowly. Painfully. It's the nature of warfare.

Until that moment, I had often wondered what my dad was thinking when he rushed into that bank. Now I knew. Rather than relay what did or did not happen, let me tell you what I do and don't remember as best as I can piece it together. It's easier that way. Although, while I won't knowingly lie, I can't promise you it's all true.

\*    \*    \*

I don't remember the impact of the bumper on the front of the building, or climbing out through the cracked windshield or crawling down the hall, below the smoke toward the sound of gunfire. I do remember turning a corner and finding four men at the foot of the stairs holding rifles and shotguns and that I was glad I saw them before they saw me. I don't remember crawling up the stairs but I evidently did because I ended up on the second floor staring at a barricade of desks and chairs and Captain lying on the other side. When I got to him he was bleeding out of several holes and told me to do something that I wasn't about to do, i.e, "Get the hell out of there." I don't remember throwing him over my shoulder and running down a back fire escape but I do remember hearing the alarm. I don't remember shooting, I don't remember reloading, and I don't remember being shot in the leg. I do remember a bullet tearing through my shoulder because my arm went limp, I couldn't hold the rifle with my right hand, and I wondered who just stuck me with a hot poker. I don't remember the five guys that came around the corner, only that I stepped over them and that the smoke was black and thick. I don't remember running the rifle empty, or emptying my 1911 and the four magazines I carried in my vest and the one on my belt. I only know that when I looked down, they were gone and the slide was locked back and barrel smoking. I don't remember running out the back, carrying the captain over my shoulder but I do have a vague recollection of trying to get down to the river, thinking if we could make it there, we'd be okay. Lastly, I remember thinking that wolves travel in packs and that's about when the lights went out.

I think I must have been out a while because when I woke up, parts of my leg and back were warm. There was an odd, sucking sound coming from my chest and breathing was more difficult than it'd ever been. I remember somebody dragging me, then a flashlight, seeing several sets of hands and people speaking in loud voices. I remember the passing smell of smoke. I remember the captain cussing me for being such a "damn fool" and then him telling somebody to tend to me and not him. I remember my legs lying in the river and my chest propped up on the beach.

I remember the sound of silence and yet I could see Sam, in my face, screaming at me. She was crying. Saying words that did not make it past my ears.

I remember pressing my finger to her lips and whispering, "You talk...a lot."

I was so tired. All I wanted to do was go to sleep. I remember thinking I should be hurting but I wasn't. I couldn't feel a thing. The tunnel was closing in. She was screaming louder now. I opened my mouth. Pushed hard but the words were all stuck together. She kissed me. Blood on her lips. I didn't like that. I wanted to wipe it off. I tasted tears. Salt and blood. I told her, "Bury me in the Brazos."

"I will not!" She cracked. "I'm not burying you." She shook her head. "Don't you do this to me. Please, Cowboy. Please." She slapped my face. "You do this and I'll kill you myself."

I remember laughing. "I think they already beat you to it."

She kissed me again. Wet. Tender. Salty tears. I remember staring at my chest and watching the red pour out. I remember having the thought, "That's not good." Then I watched it mix with the river. Carried downriver. By next week, or next month, I'd be in the Gulf of Mexico. And for reasons I can't explain, I liked that.

From there the perspective changed. I saw me not through my eyes, but from above. Sam slapped my face. Still screaming. I couldn't hear her. I couldn't hear anything. She said, "No you don't! Don't you dare roll your eyes back in your head. You are not allowed to leave here without me." She said some other stuff but it was all a jumble. Echoes without distinction.

I remember thinking I would miss her and how I'd rather be swimming under moonlight. Then I looked up, saw the clouds, and knew we'd have seen no moon. The darkness came as the breeze from the propellers washed over me. Sleep came heavy. I could hold it back no longer. I don't remember them lifting me up, taking off, the sensation of flying, news crews, cameras, or lights. I don't remember somebody holding my hand but do remember it had a familiar feel. I don't remember the paramedic asking me if I was allergic to anything but I do remember telling him, "bullets." I don't remember him pushing the IV needle into my arm but I do remember him standing over me, squeezing the fluids bag with two hands and forcing them into my arm. I don't remember them charging the paddles and screaming "Clear," but I do remember my teeth clenching when the charge hit me. I don't remember chest compressions, but I do remember staring at a tattoo of Donald Duck on his right bicep and wondering if his name is Donald. Why else would you have a tattoo like that? I don't remember bright lights in the operating room, people screaming, more chest compressions, more white paddles, and I don't remember the doctor standing back, his scrubs splattered in red, and recording the time. I don't remember losing the feeling in my fingers and toes or the metallic taste in my mouth.

The last thing I remember seeing was actually two things: my blue T-shirt lying tattered on the floor. Somebody'd cut it right up the middle, straight through the "S." It was no good anyway. Prisoners had shot it pretty full of holes. The second thing was my boots. Some idiot had cut them off my feet and they lay on the ground in a puddle. They were a sorry sight. Not even Dumps would be able to resurrect them. I hoped they didn't bury me in them. What is it with emergency room doctors and my good boots? Seems like I been here before.

I'd always heard about people dying and seeing a bright light. Mine was different.

I saw my life. Flashes of it. Like a 3-D screen but no canvas. Andie. Brodie. My dad. Black Baldies. Cinch. I was in a lot of them. And a lot of the pictures of me included weapons of some kind. Handguns. Rifles. Shotguns. Yet, here I lay dying. Ironic.

Then the strangest thing happened. This little girl walked in.

# CHAPTER FORTY-FIVE

Dear God,

They been in there operating on Cowboy for eight hours. They say he lost most of his blood. They're asking people to donate. Even put it out on the local radio. I tried but mine don't work. Wrong letter. Neither does Momma's. Dumps's does. He gave double.

I met Cowboy's wife. Her name is Miss Andie. She's been crying a lot. She's real pretty. I asked her if she wanted some coffee and she shook her head. Then nodded. I handed it to her and her hands were shaking so she grabbed it with two hands. Then she kissed me on the cheek. Her face was wet. Brodie's over there now sitting next to her. He's holding her hand. His face is real red and his eyes look bloody.

There's a bunch of other Texas Rangers here, waiting. Many were at the prison tonight. They're standing in a circle. Maybe they're talking to you, too.

I'm real worried. Momma is, too. The reason my handwriting is real bad is 'cause my hands are shaking.

We're in a bad way here, but not as bad as Cowboy. They say he's a fighter, but there's a lot of whispering going on that I can't hear.

I'll bet you can. And if you can, you need to be listening.

# CHAPTER FORTY-SIX

Dear God,

Are you listening? If you're not, I'm never talking to you again.

# CHAPTER FORTY-SEVEN

Dear God,

There's people screaming at the end of the hall. A doctor just came out and shook his head. Momma's on the floor. Dumps is crying. Brodie, too. Andie is screaming your name.

I see pain all around me.

Why weren't you listening? Why didn't you do anything?

I got something I want to say to you but you got to be in there with Cowboy if you want to hear it. Otherwise, this is my last letter to you. What you do is up to you. But, if you want me to talk to you anymore, then I need you in there right now. That's my deal with you. I'm going in there and you better be there. God? Are you hearing me? I can forget what Billy done but I can't forget this.

This right here...this is the thing between you and me.

# CHAPTER FORTY-EIGHT

The flashes faded. Just before the lights went black, I remember watching a little girl—one I knew or had known—walk up next to me, and the messy table I was lying on. She was clutching something that looked like a notebook. Her eyes were big as Oreo cookies but she wasn't afraid. Wasn't shaking. I remember somebody yelling and pulling on her. I remember her pulling away, and returning to my side. She stood there, studying me. Bold as an August moon. After a moment, she lifted her hand and laid it across my forehead, like she was checking me for a fever. She leaned in, pressed her lips to my ear, and whispered over me like water. I couldn't hear what she said 'cause my ears were coming disconnected from me. Or, I was coming disconnected from my ears. Not really sure. Anyway, I couldn't hear too well. Least not what people were saying on this side of the grave. She stood there a minute, hugging my head, whispering in my ear. Talking to the man who used to be me. I watched from somewhere above the lights. Given that perspective, I'm pretty sure I wasn't in there anymore.

I looked at my hands. Or saw them. I'm not sure. I didn't lift my head 'cause I was looking down on me and I didn't move. Anyway, they appeared before my eyes. They were cut. Bloody. Splintered with glass and pieces of wood. I couldn't move my fingers. No matter. They didn't hurt. I remember wondering, how many thousands of rounds had they fired? Tens of thousands. Each one measured. Each controlled. Each intended. Then I thought of Andie. How I loved that woman at one time. How I wanted to give her all of me, yet only gave her half. Then something tore us apart. Something I couldn't see. I was sorry for that.

The moment she had passed Brodie into my arms, for reasons I can't explain, I'd shaved off half my heart. Lived out of one half. The tough, Ranger half. Why? 'Cause it was easier. Now, as that half lay dying, the other half started thumping again. The half of me that Andie had wanted and needed all along. The half that knew love and gave it—no matter the cost.

I hadn't felt this alive...ever. And yet, by some accounts, I was already dead. The blue flat line and single tone above me said so. I'd trained so hard. Wrapped my life in the study of weapons craft. Ever ready for the rescue. Willing to die, in order to live. Lying here covered in holes, my life draining out of me, it hadn't really worked out the way I'd hoped. It's a tough world. And no, it's not fair. This right here is the price we pay. I know all that. But, how then do I live? How do you really live on the other side of the rescue?

Life felt so good in the few seconds I had to live it.

When she finished, she kissed my head and closed her eyes. My blood had smeared across her cheek. I can't tell you what she said. I have no idea. I wasn't in me. I just know that something about her words, the way she spoke them was like a hook. It snatched me off the lights and shoved me back into me. A roller-coaster ride in reverse. All the current of those white paddles couldn't hold a candle to the power of whatever she whispered in my ear.

Whereas I'd been staring down on me, now, I was staring through me. My eyes. A black-and-white screen. It flickered. Sparked. The gray faded. Color bled in. The oil was mixing with the water.

I do remember that.

# CHAPTER FORTY-NINE

Dear God,

Thanks. Thanks a lot.

# CHAPTER FIFTY

The rest is a little fuzzy and you'll have to forgive me if I don't get it just right. The word "hysteria" comes to mind—people shouting, some laughing, and lots crying. Sounded like somebody was banging pans or . . . anyway the noise was real loud. Even in my bad ear. I wanted to tell everybody to calm down, but my mouth wouldn't work right. Neither would my eyes. I pushed and pushed but couldn't get them to crack. Then that little girl kissed my bloody face and my eyes flew open.

The doctor was hollering, "Tyler! Tyler! You with me? Blink your eyes if you can hear me."

I pulled the mask off and whispered. "I'll do most anything if you quit screaming in my face."

I remember the sound of laughter. The sight of people hugging. Of tears shed and wiped. But the strangest thing was the sensation inside me. My heart was pumping. Both halves. That may not strike you as a big deal, but when you've lived life with half a heart for so long, to all of a sudden have the spigot turned on full...well, you should try it sometime.

Time passed. I don't know how much. An hour. A day. Maybe two. I couldn't tell you. When I opened my eyes again, I was in a big room. Flowers everywhere. People whispering. A man stood over me. White coat. A smile. He held out his hand and dropped two small lima bean–shaped items into my hand. He said, "We took these from your leg. One new. One old. Thought you might keep them as souvenirs."

I clasped my hand around them.

I closed my eyes. Tried to remember. How'd I get back here? Last thing I remembered I was in some place with white lights and sounds and sights like I ain't ever heard or seen and...I can't even put it into words. Don't know how. All I know is I was there and then somebody spoke words in my ear, and now I'm here and I'm wondering how I got back.

Somebody raised the head of my bed. Electronically. Sat me up. I glanced in the corner and saw that little girl standing there. Clutching her notebook. She was the one whispered in my ear. Hope. That's her name. Hope. I think that's a good name for a girl. Whoever named her sure knew what they were doing.

She walked over. I swung my head left. I was real tired. Any movement at all exhausted me. I opened my hand. She slid hers in mine. It was small. Warm. Tender.

I think some people take all the pain they've been knowing their whole life and pack it down inside them where it festers, oozing pus. Gangrene of the soul. That sore then becomes them. It's what bubbles up. You can smell it. Then there's others, others who ain't never done much of anything wrong. Maybe we once called them innocent. And maybe a great wrong was committed on them. Maybe worse than most anything we can imagine. And yet, for some reason, they take that wrong and don't pack it down. Don't hold on to it. Instead, They let it go so that it can't sour them. Like a mist, it rises up and evaporates 'cause it's got no place to call home. And out of that place inside them something else bubbles up and they offer that instead. I can't tell you what that little girl spoke in my ear. I'm not sure I was in there to hear it. I think I'd already left. All I can tell you is that when she did, a crack appeared in the universe and where evil had tried so hard to pull me out, something else reached in and pulled me back. A tug of war. And evil lost.

That's a good feeling.

I whispered, "Come here." She leaned in. "Closer." She pressed her ear close to my lips. "Thank you."

She looked at me. Surprised. "For what?"

I smiled. "For coming…" I swallowed. My throat was dry. She placed ice on my lips and I pushed it around with my tongue. "…to my rescue." I raised my good arm, or at least the one that hadn't been shot, pressed her cheek to my lips, and kissed her. She nodded, squeezed my hand, and stepped back.

Captain Packer rolled his wheelchair in, banging the door. An angry nurse ran behind him. His boots rose up below his hospital gown. He rolled up next to my bed, extended his arm, pinned my cinco peso to the pillow and sat back, breathing heavy. He was pale. He'd lost a lot of blood, too. He nodded. "You dropped that. Thought you'd want it back." He tried to laugh. "It's a little charred. And there's a dent in it, but…it still means what it means."

I nodded. "Yes, sir."

I woke up a while later and it was dark. I saw a bunch of tiny blue and red lights and numbers that I assumed measured some aspect of my being alive. A fluorescent glow spilled out under the bathroom door. Water was running. Somebody was ringing out a rag or towel. My sheets were slid off me, my skin was cold. Wet. Part of me felt clean and part did not. Part felt sticky. I smelled soap. Perfume. I thought, Lord I'm dying again and here they are preparing me for burial.

A nurse stepped out of the bathroom with a small bucket and a rag. She set it next to me, and gently sponged my leg and foot. Then my stomach, groin, and arms. There was another woman, a second nurse judging by her colorful scrubs. She was helping move me around. Somebody moved the catheter coming out of me. I grunted. "Please, whatever you do. Don't pull that."

Quiet laughter rose above me. I opened my eyes and the nurse was smiling. She said, "Don't worry."

My eyes focused and Sam was sponging my leg and stomach. Wiping the blood off me. I shook my head. She leaned in. "You okay?"

I nodded. "Yeah, I just had this figured different in my mind."

She smiled. "Me, too."

I whispered, "Either of you know how to shave a man?" They shook their heads. "When you can, would you put in a call to Georgia and ask her if she'd come shave my face. I'd be grateful. This stuff is about to itch me to death."

The next time I saw sunlight, I cracked open my eyes and focused across the room. Brodie was coiled up in a chair looking at me. I nodded at him and spoke in a cracked whisper. "How's my boy?"

He unfolded and stood up. "I drew you a picture." He handed it to me. It was a crude picture of a man on a horse, tending cows. The man had an "S" on his chest. "Thought you'd like that."

He put his arm around mine. "How you feeling?"

I smiled. "Like I been rode hard and put up wet."

He liked that. "We were all scared for you."

I swallowed. My throat was sore. Like somebody'd been plungering it. "Were you?"

"Yes, sir."

"It's okay to be scared. It means you know what you're up against." He stood there. Looking at me. I said, "I been thinking..."

"Yes, sir?"

The drugs were making my head squirrelly. "How would you feel...It's totally up to you, but I'm going to need a partner and... how would you feel about going into the cattle business with me?"

He smiled. "I'd like that."

"We'd split everything. Fifty-fifty. Try to make enough money to send you to college."

He nodded. Smiling wider.

I made as serious a face as I could. "There's just one problem."

"Sir?"

"There ain't never been a cowboy yet who raised cattle without a horse, so soon as I get out of here, we're going to get a loan from the bank and then we're going shopping. Get you a horse."

His chest swelled three inches. "Yes, sir."

You ain't never seen so many flowers. I pulled the cards out of several and sent Brodie down the hall. He set them in people's rooms who were sleeping. The nurses started calling him the Flower Fairy. He liked it. My room became a revolving door, or at least the outside of it did. News media, camera crews, politicians, even the governor. They said my running the truck into the building, then charging upstairs, was the damnedest thing they ever heard of, but that I came by it honestly. I said Captain would have done the same for me. He laughed, shook his head, and said, "Knowing what I know now, I'm not so sure."

I lay in that bed, crapping in a little white bucket for nearly a week. Finally, I got so tired of it, I sat up on the edge of my bed, leaned on my crutches, and stood. Sam was sitting in a chair reading, and it's a good thing, too, 'cause when I stood, the whole world went tumbling and I almost pancaked my face on the floor. She caught me, said, "Better not try that again." I nodded and slept for what she said was three more days. My body was fighting a good bit of infection. Seems you poke enough holes in a man, drain most of his blood, basically kill him, and that happens. They pumped me full of some nuclear antibiotics, and told me to hold tight.

Georgia came by, filled us in on all the gossip and gave me the closest shave I ever had. I told her she ought to start offering it as a service at her salon. Men would be lined up out the door. She shook her head and spoke as much with the straight razor as she did her mouth. "Other than you, I don't really like too many men. Best to keep me and my razor away from their necks. I'm liable to go to work on them, especially the ones with secrets."

I nodded, my eyes trained on the razor. "Good idea."

Another week passed. My condition improved and my fever broke. As my strength increased, I began walking, or hobbling, around the fifth floor. The hole in my right shoulder made walking on crutches tough so I only used one on the left. Hope and Sam came by every day, often bringing Brodie after school. Andie did not. I heard she was living with Jill Sievert. Jill and her husband had a goodly-sized ranch where they raised and trained cutting horses. They had a guesthouse out back. I'd also heard she'd found work though I didn't know where. I never saw her but I had a feeling she'd been in to see me. If you want to know the truth, I could smell her. You sleep with someone twelve years and pretty soon you can do that. Smell where they've been.

I had a lot of time to think. More than I wanted. Because a hospital is a terrible place to try and get some sleep, my sleep cycle was all backward and upside down so I dozed during the day and sat up nights. I also found myself looking at my hands, reliving things, like they could tell me something. But they didn't say a thing. Couple of nights, I found myself looking in the mirror. Asking questions. One morning, about 2:00 a.m., I asked myself a question I could not answer. It started with "What if—" and never ended with any resolution.

Three weeks after the prison riot, they released me. Dumps

brought me a new pair of boots for which I was real thankful. Black calf with a snip toe. Paul Bond would have been proud. He said, "A cowboy without a pair of boots is like, well, it's just not right." Brodie brought me a new Resistol.

Sam knelt next to the bed, pulled on my socks, and helped me slide my feet into the new boots. She was tugging on the right boot when she said, "What size shoe do you wear?"

"Twelve."

"You have big feet."

I tapped her on the shoulder and winked. "You know what they say about a man with big feet."

She frowned and looked over her shoulder. "No, do tell."

"Big"—I paused and smiled—"shoes."

She laughed. I had grown to welcome her laugh. It was easy. Flowed liberally. And lit up a room.

I shook hands with the medical staff and thanked them for what they did. I'd been shot seven times, twice in the lungs. How they patched me up was no small task. I should not be alive. We cheated the reaper and all knew it. Brodie rolled a wheelchair into the room and the doctor told me to "sit."

I shook my head. "No thank you."

He said, "Ty, it's hospital policy."

I said, "Doc, have I been a pretty good patient? Done what you asked?"

"Yes."

"Have I argued with you once about any single thing you've asked me to do?"

He smiled. "No."

"And I've let you stick me with a thousand needles?"

"Yes."

"Then please understand." I snugged the new hat down tight on my head. "This is Tyler's policy." I leaned on my left crutch and extended my hand to the doc. "Thank you for what you done." He handed me a small package wrapped in brown paper. It was soft.

Like clothing. I peeled back the paper and found my blue T-shirt, washed and folded. Someone had sewn it together and patched the holes. He said, "Thought you might want that."

I did. "Thanks."

After the doc left, I changed into the shirt, put my right arm around Brodie, and started out of the hospital the same way they carried me in. Just with a few less holes.

Together, me and Brodie began walking to the elevator. He punched the button, the door opened, and the two of us stepped in. When the doors closed, I looked down on him. "Brodie?"

"Yes, sir."

"You don't have to be a lawman when you get older."

He looked up. "I know."

The bell dinged as we passed the third floor. It dinged again as we passed the second. "Dad?"

"Yes."

"I want to."

The doors opened and sunlight climbed the walls. "I know." He got that from me.

Sam drove us home where Georgia and a bunch of the folks in town had put together a welcome home party. Captain Packer's wife, Sophia, met me at the front door and kissed me square on the mouth. Thanked me. I sat on the swing on the porch and watched everybody fuss over me. It was a little more than I could handle. Toward dark, most everybody left. Brodie and I sat on the swing for a long time, talking about cows and horses and a canoe trip he wanted to take on the Brazos. I kept starting out across the pasture where Cinch stood by himself. Alone. May was gone. Andie had taken her.

Maybe that was a good picture of me.

Captain Packer strolled out of the house, sat down, and the three of us tested the weight limit of the swing. After a few minutes, he tilted his hat back and looked at Brodie. "Son, would you mind running inside and getting me some lemonade or something?"

Brodie stood. "Are you wanting to talk grown-up stuff and don't want me around?"

Captain laughed. "Yes."

Brodie smiled.

Captain looked at me. "Oh, and, you're reinstated. Like it or not." He shook his head. "Besides, you need the money. And what else are you going to do? You're not fit to be a normal human being. Normal human beings don't drive trucks into front doors."

He had a point.

"The DPS is giving you a vehicle allowance. You can spend it how you like on what you like. So, do yourself a favor, be a real cowboy, and buy yourself a Ford with a big diesel." He spat. "Why you ever drove a Dodge is just beyond me."

I laughed. He was really fired up.

"We confirmed that the prison riot was ordered by Chuarez. He'd hoped to escape during the confusion." He pulled a toothpick from his shirt pocket, picked at his front teeth, and spat. "He did not. Eleven prisoners died. Coroner confirmed from ballistics that I shot two." He shook his head, tried not to smile. "Some other Ranger shot the rest. A couple dozen more were wounded." He tongued the toothpick to the other side of his mouth. "Oh, and Chuarez ain't getting out. In case you were wondering."

Sometime after ten, I got Brodie to bed. He'd been running on emotion and adrenaline for the better part of a month. He crashed. My sleep cycle had not improved so while the rest of Texas was going to sleep, I was just getting going. With the house quiet, I grabbed my crutch and hobbled down the path to the river. I took my time, three steps and five breaths. Five steps and eight breaths. It took me the better part of an hour. The smells had changed. I missed my cows. I missed Mr. B. And, in truth, I missed my wife.

I walked to Dad's grave. Rolled a cigarette. Lit it, drew deeply, and laid it, smoking, atop Dad's headstone. The smoke curled up, climbing the air. Good or bad, I'd had a lot of time to think lately. And in that time, I kept coming back around to the same couple of questions. Cinch walked up behind me. Nudged me. That was his way of saying, "Come on, old man, where we going? You've always said life's clearer sitting on my back. Hop on."

I turned around, stroked his chin. "Not yet, old friend. Might be a while. Bullets and bones don't really go together." He licked my fingers. I spoke across him and Dad. "How is it that I can go charging into a burning building, bullets striking my windshield, but when it comes to love, my marriage, and my wife, I run the other way?" The smoke spiraled but he didn't answer. I leaned on my crutch, unholstered the 1911, press-checked it and felt the round in the chamber with my index finger. Then I stood staring at its dull satin finish in the moonlight. I turned it in my hand. Maybe dying brings clarity. I voiced the second question: "All the weapons I've trained with are designed to stop threats I can see, but when it comes to my marriage, I might as well be shooting spitballs." I brushed my thumb along the slide. "This thing is powerless against the thing that's killing me." I stared down over the river and struggled with the question that had been on the tip of my tongue for weeks. The one I was afraid to ask.

I got to the bank and stood inches from the water. I was pretty sure I'd never get my boots off and certain I'd never get them back on, so I shuffled in, knee deep, then sat down next to a big smooth rock and leaned into the current.

The water rose up around my neck and rolled off my shoulders. It soaked me clean through. My mind was spinning. I lay back against the rock, staring up. I can't really tell you what I was thinking. There was too much. Where to start? I thought about those thirsty Spanish boys, a couple hundred years ago, stumbling upon this river after having been lost in the desert. Maybe they were right. Things get a lot clearer when you look at life from the closer side of death.

I thought about the two women in my life. Yes, I still loved my wife. Even after everything. And, yes, I had fallen in love with Sam.

All the way. That put me in a bit of a pickle. Split me in two. Admitting it didn't make it any easier. Just brought it out under the moonlight.

I'd spent half my life fighting an enemy I couldn't see. An enemy no pistol or rifle or nuclear blast would kill. Every day I came home from work, it'd been there waiting on me. I just didn't know it, or couldn't see it, until now. Dad was right. A prowling lion.

I stayed there long enough to get pruny. Climbing out I weighed a lot more than I did when I climbed in. And it wasn't all water. I knew what I had to do and I knew it was going to hurt a lot more than being shot.

Both of us.

Time to rush in.

# PART FOUR

If you go amongst the Philistines, it's best to go armed.

—Louis L'Amour

He trains my hands for war and my fingers for battle.

—David

# CHAPTER FIFTY-ONE

A week passed. I got rid of the crutch, and got pretty good at masking my limp. It only hurt when I put weight on it so half the time I was fine. It was past breakfast. Sun was up. Brodie was fishing in the river. Dumps was working in the barn. I rubbed my eyes and pulled myself out of bed. I was tired. My strength was slow in returning. With my mind spinning 24/7, trying to rehearse the words I'd need, I slept little. No matter what I did, I could not turn it off. I showered, shaved, and told Dumps I'd be back in a bit. I drove slowly, trying to find a way out. None existed.

I climbed the steps and Sam opened the door before I knocked. "Hi." She was bouncy, happy to see me.

"Hey."

She stepped through the door and kissed me, brushing my cheek with her thumb and palm. Not liking what she saw, she read my face. I read confusion and fear on hers. A glimmer of something she didn't like. I'm afraid I couldn't hide it. She spoke softly, shaking her head. "You're not here to finish our date...are you?"

I took off my hat and shook my head.

She shut the door and we stood on the porch. Her eyes were welling up. She was barefoot and kept looking at her toes, rubbing the lime green flaking paint on the porch.

I turned my hat in my hand. "How's Hope?"

She didn't look at me. "Good. Real good. We got more guinea pigs than we know what to do with." Hope appeared in the window holding Turbo and three other little pigs. She was smiling. Sam shooed her away. I set Sam on the porch swing and stood in front of her. I had a lot to get out so standing was better.

I set my hat down, shoved my hands in my pockets. "I've been thinking about my life lately. Being reflective. Running things over in my mind. Maybe it started in that hospital bed, but it's a place I've come to. Where I've ended up." Her eyes were expectant. Big as half dollars. "I suppose you can blame Texas, you can blame my dad, you can blame me for being stubborn and hardheaded, and I guess you could even blame the Rangers and the fact that I been shot full of holes, but whatever the reason, I have reduced all the events in my life to one of two things. To something rather simple. So I can make sense of it. Maybe the more educated would say it differently but I break it down to two words: thunder and rain." She crossed her legs and swung slowly.

I continued, "These are the moments in my life. The epochs. I say 'thunder' because in those moments I've been rattled, shaken, and maybe my heart skipped a beat or two, or several. Moments when I've known that evil is real. That it is aimed at me. That I am opposed. Directly. Thunder brings lightning and lightning a storm. Storms like: Momma leaving, holding Daddy as he lay dying, finding Andie blue and unresponsive on the bathroom floor, getting shot and being set on fire, pulling the trigger on Mr. B, losing the herd and the Corvette, walking through a weed-covered garden, finding out about Hope and what happened to her, and finally…" I looked out toward the prison.

"Out here in West Texas, we get something other folks don't get. We get to see a storm coming. Get to feel the wind turn, watch the sky roll into a dark thunderhead, and marvel as lightning licks the earth from a long way off. Sometimes it takes an hour to get to us. Sometimes it's here afore you know it."

I nodded. Paused. "I've known my fair share of storms. Some would say an unfair share. I don't know. Seems about right to me. I do know that I cringe now at thunder 'cause I know what's coming. I been through it. It don't let up. But, but on the other side, if I can get there, if I can make it, if I can hold on…is, well, on that side… is the rain."

I turned. Stared west. "I did some reading once on rain. Went to the library and looked it up. There's been a lot written about it. Most is utter nonsense, but people been talking about rain since before they could write. Early philosophers thought water was everywhere. Literally. This guy named Thales thought water surrounded us cause it falls from above, if you dig you hit it, if you walk you run into it. Say what you want, but he has a point."

I turned back to her. "I guess the point I'm trying to make and not making very well is that I can make my own storms, maybe I'm a close kin to thunder, but"—I shook my head—"I can't make the rain. All I can do is stand in it when it does fall. And I have. Gladly. In those moments, I've breathed deeply. Laughed quickly. Felt tenderly. Loved completely. And cried so hard I thought I'd have no more tears only to watch one more fall to the ground. Moments where I've reached out, and somebody's hand found mine. Where good surrounded me. Where someone defended me. Stood over me. I've known these moments, too: talking with my dad behind the garage after fighting some boys after school, my first ride in that Corvette, marrying Andie, holding Brodie, Captain pinning my dad's star on my chest, picking up Dumps on the curb and watching him learn to walk through doorways without asking permission, putting José in prison." I paused. Made eye contact. "Falling for you, then falling for Hope, opening my eyes in that hospital and finally, walking out. There have been more."

She was teary. I wasn't finished. "Maybe it's in those moments that I know I'm not alone and I don't walk alone. That I won't. When the thin whisper of a veil between what I can't see and what I can is pulled back and for one brief second I get a glimpse of what will be. Where the words 'might' and 'hope' intersect."

I reached for her hand. She stood. "Samantha, you have been rain on my face. On all of me. You washed off the storm. I won't never forget that." A tear trailed down her face. I shook my head once. "But years back I made a promise to Andie. We were picking out rings. I told her if she ever lost her way, that"—I nodded, looked down— "I'd come for her. Always. I told her that. Gave her my word."

She started crying. She knew what was coming. "Sam—" She nodded, took a step back. "I told you once I saw the soul of a woman crack in half. Well, I caused the crack. It was me. If I stay here with you, I'm no different. Still that same me. Only way I can see to start over is to keep my word. To go back to the place where I got it wrong and make it right." She was nodding, arms crossed. "Sam?" I lifted her chin. "I love you. I do. But—"

She looked at me. "What about you? What about what's right for"—she jabbed me in the chest with her finger—"you."

I shook my head.

She whispered, glancing at the house. "We'll pack up. Leave first thing."

"I been thinking about that, too. You don't have a thing to be ashamed of. Neither of us do. I think you should stay right here. In Rock Basin. There's an old saying around here that when you hit rock bottom, you start over. Some folks think it's how we got our name. I don't know. Anyway, you should stay. Build a life. Be my friend. Be Andie's friend. She's gonna need it. That may be hard. May be tough. But, your leaving here—that don't feel right. You ain't done a thing wrong. Done everything right. So, stay here. Let

Hope grow up here. Brodie'll look after her. Me, too. I don't know how to do this any other way, but, if you're leaving cause you think you got to hide or be ashamed, you got no reason."

I handed her the papers from my back pocket. "I went and saw the widow. Told her what I wanted to do. She said she was going to leave this place to me anyway, so she just gave me the deed. Signed it over. I took and had the attorney make it right. It says right here that you own this place. It ain't much but it's yours. And she threw in the truck. Thought you could use it."

She clutched the papers to her chest. Shaking her head. "I knew from the moment I met you that I could never have you. Every time I tried to walk inside you, and ask you to love me, I was bumping into the shadow of somebody that'd already been there."

I watched her and the hurt in me grew. Rising up. She'd been hurt so much. I was just one more in a string of many. She stepped back, then gingerly forward, pressing her forehead to mine. "I won't know how to be around you."

I shook my head. "You be you. I'll be me. We got nothing to hide from. Done nothing I regret."

She closed her eyes. "Cowboy, I'll never find another man like you."

I lifted her chin. "Sam, don't ever hang your head around me. Not around any man. You're...you're a gentle, welcome rain."

She smiled. Wiped away the tears. Tried to nod.

I turned, walked to the steps. I knew she was looking. Wanted to know if I'd look back. I turned. My hat in my hand. "That day, on the river...you...well, not laying you down on the riverbank and kissing you until the day turned to night and the next day was one of the toughest things I've ever done." I tugged my hat down over my eyes and left her standing on the porch, clutching those papers.

I drove down to the river. Found Brodie cutting up hotdogs and baiting a trot line for catfish. I stepped out, pulled my sunglasses down over my eyes. "What're you doing?"

"Fishing." The sight of him did my heart good. He asked, "What're you doing?"

"Was wondering if maybe you wanted to go shopping with me."

"What for?"

"Something I need to get for your mom."

He dropped the hotdogs and wiped his hands on his pants. "Sure."

We drove to town and parked in front of the jewelry store. He smiled as we stepped out, walked in. We stared through the glass and I pointed at something that looked like what his mom had passed up twelve years ago. A rectangular solitaire set in a silver band. I asked, "How much?"

The man behind the counter told me.

I scratched my head. I'd never been too good at dickering for anything other than cows and old cars. "Does it have to be that expensive?"

He smiled. "Memorial Day Sale starts this weekend. But we can start celebrating today if you like. And—" He held a finger in the air. "We got a two-week return policy if it doesn't work."

I wasn't too worried about that. I had just enough credit on my Visa to make it work. I handed the card to Brodie and said, "Pay the man."

Brodie was beaming.

I steered and worked the clutch while Brodie shifted gears. We drove to Jill's. She had a large barn out back. We circled the house, and I parked. Brodie and I stepped out. I was heading toward the house, but heard Andie talking in the barn.

Evidently, she heard us, too, 'cause she came walking out sitting on top of May. Andie was wearing a hat, her jeans, a tank top, and her riding boots that Dumps had made her.

Lord, that woman looks good sitting atop a horse.

She hopped off and hugged Brodie. Holding him a long minute. He wrapped his arm around her waist and stood smiling at both of us. He nodded at me.

I cleared my throat. Looking for a starting place. This was harder than I thought it was going to be. I brushed the toe of my boot on the back of my jeans. Brodie was standing next to her, his arm around her waist, her arm around his shoulder. She glanced behind her. Her hair had grown. The ends had been trimmed. No longer frayed. She whispered. Her word broke. "Hey."

I took off my hat, hung it on Brodie's head. "I been thinking about how to say this and I don't know...so, just let me try. Twelve years ago, you married a man who promised you one thing and gave you another. He promised you his heart, but when it came time to give it to you, he gave you half. Or kept, half from you. Depending how you want to look at it." A wrinkle appeared on her forehead. I wasn't making sense and she couldn't tell where this was going. Her eyes shone glassy. I shook my head. "You and me, we got a lot of hurt here. But, I think—no, I know that at bottom, I caused it 'cause I never gave you the me that you deserved. The me that you fought for. All those nights—" I shook my head. "You dealt with the pain a long time, then when you couldn't take it any longer you tried to ease it with what you could. Yes." I nodded. "That hurts me. Images on the backsides of my eyelids that I see when I close my eyes. I don't like them. But—" I reached up and untied the string that held the ring around her neck. "Long time ago we walked into a store and you bought what didn't scare me. What didn't cost me much. You didn't ask for what you should have and I didn't have the gumption to do what I ought. I wasn't the man I should've been. Right there in that store I made you a promise. Told you I'd come for you. So..." Brodie smiled, reached in his pocket and laid it flat across his mom's palm. "Andie, I don't really know how to be all my heart is telling me I need to be but I know I want to. I know...I tried to give my heart away to another but I can't give what I already gave. So, either give me my heart back, or let's start over."

She stared into her palm. I was schoolboy giddy.

That is until Dr. Earl Johnson walked out of the barn leading a horse. He was wearing a hat he just bought, tennis shoes, khakis, and blue dress socks. His face was puffy and bruised. Andie looked

331

at him, then me. She handed May's reins to Brodie, "You hold her a minute for me?"

Brodie's jaw was hanging down around his belt. He nodded. She walked me around the barn, out of sight. She eyed the ring. Turning it over in her palm. "It's pretty."

I was starting to get a bad feeling about this.

"There was a time when it was all I wanted." She looked at me and passed it back across the distance between us. "When you were." She placed it in my hand, crossed her arms. "Tyler, you gave me Brodie and for that I'll always love you, but I don't want to live with you anymore. Don't want to be married to you." She shook her head, patted her chest. "I don't want your heart and all the ache that comes with it. You'll always be a cowboy and I've had my fill of them."

"What about...him? Earl. He's...he's all hat and no cattle." Not to mention married.

She nodded. "Maybe. But he doesn't hurt me. And I'm tired of hurting." She squeezed my hand. "Tyler, you're a good man. In some ways, the best kind. In others—" She shook her head. "No more hospital emergency rooms. No more nights alone. No more. I just don't want to be married to you anymore." She walked around the barn, kissed Brodie and pulled him to her chest, climbed up on May, and clicked twice with her mouth. Earl failed to get his foot in the stirrup on the first and second try, finally succeeded on the third, pulled himself up into the saddle, and held on for dear life while the gelding trotted after May.

I stood there, my eyes narrow, scratching my head. Andie and Earl disappeared into the trees leaving only their dust. The cloud settled on my lips and left me dry. Brodie looked at me. Trying to read my face. I didn't know what else to say. I turned to him. "I had that pictured differently in my mind." I looked toward the trees. "Saw that working out different."

Brodie nodded.

I scratched my head and heard myself talking to myself. "Dying is easy. It's the living that's tough."

\*　　\*　　\*

I don't really remember driving home but when we pulled into the drive, Brodie said, "You mind if I ride Cinch a while?"

I nodded. "Sure."

He threw a saddle on the old man and the two went ambling off over the pasture. I stood there, stumped. My thumbs hanging onto my jean pockets. Dumps walked out of the barn, saw me, and said, "Looks like it didn't go the way you were hoping."

"You might say."

He disappeared back into the barn.

I looked at my life. No cows. No car. No girl. A garden filled with weeds.

If it hadn't hurt so much it would have been comical. Problem was, it hurt. A lot. I rolled a cigarette, lit it, inhaled deeply, and blew gently into the breeze coming across my face. The smoke exited me, paused briefly in a small white cloud, was gathered by the breeze and washed back across me. I breathed in, filling my stomach. I did that several times. When I'd drawn it down to the nub, I flicked it into what remained of the tomato garden, walked to the house, slid the ring and its little blue box inside a sock, and set it in the top drawer of my dresser. The words "two-week return policy" kept ringing in my ears. I sat down on the end of my bed and put my hands on my knees. I had no idea what to do.

Brodie returned about dark. I fried some pork chops and scrambled eggs for dinner. We ate in the quiet. The only sound was the clock ticking on the wall. It got so loud, clicking and clicking, I finally stood, pulled out the batteries, and set them on the counter. About then, the crickets cranked up out the window. I stood and closed it. Dumps stirred his eggs around his plate. "You gonna take the batteries out of them, too?"

"Sorry."

Brodie was gnawing on a bone, sporting a greasy milk mustache. "Dad?"

"Yeah."

"You can take the ring back, you know?"

"I know."

"If you did, we could take the money and buy me a horse."

I nodded.

"Dad?"

"Yeah?"

He stared at what remained of his pork chop. "She's not coming back."

I nodded. "I know that."

"Dad?"

"Yes."

He stared up at me. Shook his head. "She's not coming back."

"You just said that."

He nodded. "Well... one of us needs to."

I ran my fingers through his hair. "We'll make the rounds tomorrow. See if we can find you a horse."

We finished dinner in silence, and I did the dishes while Dumps and Brodie watched a John Wayne movie. Sleep did not appeal to me so I walked to the river. I couldn't get my wife back and I couldn't go back to Sam. She'd forever feel like second fiddle. I wouldn't do that to her. She deserved better. She deserved to be somebody's first choice. Not their consolation prize.

The next morning, I drove to town. The salesman saw me walk in and his smile melted. I laid the sock on the counter. The shape of the box stuffed inside. He scratched his head. "Guess it didn't work."

I spoke matter-of-factly. "No, it did not."

"I 'magine it wouldn't really help matters for me to try and sell you something else?"

"No, it would—" I stopped short. There were six billion people on the planet. About half were female and let's say for simplicity sake, about a quarter of those were of an age that I could marry. I might bump into some language barriers but certainly, amidst three-quarters of a billion people, I could find one woman who wanted to marry a man like me. My feathers were a bit ruffled and I was borderline pissed, which is a bad combination when it comes to diamonds and money, but I turned to him, "Yes." I set my hat down. "Yes, you can."

He showed me several different rings and to be honest, I let him upsell me. I imagine Brodie would punch my man card for letting him do it but giving back that ring was like giving up for good. It was like admitting I'd never marry again. I'd already set aside money for Brodie's new horse. If I gave him that ring back and got a refund I'd spend the money on something—maybe another new horse, maybe an old Corvette—and then if a miracle happened and I wanted to get married, I'd have nothing to give and be right back where I started. So, I looked through everything he had and I picked out another ring that looked like something I'd want to give a woman. One rectangular stone bordered on each side by a small triangular diamond. Prettiest ring I'd ever seen. Cost me an extra thousand dollars. The salesman rang my card through his machine. He said, "You sure?"

"Yes, I am."

"Well, I almost hate to offer it, but if you change your mind, I'll extend your two-week policy out a few weeks, or longer, if you need."

I thanked him, drove home, put the sock back in the drawer and tried to convince myself that it was a good investment and not an emotional-compulsion buy, that even if I didn't use it that Brodie would one day and, most important, that I felt better.

Problem was, I did not. And when my credit card bill came in the mail in about two weeks, I'd be reminded of that.

The weeks passed. I started back to work. Arrested a few men. Stayed out of and away from gunfights. We found Brodie a good horse. A four-year-old paint. He named him "Dingo," for reasons I can't understand. Fifteen hands. Smart. Lively. Tender when needed. A rare find. If Brodie wasn't sleeping, he was sitting on Dingo. We went camping two weekends in a row. Loaded up the horses, packed some food in my saddlebags, and took off down the river. Slept under the stars. We talked, laughed some, and I marveled at the man that boy was becoming. Oh, and with the department's allowance—and a loan I got from the bank thanks to Mike and the fact that I'm now gainfully employed—and against the captain's better judgment, I bought a new white four-door Dodge 2500 four-wheel drive. And this time, I got an automatic. Brodie thought we'd really moved up in the world. I got the dealer to put aftermarket BFGoodrich tires on it. All the world was right.

Well…

I woke, I worked, I tried to be a father to Brodie. We spent hours setting on the horses. Me, Dumps, and Brodie tried our hand at growing tomatoes. On occasion, I slept some. Fits mostly. Never more than a few hours. I spent a lot of time on the porch, just swinging. I'm not sure why but it's where I often found myself. And I quit rolling cigarettes. Not sure why. I just did. I turned around after a week and realized I'd not rolled one in a while. So, I took the tobacco and papers from my shirt pocket and threw them in the trash. I thought a lot about what Sam told me one time. "To walk with and alongside rather than without and alone." She was right.

I'd heard she'd had a few dates from some of the guys in town. An attorney, a rancher, a real-estate broker, and a guy that owned a Ford dealership. I was happy for her. Glad she had options. She deserved them. I hoped she was happy. Brodie said Hope was doing well in school. Even got a part in the school play. *The Wizard of Oz.* Not sure what role. She'd given away four of the five baby guinea pigs. Kept one for herself, to make sure Turbo wasn't lonely. She told Brodie she was glad to be down to two 'cause seven of those things make a lot of poop.

I started driving to a nearby town to get my haircut. Figured it wasn't too polite to walk into Georgia's salon and act like nothing had ever happened. Figured that might be hard on Sam. Okay... hard on me.

Oh, and the two-week return policy came and went. No matter how I tried, I could not bring myself to take the new ring back. Seemed like it embodied so many changes. So much about me that I'd resolved to change that I couldn't take it back. I decided to eat it and let it collect dust in my drawer.

One night I was driving home and passed by that church outside of town. The marquee read, ELDERS MEETING TONIGHT 7 P.M. It wasn't audible but I swore I heard the name Frank Hamer. I pulled over, let the truck idle. Few minutes later, I attended my first elders meeting.

Ten men sat around a big table, Pastor Kyle was officiating. I walked in, my hat in my hand. No need for introductions. I knew everyone. I nodded at each. "George, Fred, Tom, Steve, Pete, Dave." I made my way around the table. When I got to Kyle I noticed his countenance had changed. He looked whiter. Pale. Sweating all of a sudden. I stood next to him, patted him on the back. "Kyle, how you doing?"

He nodded. Maybe some more of the blood rushed out of his face.

I pulled out my wallet, unfolded the yellowed confession, and stared at it. I pressed it flat, ironing out the wrinkles with my palm. I spoke to the group. "When I was a kid my dad told me a story. In 1835, a fellow by the name of David de la Croquetagne, better known as Davy Crockett, was up for reelection to the U.S. Congress from the state of Tennessee. He told the people of his district that, 'If I lose, you may all go to hell and I will go to Texas.' A man of his word, he did just that. That story stuck with me, as has that idea, that a man ought to do what he says he's gonna do. That if he gives his word, signs his name to something, then he ought to live up to it. To own it." I laid that piece of paper flat across the desk and looked at each man. "I'm sure you all feel the same way being that this is the

Lord's house and all." I scratched my head. Looked at Kyle's milk-white face. "My dad told me something else, too. He said this world is full of evil. Has been since Cain killed Abel. And there's only one way to deal with it." I tipped my hat. "Kyle." I walked out.

I heard the meeting got sort of exciting after that. Least that's what the newspaper said.

School let out and I took a few days off to take Brodie camping and fishing. This time we loaded the truck and drove along the bank till we got to a place we liked. We set up camp, and tied a few trot lines along the bank. We set around the fire, sipping RC Colas and eating MoonPies. Every hour, we'd check the lines. On Friday night, we caught so many catfish, neither of us ever went to sleep. When the sun broke the skyline, we had filled a cooler full of fish.

Brodie was buttering a biscuit next to the campfire at breakfast when he said, "Dad?"

I was cleaning fish. "Yeah."

"I saw Miss Sam yesterday."

"Yeah?"

He nodded, and spoke with a mouthful of biscuit. "She asked about you."

"What'd she say?"

"She just wanted to know how you were doing, what you were up to. Just little stuff."

"Oh." I let that set a few moments. "Anything else?"

He sucked through his teeth, buttering another biscuit. "Not that I can remember." He swallowed. "Oh, she did say something like she wondered why you were so stubborn that you never came back and asked her to marry you."

I looked at him.

He wasn't looking at me, but he was smiling, eyeing his biscuit.

"She really said that?"

"No, no she didn't. I made that up. But, I've been wondering it just the same."

I wiped my hands and sat down on the log next to him. "Really?"

He looked at me. "Yes, sir. I've been wondering why you don't marry Miss Sam."

"Well, I thought you—"

He shook his head.

"I mean—"

He shook his head again.

"You don't—?"

He put his arm around my shoulder. "Dad, you're pretty good at being a Ranger, but you're kind of dumb when it comes to girls."

"Oh. Really?"

"Yep. Now Miss Georgia said that if you had any balls at all—"

"When did you talk to Miss Georgia about this?"

"Oh, we've talked about it several times."

"You have?"

"Yep. And she said if you had any, you'd quit being so damn stubborn and marry that girl."

"When did you get old enough to cuss?"

He smiled. "About thirty seconds ago."

I pulled his hat down over his eyes and pushed him off the log. He started laughing.

"So, you're okay with . . . me and Miss Sam."

He pushed his hat back on his head. "Yes, sir."

"That would kind of make Hope your little sister."

He nodded. "Yep. Got that, too."

"When did you get so smart?"

"Dad, I watched you drive into a burning building to save a man that meant a lot to you. You been doing that your whole life. For everyone. Me, included. I don't know what Mom's problem is but it's her problem. Not yours. I love Mom, but I think she is selfish and I think you are not. You should be happy. And Miss Sam does that. Matter of fact, I like her a lot. I reckon that's all we need to say."

I put my arm around his shoulder. "You're going to make one helluva lawman."

He nodded. "What makes you say that?"

"You see black and white. Very few shades of gray."

"Dad, I see what is, and maybe sometimes, what shouldn't be, and what should."

"Come on, let's get all this cleaned up. I can't go into Georgia's salon smelling like this."

"Wait, I got something for you." He ran to the truck and came back holding a brown bag. "For you."

I opened it. Inside I found a black, hand-braided, horse-tail hat band. He said, "Dumps helped me. We measured your hat when you weren't looking. Thought you'd like it."

"Son, I can't. You should—"

"We made two."

I slid it on my hat, smiling. I didn't know what to say. "You sure?"

"I'm sure."

"I think Mr. B would be real proud."

"Me, too."

We packed up, drove home, and while he put what we caught into freezer bags, I showered and tried to get the smell of fish off my hands. I shaved, rubbed on that aftershave Georgia gave me. It was too hot to wear a jacket but I slung one over my shoulder just in case.

Brodie gave me two thumbs-up and Dumps smiled, showing the absence of his front teeth. That meant he liked the looks of things. I stepped out of the house looking like the Ranger that I was. Polished boots, ironed jeans, Milt Sparks belt, Milt Sparks holster, and a Les Baer 1911. A starched oxford, Resistol hat with the best-looking hat band in Texas, and a shiny star pinned across my heart.

I drove to town. My mind lost in what to say. When I looked down I was going ninety-seven miles an hour. When I looked up, I saw two flashing blue lights behind me. I pulled over, stepped out, and bumped into my friend the highway patrolman I'd last seen at the prison riot. He stepped out of the patrol car with his hand pressed to the back strap of his Glock. The sun was behind me so he was looking into it. He squinted and began hollering. "Step back and put your hands on the car."

I did as instructed, which exposed both my badge and 1911. He started stuttering and stammering and apologizing as soon as I took off my sunglasses. I had about six inches on him so he had to look up to see me. "Oh, sorry, sir. Didn't know it was you. The new truck threw me."

"I 'magine I was going a little fast."

"Where you headed?"

"A date, I think."

"You think?"

"Well, I reckon I'll find out when I get there."

He nodded. "I hope it turns out the way you want it. Can I do anything for you?"

"No, thanks. I'll slow it down."

"Yes, sir."

He started walking off. "Son?"

"Sir?"

"You ever thought about a career with the Rangers?"

He nodded and smiled. "Most every day of my life." He stepped into his car, honked, sped around me. I sat staring through the windshield thinking to myself: That was me, twenty years ago.

I drove to town observing the speed limit and pulled up to Georgia's. There was a big Ford diesel parked in front so I slid in behind. I licked my thumb, brushed my eyebrows back, and put on my coat 'cause I thought it would cover up my pits, which were sweating something fierce.

I climbed the steps, took off my sunglasses, and walked inside.

Georgia, standing over her chair holding a pair of shears, said, "What the hell you want?" The word "hell" sounded more like "hale" and she added two more syllables.

I swallowed. Sam was being helped into her jacket by Shawn

Johnson—the owner of the local Ford dealership and the truck parked outside. He nodded at me. "Howdy, Ty."

"Shawn."

He shook my hand. "Glad to see you up and around."

"Thank you."

"Everyone's real proud of what you done."

I nodded.

Georgia raised both eyebrows and leaned on the chair. "And?"

I looked at Sam. "I was hoping to—"

"Well, she can't talk to you 'cause she's going on a date."

I looked at Shawn, then Sam. "Oh."

I stepped aside. Shawn opened the door and I tipped my hat as Sam walked out into the sunshine. The door shut and I stood chewing on my lip. I heard laughter behind me. I turned around and Georgia was doubled at the waist. She shook her head. "Cowboy, you've got the romantic inclinations of a piece of burnt toast." She laughed. "But, I hear they're wanting to make you an elder down at the Baptist church. Want to put you on the pastoral search committee." I nodded and watched the Ford drive off. Then I shook my head and drove home.

When I pulled in the drive, alone, Brodie asked, "What happened?"

I told him.

He laughed. So did Dumps.

I didn't think it was very funny.

I was starting to get angry, so I saddled Cinch and told Brodie and Dumps they could find me at the river. I loaded my saddlebags with ammo, climbed up, hooked one leg around the saddle horn, gave him loose reins, and Cinch walked me to the river.

# CHAPTER FIFTY-TWO

The sun hung low and blood red. The earth lay hot and dusty. Come dark, I had the beginnings of a pretty good pity party going. I had cussed everybody that had ever given me advice on love or romance and every stupid thought I'd ever had about the subject. I'd sworn off women, love, even diet sodas 'cause they tended toward the feminine. I built a bonfire and threw wood on top of it until it was too hot to stand within twenty feet. I set up a target on the far bank and, in an hour, put nearly five hundred rounds through my Les Baer. When I finished, the slide was too hot to touch and my feet were mounded in spent brass casings and empty magazines. Empty, and dripping with sweat, I holstered, walked out into the water and sat down. Clothes, boots, hat, and everything. The 1911 made a hissing, steaming sound as the water contacted the hot steel.

It'd been a long time since I was that mad. And the more I thought about it, the madder I got. Somewhere in there I started voicing my opinion on Ford dealerships and the men that owned them and how glad I was that I remained loyal to Mopar. If I'd have been a drinking man, I'd have been too drunk to stand up by now.

I think I was splashing at the water, cussing my hope-filled notions, when I heard footsteps behind me. I was not in the mood for company. "Not now. Not in the mood. Go on and eat without me. I'll be along directly."

The footsteps kept coming. The fire on the bank was roaring and was probably registering on satellites in space. I turned around. The fire lit her face with an orange glow and her eyes sparkled like red candles. She passed through the amaryllis blooms, parting them with her arms, and waded in. She'd pulled her hair up and was lifting her skirt above the water.

When she got to me, she spun me, straddled me, threw her arms around my neck, and kissed me. We stayed there a long time.

When she finally quit kissing me, and I finally quit kissing her, she rested her arms across my shoulders, then slapped me square across the jaw.

"What'd you do that for!"

"That's for making me wait weeks on you and having to go out with all those idiot guys just to make you jealous enough to come get me."

"That's not why I came back. I mean, I am jealous, but I didn't come back 'cause I never wanted you to feel like second fiddle."

She kissed me again. This time better. "Tyler Steele, you ever do that again and I'll shoot you myself."

"But I didn't think—"

"Well, you thought all wrong." She shook her head. "All wrong. I been sitting in that apartment, eating Twinkies, waiting for you to walk back into my life. Then I got so sick of them I quit eating altogether 'cause every time I did, it just came right back up." I thought she looked skinnier but I wasn't about to say anything. "Then you walk in there today, looking like . . . like everything good in this world, right when I'm walking out the door with Bozo the Clown and his stupid, hooked-up truck."

I nodded and smiled. "I do like my Dodge better."

She slapped me again, this time gentler. "Hush. I'm not finished."

"Yes, ma'am."

"So, we go to dinner and I finally look at him and say, 'Shawn, you got to take me home.' So he did. Then me and Hope sat there, waiting on you. But, AGAIN, you never came. So, I drove down here at a hundred miles an hour, scaring Lord knows what out of my little girl, and then I've got to walk down here through all the prickly pears and thorns, and into this river to interrupt your pity party 'cause you're too wrapped up in your own stuff to think of me. Now my underwear's wet, giving me a wedgie, and you know how I hate wet underwear."

"Wow."

She pressed her palms to my cheeks. Drawing me closer. "You understand me?"

I nodded.

She slapped me a third time. "Don't you have anything to say for yourself?"

"Yes." I held my hand up blocking my face. "You slap me again and I'm going to dunk your head under this water."

She kissed my cheek.

I slid off my badge and laid it in her hand.

Tears, or river water, were dripping down her face. I'm not sure, but what's the difference? "Cowboy..." She held my badge in her hand. "For years I've been afraid to give myself, I mean really give all of me, to any man 'cause the only man I ever really cared about left me standing at the altar. Dashing all my dreams. My hopes. You don't have to change." She hung my badge on my shirt, running the needle through the small sewn hole. "Don't be somebody differ-ent. Somebody else. You be you." She rested her forehead on mine. "You rescued me when I thought nobody would. When I thought I wasn't worth the effort. You gave everything and asked for noth-ing." She pressed her face to mine. "If this is life on the other side of the rescue, then I want to live it. With you. But—" She shook her head. "But if you give you to me, then"—she placed her palm flat across my chest—"come heavy."

The river wrapped around me. She was trembling. Her legs were shaking. She needed an answer. I scratched my head. Shook it. "You can't live in West Texas without a horse. You do that very long and people'll think you're weird."

She laughed. Wiped her nose on my sleeve. "Then you can buy me a horse."

I took her face in my hands, brushing away the tears with my thumbs. Our laughter echoed downriver. I said, "Might ought to get Hope one, too."

She pursed her lips. "Might. Probably should."

I shook my head. "This could turn out to be an expensive proposition."

She kissed me. "Yep. Probably will. And it only gets more expensive with time."

"How so?"

"Little girls grow up. They fall in love." She touched my nose with the tip of hers. "Somebody gives them away."

I'd never thought of that. The smile spread across my face. "I'd like that."

She tapped me on the shoulder. "But don't get ahead of yourself."

"Samantha?"

"Yes."

"Like it or not, life is a battle. We wake up in this smoldering hellhole every day, searching scorched earth for—" I held her hand in mine. "What I'm trying to say, and not doing a very good job, is...will you ride the river with me?"

She cried and laughed at the same time. It was a release of emotion she'd been holding a long time. Maybe most her adult life. She nodded and chose her words. She placed her hand on my chest. "Thunder." Then placed mine on hers. "And rain."

I set my hat on her head, stood, lifting her out of the water, and carried her back across the river. She climbed up on Cinch. I stood there, staring. Firelight danced across her face. I climbed up, put my arms around her, and we eased toward the house. It was a good picture. One I wanted to remember. I closed my eyes and let it burn itself onto the back of my eyelids. Moonlight cast our shadow across a cowless pasture. A breeze rolled across us. Texas rolled out beneath us. Blue skies in the distance. The smell of rain in the air.

# CHAPTER FIFTY-THREE

Dear God,

I been thinking and I think you do a pretty good job with all you got going on. I mean, I don't know how you keep it all straight. There's a lot going on down here. If nobody's told you today, you're doing a good job. There were times when I didn't think so. Billy Simmons. Mr. B. Cowboy getting all shot up. And I still don't know why that stuff happens, but even after all that, well, the papers said Billy Simmons is in prison for three lifetimes, which—by the way—doesn't really make sense. How do you serve the second after you're dead following the first. Why don't they send him to prison for the rest of this life? Anyway, Mr. B's mound is covered in grass and next year Brodie said it'll be covered in bluebonnets. And, as for Cowboy, well, just look out there.

Momma and Cowboy are riding back from the river on Cinch. She's sitting up in front of him. Sideways. His arms are wrapped around her. She's soaking wet. He is, too. They're laughing. She's wearing his hat. Looks like Momma found a home for her heart. You can read it on her face. It's like all the pieces finally fit together. Do you think maybe this time things could work out? Momma really deserves to be happy, and Cowboy, too.

I know I'm young, and that I don't know all that adults know but I know this—there were times when I looked around and all I saw was bad. Bad stuff. Bad people. Then, for reasons I can't figure, something happens and Wham! It all turns around. The bad is gone and the good is come.

I know you're probably tired of all my yapping. My teachers tell me I can talk a lot sometimes. There was a time when nobody wanted to hear me and all they kept saying was "shush." So, I did. Then when I got quiet, they told me I should talk, open up, express myself, so I did. I opened my mouth and started to make the words again. Now, they're telling me to "shush." Control my tongue. They need to figure out what they want. Talk or not talk? Make up your mind.

Anyway, I'm going now. Cowboy just took Momma out on the porch and handed her a sock and Lord only knows why. Now she's crying. He's kneeling. I wonder if his leg hurts? Now she's kneeling, too, and she's hugging him. That must be some sock.

I got to go. Momma's calling.

Oh, and God? Keep up the good work. Some of us are paying attention and we appreciate it.

———

Dear God,

Wow, that was fast. You're good. I mean, I know you're Good. But, you're also really good. Momma just showed me what was in the sock. And it's only been like ten minutes since we last spoke.

Thanks, a lot. I won't ask anymore today. You done a lot. You deserve a break. Maybe take a nap or something. We're going off to dinner. Brodie said we're going to Whataburger to celebrate. Dumps just put in his teeth and passed around a Mason jar with part of a bootleg in it so he must be going, too.

Hey, can I ask you one more thing? Miss Georgia, she talks tough but she's lonely and she'd really like a good man to take care of her. Sit with her while she eats dinner and scratch her back at night. Maybe rub cream on her feet. She's got these bunions and she says they hurt her after a long day. She's a real good woman, she'd make a good wife. You think you could find her someone? Haven't you got somebody, somewhere, that needs a friend like Miss Georgia? What about Shawn down at the Ford dealership? He ain't married.

Oh, Turbo wanted me to let you know she's doing just fine and she likes it here. She just walked across my notebook and dropped a turd. That means she's happy.

---

Dear God,

Momma married Cowboy today. They stood beneath what's left of the marrying tree while Mr. Dumps, Brodie, and I stood there staring. The preacher said some real nice words. Momma looked so pretty. Miss Georgia had done her hair all up. Momma was wearing jeans, her new boots, a white linen shirt, and a cowboy hat that Cowboy had given her. But Cowboy slipped it off her head when he kissed her. And she kissed him back, too. It was a good kiss. Not that I really know about such stuff. But they kissed a long time and one of her legs came off the ground like they do in the movies. Momma's ring sure is pretty.

Lots of people came. Bunch of men wearing white hats and silver stars. Cowboy hung his daddy's Stetson and holster over the iron cross at his grave. Like, he wanted him there. I guess he was, too. Miss Georgia's mascara ran all over her face. Looked like a raccoon with orange and purple hair. We all stood out there, circled around the tree. Cowboy said a few words, thanked everybody. He talked to Brodie. Told him, right there in front of you and everybody, how proud he was of him. Said every good thing he ever did and ever hoped was wrapped up inside him. That Texas ain't never done no better than Brodie Steele. Brodie blushed. Then Cowboy talked to Momma, told her how he loved her. How he's sure glad he bumped into us on the interstate.

After the ceremony, Cowboy walked us all to the barn where he swung open the door and walked out Momma's wedding present. A jet-black mare that stands a little over fourteen hands. Prettiest horse I've ever seen. Momma couldn't believe it. Just stood there with her hands over her mouth. Dumps had found her an M. L. Leddy's saddle. Fits her real good. Brodie said that's a big deal. I just have to take his word for it. Momma said she was gonna name her, "Goodness." 'Cause, she told everybody, that's what she'd found in Tyler Steele. I kind of think it's a dumb name but then so is "Turbo" so who am I to talk.

But, that's not the best part. Close, but not really. After Momma got Goodness, Cowboy came over to me, grabbed my hand, and led me outside the barn and around the back. Brodie walked alongside. He was smiling. Cowboy turned the corner and right there in front of everybody he put his hands over my eyes and said, "Don't look." And I didn't neither. And when he took them away, Brodie was standing there with the prettiest bay mare I'd ever seen and they'd tied a red ribbon around her neck. I couldn't believe it. She was beautiful. Had little white patches just above each hoof that looked like she was wearing socks. Cowboy picked me up, just like he done

Momma and he set me on top of that horse and he fixed my stirrups and when he was done, he told me I could name her whatever I want so I asked him if he thought Socks was a good name and he said he thought it was a real good name. And then all four of us rode down to the river.

It was the best day of my life.

Anyway, they're gone now. Went on a honeymoon. Momma and Miss Georgia had gone shopping for some new night-gowns. Momma told me that Cowboy would like them a lot. But I don't know why. She's the one that's got to sleep in them. I saw them and they don't cover up much. The bottom of her butt shows out the back. Might as well wear nothing but, any-way, they've gone up to a cabin in the mountains of Colorado. Be gone a week. Miss Georgia and Dumps are taking care of Brodie and me.

God, I know I'm always bugging you with little stuff that prob-ably don't amount to a hill of beans in your book but I think I've learned something. Something I think might be impor-tant. Like the kind of stuff grown-ups learn. Maybe it's what makes them grown-ups. And it's this—sometimes it's hard to see what could be, what we hope for, through the hurting part of what is, 'cause sometimes stuff hurts so much that we can't see nothing. But then sometimes what we hope for, well, seems like if we hope it long enough, hard enough, deep enough, it becomes what is. Not always, but sometimes. Maybe that's the thing about hope. Maybe it's sort of something special. Like it's the thing that makes the difference. Maybe it's the kind of thing that bad stuff can't kill. Can't get rid of. Not never. No matter who does what to you. Sometimes I wonder if that's what Momma was thinking when she named me. Maybe she'd gotten here, too. Maybe she got here first.

I may be getting ahead of myself, but I had one more thought and it's this—while I think we need hope, I think you need it, too. Like, you need to know that we do. That we still do it. That we're pulling for you 'cause, well, where else can we go? Who else is going to listen? Where else would I take it? And I think the older people get, the less they do it. I think they want to, but I think they're afraid. It's like they bit into a sour apple and now they won't eat no more apples at all. Which is stupid if you think about it. That's like saying that just 'cause you had one sip of sour milk that all milk is bad. Well, that's crazy. I've had a few bad apples, even bad milk, but I've had lots more good. What if I'd have thought that back at the Ritz and never sipped the cream? Just where would I be? It's weird. You got to figure this out to be a grown-up. But once you become one, you got to turn right back around and be more like a kid again. Doesn't that strike you as strange? It does me. Like you got to be both when you can't be but one. It's tricky. Anyway, that's what I think.

I'm going now. I'll write more tonight. Dumps is taking us to Whataburger. They got good cheeseburgers. And lime-ades. And French fries. And chocolate shakes. They put whip cream and a cherry on top. I like being with Brodie. He's a good cowboy. You ought to see him on a horse. I ain't never seen nothing like it. And now that he's my brother, he don't treat me no different. I was worried that he might, that maybe he was too cool to hang out with his sister, but he don't. He opens doors for me, tucks his shirt in, takes off his hat when he walks inside, washes his hands before dinner, holds my foot when I'm trying to get it in the stirrup, lifts the seat before he does his business, shakes hands firmly, and looks people in the eye when he's talking to them. He don't cuss, he don't spit around me, and he don't never walk in front of me but always beside me. All this to say, that I like West Texas. Everything that's good and right and is what it ought to be—well, that's all wrapped up in this thing you made called a "cowboy."

# EPILOGUE

Dear God,

I'm sitting here in Momma and Daddy's house. On the end of
Brodie's bed. Lace and white silk draped about me. My train
is nearly ten feet long. Daddy's coming to get me in a few minutes. Walk me out across a sea of blue to stand beneath the old
tree. Hand me over to Peter. There was a time when I thought
this moment was not possible. That maybe I wasn't worthy of
it. Now it's here and it seems surreal.

Daddy's so proud. You can see it on him. Momma bought
him a new white Stetson. He looks so handsome. The gray
hair above his ears just shows below the brim of the hat. And
Momma made him a hat band out of Cinch's tail. She's been
keeping it since he died.

This room brings back lots of memories. I used to play
Legos over there. Watch movies up here. Talk on the phone
over there. Brodie's aftershave is hanging on the air. He'll

be graduating soon. Getting his appointment to DPS. Says he's joining the narcotics division after he "pays his dues." A fourth-generation Ranger. Have mercy. Says he'll come home on the weekends and help Daddy run the business. The two of them got more cows than they know what to do with and every time land pops up for sale next to the Bar S they buy it. It's nearly three times the size it was when I was a little girl. And Momma's house is so pretty. Just look at all she's done to it.

Daddy said the governor's coming to the wedding. And so is the actor who played Daddy in the movie about his life. Some of the cast and crew. I never imagined. A lot of people love him.

In all the busy-ness, I hadn't seen him much, so a few days ago, I went looking for him. Wanted to try on the dress and let him be the first man to see it. I pulled on my jeans and started looking. Took me nearly an hour. Found him down at the river. Sitting in the middle as usual. Surrounded by his Bradfords and Black Baldies. His head and shoulders the only thing sticking above the waterline. I laughed. He stood up. The Marlboro man soaking wet. Walked over to me, picked me up, and carried me out into the middle. We sat there, just the two of us, leaning into the water.

I got to thinking. About Daddy and how we all met. I found myself shaking my head. Where would I be without that man? Where would Momma be? There is no telling. And Brodie? You would know better than anyone how lost I'd be without him. There was a time when I was worried that he might be upset that I was marrying his best friend but I think he's okay with it. Actually, think he likes it. Maybe, in some way, he feels responsible. I think my marrying Peter allows him, in a way, to pass me to another. Hand me off to someone he trusts.

There in the water, I got to watching Daddy. Still so hand-some. Still skinny, still strong, still loves Momma, still brings her down here under the moonlight, still makes her smile, still brings her flowers, still loves riding with her, still. Little has changed. I was thinking back today, way back, and I could not remember that guy's name that Momma was dating. The one that made the movies of me and Momma. I think it was Bob or Brandon or seems like it starts with a "B" but, no matter, Daddy got rid of him, too. Last we heard he was still serving his first lifetime.

We've come a long way. All of us. Sometimes I just scratch my head. I am amazed.

I was at a wedding party yesterday, stealing a few minutes to myself, when my ring bearer walked by and asked me about this notebook. He's so cute I could just eat him. He fingered the worn edges, turned his nose up and said, "What's that?"

I said, "My journal."

"What do you do in it?"

"Write letters."

"To who?"

"God."

He chewed on his lip, looked down, then up at me. "You know him?"

I nodded. "A little."

He looked over each shoulder, then lowered his head and asked, "What's he like?"

About then Daddy and Brodie walked by. Such presence. One a spitting image of the other. He watched them, jaw open. I pointed. "He's like them."

"Oh." Eyes wide. "Wow."

Gotta go. Daddy's knocking on my door.